General Ludd

General Ludd

by John Metcalf

ECW PRESS
Downsview Ontario

Canadian Cataloguing in Publication Data

Metcalf, John, 1938-
  General Ludd

ISBN 0-920802-30-3 deluxe   ISBN 0-920802-24-9 bd.
ISBN 0-920802-22-2 pa.

I. Title.

PS8576.E82G46   C813'.54   C80-094492-5
PR9199.3.M47G46

Earlier versions of Chapters 1, 2, and 8 appeared in *The Tamarack Review* and *Canadian Fiction Magazine*. Chapter 14 appeared in *Love and Money* edited by David Helwig.

This book was typeset by Erin Graphics Inc. and printed by the University of Toronto Press.

Published by ECW PRESS, Stong College, York University, Downsview Ontario M3J 1P3.

For John Newlove

Also by John Metcalf

New Canadian Writing   1969
The Lady Who Sold Furniture   1970
Going Down Slow   1972
The Teeth of My Father   1975
Girl in Gingham   1978

Chapter One

They are, I thought sadly, what they eat.

In the centre of the festive board stood a large stainless steel utensil of sullen coleslaw. At the far end of the table was displayed an assortment of cheeses which at the last moment a female graduate student would have been dispatched to purchase because nobody had remembered. There would be no good Canadian cheddar, no Cherry Hill, no Forfar. There would be the usual unripe Brie and Camembert and goaty stuff past its prime and stuff wrapped in withered leaves and stuff tainted with nasty herbs. None of the cheese would have reached room temperature.

The plates were paper, the knives and forks plastic.

But the wine was Canadian. *All* of it. And all of it *would* have reached room temperature.

Warm Duck.

I was being inducted for the fourth time as Writer-in-Residence at a Canadian university. St. Xavier's ten years earlier had been a small Catholic liberal arts college. It was now secularized and grown big. In return for the right to grant its own degrees it had sold its independence for the pottage of government support. On its once gracious grounds now squatted the concrete bunkers of new disciplines.

The Reverend Father President was welcoming me interminably. He was short and fat in black with a large silver cross reposing on his chest. James Wells, he had assured the thirty-some people in the Faculty Club, needed no introduction. My fame had, according to him, widely preceded me; my poetic honours and accomplishments were an adornment of the nation's culture — nay — were of its very fabric; my five collections of verse were surely familiar to all. He read their titles from a piece of paper.

As all would agree, it would be merely tedious to rehearse further — the Governor-General's Award at so young an age, the distinction of translation into Finnish and Dutch . . .

(Of the five collections, two still in print; last royalty cheque $117.63.)

The Reverend Father seemed set fair for a voyage into metaphor.

Parnassus popped up.

Apollo appeared.

I stood beside Hetherington, the chair person of the English Department, head modestly bowed. He was British and was wearing a tweed sports jacket with inevitable leather patches on the elbows. He was the only member of the establishment I'd met so far. I'd been ordered by mail. Last academic year playing to capacity crowds at Western Ontario — opening this week in Montreal. Hetherington, for some unknown reason, was holding an economy size bottle of Johnson and Johnson's "No More Tears" Shampoo.

The Reverend Father President hoped that the leaven of creativity would cause, if he might be pardoned the trope, the academic dough to rise.

(Polite laughter.)

Was it fanciful, wondered the Reverend Father, to imagine invisible among them Calliope and her Sisters?

The English Department, if it was like most of them in Canada, would be made up of seventeen Americans, four Englishmen, and three Canadians with the Canadians optional. The department would be united only in its indifference or hostility to the Writer-in-Residence.

I've often wondered why they go through the motions of having Writers-in-Residence. There's the zoo aspect, I suppose. And the Public Relations aspect — not only Learning but Culture too. As the Canada Council pays half the shot, they're getting all that Leaven of Creativity and Calliope and her Sisters and a funny man you can stare at for half-price. I really don't know. It remains a

8

mystery. That they believe in patronage, pure or otherwise, is a preposterous fancy.

But more intriguing—the *how* of it!

I imagine their Departmental Meetings.

What about Malcolm Lowry? One sees his name in journals.
Who's he?
How about a woman this time?
He's dead, isn't he?
Is he?
Pardon? Is who what?
Dead.

They hadn't assigned me an office yet but I knew where it'd be. It would be opposite the men's washroom. It always was. Who with tenure or on the regular strength would accept an office next door to or opposite a room which flushed itself loudly every three minutes and smelled of Fresh Pine?

The Reverend Father President seemed to be concluding. He said 'community' and 'educational process' and 'stimulating interchange' and 'shelter within the academic fold' and then there was polite applause and then the wine was broached.

I was foolish enough to be disappointed about the wine. London, Ontario, yes, but I'd have thought that Montreal could at least have risen to something from Algeria.

The faculty stood in defensive groups wishing themselves elsewhere or in some cases, perhaps, wondering where they were.

Hetherington, still holding his bottle of "No More Tears" introduced me to face after face.

'... our Chaucer chap ... our Drama man ... our Remedial Team ...'

A Dr. Gamahuche, described by Hetherington as a Renaissance man, hoped that the Academy with its analytic disciplines would not prove inimical to the more intuitive and fluid processes of poetic composition. I told him I hoped so too. Hetherington said that Dr. Gamahuche published frequently in *PMLA*. I made Dr. Gamahuche my being-very-impressed face.

Poor dreary sods—the whole of their lives conducted with the logic of the Mad Hatter's Tea Party with higher and higher qualifications demanded of them to teach increasingly abstruse material to more and more students who find the *Reader's Digest* baffling in its complexity. Most of them honestly think they're doing a valuable job—and so they are. But it isn't the job

9

they think they're doing. The more people they manage to intimidate or delude, the further off is the day when the will of the people will be expressed — a free TV in every pot and buggers like me to the wall.

"And *this*," said Hetherington, "is my wife, Julia."

I took the limp hand she proffered. The fingers were covered with rings of native workmanship and her finger-nails were dirty. She had a strangely *bundled* appearance. She was wearing a sort of khaki-coloured shawl with a lace edge and the shawl was secured on her meagre chest with a silver thing the size of a plate that looked like a Chrysler hub-cap. Her skirt was floor-length and mothy velvet, her hair unkempt and slut-coloured.

"When my husband dragged me to America," she said in an excruciating Oxford accent which was enough to raise the hackles on a dog, "I learned *they* had a literature and now he's brought me here I'm informed there's a Canadian one too. Personally, I never finished Thackeray," she said. "Not that one would wish to. Or would one?"

"Julia!" said a rude, fat woman. "Where have you been hiding?"

"Well, I've just finished a baby," she said. "But it expired."

I indicated my empty glass, did my charming smile, and eased myself away.

A young man standing on the other side of the drinks table took off his spectacles and downed three doses of Duck in quick succession and shuddered.

Julia's voice carried. Her shawl, it turned out, was a dyed tablecloth, her skirt part of a pair of curtains and she'd found this immensely clever little artisan who *did* such things, brazing or whatever they called it, something mysterious anyway, who'd ingeniously affixed a *pin* . . .

It was impossible not to listen.

It *was* a hub cap.

"You're the poet," stated the young man with the spectacles.

I nodded.

"I haven't read any of your stuff," he said. "Fact is, I've never heard of you. My name is Frederick Lindseer, assistant professor, Freshman Survey, one-year terminal contract but extended till Christmas because the guy broke his leg and both arms."

"What guy?"

"The sabbatical guy."

10

He was, I realized, pissed to the gills and I envied him. If I drank enough Duck to blur the edge of the evening, I knew I'd have the screaming runs the next day.

Julia's voice penetrated. The sort of *wings* on it had reminded her of Pegasus or Mercury, if one saw what she meant, and the idea of its being a piece of a *motor-car* had tickled her fancy rather. The juxtaposition of the classical with the . . .

"The guy before you," said Lindseer, "the writer guy, can't remember his name, he said to me in the washroom that his writing was dictated by the rhythms of his inner life."

"Perhaps he was making a pass?"

"You don't, do you?" he said earnestly. "Have rhythms in your inner life?"

I assured him I'd rather have piles.

"I was at University of Maine," he said. "Wrote a Ph.D. thesis on Thomas Wolfe. It's called *Thomas Wolfe in Germany*. Why?"

"One gets trapped into things," I said.

"I hate the garrulous bastard," said Lindseer. "You know what I'd have done if I'd been Maxwell Perkins? I'd have fixed to have his fingers smashed in an alley."

'I do believe,' fluted Julia's voice, 'I'm becoming a trifle tiddled.'

"What *did* he do in Germany?"

"Went on vacation with a piece of ass. Listen," he said, "you want to know what I think? I can just see it. Oranges, grapefruit, lemons, tangerines, lots of green tissue paper. All nestled in green tissue. Avocados maybe. That's what I'd like. And the name."

He sketched curlicues in the air.

"Lots of bright colours — not *gaudy* in any way. But *bright*. Not a big place. Select. And it'd say:
Fred Lindseer's Fruits."

"It sounds good," I said. "Do it before it's too late. Have some more Duck."

"I applied to forty-seven places before I got a terminal at this shit-heap," he said. "And after this, after Christmas — I guess it'll be back to the States and trying junior colleges, high schools even — I'm twenty-seven now so that's, so that's thirty-eight fucking years before I get my soc'al security. Thirty-fucking-eight years talking Thomas fucking Wolfe."

"Fruit," I said. "Go into fruit. It's more honourable."

He swilled some Duck in moody silence.

11

I was watching a woman at the cheese end of the table. She was small with black hair cut very short, cropped almost, and a funny monkey sort of face and a nice grin. I hadn't noticed her before. She was suddenly the most attractive woman in the room. She had the figure of a girl but her face was older, the faint lines attractive. On her brow there was a white scar. I watched the jut of her breasts under the black sweater. She was pouring wine for people and chatting to a middle-aged man who was wearing a hearing aid and kept inclining towards her.

Unusual for me, that sudden attraction.

I've had my fill of women. Most poetry is written by neurotic girls. That which isn't is written by neurotic wives who wish to leave their insensitive husbands. All over Canada from coast to coast in city and in hamlet there's a multiplicity of Edna St. Vincent Millays *yearning*.

It's a depressing thought.

This Writer-in-Residence racket is a strain until you learn the ropes, until you realize that many of these creatures consider you a therapist, the resident Miss Lonelyhearts, less *base* than other men, a being sexual in some *purer* way.

Shelley with prick.

There had been, in the past, until I'd learned better, entanglements.

A broody one from Winnipeg with a very small left breast and a large right breast had locked herself in my bathroom and tried to cut her throat with my *Philishave*.

It all interfered with work.

'I can tell the precise moment at which I'm ovulating,' said Julia's voice. 'I can feel a distinct *ping*.'

Lindseer had been brooding.

"What do you think about avocados?" he said suddenly.

"Definitely," I said. "A fruit store without avocados could by no stretch of the imagination be called Select. You might not sell many but you could always say, 'Would you care for avocados today?' It'd make people feel inferior. Which is necessary."

Lindseer nodded slowly. He filled his glass again.

"*But*," I said, "you nestle the avocados in *red* tissue paper."

"*That*," said Lindseer, "that is just . . . Fred," he said. "Call me Fred."

"Fred," I said, "you wouldn't have anything to drink, would you?"

12

"I finished it in my office."

"Ah, well," I said. "Pass the Duck."

The squits it would have to be.

"Cosimo's taking him away now," he said.

"What?"

"The President. He's on the sauce and they don't let him loose anymore."

"Who's Cosimo?"

"That big guy."

I watched the Reverend Father President being shepherded out — a smile here, a nod, a word or two there — by a man who stood about six foot seven and who had a brush-cut and was wearing a plaid madras jacket — the sort of jacket that makes North Americans disliked in Europe.

"There were all sorts of rumours," said Fred. "Juiced in the men's residence at night. Women's clothes. Flopping his dork out. That sort of stuff. So the Provincial put the skids under him and Cosimo's the real wheel now."

"Provincial? You mean Cosimo's a Jesuit too?"

"And how! Cosimo O'Gorman S.J. — a bastard natural born. When old Cos came in the first thing he did was ax nearly all the Classics Department. Not contemporary, right? Not relevant. *Old* stuff. And no fuss because they were all S.J.'s and they do what they're told. So he replaced them with a Business Administration Department. So the enrollment goes up, right?"

"Right."

"So next, he chops the Theology Department down to two guys. Who gives a fuck about Theology, right? Same thing. All Jebs. No union. So now he has some money in hand. So he sets out to build up something that *is* contemporary and he builds this whoring great department called the Communication Arts Complex. Up goes the enrollment again."

"In like Flynn," I said.

"CAC," said Fred.

"What?"

"Communication Arts Complex. They've got tens of thousands of dollars of hardware over there. Video stuff, TV cameras, recording studios, sound mixing studios — Christ knows what. Kids like it. It brings in fees. It's *logical*."

I nodded.

"Five hundred kids over there," he said, waving a wild arm,

13

"five hundred moron kids who're all going to fuck off and be Fellini except they've never heard of him. It's *logical*. They can't read. They can't write. So they press buttons."

"This Cosimo," I said, "sounds like a sweetheart."

"Cosimo," said Fred, "is an operator. And money! Jesus, he raises money like a dust-storm. Alumni, Foundations, Corporations—you name it, Cos is in there."

He placed his glass on the table with drunken care.

"I will now," he said, "give you Cosimo's CAC speech."

He composed his face.

"No man," he intoned, "is an island entire unto himself. Communication is the bringing together of people. The bringing together of people is a kind of Love. God is Love. Therefore Communication is a part of God's Will and Essential Nature. Radio and TV are therefore God."

"Seems to touch all the bases," I said.

"Cosimo O'Gorman," said Fred thoughtfully, judiciously, "is a cunt."

We were silent for a few moments. Julia Hetherington had hauled up her velvet skirt and was indicating to a woman and two men certain veins.

"Have you been there yet for dinner?" said Fred, jerking his head in her direction.

"No."

He laughed.

"You will," he said. "You will." The thought seemed to give him a lot of amusement.

"Tell me," I said. "Hetherington introduced me to two people he called the Remedial Team..?"

"Laurel and Hardy," said Fred. "Fatty and Squeaky. Them over there."

"Don't point."

"If you can't read or write," he said, "you're accepted into *Remedial One* and get a credit towards your degree."

"A *credit*?"

"Why not?" said Fred. "You got to be democratic. They do the work—they get the credit. They have workbooks—like in grade school?—a camel is blue, green, an animal, none of these. Place your tick in the appropriate box. Right? And then they come to me for the Survey. The *Prologue* to the *Four Quartets*."

"Then what?"

14

"Then I fail 'em. They look at the first line of the *Prologue* and they can't see anything funny about the spelling. So then they go back to Laurel and Hardy for *Advanced Remedial.* And they get another credit."

"And *then* what?"

"I fail 'em in the Survey again and the marks are sent in to the Dean and the Dean says what is all this shit you can't fail 99% of the students unless you're a crumby teacher so smarten up asshole and he gives the marks to this genius in the Business Administration Department who performs a very complicated mathematical procedure that adds forty to everyone's score and they all pass."

"*All* of them?"

"The customer, old buddy, is always right."

"Fred, you're shitting me."

"Well, O.K. Pass mark is 45. They add 40. And maybe still fifteen or so flunk out. Like the ones that *drool.* So then they convene a full Department Meeting and the flunk papers are reviewed.

Someone says, 'That's a word, isn't it? Isn't that an *and*? And old Hetherington'll say, '*It's very* neatly *written.*' Right? So they pass ten more of the fifteen. And do you know what the five droolies who flunk do?"

"I couldn't imagine," I said.

And I couldn't.

"Well they appeal their case to the Student Ombudsman — he used to be the Host on a Hot Line Show — and he defends their rights and human dignity and then old Hetherington clucks about and agitates himself and agrees that no one ought to bear the stigma of failure so they pass them too."

"Fred," I said. "You're all right. But get into fruit while you're still young enough."

"I'm going to get some cheese," he said. "Perhaps it'll stop me from throwing up."

As he moved along the side of the table, the woman with the monkey face looked up and then smiled at me and nodded. I raised my glass in salutation and smiled back. She was lovely. The hearing-aid man stooped again and monopolized her and I felt suddenly angry with him.

I surveyed the throng, the gleam of spectacles, the chitter.

There are a few scholars left, I suppose, but these were the sort of academics who when they read anything at all read earnest

Pelican books called *Kinship and Family Structure in Notting Hill.*

Fred came back with a paper plate and a plastic knife. He dug into the slab of cheese and the knife snapped.

"Good to have you with us," said a passing man.

"That's Norbert," said Fred. "He's one of your lot."

"What do you mean, 'my lot'?"

"The Canadian literature lot—there's four of them," he said. "But three are from the States and one's Canadian and the Canadian one won't have anything to do with the American ones because they're American and not Canadian. And the rest of the Department shits on all four of 'em because they reckon the Canadian stuff's a load of crap."

"And which is the Canadian one?"

"The fat broad over there in the green dress."

He pointed.

She oozed flesh.

"She is called Ms. Mary Merton and she is a very big pain in the ass," he said. "She teaches a course called *The Image of the Woman in Canadian Fiction.*"

"Say no more," I said.

"And another called *The Gynocentric World View* and she runs the Women's Drop-In Centre and makes Department meetings longer."

She was wearing a large white button with the biological symbol for 'female' on it in black and came close to needing to.

"And the guy with the see-through blouse?" I asked.

"That's Malcolm," said Fred.

"What's *his* field?"

"Buggery."

Fred was becoming swaying drunk. He'd been eating the cheese with his fingers and was now smelling them with a disgusted expression.

"And tell me, Fred," I said as casually as I could, "who's the woman at the other end of the table—the one with the black sweater?"

He turned and stared.

He gave a contemptuous laugh.

"That," he said, "that's the Department Bicycle."

I stared at him.

"Would you care to elaborate on that?"

"Oh, Christ!" he said. "Good night."

I turned and Cosimo was towering over me.

"Welcome aboard," he said, pumping my hand. "I'm O'Gorman, Director of the Communication Arts Complex so we're in the same line of business."

"Business?"

"Communication," he said, "though *we're* not print-oriented. Linear's a dirty word in *my* Department."

He laughed.

I laughed.

He sketched a playful punch to my shoulder.

"Come over any time," he said. "I'll give you a tour of the plant."

"I'd really like to do that," I said.

"Feel free," he said.

He waved a cheery good night.

I moved down the table and held out my glass to the woman in the black sweater.

"May I?"

As she poured, I said, "I'm Jim Wells."

"I'm Kathy," she said, "Kathy Neilson."

"Like the chocolate bar," I said before I knew what I was saying.

She had small hands with rather stubby fingers.

"Have you read Hugh Johnson's book on wine?" I said.

Her eyes were dark brown.

"No," she said.

"Marvellous title. It's called *Wine.* You couldn't get much more authoritative than that."

I felt myself to be babbling.

"Do you know what he said about Canadian wine?"

"Tell me."

"He said it was the nastiest wine in the world. 'The foulness of the taste is what I remember best', he said. And that," I said, "was even before they'd *invented* this."

I raised the glass to her and then considered the contents.

"It reminds me of that famous story about Bismarck," I said. "After the Franco-Prussian War, Bismarck said to the Kaiser — or perhaps it was the other way round, 'We ought to toast this victory in champagne' and then the Kaiser said to Bismarck, 'We ought to toast it in *German* champagne.' And then Bismarck or it might have been the Kaiser said:

'There *are* limits to nationalism.'"

Kathy smiled.

"True story," I said.

"You're a mine of information," she said.

Her eyes had lovely crinkly corners. I found myself thinking to my delight and dismay that she looked like a pixie picture in a child's book. I wondered if I could possibly be drunk but knew I wasn't.

"I suppose you get sick of the subject," she said, "but I like your poems very much. Well, not *like* because they're not . ."

"Amiable?"

"But I do admire them."

She blushed.

"Had you read any before?"

"No," she said. "Have to admit. But I bought them when it was announced you were coming."

"*Bought?*" I said. "You *are* a curious kind of academic. They usually request 'desk copies'."

We were smiling at each other.

"Ah!" said Hetherington. "There you are. I do hope I'm not interrupting but I thought I'd better have a word with you if I may . . ."

He took me by the elbow and steered me away a discreet distance. I glanced over my shoulder and she pulled a funny face.

"I've found an office for you but we seem to have run into difficulties with Supply and there's no desk. Working on that now though. Doesn't do to be too peremptory with Supply. Touchy lot."

He smiled vaguely.

"But what I wanted to mention was this. Your predecessor dealt with the chap—what *was* his name—and so did the writer before that, and it's become something of a tradition I suppose. And as soon as we've fixed you up with a desk, he'll be bound to be along to see you so it's a case of Be Prepared."

"What is?" I said.

"Well, you see, there's this chap. The thing of it *is*, he's Jewish," said Hetherington. "A Jew," he added, as if in amplification.

"What about him?"

"Well, you see, he's in his fifties. Had a bit of a rough time."

"Rough time?"

"Concentration camps and all that sort of thing," said Hetherington.

18

"Yes?"

Hetherington studied his shampoo bottle.

"Well, you see, the chap's a poet. Evening student, actually. Technically. Rather an odd bird. He's been around here for about ten years I gather. Bit of a fixture. Takes courses every year but he never does the work, you see. And at exam time — well, he just hands in a batch of these poems and people tend to pass him because, well, he's had rather . ."

"A rough time," I said.

"Exactly!" said Hetherington as though I'd produced a brilliant phrase which neatly summed up something he'd been groping for.

"And then," said Hetherington, "the poor fellow's disabled."

"What do you mean 'disabled'?"

"Polio, actually."

"Oh, no!"

"Though he's *amazingly* mobile," said Hetherington. "In his chair, I mean."

I nodded.

"And then to top it all off," said Hetherington, "there's his heart."

I raised my eyebrows.

"Yes," said Hetherington, "dickey."

"Well . . ." I said.

"And I expect he'll be one of the first to pop in to see you and the thing of it *is*, he doesn't speak, well, *standard* English and if you hadn't been forewarned, as it were, you might have thought his poems — well, not up to scratch."

"So you want me to talk to the guy and whatever I think just pass him along."

"That's it, really," said Hetherington. "In a nutshell."

"I suppose you didn't get anywhere with my objection to giving grades?"

"Frightfully sorry," said Hetherington, "but the Dean was obdurate. We tend to have this little clash every year and I do, of course, relish the absurdity of the . . oh, and by the way, the chappie's name is Zemermann."

"Zemermann," I repeated.

"Itzik," said Hetherington.

"Pardon?"

"Itzik Zemermann."

19

Chapter Two

A pleasant week had passed since my induction. I'd been into the university only once and briefly. I had explained to a helpful girl in the payroll office the special nature of my status within the structure of the university and the special nature of my arrangements with the taxation authorities and she had helpfully agreed to issue my pay cheques without deduction at source. From the university book-store I obtained some light reading and an enormous *Dictionary of Saints* — all of which I charged to the English Department.

Other than this brief foray, I'd read, worked on a poem, pottered about the neighbourhood, and made several starts on my idea for a money-making novel. Hetherington had still not managed to obtain a desk from Supply and my calculated daily phone calls of enquiry from the corner store had shredded him to gibbering apology. We had already established that I would make myself available to students only one and a half days per week owing to the pressure of my own creative activities but his guilt about the desk could doubtless be pressed to further gross advantage.

I love the middle class.

'-In-Residence' is just a form of words. It's never offered. Two days before my induction, I'd come down to Montreal from a cottage in Ontario where I'd spent the summer with friends and found a room in a part of Montreal near the Forum where cheques were not looked on favourably and leases not required, the sort of area checked first in an intensive manhunt. The room was on the top floor of a three-storey building. On both sides other old buildings were being demolished in preparation for high rises. The room contained a washbasin, a kitchen chair, and a bed with a sagging mattress. A once floral curtain screened off the fridge and a hot-plate. Share leprous bathroom. But it was the wardrobe which had decided me before rent was even mentioned. It was massive and ancient, brass handles and beaded trim, and reminded me of an upended coffin or sarcophagus — the sort of coffin in which a mafia capo might have been buried in some remote Sicilian village.

I'd beaten the Gagool-like creature who ran the place down to sixty-five dollars a month and as soon as I'd pressed money into her claw and hustled her out, I'd taken off my shoes and got inside the wardrobe and closed the door.

It had only taken a couple of days to discover the essentials — the whereabouts of a breakfast place, a twenty-four hour a day café, the nearest liquor store, a dry-cleaner's and shirt place, and which of the local grocery stores sold beer after hours — in this case a dingy emporium full of dusty cans of pet food and run by two limpid-eyed Lebanese. Price plus fifty cents if you picked it up; a dollar on the top if delivered.

In the room opposite mine across the street lived an old man who spent most of the day in his undershirt leaning on his window-sill and drinking beer. He shouted at passers-by, obvious insults though I couldn't make out the words. Fur coats and ornate hats with poodles and daschunds he just yelled at and when they looked up he pointed at them and cackled.

On the corner of the street grew a vast maple which the city had forgotten to cut down and grey squirrels ran along its swaying outer branches and launched themselves onto the cornice and ledge of the old man's storey and scampered along to his open window where he talked to them and fed them bread. The more timid ones took it from his hand but others hopped over the sill and sat on his table.

My ancient little fridge was humming away, stocked now with forty-some Labatt's Blue and the wardrobe contained, besides my two suits, two twenty-sixes of Cutty Sark. The mid-morning September sun was lying in a band across the uncarpeted floor, and I was propped up on the bed drinking beer and reading a history of the Luddite movement. And day-dreaming.

In the evening I was to give my first reading at St. Xavier's, an event open to both university and public, to be followed by a reception in the Faculty Club.

I felt a bit disappointed with the Luddites. I'd had the impression they were an anarchic group bashing machinery to buggery for the pleasure of it and generally trying to stem the Industrial Revolution, a project which would have received my full support. But it turned out that they were merely after higher wages and better working conditions — forerunners of the rise of unions. All very worthy but my interest in politics was exhausted long ago.

I flipped the page and found a facsimile of a letter written to a foreman of a jury which had convicted a group of Luddite rioters.

The letter read:

Mr. (undecipherable scrawl) — Late foreman of a jury held at Nottingham 16 March 1812

> Sir,
> By General Ludd's Expre/s Commands I am come
> to Worksop to enquire of your Character towards
> our cause and I am sory to say I find it to
> correspond with your conduct you lattly shewed
> towards us, Remember the time is fast approaching
> When men of your stamp Will be brought to
> Repentance, you may be called upon soon.
> Remember you are a marked man.
>   yours for Gen Ludd
>   a true man.

I was charmed by this letter, a model of what such a letter should be. I got up off the bed and leaned on the window-sill looking down into the street. I raised my bottle to the old man in salute and he shouted something angry-sounding but I couldn't hear. I thought of a long list of people to whom I would like to send such a letter, other *soi-disant* poets, numerous book-reviewers, my publisher, the criminal who runs his accounting department, and a certain Mr. Archambault at the Taxation Data Centre who sends me repetitive letters which I now return with *Deceased* written on them.

I leaned there thinking about my novel, a comedy-thriller set in Canada. I envisaged large paper-back sales and a scramble for the movie rights. I'd started it six times and now had the title and half a

22

page complete. Money was the spur; it was the actual writing of it that bored me.

Most of the thriller would have to be set in Ottawa which was an obstacle to credibility before I'd even started because a best-seller needs scenes of naked lust and lubriciousness and it is very difficult to imagine depravity of any kind in Ottawa. For those who *live* in Ottawa, depravity is Hull.

And again, most of the thriller clichés I could filch from other writers just aren't convincing in a Canadian setting. Skullduggery on trains, for example. We've got more miles of track than the whole of Europe put together but we lack border crossings and customs posts and men with metal teeth and shiny boots demanding papers. All that happens on Canadian trains is that drunken Maritimers press old sandwiches on you and after you've declined with thanks and they've challenged you and everyone else in the coach to fight like a man they sprawl asleep in their spittle and then the conductor comes and takes away their bottle. Not exactly the stuff of Eric Ambler, Len Deighton, or Gavin Lyall.

But I was pleased with the main outline.

The Canada Council is actually the front for Canadian Counter-Intelligence and is run in typically Canadian fashion by an Englishman called Commander Swann. Commander Swann was the Third Man in the Burgess and Maclean Affair—not Kim Philby as many thought—and so is actually a Top Soviet Agent. He is also a ferocious homosexual and drinks after-shave lotion. Canadian Counter-Intelligence (or, to give it its correct title, Intelligence Canada) receives word that an important KGB Agent with many secrets and specific knowledge of Soviet Agents in Canadian High Places (i.e., possibly Swann himself) is coming to Canada with the Bolshoi Ballet and wishes to defect. No one, however, knows who the man is. Swann's job, ostensibly, is to identify, secure, and debrief the defector; his actual job, of course, to kill him. This involves the serial murder of half the Bolshoi Ballet thus provoking International Incidents etc. etc. until Swann is unmasked by his Arch-Rival, the Commissioner of the RCMP — another Englishman with whom Swann has been at St. Crispin's Prep School, Eton, and Oxford. In a stirring denouement, Swann is trampled to death during the RCMP Musical Ride during the Calgary Stampede.

I thought it was quite a good plot as plots go but it was really the details which were amusing me. Agents sent in their reports in code on application forms for Senior Arts Grants and as the activities of the actual Canada Council and Intelligence Canada sometimes became confused, bewildered residents of remote Canadian villages were from time to time awarded large sums of money to cover the Baptist Church with sheets of transparent plastic or construct vast sculptures from empty Javex bottles. Conversely, agents in the field were sometimes reminded that they'd omitted the names of three other writers or painters as referees.

A further embroidery was that I'd decided to give all the Agents the names of prominent Canadian writers.

All I'd actually *written* so far was:

THE MUSICAL RIDE

All was quiet on the third floor of The Canada Council offices on Sparks Street in Ottawa. The Duty Officer, Captain Alfred Purdy, was reading with fascination the Letters from Our Readers section in Penthouse.

"I, too," he read, *"like G. T. of Staffs, am sexually excited by the sight and smell of wet fish."*

The door crashed open and in strode Commander Swann in a towering rage. Purdy removed his habitual and disgusting cigar.

"Are last night's signals filed!" bellowed Commander Swann. "They are not, sir! And why not? Because, Mr. Purdy, you are idling! You are as usual, reading smut! How many times must I tell you?"

He pounded on the desk.

"Do it Swann's Way!"

"Do it Swann's Way!"

"But Commander . . ." said Purdy.

"And where are those other incompetent swine? Where's Hood, Blaise, Smith, R.? If they're having it off again with those secretaries up at the Art Bank, by Christ, I'll have them posted. I'll post them, Purdy. No mercy on the buggers. I'll post them north of Hudson's Bay on an ice floe."

"Smith, R. was seconded, sir, to the RCMP."

"What in hell for?"

"They requested help, sir, in compiling a National Index of Rumanian restaurants."

Commander Swann made a strange whimpering sound.

"Purdy," he said, "there are times when I could be driven to

24

saying a naughty word."

I turned back into the room and considered my coffin-like wardrobe. It was time to get dressed and investigate a new restaurant for lunch. I was looking into the tarnished mirror and knotting my tie when I was startled by the sound of exploding glass. I reached the window just in time to see the old man opposite chucking another empty into the middle of the road.

I grabbed up my jacket, put six bottles of Blue into a shopping bag and hurried down the stairs and out. I stopped in the middle of the street to kick the larger fragments into the gutter and then went into his building and figured out which must be his room.

I knocked on the door.

There was no sound.

"Hey!" I called. "Are you in there?"

There was no answer but I heard some faint noise.

"Quit chucking bottles, you stupid old fart. You hear me?"

I waited a moment.

"They'll come and throw you in the tank," I said. "Understand? I've brought you some beer. I'll leave it outside the door. But quit throwing stuff or they'll take you down to Station Ten and flush your head in the john."

He cackled inside the room.

Then his voice said:

"I seen you, sonny."

I waited for a few more moments in the gloomy hallway and then I went down the stairs and out into the sunshine again. I found a pleasant Italian place for lunch and ate cannelloni which was good and drank a carafon of the house wine which was plonk of the worst kind. Especially imported, the proprietor assured me, and from the taste of it by tanker. I sat there when I'd finished eating and ordered cappucino and cognac. The word 'plonk' made me think of the word 'rotgut' and I took out my notebook which I always carry to record observations, brilliant thoughts, snatches of overheard conversation.

I flipped through the scribbled pages until I found space and read at the top of the page:

'Male redwings come north first in the spring. Females follow later. Why? Males flock together—don't seem to be staking territory.'

Under that it said:

25

'Buy tooth-paste and Lavoris.'

Then a telephone number I didn't recognize.

Then:

'City snow-banks in early spring rotted and holed by the sun look like dirty coral.'

I wrote down 'Plonk' and then 'Rotgut' and then 'Rotgutt' and then 'Rotgutt Plonk' and finished by underlining the words *Herr Rotgutt Plonk*. He could be a swinish East German Trade Mission man in Ottawa in liaison with Commander Swann. A rigid Prussian type who wore a corset and had a distasteful relationship with a sensitive boy called, called what? Called *Axel*.

I jotted down:

In the dim bedroom Herr Plonk unlaced his corset and said with heavy humour, 'It is the time now to grease the Axel!'

I doodled.

I was still trying to puzzle out what Canada could have sent to Russia in exchange for the Bolshoi. The only thing that had occurred to me so far was Stompin' Tom Connors.

I sauntered along St. Catherine Street looking into the junk-filled windows, Indian imports, incense and candle stores, poster stores, record stores, shoe stores full of boots and shoes with vast heels which all looked as if they were made for a population with mass orthopedic deformity. Souvenir stores full of souvenirs of Canada — toy mounties, toy seals, key-rings, vibrators, and dildoes embossed with scarlet maple leaves.

An unconscious drunk in a doorway who'd pissed himself, a dark stain meandering across the grey sidewalk.

Panhandlers.

Black men strutting in Detroit ponce outfits.

In front of an electrical appliance store a lobotomized crowd gawped at seven colour TV sets each showing the same programme in differing unnatural hues.

The summer at the lake had weakened me, the sound of water lapping on rock, the slow flight of blue herons in the evening light. I wasn't ready for all this grunge and noise and dirt, for the flotsam and jetsam human and material of these cities all alike where I had to scavenge for a living. I wasn't ready to admit once more that I lived in a country in which there was not one good book store, a country in which every half hour millions of radios informed the inhabitants whether it was hot or raining, a country where the unconscious desire of most citizens is to see from coast to shining coast one uninterrupted shopping mall. I wasn't ready to admit once more that I lived in a country where green coca-cola bottles are collected as antiques.

The first bookshop didn't carry poetry at all. The second had five copies of my last book, obviously their unsold first order. I signed my name large in them with my felt pen to render them unreturnable to the publisher, thus ensuring my royalty, then introduced myself with bonhomie to the manager and informed him of my gracious gesture. He was obviously aghast but managed a weak smile as we shook hands.

I love the middle class.

I then discovered a pleasantly seedy tavern on Guy Street mercifully lacking a TV and juke-box and sat in the gloom, day-dreaming, drifting, drinking slow draft. Enough work for one day.

Signing books unasked in bookstores had been one of John Caverly's dodges. He'd been much in my mind lately, my coffin wardrobe perhaps with its suits — 'protective colouring' he'd always called them. Strange business the poetry game — dependent on the lottery of grants, offers from universities, the vagaries of the reading circuits, windfalls. Even this quiet tavern brought him alive before me. We'd been drinking together one late morning in just such a place as this when a crowd of university kids had come in, shouting, laughing, singing eventually and John had risen in genuine outrage and shouted, "Be quiet! There are people in here trying to get drunk!"

He was one of the few men I've ever really loved. He was ten years older than me. He killed himself just over a year ago. It must have been during one of the black times when he felt he'd never write again, too old and fierce for anything else, nothing more to say, brains scrambled with the strain of saying it.

Remaindered.

We shared a ratbag apartment in Vancouver for a while in the middle sixties after I'd left my wife. I often think of his pronouncements, recall his anecdotes, see his face.

'Always demand double what they offer.'

'Never pass up a Fringe Benefit.'

Our most amazing Fringe Benefit was the incredible occasion when the Chargex Gnomes mailed unsolicited credit cards to hosts of unlikely people. There was one addressed to John in our mailbox. He read the accompanying advertising as though stunned. It took time for the magnitude of the thing to sink in. The mail boxes in the foyer of the apartment building were the kind that the mailman opens with a single key, the whole face of the affair lifting up to reveal the interiors of the individual pigeon holes. John raced back upstairs, got a stout screwdriver, and can-opened the single lock. We collected all the Chargex cards there were. We did a friend's building too.

In three days we worked twenty-seven cards.

'For people like us,' John had said, 'there are no pensions.'

His early books fetch high prices in the first-edition trade.

'Royalties.'

'Free-lance.'

Wonderful words. A knight riding out on a white steed gaily caparisoned. A May morning. An illumination from a Book of Hours. But the hours and years don't work out that way. There's little of nobility in hack editing, newspaper work, reviewing, ghost-writing the autobiography of an insane Alberta meat-packer as I did. That illuminated pathway of red and white roses intertwined leads inexorably to Grub Street.

I sucked foam off the top of the beer.

Free-lance my ass! 'Mercenary' would be more accurate. 'Routier'.

I store manuscripts and a few books with a friend in Edmonton. My only other possessions are clothes, current manu-script, and a typewriter. As I have no intention of ever again being employed in an actual job, I've made it a rule to save on inessentials and always maintain between six and seven thousand dollars in the bank to cushion bleaker years. For years I lived meanly from necessity. Now there's no longer any real need but it's become habit and there's no spur to change.

Beer brass in the glass.

When my first book was published after years of the little magazines, I quit my job. I was married then. I was working as a Personnel Officer with Macmillan-Bloedel, a pleasant enough way of passing the time, scrambled by lunch and smashed by five, but it interfered with reading and writing as I was called upon to talk to people who alleged that their burning ambition in life was to be employed by Macmillan-Bloedel.

The whole bloody marriage was going down the drain. Marjorie was beginning to realize that hubby's hobby had consequences, wasn't like fret-saw work in the basement or wholesome like golf. She'd been an art student when I'd met her but with marriage had succumbed to some atavistic demand for chintz furniture and life-insurance. I had to shut her out more and more to get the space and silence. She became resentful.

The night that actually finished it remains in memory, a night like a scene from a Mack Sennett comedy though it wasn't funny and it wasn't silent.

I was sitting in the arm-chair in the living room reading Robert Graves. She was sitting on the couch doing nothing aggressively. Then she got up and switched on the TV, a gift from her bloated mother. It was the Ed Sullivan Show and a strange child with a big head, possibly a dwarf, was playing some improbable Bach-sounding fugue thing on an enormous harmonica. I asked her to turn it off. She refused. I put down my book, crossed over, and pulled out the plug. She got up and plugged it in again. I then went into the kitchen and found the pair of chromium-plated poultry shears, a wedding present from her ginger-coloured cousin, went back to the TV, unplugged it, and cut the wire. I then went back into the kitchen and rootled out the tool-box she'd given me as an anniversary gift in the hope I'd fix something and with the claw-hammer ripped off the back of the TV. Then, using the chromium-plated poultry shears, I snipped through all the multitude of little coloured wires one by one. Then I broke all the tubes. The screen itself was resilient and sustained several heavy blows from the hammer and cold-chisel.

I found myself wondering about Marjorie and realized that I didn't even know where she was or what she was doing. The divorce petition had cited mental cruelty—presumably my silence and the wanton destruction of her TV. I don't know. I wasn't there. I found myself picturing the curls of pubic hair her bathing suit betrayed—something that had always made me feel unaccountably horny.

I found myself thinking yet again of Kathy Neilson, of the disarming innocence of her grin, of Lindseer.

I found myself thinking of John Caverly's face, the deep lines from the corners of his mouth.

My mood was dipping. I was, I realized, brooding on mutability, the infinite variety of life's rich pageant, the sadness of the young in one another's arms.

And as a cure for *that* mawkish maundering, I stepped out into the startling sunshine and bought a new tie with blue stripes to wear at the evening's reading.

Chapter Three

I stood at the back of the auditorium and surveyed the house.

"I'll..just..ah..." said Hetherington and went away.

Twenty-five's an average crowd for these cultural binges. This was a positive multitude. There were the members of the English Department politely doing their duty, a large number of students (most of them, I suspected, in compulsory attendance from cancelled evening classes), a couple of young Montreal poets I recognized with a horde of their hangers-on, some odds and sods of the general public. More than a hundred altogether, maybe close to a hundred and fifty.

No sign of Kathy.

But my eyes were drawn down over the crowd to the front row where on a makeshift platform in the centre aisle stood some sort of large movie camera on a tripod. People were clustered about it. On the stage itself stood a table and on the table were microphones and a tape recorder. I strolled down the side aisle to the stage and put my books and typescript on the table.

"Are you the speaker?" said one of the movie youths who was wearing a scarlet bandsman's coat with gilt frogging and white corporal's chevrons.

I nodded.

"Just stand where you are," he said. "Don't move."

Spotlights suddenly blazed on with blinding power. The corporal consulted a light meter and then kneeling on the edge of the stage conferred with another movie youth who had a plastic disc with a smaller plastic disc stapled to its centre. I don't know what they're called but the Royal Bank once gave me one which when you turned it to, say, Edmonton, on the outer edge, gave you Edmonton's population in a little box on the inner disc.

"Get a level from him!" shouted a voice from the darkness beyond the light.

I never cease to wonder at the priestly self-importance of people involved in filming things. It exceeds even the self-importance of people involved in theatricals. And even more amazing is the acquiescence of those being filmed.

Your children, Mrs. Thing, are lying squashed under this bus. Tell me ...

And they do. They do.

"Are you in charge of all this?" I called to the corporal.

"I'm a technician," he said.

"Only carrying out the orders of your superiors, eh?"

"What?"

"Who *is* in charge?"

"Professor Ross. Him. Coming across."

I narrowed my eyes into the light.

This Ross, when I could see him properly, looked thirty-ish and hairy and was wearing a sort of denim suit which was hand-embroidered with zodiacal signs. He clambered up onto the stage, approached me, then suddenly stooped and backed away from me drawing a chalk square on the floor behind the table.

"I don't want you outside this frame," he said. "O.K.?"

"How do you do?" I said.

This witty thrust did not seem to penetrate.

"Nervous?" he said.

"Not at all," I said. "I'm .."

"Just be natural," he said. "And you know on film it's not like on stage so lay back on, you know, like the hands and ..."

"I was about to say," I said, "that I was delighted to meet the person in charge because none of this was agreed upon and I wanted to enquire if you were paying a fee or a royalty."

"Fee?" he said.

"Or royalty?" I said.

"But this is educational," he said.

"Oh, I'm sure it will be," I said.

"No," he said. "I mean it's for educational use."

I said nothing, just looked.

"For the Communication Arts Complex," he said. "For the Visual Archive."

"You mean," I said, "like xeroxing books?"

"Right!"

He really wasn't worth playing with and as a public reading was an understood part of my contract and this cinematic tomfoolery an insolent *fait accompli*, it would have been awkward then and there to demand cash on delivery.

I retired to a chair at the rear of the stage. Two minutes to go. Sad to think that I earned more for reading aloud for an hour than I did from a year's book sales. Pipfart and Squeakstrut were now playing with wires and cables, sticking them to the floor with masking tape. One stuck a jack plug into the innards of the tape recorder. This piece of hardware put me in mind of ageless tavern anecdotes:

. . . and then he pulled out his jack and while it was still steaming she said . . .

Hetherington materialized on stage and launched into a meandering introduction — the usual blather and then the twaddle about my being willing to 'entertain' questions at the close of the reading. Pure assumption on his part. I wasn't.

Entertain!

I gave up such 'entertainment' two or three years ago — as soon as it was safe to do so. The questions were always the same. My answers were always the same. The questioners were always concerned with autobiography, inspiration, and what they felt to be the lack of recognizable form in my work. Turds and turdlets, impertinent and opinionated. But as I live off public money, *their* money, my answers were always modest, rueful, humble and shy.

Smile and smile and be a Poet.

What can one say to a congregation of lovers of Poesy who suffer from a collective tin ear? To those who wouldn't notice internal rhyme, assonance, dissonance, or apocopated rhyme if it was rammed up their ass.

So now I just perform. Personality is all. Be fucked if they understand a blind word of it but they share the illusion of participating in Higher Things which is all they really want anyway. Anything else is too much like hard work. Row upon row of Big

Macs. If they had any real interest, they'd *buy* the books and read them decently at home.

I always judge my readings to a fraction under an hour. I was about half way through and stopped to pour a glass of water from the carafe—not because I was dry but to allow a few seconds to pass, to rest them, before I moved on to some stronger stuff.

As I moved back to the lectern from the table, having abandoned my cage of chalk, a horse-faced woman with her hair in a bun appeared from the darkness and handed me up a note.

I glanced at it and nodded.

She simpered like a ravaged Joyce Grenfell and disappeared into the darkness again.

The note said: YOU ARE BEING SECRETLY RECORDED.

Poetry seems to attract them like flies.

I enjoy the actual reading itself though. It's pure performance —an art utterly distinct from writing. I was working this audience exactly as I wanted though it wasn't one of the better halls I've played—the voice, even with amplification, was tending to fall soggy about three quarters of the way to the back and I was having to pitch higher than was comfortable.

They'd had their thirty minutes of charm and anthology-fodder and I was preparing to shift gears into something declamatory, highly rhetorical, repetitive and hypnotic. They were softened up for a working-over, all stops out, two of the long historical poems, very moving. And then like a hart to the cooling bar for a large brandy. I was thinking of pizza and Kathy. With anchovies.

I wear my watch on the inside of my wrist so that I can glance at it unnoticed while I'm working—it's a trick I picked up from watching musicians in bars and night clubs. Watching the time on the middle of intricate solo fingerings when the emotion generated is at a peak—I enjoy that paradox. A good performance is always calibrated seduction. One evokes emotions one does not feel— actors, singers, dancers, politicians, poets—every single one a feigning whore. I enjoy that too.

I gave them the works.

Lovely the voice, lovely the flow of words, the sudden denial of the ear's expectation, the rise, the climb, the house of words like a card castle building, building, bound to tremble, tumble, saved sudden, turned, inverted, the melody resolved, restated, rest.

Sustained applause.

Modestly bowed head for a moment, a mouthed 'thank you', a

33

smile.

'More! More!' from many voices.

Fuck you! What do you want for free?

I stepped down decisively from the stage to forestall the 'entertainment' of questions.

"I'm sure I'm speaking," said Hetherington, "on behalf of us all . . ."

Blah. Blah.

"So let us adjourn to the, ah, Piernian Springs, as it were, of the Faculty Club where there is a Cash Bar."

There were a couple of books to sign. I always think of Faulkner as I smile and write — *with best wishes*. When asked at a party to autograph some books, he said, 'I only sign books for my friends.' All very well for him though — people *bought* his books and Hollywood paid him while he stayed at home and got pissed.

A student asked me for my autograph. He said he'd cut his evening class in Theology and Ethics to attend. The only thing he had with him to write on was his course text-book so I scrawled my name on the half-title of *The Parables of Peanuts*.

Strange business, readings. Paid for by The Canada Council, of course, or else there wouldn't be any. They're not really worth it for me any more unless they're local or the going is getting rough. $125.00 plus travel expenses which usually works out to three days of lost work for about $41.00 per day. Day getting there, day getting back, day recovering while the mind clears itself of flying, drinking, talking, and smiling.

It's always the same. Met at the airport and driven to the hotel suffering from Air Canada chicken. In the hotel you can't turn the heat in your room below 100° and there are watercolours on the wall of Peggy's Cove. Introduced to all the CanLit noddies, dinner in some foul restaurant where the menu's French but the food isn't. The reading. The entertainment of questions. The reception. Driven back to the hotel by somebody who feels compelled to point out all the local landmarks which you can't see even if you wanted to because it's dark.

A lousy night's sleep because of the festive conventioneers who are vomiting in the corridors and knocking on your door and then saying sorry they were looking for good old Mabel.

And then back to the everywhere identical airport where you board, drink too much, eat the chicken and the potatoes sculpted into small balls and read *Sports Illustrated* because the buggers up front got the newspapers and the two copies of *Time*.

But readings aren't all bad. If I've worked an audience well, it gives me an adrenalin jolt and afterwards I feel an exhilarating tigerish tension which takes hours and hours to wind down and I always drink heavily—though often to little effect.

The mob was clearing, wending its way to the Faculty Club, and by the time I got there the place was jammed but old Hetherington had secured me a double brandy. He's only a couple of years older than me but to think of him as 'old' Hetherington seemed inevitable.

He was.

"Jolly moving, I thought," he said.

I downed the brandy and, waylaid by congratulations, made for the bar again. I couldn't see Kathy anywhere in the crush and realized I'd been looking for her all evening, had been extending myself up there for her. I struggled forward.

"Hey, like that was just great," said a hairy student clad in farmer's garb, "that last one. Heavy."

"Thank you," I said. "I'm glad you enjoyed it."

Encroachment year by year of brush on what little there ever was of cultivated land, prickly ash and spindly saplings—severe need for a chain saw and a deluge of brush spray. The last standing blocks of dressed stone thought to be the work of giants.

Where the *fuck* was Kathy?

I got another double brandy and a bottle of Blue and stood there juggling glass and bottle and trying to get at my wallet without losing the liquid in the jostle. I was jammed against a dessicated menopausal creature who was describing to another thing how she'd motivated her eighteenth-century class. She'd run two time-blocks together and every member of the class had had to make, bake, or buy something typically British—muffins, scones, ginger-snaps, Parkin cake, Coventry Godcakes, Bath buns, marmalade—and then they'd all sat around in groups of six and shared a typically English tea. The experience, she felt, with so many of them being *foreign*, had brought them closer together and, dared she hope against hope, added another dimension to Swift and Jane Austen.

Did the other thing realize that Parkin cake was associated with Guy Fawkes? And the triangular Coventry Godcakes with the spires of Coventry's churches? *Most* interesting. And they had located all the place names on the map.

35

And then I saw her, a white blouse, on the far side of the room. The earth didn't move exactly, but I did, glass held high through the press.

"Excuse me."

'. . . surely must be treated in a holistic way to be made comprehensible . . .'

"Excuse me."

'. . . not really sure if it could be classed under the heading of narratology . . .'

"Excuse *me*."

"Hi," I said. "I've been looking for you."

"Oh," she said. "Why?"

"Not looking for you *for* something. Looking for you."

"Oh," she said.

We were staring at each other.

Then she said, "Good."

"Yes," I said.

"Do you always behave like this with women? So direct, I mean."

"No. I've been thinking about you all week."

"You don't know anything about me," she said.

I shrugged.

"I went to your office," she said, "but you weren't there."

"And what would you have done if . ." but broke off as I saw bearing down on us the hearing-aid man.

"Oh, *Christ!*" I said.

She put her hand on my arm.

"Don't," she said. "He's retiring next year. He's nice. He's my friend."

"Good evening, Kathy. Good evening. We haven't been introduced."

"James Wells," said Kathy. "Henry Benson."

We shook hands.

"I attended your reading," he said. "But some of your . . ."

He tapped the battery of his hearing-aid helplessly.

"I hope you won't consider me rude," he said, "but when I was young I had a great admiration for Roy Campbell, a conviction I no longer feel. And now my younger self surprises me. I devote myself now to Shakespeare."

"Do you always express yourself so elliptically?" I said.

"Usually, now," he said, his eyes taking in the room, "I don't express myself at all."

"Usually," said Kathy, "he turns his hearing-aid off. Don't you Henry? And don't pretend you don't."

"What was that, my dear?"

"In the main," I said, "I'd go even further than that. It's premature to teach the work of *any* living writer—but Tennyson, Hardy, Kipling, even later, were read and *bought* by a public which also *bought* contemporary painting and sculpture, which . ."

He nodded to cut me off.

"Yes," he said, nodding again. "Yes. There is point there. We are doubtless at the end of something. Perhaps we've been at the end of something for longer than we care to admit."

He smiled suddenly.

"Forgive me," he said. "Kathy is a solace to me but I sense that I'm intruding."

"Don't be silly, Henry," said Kathy.

To me he said, "Every lunch time I am to be found in here drinking far too much sherry. Perhaps one day you might care to join me?"

"It would be a pleasure," I said. "We can talk about the *Georgiad.*"

"Or just drink sherry," he said.

And then to Kathy, he said,

"Quite unlike last year's mountebank."

We watched him as he ambled his stooped way through the crowd.

"You like him," said Kathy. "I can tell."

Round her neck was a fine gold chain which disappeared into the neck of her blouse.

"Perhaps I was just being polite."

"No, you weren't," she said.

"What makes you think you can tell?"

"Mr. Wells? I did just want to say how much I enjoyed your reading."

I turned and recognized what Lindseer had called Hardy of the Remedial Team.

"Thank you," I said. "I'm glad you enjoyed it."

She looked like a less wrinkled Margaret Rutherford.

I started to turn back to Kathy but she interposed her bulk.

"I was hoping," she said, "you'd come to one of our ModComs in Listening Skills."

"Your *what?*"

"Modules in Speech Communications and Listening Skills," she said.

"I'm sorry," I said, "I'm not sure what you're talking about."

"Well, we have two basic Modules—Speech Communication and Writing Skills, you see."

"No. I'm afraid I don't. At all."

"Well in the Writing Skills Module—apart from the programmed workbook, we seek to avoid externally imposed exercises and contrive to place our students in functional writing situations. We find that . . ."

"What," I said, "is a 'functional writing situation'?"

"Diaries," she said, "and telegrams."

"What's all this got to do with me?"

"Well I was thinking of you more in the context of the Speech Communications Module," she said.

"Were you?" I said.

"If you could read to them—something short, of course, and not too . ."

"What for?"

"Well we're always seeking ways to enhance their effectiveness as interpersonal communicators and your input . ."

"What do you *mean?*" I demanded. "What in Christ's name is an interpersonal communicator?"

She didn't even flinch.

Impervious old sow.

"One of our major problems in remediation, you see," she said, "is speech *motivation.* Many of our remedials are from ethnic backgrounds and of low socio-economic status, and all of them are culturally deprived and so I thought of you in terms of a *motivator.*"

"*Did* you?"

"So my thinking was that if you could read to them for a few minutes—their attention span is inevitably brief—within that verbal context a *natural* interpersonal interchange might be effected."

I stared at her.

"So far as I am able to understand you," I said, "which is not very far, you wish me to read a poem to the students you teach and then let them ask questions. *Is* that what you mean?"

She nodded.

"Then, my good woman, you should say so."

I held her eyes with mine.

"The answer is 'No'. And may I recommend to you the use of the words *poor, foreign, ignorant, conversation,* and *working-class.* And may I recommend further, that you earnestly apply yourself to the works of H. W. Fowler, Eric Partridge, and E. B. White."

Her face had turned a mottled pasty colour, interestingly like a steamed plum pudding.

"I've *never* been so insulted!" she said.

"Then, madam, you have been extraordinarily lucky for far too long."

Her indignant buttocks marched away.

"Good God!" said Kathy. "Do you do that very often?"

"Only under the influence of drink and extreme provocation."

I set my glass on the window ledge.

"I can't stand any more of this place tonight," I said. "I need a quiet drink in soothing surroundings. Coming?"

Chapter Four

The taxi-ride had sped with chatter and gossip. Malcolm suffered an unrequited love for George Norbert; Julia Hetherington had six children and had once voluntarily committed herself; Mary Merton, on political grounds, wanted more than anything else to be a lesbian but couldn't find anyone to take her on; Dr. Gamahuche, the Renaissance man, collected matchbox labels and edited a magazine for phillumenists called *Lucifer*.

I approved of the red leather luxury and deft obsequiousness of the Ambassador Bar. The canapés were good too. Kathy was sipping Pernod and I was drinking scotch. She was in the middle of a story about an awful poetry reading she'd attended at St. Xavier, a famous American poet, she couldn't remember his name, a big man, extremely bearded and sweaty, some sort of Black Mountaineer who'd recited poems with long gasps and indrawn wheezes between lines and even words and afterwards in the faculty club people had been talking about poetry structured in breath units but it turned out he was suffering from emphysema.

Kathy was inspecting me over the rim of her glass with those dark brown eyes. Unlike the first time I'd seen her, the effect was enhanced by eyeshadow and mascara. It occurred to me that I'd like to lick it off.

"Is it true," she said, "that you have a despairing world vision?"

"*What?*"

"Well? Is it?"

"I wouldn't know what a 'world vision' was."

"And that you observe with ironic grace a bleak and desolate landscape?"

"You've been reading dust jacket copy," I said. "Do I *look* as if I have a despairing world vision?"

"There are all sorts of stories about you," she said.

"Nonsense," I said. "People like to invent stories about poets because they think poets ought to be like what they think poets ought to be. It's all Dylan Thomas' fault."

"So it isn't true you set fire to the faculty lounge at Dalhousie University?"

"I was completely exonerated," I said.

"And the funeral in Fredericton where you . ."

"How do you manage to keep looking so gorgeously *fresh?*" I said. "Like a wedge of lettuce, a bite into a radish . ."

"The funeral," she said. "You didn't, did you? Present the ashes to a darts team as a trophy?"

"It was all a misunderstanding. The urn *was* inadvertently left in the Legion Hall," I said, "but tell me. How well do you know Fred Lindseer?"

"Fred? Not particularly. Just through the college. Why?"

"Just wondering," I said.

In the seven years since I'd left Marjorie, apart from casual dippings of the wick, I'd managed to live with four different women for longer or shorter periods of time, sometimes quite happily, always ultimately disastrously. The pursuit of poems always got in the way. I felt there was nothing that humans could do, no contradiction which could surprise me for long, but there was something about this one, this Kathy Neilson, something that didn't make sense . . .

A loud mutter at the next table made me turn. I found myself looking into the glaring face of a large black man. He was wearing a gay orange and blue dashiki with a black tie round his bare neck.

"Pardon?" I said.

"I wasn't talking to you," he said. "I was talking to *me.*"

"Sorry. My mistake. Why are you dressed like that?"

"It's the costume of my country," he said. "The *native* costume."

"Don't talk balls," I said. "You're not African. You're from

41

Barbados."

"*I* know that," he said, "but they not knowing."

"The *tie*," I said.

"They embarrassing me," he said. "I explain them this was a jacket in my country but they not letting me in without a tie and they give me this tie so I thinking, all right man, you embarrass me *I* bloody embarrassing you and sit here and get drunk drunk."

"Good for you," I said.

"I been here making a disgrace," he said proudly, "since six o'clock."

At that moment a large, florid man wearing a hounds-tooth check suit and carrying a brief case and a rolled newspaper strode into the bar. He radiated middle-aged good health.

Still walking across the room, he called to the barman in a booming voice,

"Good evening, Charles. A couple of jiggers of the usual and don't be niggardly!"

"That going *too* far!" said the dashiki man heaving himself upright.

I watched their trajectories to the point of intersection. The blow had a fruity sound and we stood to see the hounds-tooth man sitting on the floor his hand over his nose.

"Who *you* calling niggardly!" said the dashiki man.

"Purse?" I said to Kathy. "I think we'd better be going."

"And in future," I said sternly to the hounds-tooth man, "try to curb these racist outbursts."

I took the dashiki man's arm and hurried him towards the exit. The barman was watching us and speaking closely into the telephone.

"Thank you, Charles!" I called back.

I flagged a passing cab and bundled the dashiki man into the back.

"Got cab fare?"

"Right bang on the nose," he said.

"Well he certainly does now," I said. "No doubt at all."

As the cab pulled out into the stream of traffic, the black tie was thrown from the window.

"Well," I said, "we'll have to find another bar now."

"Don't you think we've had enough?" said Kathy.

"Enough? What kind of talk is that? The night is yet young."

"I was frightened," she said. "I thought he was going to hit *you.*"

"Why would he want to do that? Besides, you can always tell."

"*You* might be able to," she said.

"Where's the next nearest nice bar?"

"Well . . ." she said. And then, "What's amusing you so much?"

"I was just thinking about that man. A very salutary lesson. Works hard all day clawing his way even further up the ladder of success, feels up his secretary, plays squash, sunlamps, dines out, strides into *his* bar to be served by *his* barman with a couple of quick ones before going home to the wife and offspring and suddenly a damn great nigger punches him on the nose. His very world shaken. Here today; gone tomorrow. A house built on sand. What's this place like?"

"I've never been in there," she said.

It was dark and Russian inside with cossacky waiters in boots and bloomers.

"I read about this in a James Bond book," I said, grinding black pepper onto the surface of my second vodka. "It's supposed to be the way the Russians do it. You have to let it all into your mouth at once and sort of sluice it about your back teeth to mix the pepper and then spurt it out again into the glass and then swallow in one."

It was long moments before I could speak again.

Kathy was watching me with an amused interest.

"'One should try everything once'," I croaked, "'except incest and folk-dancing.' Arnold Bax. *Penguin Dictionary of Modern Quotations*."

And then, as breathing became easier and inner warmth spread, I said,

"Jesus Christ! We'd never beat the buggers in a fair fight."

I saw her glance at her watch.

"Are you tired?"

"No. Not particularly. But if you keep on drinking like this . ."

"The Leith police dismisseth us. Peter Piper picked a peck — need I go on? My dear girl . ." I said.

"You," she said, "are forty. I'm only four years younger than you. I'm not exactly a girl."

"I'm a rose-red poet half as old as time," I said. "You're *hundreds* of years younger than I am. And you have very grave and beautiful eyes."

"I have an advantage over you," she said.

"What's that supposed to mean?"

"I've read your poetry. I've been reading it all week."

"And?"

"Underneath all that ironic grace and desolate landscape stuff, I suspect you're just a plain, horrible old romantic."

"That's your diagnosis, is it? And you worry that I'm getting a little long in the tooth to play the roaring boy?"

I patted her hand.

"Little Mother of All the Russias," I said.

"In a few more years," she said, almost reflectively, "you'll be using pancake make-up to disguise the veins in your nose and washing your eyes every morning with Murine."

"Ho, *ho!*" I said. "For a lady in a crisp white blouse you have a surprising range of knowledge."

She shrugged.

I was trying to sort out what I felt about her and felt confused. There was the vagrant thought that she frightened me. I was enchanted by that grin, the grace of her carriage, the gravity of her face in repose. But the maggot of Lindseer's comment was hollowing away at my pleasure. There was something about her, a serenity, a strange reserve, a modesty even — I didn't know *what* it was — impossible to reconcile with Lindseer's contempt. Nothing made sense. I should have waited. A week's patience would have answered any questions. But something demanding in me wanted to see the colour of the blood that flowed.

"So how about it, Jim? Would you order me a coffee?"

"A coffee," I repeated.

"'Sufficient unto the day'," she said.

"Is it my turn?" I said.

"What?"

"I said, 'Is it my turn?'"

She stared at me.

"'Take therefore,'" I said, "'no thought for the morrow: for the morrow shall take thought for the things of itself.'"

I set my glass sharply on the table-top.

"I did *not*," I said, "come out to play paper and pencil games with you. I'm relaxing. I've been working. Hard. I wanted your company."

"*I* didn't start quoting things," she said. "*You* did."

She returned my stare with an annoying composure.

"You're right," I said eventually. "I did. I'm sorry."

"I wanted your company, too," she said. "I know you've been working — and I can only guess how hard but there's something about you when you've been drinking. I don't know — a sort of violence that's frightening."

"What on earth have I done that's violent?"

She shrugged.

"The way you got that man out of the Ambassador so quickly as if you knew what you were doing and you chopped that awful Mrs. Phillips to pieces earlier — oh, I don't know. It's as if you're getting more and more angry inside and might explode at any moment. That's the sort of feeling you give me. And I don't know what the anger's about — and that's frightening too. As if . . ."

"Oh, Holy Christ!" I said. "Look! A gypsy with a violin. And another bugger with an accordian. We've got to get out of here."

As the commissar was producing a taxi, I said, "So it's a deal. No more anger and just one last drink without gypsies."

To the taxi-driver I said, "Would you take us to the Mocambo, please?"

"Where's that, the Mocambo?"

"I have no idea," I said. "You could look it up in your street directory or call your dispatcher."

"I don't know any Mocambo," he said.

"In every North American city," I said, "there is a sleazy night club that features third-rate bands, variety acts, and strippers. It is always called the Mocambo."

"Oh!" he said. "You mean the Show Bar."

"That's the place," I said.

"They play that Danube thing," I said.

"Who?" said Kathy. "The Show Bar?"

"No. Gypsies," I said. "Close to you."

He drove us towards an increasingly dismal part of Montreal which was near the docks and a marshalling yard. On the way, I took Kathy's hand in mine and said, "I'm sorry. I didn't want to quarrel."

"Nor me," she said. "I very much don't want to."

"Why?" I said.

"I don't know," she said.

"We won't stay long," I said.

We were silent.

"You're a bit overpowering," she said. "But you know that, don't you? You use it, I mean."

45

I stared at the appearance and reappearance of her pensive face in the strange shadows of the back of the cab.

"I only know it sometimes," I said. "Or feel it. Only sometimes."

As I paid the taxi-driver I studied the neon which stuttered on the marquee. Playing tonight were The Blue Men, Mister Mugs, and the star attraction, Miss Ora Felony.

At the wicket in the narrow hall, I showed my identification card to the hag in charge and said, "Press". Fifty-ish rock was blasting from behind the padded doors. The horrible woman pressed a buzzer and a burly character in ill-fitting evening dress appeared.

"Press," she said.

"Mr. Haine's off, eh?"

I made as if to proffer the plastic card but he beckoned.

The noise could be felt. He bullied his way through the gloom and crush, cleared a front table, and gestured for a waiter. I nodded my thanks. Kathy bellowed into the waiter's ear for a Coke, I for a Molson Export.

The Blue Men actually were blue. Their suits were blue, their shirts were blue, their shoes blue suede. Even their hair was blue, a light powder blue and blow-swept into lacquered blue cotton-candy crests. There were seven of them. Apart from the drummer who was relatively stationary, the three guitars, fender bass, and two saxophones marched and counter-marched as they played. They also jerked, bowed, hopped and twisted in unison.

We must have caught the last number of their set because the lead tenor advanced to solo with raucous renditions of a medley of Little Richard and Fats Domino standards while kneeling, running on the spot, removing his jacket, and lying on his back with his legs kicking in the air. Behind him the while, his followers in phalanx swung left, swung right, left leg *kick*, right leg *kick*, formed line, advanced, retreated, playing endlessly the same riff over and over.

Then, as the house lights rose to something near the level of the false dawn, the Blue Men battered a few choruses of 'Blue Suede Shoes' at triple tempo and ended with an epileptic attack of drummery and a sort of chord.

There was a brief silence.

Recorded music came on at a bearable level. Conversation became possible. A chair was wedged into my back by one of the waiters as the iron tables were hauled closer together to accommodate the thickening crowd.

"I didn't know you worked on the paper," said Kathy.

"I don't."

"But this," she said, peering at the plastic card, "is dated for this year. For the Winnipeg *Gazeteer*."

"I worked there once," I said, "and a friend renews it for me without the actual blessing of the management. Good for everywhere in Canada except Winnipeg. They know all the boys there and they'd probably check you out. It's no good for political things either. They're tight on them."

"Why bother with it now?"

"In my younger days," I said, "before my world shattering fame had spread as far as Montreal, it afforded me *entrée* into warm places where there was often free food. And enabled me to observe with ironic grace conventions of dentists and 4-H Clubs. I use it now to watch movies and car-crashes."

Kathy was staring about the gloom.

"I've never been in a place quite as crummy and tawdry as this," she said. "It *smells* in here."

"The view from the Ivory Tower usually excludes the Mocambos," I said. "Too high up."

She didn't reply.

"Rapunzel, my sweet Rapunzel, let down your hair and I'll give you a nice guided tour. Let us start with the bar. The bar, you will observe, runs three sides of the stage. Observe more closely and you will notice that in spite of the eager crush, there are spaces at the bar. Those stools which *are* occupied are occupied predominantly by ladies. Every few minutes or so a gentleman will sit next to a lady and after some jovial conversation, a drink taken, a drink bought for the lady, the lady and gentleman will disappear. However, the stools thus vacated are not taken by the pressing throng but, at some unobserved signal from the barman, by yet more ladies. These ladies are ladies of ill-repute.

The black gentlemen in the floppy hats and lavender suede thigh boots are very occasionally charged with living off the avails of prostitution. This year, the gentlemen in funny clothing are all drinking Glennfiddich or Glenlivet. Why, I don't know. Appearances to the contrary, they are not from the U.S.A. They merely wish they were. They are from Jamaica. They have not yet graduated to wearing openly their little coke spoons on their necklaces.

47

Many of the audience — mainly that black part on the left hand side — are not strictly audience at all. They come to see and to be seen. They are, one might say, part of the show. Just in time for the last set, the transvestite brigade arrives. They are given to squabbling. Sometimes a tolerant bandleader will allow one or more to sing with the band. They sing 'Moonlight in Vermont' and 'Misty'.

The strong wafts of pot, always described in fiction for reasons unknown as, 'the sweet, sickening smell of' indicate the presence of a part of the student body working their way through college by hawking lids, uppers, downers, or their arseholes — the usual recognition signal for the latter activity being a request for a light or cigarette.

That forlorn gentleman two tables over to your left with rings on every finger and draped with lengths of sturdy iron chain is not some modern version of a medieval penitent. No. He is, if one may still use such an opprobrious term, a pervert — a pervert in full regalia hoping that another clanking loony festooned with bits of old iron will appear so that they may repair to the boudoir where they can suffer and inflict the wounds of love.

The waiters in all Mocambos are chosen, not for their grace, dexterity, speed, or ability to give the correct change, but because they are all ex-wrestlers or punchy gym-fighters capable of dealing quietly with those drunk enough to become recalcitrant. There is, however, rarely any violence in places such as these as too many interests work together to maintain them as places of business and convenience."

"And *this* is depravity, Jim? This smelly bar? Am I supposed to be impressed? Or are we working up to another bout of anger?"

"Where was I? Yes. Convenience. The conveniences are always concessions. An aged servitor sits inside by a tray of towels, chewing gum, and prophylactics. He offers towels on which one can dry one's hands after one has already dried them on a paper towel. For this non-service, one gives him never less than a quarter. His other activity is to brush invisible dandruff from one's collar and shoulders. This he invariably does while one is in the process of urinating. He performs this task with vigour and causes one thereby to urinate on one's shoes or trouser cuffs.

In the cubicles of his domain, aging gay gentlemen remove their dentures the better to suck the organs of younger gay gentlemen. This lavatorial tryst is, for reasons unknown, called the

48

'tea-room trade'."

"Jim?"

"Over to your right . ."

"Jim!"

"You're interrupting me just as I'm gaining eloquence."

"Why do you come to places like this?"

"You didn't like 'lavatorial tryst'?"

I took out my notebook and wrote it down. Added 'against the porcelain pissed'.

Possibilities there.

"Why Jim?" said Kathy again.

I stared at her.

"Ah!" I said. "How shall I answer thee, Rapunzel? Let me count the possible ways. Shall we say, *nostalgie de la boue*? Or shall we say because I like to observe the activities of the denizens with ironic grace? Shall we say that I am, perhaps, a part of them? May we, *dare* we say, it is the microcosm of the world in which we live? Isn't 'microcosm' a word much used by literary critics?"

"*Why* are you needling me, Jim? *Why* are you trying so hard to be hurtful?"

"Perhaps we might say I'd rather be here getting drunk with a lot of whores who confess themselves as whores than be with the whores by whom I'm employed. And for whom I whore."

"If you feel that strongly, why do you work in universities?"

"What alternatives do you suggest?"

The hominid who'd be keeping us steadily supplied with Coke and Molson Export free of charge appeared again and slammed down two more graceful bottles.

"Rapunzel!" I said. "You've given me a wonderful idea! Why didn't I think of it before? I'll retire. How simple! And live off the avails of my gracefully ironic observations."

"Besides being smelly, it's very *sticky* in here," she said. "Fresh air would be a relief. If you want to perform, you'll have to find yourself another audience."

She tried to push back her chair.

"Fuck you, Kathy Neilson. In your crisp white blouse. Because you work for them, *are* one of them. Because, pathetic as it sounds, I think I'm falling in love with you. And *that's* something I can do without."

She was trying to free her coat from the chair back.

I clamped my hand on her arm.

"Excuse me," she said.

"No," I said. "You can tell me this. How well do you know Lindseer?"

"You're hurting my arm."

"Lindseer."

"What *about* him?"

"You said you knew him through the college. More. Tell me something else."

"I don't understand. He took me out for dinner one night and other than that.."

"And what happened?"

"You're *hurting* me," she said.

"I couldn't care less," I said. "What happened when he took you out for dinner?"

"What business is it of yours? What do you *want*?"

"Just tell me."

"We went out for dinner. We had a pleasant time—he can be very funny when he wants to be. I invited him back to my apartment for a drink, coffee, a cup of tea—whatever. Somehow he got the idea in his head that the invitation went further and he became persistent. And then extremely unpleasant. And I had to more or less throw him out."

"Kathy," I said. "*Listen!* You *must* listen to me. Lindseer said something to me about you—something venemously unpleasant."

"Will you please let go of my arm?"

"I'm sorry. I had to know more. *Had* to know."

"Am I free to leave now?"

"Kathy, for Christ's sake! I'm sorry. Please."

The lights went out.

"*Please.*"

SHOWTIME!

To recorded razzle-dazzle big band music, a small, depressed looking man advanced into the spot. Kathy's shape had not moved. The small man was wearing a kind of lion-tamer's uniform and leather riding boots. He bowed. He clapped his hands. Mister Mugs planed forwards on a skateboard. Mister Mugs was a doleful chimpanzee and more grey and dirty pink in an unpleasant way than hairy. He was wearing a derby and striped pantaloons with suspenders.

"Is *that* all you can do?" said his trainer, stripping the cellophane from a cigar.

50

Mister Mugs then balanced on one leg and stretched out like a scurvy ballerina.

"MATCHES!" shouted the Mugs man.

Mister Mugs waddled to a table and came back with a huge box of matches that said MATCHES on it. He opened the box and extracted an eighteen inch match which he struck fearfully and applied to the Mugs man's cigar. Then suddenly snatched the cigar and puffed happily on it.

"I guess he's so lovable," said the Mugs man, "I can't deny him *anything*. Of course, *he* can't deny anything either."

The spiel was not inspired.

There was a lot of it.

Mister Mugs rode a tricycle, a bicycle, a monocycle, identified the numbers one to five by tapping the required number of times with a pool cue, and, as the finale, played "London Bridge Is Falling Down" by selecting the correct bells from a tuned row and shaking them. He scratched his scaly skin between bells, picked his nose with delicate finger, and bared his yellow fangs in an anguish of simian concentration. It all took a long time. When he'd finished, he applauded himself vigorously. The audience was more restrained.

The house lights rose.

"Poor thing!" said Kathy.

"I should think he's about ready for *Advanced Remedial*," I said.

She pushed the new beer bottle to my side of the table.

"Peace?" I said.

"What did he say about me?" she said.

I shook my head.

There was silence between us.

A couple of unidentifiable rock records played.

"What are you brooding about now?" said Kathy.

"It's sad, isn't it?" I said. "When you think about it? You learn to play an instrument, join a band, practice, learn how to play that instrument while marching about and jumping up and down — years of effort. Dye your hair blue at the cost of any normal social life. And then end up with second billing to a not very good chimpanzee."

"Are you being metaphorical?" she said. "In some subtle way? Another eruption?"

"No. Just thinking about Blue Men and chimpanzees."

SHOWTIME!

51

Darkness fell.

At the rear of the stage there was a dim shuffle of Blue Men and then to the strains of "If You Were the Only Girl in the World" played as pianissimo as the Blue Men were capable of, out into the spot stepped Miss Ora Felony in Victorian costume and parasol. With much mincing, parasol twirling, and shows of shy, shamed reluctance, she removed layer after coy layer of bustle, shift, chemise, slip after chiffon slip, until she stood revealed braced in bra and so many black garters, garter-belts, corselets, and frilly folderols that she looked as if she'd been trussed for multiple injuries by a fetishist member of the St. John's Ambulance Brigade.

These endless dressings were then peeled off to the accompaniment of "A Bicycle Built for Two" until Miss Felony was reduced to naked knockers and a G-string. With a chorus-girl kick, she slipped the parasol between her thighs, half opened it with phallic flick and thrust, and the lights went out.

When they came on again, coloured spots were revolving, bathing her in reds, blues, yellows. The shape of the last Blue Man was filing off. The spot settled into a soft rose. A second rose spot intensified behind her. Its cone of light grew larger and encompassed a gigantic black man sitting behind three drums and clad in a leopard skin loincloth. White strips of fur hung from his waist. He began to play a simple and monotonous rhythm. Miss Felony swayed to the pattern of sound.

The audience quietened.

The drumming increased in tempo and volume, interesting arhythmic notes sounding on the tuned drums. Miss Felony started to stroke her swaying body. The drummer's finger-tips, palms, the edges of his thumbs were flashing over the skins. He was grunting and uttering falsetto cries in emphasis and counter-rhythm. The rhythms he was building were becoming hypnotic. From his bushy hair, rivulets of sweat began to run down his face and glistened on his dark skin. Glistened on his massive chest.

The spotlight on Miss Ora Felony hardened into a yellow. She was now holding a boa-constrictor. She draped the snake around her neck so that its head curved near her breasts. Then, moving with the tempo of the drums, softer now and slower, she began to caress the snake, fondling it, teasing its neck and head with finger-tips towards her nipple. She eased its length across her shoulders, guiding its head down between her breasts, passing its head back and forth across her navel. Her mouth opened and she moistened her shiny lips. The gleaming fluid weight of the snake seemed to flow down her body. Holding the snake's neck with both hands, with grind after grind, she brought its head closer and closer to her plump pudendum.

The drums slowed now, the rhythms like a heart-beat, steady and alive. With soft moans she worked the snake between her thighs. The drum beats thickened. The snake grew out along her braced forearm, uncoiling slowly, rolling from her thigh upwards. The drummer was grunting now and the drums started to urge her, louder, faster. Her hands sliding, seeming to tease, she guided the snake's questing head up the length of her body, between her breasts, until she was holding the snake's neck level with her head but at arms' length. Its tail was coiled round her ankle.

The black drummer's eyes were rolling. His body shone with sweat. The drums urged, edged, urged. Slowly, Miss Felony brought the snake's head closer and closer to her face. She was moving now in a patterned abandon of obedience to the drums. Her mouth opened and she licked her lips. The snake's body looped in fat, glistening rolls around her arms and waist, the thick rolls turning, tightening. One drum now was pattering a continuous mutter, the other, against its rhythm, was urging faster and faster a single throb. Her tongue flicked the side of the snake's head. Her tongue teased the top of the head. A thread of saliva glinted in the light. The opening lips came closer. Finally, Miss Felony took the snake's head deep into her mouth, her thighs thrusting, thrusting. The drums flashed into a frenzy of mounting sound and then were silent with a single resonant knock as the lights were killed.

The applause was wild, whistles, shouts.

When the pink lights came on again, the snake had disappeared. Miss Felony took her plaudits, pointing back at the black drummer.

"Kingo!" she called. "Kingo!"

He rose to his great height and spread his arms.

A Blue Man came forward and draped a cape around Miss Felony's shoulders.

The applause continued as she and the huge drummer left the stage.

The house lights came up.

Our waiter deposited two more bottles.

I glanced at Kathy.

"White woman speak with forked tongue," I said, feeling oddly embarrassed.

"Wasn't the drummer good!" she said.

"Not at all bad," I said, feeling very grateful that the pair of them hadn't returned for some unimaginable encore.

"Was *he* from Barbados, too?" said Kathy.

"No. He genuinely *was* African."

"Hope you'll forgive the intrusion," said a voice which belonged to the chair which had wedged itself into my back. "Couldn't help overhearing your remark. Difficult not to. I'm by way of being a bit of an old Africa hand myself. Definitely African. Yoruba drum patterns when they were genuine but the fellow wasn't Yoruba. Nor were the drums. Not the real thing."

"Won't you join us?" I said, feeling grateful for the interruption. I still felt embarrassed being with Kathy not knowing how she'd been affected by the grossness of the act. And not drunk enough not to care. And not sure still whether she'd forgiven my earlier nastiness.

His joining us involved turning his chair and moving a foot closer. He was wearing a grey suit and his white hair was turning yellow in front.

He held out his hand.

"Harrris Armsby," he said.

I shook hands and performed introductions.

"As I was saying," he said, "not the real thing. They usually play with curved sticks, you know. Listened to them nearly every night of my life. This fellow was playing the sort of thing a six or seven year old would play on a *kannango*. Not Yoruba. Has a more southern look about him.

Pardon? What part of Africa, my dear? In my years, most parts. But the North West, mainly. Seems I've lived there all my life. District officer during the late twenties and thirties and then desk-bound in ghastly Accra."

He raised a finger at a passing waiter.

"If I'm not boring you," he said, "I could . ."

"Not at all," I said.

"Fearful of that," he said. "Of becoming an old bore."

"Don't feel that," said Kathy.

"Well," he said, "the Yoruba master drummers, you see, come from families of drummers. Father to son. Not like being a musician here. The drum is a god. And the drummers are its priests. The Yoruba drummers call the god Ayan. They were my people, you know, the Yoruba. Damned fond of them."

"The Captain," I said to our waiter, "is a musicologist and of our party."

"Eh?" said the waiter.

"Him. He's Press."

"Oh. What is he?"

"What are you?" I said, indicating his glass.

"Scotch," said the Captain.

"Double," I said to the waiter.

"Where was I? Oh, yes. Ayan. All the drummers are called Children of the House of Ayan. Start 'em off as tiny little beggars, banging away. And all the drummers have Ayan as part of their name, you see. Might be called Ayaniji or Ayanwummi. That sort of thing. Now the fellow tonight was playing a kind of *kannango* — trainer drum for kiddies. Learn how to change pitch on that, you see. And when the nipper's good enough they say to him on some ritual occasion:

'*Eni t'o ba mowa we a ba' gba jeun.*'"

A scotch appeared in front of him.

"Means something like:

'Now you know how to wash your hands you can eat with the adults'. Join the other chaps in the orchestra, sort of thing. Then he has to learn the *iy'alu*, the *omete*, and then the *gudugudu*. The *iy'alu* is the mother drum — does the talking — bit of a joke there. And the *gudugudu* is the father drum. The *omete* drums are a sort of well, *chorus*, you might say. Then there's the *kerikeri* drum and the *bata*. On and on."

He poured his scotch down his throat, an action I've seen once or twice performed by beer drinkers but never with undiluted spirits.

"The villagers *sing* the words, you see, while the drums, all different pitch, *play* the words. All very complicated. Damned complicated. I'm not boring you?"

I signalled the waiter.

"Of course," he said, "after thirty years or more, gets a little wearing. One sometimes puts the old 'Jupiter' on the phonograph at full blast to drown it out. Edna couldn't stand it. The drumming. Just noise to her but she never tried to listen."

"But what do they play *about*?" said Kathy.

"Oh, there's always something going on. Secret societies, initiation, parties, general booze-ups of a religious nature. What happened during the day. No end to it."

More scotch and beer arrived.

"This is extremely decent of you," he said.

"My pleasure."

"God!" he said. "I miss Africa. Never happier. Realize that now. I went back to England when they retired me. Truth to tell, couldn't stand the bloody place. Everything changed. They all go out every day at eight-thirty and get rained on and then they watch bloody television all night. And on Sundays they polish their little cars. Beer's revolting. Nothing but fizz and chemicals. Shepherd's pie. My sister in Eastbourne. Ever been to Eastbourne? Take my advice. No children of my own. Everybody bloody rude. Coins absolutely incomprehensible. A pound's a pound but it isn't a pound. New P—damn good name for it. Metric nonsense. Lot of French rubbish. The whole place covered with bloody great roads."

He shook his head sadly and downed another scotch.

"Colonial pension. War disability pension. Old age pension. A bit tucked away. So I thought of years of bingo and shepherd's pie and I—ever had a thing called a Wimpy? Kind of food? Well, anyway, so I thought, a joke's a joke, as they say, but bugger a pantomime. Sailed for foreign climes. Pastures new. Just as bloody boring here."

Yet another scotch appeared and disappeared. His adam's apple didn't even flicker.

"When the war came along, I volunteered right away. Requested transfer. Tired of settling disputes about whose bloody goat ate whose bloody yam and trying to stop the buggers from cutting the telephone wires. Made copper bracelets out of the stuff. Thankless task. Get it back up, next night they'd have it down. So I was ready for a touch of excitement. Back to England. Kitted out. Hung about for bloody ages playing silly buggers. Then popped over to France. Minute we landed, I copped a blighty one. Shot in the arse."

He roared with laughter.

"Cheers!"

"Bored with the whole bloody thing then. Lying on my tummy in Maidstone. Went back to Africa and bloody glad to get there. And all I had to show for it was three holes in the old BTM. One of Nature's and two of Hitler's.

Then Edna died. No point in lying to yourself, is there? She'd never been very strong. Painted a lot, you know. Watercolours.

They were drumming the evening she died—some sort of *Gelede* thing probably. Seemed to have been going on all day. One forgets. I was holding her hand and she whispered to me,

'They're drumming again, Tom.'

Then she just slipped away. Why she called me Tom, I'll never know. Always *used* to call me Jimbo. Don't know why she called me that either. But there you are. She'd been rather odd for years. Couldn't take her down to the Club when we were in the old metropolis—one gin-and-It and she was off. Threw a dart at a barman. Spent most of her time with Chap, our houseboy. Tower of strength, Chap. Efik, you know. Cross River people. But she *could* whip up a good curry—I'll say that for her. Cleared the old passages in no time. The real truth of the matter, no use in beating about the bush, she was absolutely potty. But Chap—God, what a good man Chap was. Used to sit by her bed hour after hour while she read aloud to him. The Bible a lot. Beatrix Potter towards the end. He didn't understand a word of it of course. Just as well really.

And when she died, his heart was broken. Painted himself with red and white clay and sat by her grave for three days howling like a dog. The missionary fellow dropped by—complained about it. Know what I told him? Told him to go and pray for her soul or I'd take his dentures out and stamp on 'em. Never did like vicars and so forth near my chaps.

Chap wasn't his real name, of course. We'd just shortened it. His real name, Christened and baptized, was Second Book of Kings, Chapter One."

He gesticulated with his glass at our waiter.

"Never could sort out what he actually believed in. So far as I could gather, he thought Jesus was a chap who lived in England and Edna was his local representative.

Spine started to play up. Elevated and transferred to a bloody desk job in ghastly Accra. Chap wouldn't leave me. Gave him plenty of dash when I had to retire—damn near broke my heart. He married an Ibo woman or Ibibio—she drove a lorry anyway."

He fell into a brooding silence.

I excused myself and wended my way to the washroom. As I urinated I braced myself against the tiles with my other hand so the servitor only managed to make me wet the toe cap of one shoe. I rewarded him with a quarter.

As I sat at the table again, the Colonel was saying,

"Up in the north country, they're all Muslim of course. My

57

fellows thought Muslims no end of a joke. Had songs about 'em, special dances where they danced the way they thought Muslims looked. Never was very keen on 'em. Those revolting boys lounging about dyed up to the eyebrows in henna. Most of those Muslims, those I had to deal with at their courts — women wouldn't have got a look in! Give those chaps a boy anytime.

They *preferred* boys. *Preferred* them."

"Why?" said Kathy.

"*Tighter*, my dear."

"Oh," said Kathy.

"You must be used to seeing snakes, Colonel," I said quickly, feeling again that unusual embarrassment.

"Don't follow your meaning, old chap."

"I meant tonight. Snakes. You must be used to snakes."

"Got you," he said. "Snakes. Oh, quite. No. Saw hardly a one in all my years. Run over on the road occasionally. Hate the bloody things."

"Well, let's go and look at tonight's," I said. "I think the Blue Men are coming back."

"Ups-a-daisy!" said the Colonel gaily. "Three bags full, sir. Game for anything. Only come to places like this for a nightcap and a little liveliness. Nothing worse than a poof with blue hair."

We made our way to the performers' exit which was guarded by a primate in evening dress. Miss Felony's dressing room was the second down a corridor stacked with crates of soft drinks and cases of beer. The rear of the premises remained warehouse unconverted and cold. The Colonel lurched.

"Old wounds," he remarked to a pile of crates. "Play me up sometimes."

"Press, Miss Felony," I called.

Her dressing room was larger than usual, mirrored with light bulbs, a high power unshaded light hanging from its flex overhead. She was wearing a terrycloth housecoat. Her African drummer was sprawled in a busted arm chair smoking a cigar. He was clad in a paisley dressing gown and woolly slippers. The room, partitioned off from the cavernous warehouse behind, was heated by two electric heaters and smelled of make-up, sweat, and stale perfume.

"Madam," said the Colonel, bowing unsteadily, "an honour."

"Do forgive my not getting up," said the drummer, "but I'm feeling a trifle seedy. The onset of a cold. I'd give absolutely *anything* for a mug of cocoa made with hot milk."

"*Onim deefo kukudurufu!*" said the Colonel.

"I beg your pardon?" said the drummer.

"*Bojuwole ko toju awon omo re etitan ni gbeyin eyin!*" said the Colonel emphatically.

"I'm afraid, sir, that I'm unable to understand you."

"*Oyùnworià, Isirikokota!*" said the Colonel.

"Is your friend quite well?" said the drummer.

"Good God!" said the Colonel. "The fellow speaks English like a native."

I felt things were getting out of hand.

"May I," I said, "introduce Miss Neilson, a noted herpetologist. And General Armsby here, late of Africa. The General, having sustained fundamental injuries in the war, is now retired and devotes himself to the study of African music."

"Apart from being *born* in Africa," said the African removing his afro, "I was brought up entirely in England actually. Boarding school and so forth."

"Just noise to Edna," said the General, "but she never *gave* herself, you see. With her it was always daffodils."

"And the year I came down from Balliol they shot Pop for peculation and the ready ceased to flow. Even Gabbitas and Thring couldn't find me a niche. So there I was faced with teaching grubbies in a secondary mod or collecting tickets on the Underground. Anything, thought I, rather than either. I'd played drums at Oxford with the Carfax Rhythm Kings so upon ending up on these wilder shores, a drummer I became."

"I think you'd better get a crate and let the old gentleman have your chair, Harry," said Miss Felony.

"A tragic tale," said Harry. "From mud hut to rags."

"What about me?" said Miss Felony.

"Honoured, madam," said the General. "But what about the *kannango?*"

"The drum things, do you mean?" said Harry. "From a Folkways record, actually."

"Needless to say," I said to Miss Felony, "we were fascinated by your act. Rarely have I seen a stripper perform with such abandon, such artistry."

"Exotic," she said.

"I'd go further," I said. "Almost unbelievable."

"No," she said. "*I'm* an exotic not a *stripper*. Or you can use . . ." She rummaged about in a sequinned purse and came out

59

with a card which had written on it in ballpoint capitals ECDYSIAST.

"Our agent insists on that," she said. "Exotics get paid on a different scale, you see."

"And justly so," I said.

"Although not strictly accurate," said Harry. "I've always wanted a reporter to use the word *figurante* or *coryphee*."

"Would you like a drink?" said Miss Felony. "We've only got gin. We ran out of mix. Why don't you go and pinch some more, Harry?"

"It's the mix that's bad for you," I said.

"Because I'm not feeling very well, Charmaine," said Harry. "That's why."

"Well be a pet and plug the kettle in, then," she said. "We'll have it with a drop of warm water. You never do *anything*."

"You've no idea," he said, "how positively *exhausting* it is being primitive."

"Sometimes," she said, "I think you're almost as bad as Mimi."

"Oh, poo on you!" said Harry.

"Most gracious of you," said the General. "Never could refuse a lady."

"He's got manners, Harry," she said, "even if he *is* pissed."

"Poo, poo, poo," said Harry.

"Sun's over the yardarm," stated the General.

We drank to each other's health in warm gin. I watched Kathy's face as the fumes hit her.

"Isn't this *comfy!*" said Harry.

"Now about this snake," I said.

"Don't you *hate* mornings?" said Harry. "All those milkmen."

"You'll have to wait a bit," she said. "He's still in the fridge."

"In the *what?*"

"Well it quietens him down, you see. I pop him in for half an hour before I go on and for half an hour after I come off. Quietens him down. That and plenty of food."

"Well let's start off with your career," I said. "How you came to be an exotic. And about the snake, of course."

"You'll give us a good notice, won't you?"

"Certainly. More. I want to do a piece."

"Personally," said Harry. "I'm quite happy with 'savage' and 'primitive' but *figurante* does have a certain . . ."

"I'll definitely work it in," I said, taking out my note book.

60

"I've always wanted to use *poses plastiques* so I know exactly how you feel."

"Lovely," he said, wiggling his woolly slippers.

"And if we're going to use *figurante* for Charmaine, I think we'd better have you as the son in exile of a paramount chief. Do you like 'paramount'?"

"I used to be shaded under *huge* umbrellas," said Harry.

"And the General translated," I said.

"My pleasure," said the General. "Absent friends," he added draining his glass.

"And whenever I was walking along and got tired my retinue had to go down on all fours for me to sit on them," said Harry.

"Sounds like Ghana, Benin," confided the General in a loud voice. "Though he still looks more southern to my eye. No Arab in *him*."

"Certainly not recently," said Harry.

"*I started*," said Charmaine.

"I'm so sorry," I said.

"I started," she said, "as a single. Parasol strip on the Main and in the East End and some of the French clubs up north. *Miss Bounty*, I was then. All the really top clubs were belly dancers then—Arabs from Trois Rivières, if you know what I mean. But I was doing very nicely. Plenty of work. And I didn't have the weight for the belly anyway. And it went on like that for about five years but then everything began to change. All the clubs started to change hands—even the small ones that hadn't been before. You know. The old Silver Dollar went for slot machines and The Rodeo got bought out by the Chinamen. It's The Lodeo now and they have their own sort of things in there. It was rougher but things settled down until the transvestites ruined it all. Suddenly everyone wanted transvestites. So Lenny had me doing doubles with a transvestite juggler called Mimi the Barmaid—oh he *was* a bitch—and then a lot of clubs began to go for Amateur Nights and they were more popular *and* they were free so . ."

"What sort of Amateur Nights?"

"You know," she said. "They're very popular down East Montreal."

"Tell me."

"Well, you know. Getting people up on the stage singing and dancing that aren't right in the head."

"Mentally retarded?" I said. "Idiots?"

"Simple," she said. "And they pay them with Monopoly money so all the professionals were getting squeezed out."

"Times were becoming hard?"

"So Lenny called me in, he's my agent . ."

"One of nature's gentlemen," interrupted Harry.

"Thank you sir," said the General. "You honour me."

"So Lenny said, Charmaine, he said, we've got to change your act. We've got to change your name. He said, Charmaine, you've got it all, he said, but we're in trouble. Your legs are lovely, he said. Your behind's a treat. And your mammaries — words fail me, he said. But, he said, are mammaries enough? They're fickle — the audiences. They want more. He said I had to be more — what was it, Harry?"

"Knowing him," said Harry, "I expect it was 'explicit'."

"He's a gentleman, Lenny," she said.

"They broke the mold," said Harry.

"Snakes, he said, is what they want. I couldn't touch one I said for love or money. So he sent me to a psychiatrist for snake-lessons. Paid for it himself every cent. Talking about them. Looking at pictures. Touching a snake skeleton. Being in a room with one in a cage. Took weeks and weeks. Until I could touch one. Then I had to look after one in my apartment. And then until I could touch one with my tongue. What *was* that word, Harry?"

"Conditioning," said Harry.

"Yes," she said. "Until I could, well, you know . ."

"Put its head in your mouth," I said.

"Well I know it's a bit rude," she said, "but a girl's got to make a living."

"Tell me, Charmaine, what do you think about when you're doing it?"

"Food," she said. "Well not now, not so much. But I did. It's cold out of the fridge and at first I tried to think of well, like sucking a carrot but really I don't think much about anything now. Though I have a few before I go on."

"Well, thank you," I said, "just a drop."

"Ladies!" said the General. "Gentlemen! Your health. Collectively."

"Same to you," she said. "Of course, Lenny didn't like that."

"Who is Lenny?" said the General.

"Shush!" said Kathy.

"Didn't like what?" I said.

62

"Me drinking. Said it'd ruin my figure and he didn't like his artistes on the juice. But he doesn't have to do it, does he? And a little drop of gin never hurt anybody. Well, anyway, before I started with it — with the act I mean — Lenny'd found Harry. He said I needed colour for the act and Harry being.."

"As in 'local colour'," said Harry.

"And we practised for hours, didn't we, Harry?"

"Hours," agreed Harry.

"And Lenny has this colour-chart thing for the lights and everything that the club has to use."

"The primitive savage sweat which courses down my gleaming bod," said Harry, "is supplied by glycerine secreted in and from this disgusting wig."

"Lenny sounds a very talented man," I said.

"Ineffable," said Harry.

"Ladies present, old chap," said the General disapprovingly.

"Would you like to see Snakey?" said Charmaine.

"Most definitely," I said.

She opened the small fridge and lifted him in a lump out of the vegetable crisper. He was as rigid and unpliable as a coil of frozen garden hose.

"You're not on again tonight, are you?" I said.

"No. Just the band."

"Well why put him in the fridge when you're not going back?"

"Well the spot lights heat him up," she said, "and the fridge calms him down for the night."

She placed the tangled lump in a wicker basket.

"*Is* he a he?"

"Ooh!" she said. "I never thought. How do you tell? I never even thought about it. Oh, I do hope he's a him. It'd be more — well — natural, wouldn't it?"

She stared down at the snake.

"Miss Neilson?" I said. "Would you care to make an examination?"

"It is definitely a male," said Kathy. "The neck markings are quite distinctive."

"Oh, that *is* a relief," said Charmaine. "Just think — I'd never even thought . . ."

"God!" said the General. "What an ugly brute!"

But his eyes were so unfocused it was impossible to tell if he was gazing at the snake or Charmaine.

"Bottoms up for a dead soldier!" she said, proffering the gin bottle.

"They did not die in vain!" declared the General.

"Steady the Buffs!" said Harry.

"Talking of which, Charmaine," I said, "and this is always good copy — have you ever been arrested or fined for indecency?"

"Only by the SPCA," she said. "Not fined. A letter of protest. Lenny was furious. He *wants* me to be arrested. It's a vegetarian," she said. "It eats eggs. There's no cruelty in eggs. *Rabbits* or something but a nice egg!"

"Cooked?" I said.

"Cracked," she said.

I made a note in my book.

"Cruelty!" she said. "I was born right here in Montreal. In Verdun."

"Ah!" said the General. "I missed that show. Just a youngster at the time. Heard my father's stories, though."

Charmaine, very angry, stared down into her empty glass.

"Cruelty!" she said. "If it's cruelty you should see between my thighs! If I pull him and the scales go the wrong way it chafes me nearly raw."

"Jim?" said Kathy. "The General's asleep."

"*General!*" I said.

"Well, just a small drop," he said, starting up.

"No, no. It's time to go."

"Go? Go where?"

"Cruelty!" said Charmaine. "It costs me a fortune for my thighs in handlotion."

We thanked them for the interview and drinks and made our way along the cold corridor echoing with good-byes to the warmth of the club.

"Why was she all orange?" said Kathy.

"Water-solvent skin base called Golden Glow," I said. "Otherwise they look like slabs of veal under the lights."

"How do you know that?"

"I forget," I said. "Perhaps I made it up."

I seated the General at the bar.

"I don't want to go home," said the General. "Reminded me of Chap. That chap. Poor Edna. She was an Anglican, you know."

"General," I said. "It has been an honour but I'm sure you'll understand if I tell you that Miss Neilson and I have a pressing engagement."

"Delighted!" he said. "Delighted. And when is The Happy Day?"

I patted him on the shoulder.

I was feeling full of a spreading happiness. The world seemed full of possible diversion. I was feeling expansively drunk.

"For my friend, the General," I said to the barman tossing a bill onto the bar, "a double cognac. From an unopened bottle."

I touched to his glass the print-smeared glass which was still somehow in my hand.

"They shall not pass!" I said.

"They did," said Kathy.

"What?" I said.

"Bear him children!" said the General loudly and to the interest of two nearby whores. "And the secret of married life is simply this: *E je gba kadara.*"

"Thank you," she said and kissed his cheek.

Our destination was a delicatessen. We were in a taxi. I had an impression of a huge window full of vast bottles of yellow and red pickles, pyramids of bagels, hecatombs of smoked meat and pastrami studded with spice, golden fish and silver paper, and obese, dark, hanging salamis.

Chapter Five

I awoke in a white room to the mutter of distant typing. I was lying in a double bed. Facing me was a window. Hanging inside the recess of the window's white woodwork was a fern in a brass bowl. The sunlight burnished the bowl, glowed on the fern fronds. The green of the fern was strong but delicate. I stared at the white planes and angles of the casement corner, the curve of the glowing bowl, the emerald fern. The sunlight held them timeless like an intense detail of a *trompe l'oeil* painting. It was imperative that I concentrate on them, incorporate them, before the sudden beauty vanished, before clouds broke the spell.

No need for a notebook. Things seen in such a way burn in my memory. These things seen, would, I knew, appear at some time in a poem. As seen now, transmuted perhaps, translated. I didn't know how I knew but I'd learned not to think about it.

On the white window sill below the fern stood a massive brass pricket candlestick. It had an ancient, ecclesiastical look. One, perhaps, of an altar pair. A heavier colour than the bowl. On the white wall opposite the bed hung a Chinese scroll painting on yellowing silk, leaves, branches, mountain peaks, the suggestion of mountains beyond them. Near the bottom of the painting, three tiny figures were crossing a bridge.

I lay there without moving and allowed the colours and shapes to soak into me.

The bed was comfortable. Clean white sheets. A dove-grey blanket with a single blue stripe across it. I moved a leg and an arm and felt myself to be naked except for my underpants. Anything but slight movement seemed unwise. I had a definite hospital feeling. Tongue like a dead tie, eyes sunny side down. I could not see my clothes. I extracted my arm from the tight-tucked bed and studied my watch. It said 9:30.

"Hello?" I called.

The typing noise stopped and I heard the scrape of a chair and then Kathy appeared. Her head was turbanned in a towel. She was wearing jeans and a blue shirt loose over them.

"Good morning," she said. "And how do we feel today?"

"We don't know yet."

"I'll make some fresh coffee," she said.

There were sounds from somewhere else and then the roar of a coffee grinder. The smell of the ground coffee coloured the room. I lay there helpless. She was singing and humming.

I stared at the fern and the strange shapes of its shadow.

She came in with two mugs of coffee and set them on the bedside table.

"My one extravagance," she said. "I just can't drink instant coffee any more."

"You should have lots of extravagances," I said. "It's more fun."

I heaved myself up a bit and managed a few sips before falling back. She lighted two cigarettes and put one in my fingers. Then she sat on the edge of the bed.

"How long have I been asleep?"

"About five hours."

"It's not enough," I said.

As I leaned towards the trembling coffee mug I noticed she wasn't wearing shoes.

"Your feet are nice," I said.

"You look really revolting," she said. "Do you *feel* that bad?"

"Worse," I said.

"You seemed O.K. in the cab," she said. "It must have been the beer in Maxie's. Delayed action or something."

"Maxie's?"

"Where we went after the Show Bar."

"Oh, *Maxie's*," I said.

67

Her dark brown eyes studied me. She seemed suddenly amused.

"You don't remember, do you? Why you're here and not at your place. And the wrestler? And the two Greek waiters?"

"No," I said.

"Would you like to hear about it?"

"No," I said.

"When we went in," she said, "there was a huge fat man at the counter with a completely shaved head. You insisted that he was a wrestler called Gilles 'The Fish' Poisson and that you'd seen him fighting somebody called Tarzan at the Forum."

"Tarzan Tyler," I said.

"You persuaded him to come and sit with us and you ordered him three pastrami specials because you said he had to keep his strength up."

"Christ! I must have been drunk."

"And he kept on insisting he'd had ringworm and was employed in the carpets department at Eaton's. And *you* kept on insisting that you understood and respected his wish to remain incognito. And you'd gone and introduced me as a noted herpetologist and he obviously thought that meant some kind of doctor because he wouldn't stop telling me all about his ringworm."

"I hope we didn't touch him," I said.

"Then," she said, "when the food came, you said the french fries were McCain's frozen french fries and were not acceptable. And the waitress said they were the only kind there were and you said you didn't wish to bandy words with her and demanded to see the manager."

"The correct line to take," I said.

"When you're drunk," she said, "you don't talk—you *orate*. And in the most grandiloquent way. It's embarrassing. There was a particularly elaborate one that involved grapes withering on the vine and McCain's being the Mark of Cain. And I think fig trees being blasted came into it somewhere."

I flapped a hand at her.

"Anyway," she said, "you informed the manager that frozen french fries were a disgrace, a blot upon an otherwise admirable establishment. You went on about it and he just waited till you'd finished and then he said french fries were french fries so what was the big deal? And then you *really* got going. You said frozen french fries were a blight spreading across the land and were a symbol of the spiritual malaise from which Canada suffered."

I nodded approvingly.

"You demanded to know how poetry and the arts, how civilized society itself, could grow and flourish if the basic things of life such as lovingly prepared food were denied the citizenry."

"And what did he say to *that*?"

"He said to put ketchup on."

"You see!" I said. "I was provoked."

"And why didn't you shut up anyway? And *then*," she said, "starting with a general attack on North America for its lack of an indigenous cuisine, you mounted to accusing him of pandering to debased tastes. Then you accused him of deliberately setting out to debase taste. Then you called him a whoremonger in a monkey suit. And by then another manager had come and it started getting more complicated and obscure."

"What do you mean 'obscure'?" I said. "I'm never obscure."

"Well, you were trying to associate frozen french fries with watching television and reading bad books and bad money driving out good."

"Nothing obscure about that," I said. "It's obvious and true."

"And then," she said, "he called two Greek waiters to throw you out."

"Was I wounded?"

"No. I saved you," she said. "I calmed him down. I said I was a medical aide and that you were out under my care on a three-day pass from the Allen Memorial Institute."

I stared at her.

She grinned and the grin grew into a smile.

"I've never done anything like that before," she said. "I've been thinking about it all morning and I'm still pleased with myself. I think usually I'd just have watched or been carried along with what was going on. But I knew that if anyone touched you, you'd have hit them. And I wasn't going to have you hurt. And it was easy to do. I didn't really *decide* to do it. It wasn't *me*. I was a noted herpetologist with this person under my care. And it was easy—it was like being in a play. I even enjoyed it in an odd way. It's being with you," she said. "It's catching."

"I hope I denied this?" I said. "This business of being insane."

"No. You were trying to incite Gilles 'The Fish' Poisson to tear them all apart with his bare hands and *he* kept on saying, 'Look! I don't even know this guy. I'm sitting at the counter. All it is, he bought me a sandwich'."

"The coward!" I said.

"And the manager kept on saying, 'Look, lady. Just get him out of here, all right? Just get him back to the funny house, no insult intended. Lady this is a *restaurant*.' And you'd collected a large crowd by then and . . ."

"Have you got any aspirins?" I said.

"And you stood up and rapped on the table with an empty beer bottle and started quoting that Wordsworth thing about taste from the *Preface* and while you were declaiming *that* in a sort of Jeremiah way, the manager was saying, 'Lady, *please*. This is a *restaurant*' and Gilles 'The Fish' Poisson was saying, 'I don't even *know* the guy' and some kids were shouting 'Right on!' and 'Leave the old guy alone!'"

"Old!" I said.

"And a woman kept saying, 'Are they making a movie?' 'Is it a movie?'"

"Aspirins?" I said again.

"And then the taxi," she said. "We were obviously off on a guided tour. You kept on saying, 'I'll recognize it when I see it'. So I brought you here."

As she was going out, she said, "Oh! And if you were wondering—I slept on the couch."

I closed my eyes.

When she padded back with the aspirins and another mug of coffee, she had a book with her. She settled herself on the end of the bed, found the place she was looking for, ran her finger down the page.

"This was it," she said. "How on earth you remember things . ."

"Photographic memory," I said.

"Funny you couldn't remember the name of your street," she said.

She started to read:

'For a multitude of causes, unknown to former times, are now acting with a combined force to blunt the discriminating powers of the mind, and, unfitting it for all voluntary exertion, to reduce it to a state of almost savage torpor. The most effective of these causes are the great national events which are daily taking place, and the increasing accumulation of men in cities, where the uniformity of their occupations produces a craving for extraordinary incident, which the rapid communication of intelligence hourly gratifies. To this tendency of life and manners the literature and theatrical exhibitions of the country have conformed themselves. The invaluable works of our elder writers, I had almost said the works of Shakespeare and Milton, are driven into neglect by frantic novels, sickly and stupid German tragedies, and deluges of idle and extravagant stories in verse. When I think upon this degrading thirst after outrageous stimulation . . .'

She slapped the book shut and grinned at me.

"If you could only have heard the counterpoint to that," she said, "the manager, the comments from the crowd, Gilles 'The Fish' Poisson saying 'I was sitting at the counter. He comes up to me . .'"

"It isn't funny," I said.

"You should have been there," she said.

"That's what we've lost," I said. "Dignity, clarity, cadences. And we're left with exactly what he described — in spades."

She inspected me, the only word for it, her face taking on that grave, considering expression.

"You don't just think these things, do you?" she said slowly. "I mean, they're not just ideas or intellectual positions for you, are they? They're things you really *feel*."

"You got it, Tootsie," I said, "me and de Tocqueville both."

"So *that's* what some of that violence is," she said. "That dangerous feeling."

"At times," I said, "you remind me of an intense fifteen year old. When they've just understood something or they're being earnest about injustice. You also look about fifteen. And you're making my headache worse."

"Hmmm," she continued, obviously pursuing her own line of thought.

"Stop staring at me," I said. "It's like being in a toy shop with an outsize Easter Bunny."

"Hmmm," she said again.

"I suppose I ought to apologize," I said. "For embarrassing you, I mean."

"What? Oh. Well I *was* embarrassed at first but then I wasn't. I've never been a noted herpetologist and a medical aide in one night before. I think I liked it."

I wanted to squeeze her foot but I didn't have the strength.

She glanced at her watch.

"I've got a tutorial at twelve," she said, "and some work to do before that and I've got to dry my hair and get dressed. You know

71

it's Wednesday, don't you?"

"What's Wednesday supposed to mean?"

"This is your first afternoon—your office hours start at one."

"I have to *go* there? Today?"

She was taking clothes out of the closet. I saw my suit.

"So I'll leave you the key and when you feel better you can lock up after you and give me the key this afternoon. I'll be in my office."

I grunted.

"Isn't it supposed to be one of the things about alcoholism?" she said. "One of the Five Signs or whatever it's called?"

"Isn't what?"

"Black-outs?"

I closed my eyes.

She went out and I listened to the whoosh of her hair-dryer and then the *brrrr* noise it made as she put it on something to use comb or brush. I could picture her movements exactly having seen them performed by many other women. I wondered vaguely what it was like being a woman, dressing, putting on make-up, hair-tending, as if each day were an appearance on a stage. And how much of every movement was calculated and what it felt like to be under continuous sexual observation. Which led to probably fascinating thoughts about what women were when they weren't on stage. I'd often wondered about it. Wondered even if they ever weren't. But my head hurt too much so I closed my eyes and listened to the inside of it.

As she'd leaned forward to set the coffee mugs on the table, I'd caught a glimpse under the blue shirt of her navel. It was a nice navel and I like navels but even thinking about *that* was painful. In spite of the aspirins, my headache was obliterating and my body felt as if I'd had a jolly night with the Gestapo. I curled up and clutched my limp member to comfort myself. It felt like a plasticine afterthought.

My earlier efforts at courteous conversation had been a mistake. They had taken their toll. I felt very bad-tempered. Oblique temperance lectures in the early morning, boiling stomach acids sloshing about, the prospect of having to get up and go out and *do* things, and now, intimations of a bowl and rim spattering explosion of diarrhea.

I wondered vaguely, too, through the hammering pain if at forty I was undergoing some distasteful menopause or experiencing the grand climacteric twenty-three years early. Or if it was simple senility. There had to be *some* explanation. The symptoms were impossible to ignore. A disgusting access of sentimentality being the main one. Babbling in my cups of love. Thinking of this woman I hardly knew as a bunny rabbit, a chocolate bar, a fucking pixie for Christ's sake! Wanting to squeeze her foot. Feeling happy with the intimacy of her lighting a cigarette for me. This was not the Jim Wells of old, the old ramrod dying of women, Wells the scourge of pudenda.

"You know, Jim," she said, coming into the room and opening the closet *rattling* things, "it'd be the decent thing to do if you *did* write a piece about Harry and Charmaine."

Write and thank Grandma for the nice birthday socks.

I opened my eyes and glared at her now black corduroy rump.

"What were you typing?" I said. "Before."

"Just some notes."

"As long as you weren't writing fucking *poems*."

"No. I was writing about somebody else's poems," she said, "and if you're not careful, you grumpy sod, I'll tell you some of the more passionate declarations you made in the taxi."

She hurried out again.

Then she seemed to be hurrying in again. She stood in the middle of the room holding a pair of black shoes.

"I suppose you *would* feel that way," she said, "having to fight against it. And I never think much about things like that because *my* work's so remote from it."

"What are you *twittering* about?"

"About taste and so on. I'd never thought about it really. From your point of view, I mean. You know, about readers and audience and selling books and so on. It's quite interesting."

"We ought to have a chat about it one day," I said.

"I've got to rush," she said. "Key's on the table."

I listened to her receding footsteps.

"*Where am I?*" I called.

"Ten minutes from the Forum by cab. Bye!"

The door slammed.

I closed my eyes.

It was imperative to get moving.

I'd been sweating out the booze and my skin felt as if I'd been rubbed all over with a fine grade machine oil and then dusted with powdered brick. Any exertion and I'd crack. In her bathroom mirror I looked at my Looney Toon eyes. I inspected her bathroom cabinet. I always look in women's bathrooms. Perhaps it's a kind of perversion. Hers contained nothing of any interest. Make-up. Some tablets that said three times daily and a squishy old tube of something. I'm always hopeful of finding some amazing sexual device.

I remembered another painful morning in another woman's apartment years before. I could still taste the greasy shock of it and the dry heaves over the washbasin and the spitting. In her bathroom cabinet I'd found a small, rusting, leg razor matted with hair and a new toothbrush. The toothbrush had been so cunningly sealed into its plastic box that I'd had to stamp on it to smash it open. And then, bristles arrested, my mouth had filled with the sudden realization of Delfen Spermicidal Gel.

Imperative to get moving, work to be done, thank Noddy Hetherington for my desk to make him feel worse, chat up the secretary, generally show the flag and give the impression of furious creativity.

The kitchen was so narrow it was almost a galley. The main room was large — one of those living room, dining room affairs with an arch between. The living room had a couch and armchair and a fireplace beside which was a pile of birch logs on the tiled hearth. A vase of bronze coloured chrysanthemums stood on the coffee table.

The dining room part was equipped as an office. The walls were solidly shelved. A desk and typewriter. A filing cabinet. I glanced along the books. The major works. The major references. Masses of critical bumph. Horrible journals. On the bottom row a lot of calf and gilt. At some cost, I stooped to read a title. Sermons. On the desk were some folded galley proofs. I didn't look at them. I'd looked in her bathroom and galleys were a bit like reading letters though I'd have looked if I'd been feeling better. On top of the typewriter sat a green Victorian book bristling with paper markers. I looked at the title page. George Herbert. *The Temple; Sacred Poems and Private Ejaculations.* I knew I wouldn't have the strength even for that.

I locked the door, went out, it was an old apartment building on a street with trees, walked downhill in unwelcome sunshine. I flagged a cab and relapsed until the driver said I was where I wanted to be. In my room I had an immediate desire to climb into my wardrobe and close the door. I imagined my corpse in the wardrobe surrounded by my regalia, a pen and typewriter, piles of soiled feminine underwear, launched into a strong current like a Viking pyre.

Taking clean clothes, I bolted myself in the communal bathroom with its probably endemic athlete's foot and drug-resistant fungal spores. I washed my hair with something called Breath of Pine. A brief, gagging swill with Lavoris. Two freezing bursts of spray for the pits. Where I'd walked, it was possible to make out the pattern of the linoleum.

The pain, compounded now by nausea, was reaching crisis point. Standing in front of my mirrored wardrobe and knotting my tie with shaking hands, I thought of St. Ignatius of Loyola. According to Loyola, Xavier was the stiffest clay he had ever molded. My clay, I thought, was more like liquid slip. Stiffening was what it needed. A couple of St. Xavier's Bloody Marys were my only hope of salvation. And at that it would be a miracle high up in the Lazarus class.

I sat in my office.

Nothing happened.

Irregularly, the door of the washroom opposite banged like a rifle shot — the shushing device at the top doubtless removed by some student prankster.

Outside my window, squads of very big boys were running plays and knocking each other down — the famed Conquistadors from the Physical Arts Complex with a budget reputedly twice that of the library. They were being coached by the Director of the Physical Arts Complex, a large moron with a very loud voice upon whom, according to the Calendar, a college in Louisiana had conferred a doctorate. I closed the window to muffle their hupping and bellows.

Four Bloody Marys in the soothing company of Henry Benson had sealed the exposed nerve endings and restored my humour. A conversation with Henry Benson was a matter of such delicacy and obliquity that meanings approached and retreated like the formal movements of a minuet. I had, however, by the rudeness of direct questions, forced some very interesting information from him.

Kathy, it turned out, was the star academic attraction of the whole arts side of the dump. She had been selected for the honour

75

of preparing an annotated *Complete Works of George Herbert* for the Oxford University Press. Apparently there existed no reliable translation of his Latin poetry and his prose works were not in print. Neilson was her married name. She had been a widow for three years. Her husband and six-year-old son had been killed in the car crash which had left the ridged, white scar on her brow. She had first come to St. Xavier because her husband was working as a geologist for the Quebec government and she had remained at St. Xavier... inertia might possibly account... She had become, perhaps, though understandably, too self-contained, withdrawn... reaction to the terrible personal...

Further than this it was impossible to go without violating Benson's sense of decorum. There had hovered round the edges of his conversation unspoken pleas.

I lapsed into drawing a frieze of stick figures on my nice new stationery. My jolliest smile had extracted from the secretary, physically an unfortunate specimen, lots of paper, letter-head, nice coloured markers, and the method of making long-distance phone calls. It was a pleasing system because, as far as I could work out, untraceable. One merely claimed to be Hetherington.

I did a row of stick-figures having sword-fights.

Benson's information made sense of her apartment. The grimly professional study. And the submerged side of her personality which the white bedroom with its beautiful objects carefully chosen hinted at. I allowed my mind to luxuriate in the radiance of the fern in its brass bowl.

With my Royal Blue marker I wrote:
Kathy Neilson.
And then:
Katherine Neilson.

I thought of her body but felt no lust. I was lost in an adolescent haze of generalized desire.

I did not want to think of her dead husband. I did not want to think of her dead child.

Suddenly the door opened and a muttering man in overalls from Supply shambled in. He stared at me. He consulted a clipboard.

"You're not McCready, R.," he said.

"True," I said.

"You were last year," he said.

"I wasn't, you know."

He looked puzzled and shambled out again.

I swivelled on my chair for a bit.

Flipping through my *Dictionary of Saints* I came upon St. Creophothus martyred in Thrace in 1407. Publically buggered to death for theological reasons.

(Cross-reference to Bogomil, Heresies of)

I investigated Bogomil.

My desk was nice. In one drawer was a pile of term papers dating from nineteen hundred and seventy-two. I looked at the top one. It was three pages long and preserved in a glassine binder, the third-year work of one Sandy Rowson. It said:

A Study of the Poetry of John Donne

"The poetry of John Donne was mainly written in the seventeenth century. John Donne was British by birth. He was also a priest. His poetry is Metaphysical poetry. According to the dictionary of which I made use in my research (Webster's New World Dictionary, College Edition. 1959. The World Publishing Company.) the word Metaphysical means — 1) of, or having the nature of, metaphysics; of the nature of being or essential reality 2) very abstract, abstruse, or subtle: often used derogatorily of reasoning 3) based on abstract reasoning 4) beyond the physical or material; incorporeal, supernatural, or transcendental 5) fond of or skilled in metaphysics 6) designating or of the school of early 17th-century English poets, including especially John Donne, George Herbert, Richard Crawshaw, and Abraham Cowley, whose verse is characterized by very subtle, highly intellectualized imagery, sometimes deliberately fantastic and far-fetched: term first so used by Samuel Johnson.

It is my definite opinion that of all these definitions it is definition number six that is the one that concerns us most at this point."

In the margin by this sentence was a large red tick.

I swivelled on my chair for a bit again.

A knock on the door interrupted my contemplation of the oak hat stand.

A nattily dressed boy came in and enquired if he'd found the right Mr. Wells — Mr. Wells the Poet-in-Residence. He was, he said, in search of information and a favour. I waved him to the other chair where he seated himself with assurance. Against the side of the chair he propped a pigskin briefcase of impressive slimness. He had about him the aura of an embryo life-insurance salesman. I wondered if he was one of the barracudas from Business Administration or Engineering cruising in search of Mickey Mouse credits.

"And how can I help you?" I said.

"My name's O'Malley, sir. Martin O'Malley. I'm in my last year of Communication."

"I often feel that way myself," I said.

"Pardon?"

"Do go on," I said.

"Well, you see," he said, "I'm in Sound."

"Sound?"

He explained that the Communication Arts Complex was divided into Sound and Visuals. After much questioning and confusion on my part it turned out that Sound meant, roughly speaking, radio and recording things with tape-recorders.

"And so how can I be of assistance?" I said.

He explained that those who were about to graduate in Sound were faced with what in another discipline might be called a dissertation or thesis. In Sound, this took the form of producing a two- or three-minute assembly of Sound which might be Voice, Sound-Collage, Voice Over Sound, or some sort of mixture of all three. The requirements of the piece were that it be up to professional standards.

"And what exactly are professional standards?"

"Acceptable," he said, "to a jury of professional broadcasters."

"And who *are* the experts?"

"Well, they're chosen by Father O'Gorman. He has very close ties with all the local media, of course, and in Sound they're drawn from the half-dozen or so English-language radio stations."

"The horse's mouth," I said.

He looked blank.

"They have the day-to-day experience," he said. "As Father O'Gorman always says — you'll never make it in Radio if you don't have your finger on the pulse of Radio Land."

"So who *are* Father O'Gorman's experts?"

"Well there's Percy Hendry who's the Happy Morning Host for CUNY and then there's CUNY's Allen Preen — he's the Candid Opinion after the six o'clock news. And the third judge is Norman Gigolino from CRUD."

"And what does Mr. Gigolino do?"

"He's the Evening Hot Line Moderator."

"I see," I said. "And your work has to measure up to the standards of this trio?"

"Well, there's more to it than that, Mr. Wells. It's not just passing the course. Nearly everyone does that. But we're all shooting for what Father O'Gorman calls 'Making the Big Three.'"

I looked at him.

"They pick the best three Audios of the year and give them air-time as a Community Service. Father O'Gorman introduces a special half-hour slot and talks about the work of the Complex and its relationship to the Community, you see, and then the three students whose work is featured get to work on one of the stations for two weeks as a reward for excellence. And to be frank about it, sir, that looks pretty good on your résumé when you apply for jobs."

"I suppose it would," I said.

"Three years ago," he said, "one of our students got a permanent job with CUNY because of his Audio. But that's the only time that's ever happened. His piece was so good that Father O'Gorman still uses it for a teaching aid."

"It must have been truly exceptional," I said.

"It hurts to say it," said the boy with a rueful smile that would take him a long way, "but it was really something else. It was called *With a Little Help from My Friends*. A Public Service Message. Statistics and snatches of the Beatles fading in and out with street interview mix."

He shook his head slowly in admiration.

"It was on the growing menace of V.D."

"Relevant," I said. "Timely."

"But most of us have to try to get jobs on stations in small towns and work our way up."

"The Horatio Alger spirit," I said.

"Pardon?"

"And where do I come in?" I said.

"Well, sir," he said. "I've thought of something that's different. The cultural angle."

"The cultural 'angle'?"

"I found one of your poems, sir, in an anthology. It was about snow."

He took a sheet of paper from his pigskin briefcase.

79

"*Snow, falling*, sir."

"Oh, yes. I remember that," I said.

"What I wanted to do, with your permission, of course, sir, was to assemble a collage of snow-associated and snow-related sounds with the poem voice-over."

"Hmmm."

"Wind, sir, the sound of shovels on sidewalks, the cries of children playing, the crunch of footsteps on crisp snow, the sounds of car horns muffled in the distance, sir, tires spinning..."

"I haven't looked at the poem in years," I said, "but as I recall, it was an extended metaphor of the end of a love affair."

"It has a lot of potential," he said.

"What I'm trying to suggest," I said, "is that it isn't about *snow*."

"But it's full of snow images, sir."

"In a sense," I said, "it is but.."

"I can *hear* it," he said. "You see, sir, I think I can make the words on the page come *alive*."

"Alive," I repeated.

"It's a whole new dimension," he said.

"O'Malley," I said, "you have my blessing."

"Thank you, sir," he said, zipping up his briefcase, "thank you very much."

Just as he reached the door, I added,

"Come and see me on Friday to negotiate copyright."

When the poor, stunned fucker had finally gone, I did a few more half-hearted stick-figures but couldn't concentrate. Even writing *Kathy Neilson* with an orange marker failed to soothe me. My rage and blood pressure were mounting in tandem.

My mind could not accommodate the unholy alliance of CUNY, CRUD, and CAC. The idea of a 'degree' officially blessed by a rabble of glib, semi-literate salesmen of carpets and groceries, ratified by snake-oil hucksters, flim-flam men, the Elmer Gantries of the sick, sad dregs of Radio Land ... My mind drifted in a day-dream of retribution to be visited upon this Cosimo O'Gorman, this false priest in commercial clothing, a day-dream violent like most of my day-dreams, final, cleansing in its utter carnage, apocalyptic.

The summons to assemble would go forth...

To all True Men by the Exprefs Command of General Ludd...

There was a knock and a thud and a fumbling at the door and

it swung open to reveal a man sitting in a wheelchair. On his lap was a bulging briefcase. He manoeuvred the wheelchair through the doorway, stopped, twisted his torso round violently and pushed the door shut behind him, trundled forward.

I stood up.

From his broad shoulders hung the single paunchy mound of his chest and stomach. His left arm was stick thin, the wrist and hand wasted. Both legs were thin and useless, the cloth of his trousers loose on his thighs. His glasses were thick and smeared. They had slipped with the exertion of his entrance and he pushed them higher on the bridge of his nose with the ball of his thumb.

He stretched out his right hand.

"Zemermann," he said.

I shook it.

"How do you do, Mr. Zemermann?" I said. "Mr. Hetherington mentioned your name to me."

"Not *Mr.* Zemermann," he said. "Call me please Itzic. Should poets be so formal with each other?"

I nodded and smiled.

He must have been a tall, powerful man before being stricken by polio. In spite of the wheelchair and the wasted limbs, he still gave an impression of energy and strength. His handshake had been crushing.

He lifted the briefcase from his knees, set it on the floor beside the chair, levered himself with his right arm into a higher position.

"I've been looking forward to this day," he said, "this day when I shall meet Mr. James Wells. This to me is a special day. I am your student. You are my teacher. From you I am coming to learn."

"I'm sure it will be a pleasure for both of us," I said.

He stared at me through his thick spectacles, owlish, solemn, rumpled in his brown suit. He took his left leg with his right hand under the knee, lifted it up, and dumped it into a new position on the wheelchair's footplate. His kneecaps were like huge swellings.

"Who," he demanded, "*is* Itzic Zemermann?"

"Ah . . . ?" I said.

"My name, Mr. Wells, is Isaac. Itzic is a name of fondness. It means 'Little Isaac.' All my life I have been called Itzic. To understand me, to understand my work, you must know something of me. Who *is* this Itzic Zemermann? Who *is* this man who sits here? Where does he come from? What is the story of his life? Of the life of a man," he said, raising his forefinger, "*is* art made."

81

I nodded.

"In front of you, Mr. Wells, is a Jew. A Jew from Poland."

He stared at me.

I nodded again.

"I was born in Lublin. For nearly twenty years Lublin was my home, my world. As a child the courtyards and alleys echoed with my name. 'Itzic!' my mother called. 'Where are you hiding, Itzic?' In the evenings among the market stalls we played. At the *cheder* Itzic stood to recite his lessons. I grew older. The Jews of Lublin made garments, Mr. Wells. Itzic too made garments. We were not poor. We were not rich. But life was rich for Itzic. My family was my happiness, my warmth, my wealth."

He continued to gaze at me.

He started to struggle with the jacket of his suit, working off the left shoulder with his right hand, tugging down the left sleeve, heaving his bulk to his right side until he had freed his left arm. Then he canted over to his left and with great effort and contortion got the jacket off. He then brought his right wrist to his left hand. The withered, twisted fingers scrabbled at the button on his shirt cuff, faint movements like the legs of a dying insect in a jam-jar.

"In August, 1942, Mr. Wells," he said, holding me with his eyes, and pushing up the shirt sleeve of his right arm to reveal blue tattooed numbers, "Itzic Zemermann vanished and became what you see."

He leaned out from the chair and thrust his forearm within inches of my face.

"His home in Lublin was taken from him. His family was taken from him. His name was taken from him. He became this number. Little Isaac was given a new home. His new home was called Treblinka."

"I have read of Treblinka," I said, feeling inadequate to the situation, not knowing what to say, embarrassed, ashamed.

He pushed down his shirt sleeve in silence and the fingers started their slow movements at the buttonhole.

"Can I help you with..?"

"To read, Mr. Wells, to read of Treblinka, to read of Auschwitz, Birkenau, Chelmo, Majdanek, Sobibor—to *read*, Mr. Wells, is not to know."

I nodded again.

"It is beyond imagining," I said.

One of the tattooed numbers on his forearm, a number 7, had

been written in European fashion with a bar across the downward stroke. I wondered why I found that so peculiarly shocking.

He nodded his head.

"Oh, Itzic was clever!" he said. "In 1942 the Jews of Lublin were sent to Belzec but clever little Itzic ran away. But where to run, Mr. Wells? Where to run? So instead of Belzec for Itzic it was Treblinka."

He leaned back against the blue canvas of the chair.

"Three million Polish Jews died," he said, "but Itzic Zemermann survived."

"What can I . ."

"What," he said, "what happened next? Armies happened, hospitals, from strange place to strange place, and then the UNRRA camp, waiting, waiting. Quotas were full they said. Even the allies did not want Jews. And then, Mr. Wells, a miracle! Canada accepted me and Canada became my home. Life was not easy, Mr. Wells. I learned to speak the English language. I worked and worked. I married. My wife and I ate little. Still I worked. All our money we saved. And then . . ."

He indicated his wasted legs.

I shook my head.

His ankles were puffy, the flesh bulging over the sides of the suede shoes. The feet hung on the thin legs like big boots on a rag doll.

"But in the hospital, Mr. Wells, a plan came to me. And this plan drove me on through all those hours. My plan was meat and drink and sleep to me. Always my plan."

"And what was your plan?"

"What was my plan? What was Itzic planning? What *was* this plan?"

I found I was shaking my head again.

His magnified eyes held mine.

"A parking lot was my plan," he said. "A parking lot."

"A parking lot," I repeated.

"Why a parking lot, you want to know? Why should Itzic want a parking lot? Because, Mr. Wells, a parking lot even Itzic sitting down could do. Because a parking lot makes money. But what else does a parking lot do? *Time* it gives, Mr. Wells. Time to read, to think, to write. I'm sitting in my hut day and night and reading. Poetry! History! Politics! Everything I read. My customers would laugh and say, 'There he is, that Itzic, reading, always reading!' But what is Itzic seeking? What is the plan *behind* the plan?"

He reached down and hauled up the briefcase. Holding it steady with his left arm, he undid the straps and buckles with his right. It gaped open towards me. It was full of books, papers, and on top of them a folded rubber hot-water bottle which flopped out and fell on the floor.

I picked it up for him.

"Sometimes," he said, "I can't get to a washroom."

"Ah," I said.

"Ah!" he said.

He took out a book.

"*This* was my plan," he said.

"A book!" I said.

"What better can I give my teacher?"

"Thank you very much," I said. "I'll read it and treasure it."

The book was called *Songs of a Survivor*.

It was published by the Vantage Press.

His unerring eye caught mine.

"Yes," he said. "I was forced to publish it myself. From my savings I paid. The magazines rejected me. We are overstocked they say. Then I tried all the publishers. They rejected me. Poetry does not make money they say in their excuses. Always rejection. Always some excuse."

He shrugged.

He began to fight his way into his jacket.

"It is part of being a Jew," he said. "Christians do not want to know of our suffering. They would like to forget."

He settled the briefcase on his lap.

"You are here all day on Friday," he said. "Then we will talk. And I will bring you new poems to read. Such poems I will bring you!"

With his right hand, he hauled his feet further in on the footplate.

"I'll look forward to it, Mr. Zemermann," I said.

"Itzic! Itzic!" he said chidingly.

"Itzic," I said.

I held the door for him and watched the rhythmic bobbing of his head and shoulders as he pushed himself along down the corridor. I went back into my office and sat staring at the oak hatstand thing with its four brass hooks.

I opened his book.

After the title page and contents page were printed three letters of commendation. The first read:

'The poems of Itzik Zemermann are indeed the poems of a Survivor. His unquenchable testimony to the Jewish spirit shines in every line.'

> Rabbi Shmuel Y. Yankelvich
> Bar Ilan University
> Tel Aviv

The second read:

'Itzic Zemermann will never let us forget the sufferings of Our People. His poems are a conscience to all who let Time dim the horrors of the Holocaust.'

> Rabbi Solomon Kane
> Temple Beth Israel
> Montreal

The third read:

'Dear Mr. Zemermann,
      Thank you for your little book. Your verses are utterly unlike any verses on the Holocaust I have ever read. Publishing funds are limited here however, but *Ani m'achel lecha mazal tov*.'

> Professor Arnan Yacobi
> Hebrew University
> Jerusalem

I read the first poem.
I stared at the oak hat-stand thing.
It was a quarter to four. In fifteen more minutes the bar would open again.
The first poem was called "My Grave".
It read:

> *My grave is in a lonely place*
> *And I shall leave without a trace.*

85

When my song is sung
No bell shall be rung.
Only the wind may hear my lay
And see me go away,
With not much glory,
For I shall have told my story...
How my family is buried in lime,
And I must write about it all the time.

Chapter Six

Since that morning of my awakening in Kathy's apartment, the passage of days blurred. Each day was a suspension of real time, an impatience for evening to arrive, evening, and with it, Kathy. We had gone to restaurants. We had gone to movies. Against all instinct, I'd even agreed to go to the Place des Arts to watch a Noh play. Noh plays offer two main actors, a *waki* and a *shite* which, as far as I was concerned, just about summed the matter up. The company was performing truncated versions tailored for Western audiences. The truncated version lasted for three and a half gruelling hours of deeply significant gesture.

I was obviously in love.

To please Kathy, I'd called my newspaper contact in Winnipeg and through him established a circuitous in with the Montreal *Herald*'s Entertainments man, circuitous as the *Herald* was one of the four largest and most influential papers in Canada and the Entertainment's man one of the paper's superstars. His effluent polluted six or seven pages per week. The world of rock was his.

I duly wrote a piece on Harry and Charmaine which included the words 'figurante' and 'paramount chief'. I batted it out right there at his desk. He ran it the next day. He was a tall, emaciated lovely of about thirty who a few years earlier had been at the epicentre of an acne blast. About his neck hung an amulet pouch and a necklace of fangs and molars. His hair stuck out and about like a clown's fright wig. He wore vast aviator spectacles whose blue tint enhanced the yellow of his teeth. I adapted myself to his semi-aphasic style of utterance, dotting every sentence with 'like', 'man', 'shit', and periods of profound silence.

I gave the impression I had paid my dues.

In return for my encroachment on the world of rock, I was forced to listen to his disjointed theories in the *Herald* cafeteria about food and the principles of the digestive system—what he called The Tube—and an account of a concert he'd just covered given by a psychotic group called Snatch where the road-men had laid on a scene in a motel afterwards with skag and poppers and what he called 'diddily-gash' by which I understood him to mean girls under the age of twelve. It was his conviction that you couldn't better pre-tit poontang.

As he said:

"If it's old enough to bleed, man, it's old enough to butcher."

After a ritual ghetto slapping of palms, I left him there chewing a bran muffin and a heap of grated carrot.

As I was in the building and had ascertained the absence of the Book Page Editor, I executed a rapid sortie into the literary cubicle from which I removed five review copies of fat art books which I sold to a used-book store the next afternoon at close to half-price.

I filled in the days not spent at St. Xavier by reading, sleeping, trying to write, wandering the museum on Sherbrooke Street. I loitered in the many art galleries. I regard it as my duty to stir them about a bit. In the more hushed and sepulchral galleries, I made sudden and loud derisive sounds. On leaving, I always made cheerful summations of the exhibitions to the ethereal creatures who graced the reception area.

In other galleries less sanctified, sycophantic young salemen and model young women showed me their wares. I admired the cool intelligence of the various pyjama stripes they hauled out for my inspection but suggested that perhaps, just possibly, *this* stripe might be tinged by a certain quality of . . . sentimentality? . . . which to some extent might be said to vitiate . . . They hastened to qualified agreement and dragged out more canvases from their stock. Such minimalist discussions were a soothing prelude to lunch.

In the several antique shops, I examined Arabic bowls decorated in Kufic script, cased pairs of duelling pistols, here Greek pottery, there Egyptian faience. I'd realized long ago that the acquisition of such beautiful objects was not compatible with remaining free and relatively unemployed but I was drawn to the intimacy of handling them.

In a used-book store I'd found an affordable treasure in their 25-cent-bin entitled *The Vegetable Way to Health*, a priceless volume written by an aged American maniac whose theories and style delighted me. There was an especially fine chapter which thundered in a deranged baroque against the practice of circumcision. The chapter was entitled "The Slaughter of the Prepuce".

Lying on my bed, day-dreaming, I had come to imagine *The Slaughter of the Prepuce* as a vast canvas in a stiff, neo-classical style like the worst of David. For some reason or other the events depicted were taking place in a turgid desert. The background was dotted with pointlessly broken columns. Impassive soldiers stood about in a triangular composition. On one side of the painting, the weeping Mother in rigid drapery was being restrained by a degenerate NCO. On the other side, the Father stretched his arms beseechingly towards the Naked Babe in the foreground where the larger-than-life Centurion was about to slice the end of its winkie off.

I'd toyed with *The Musical Ride* and filled several pages with scribble but my heart wasn't in it. The only real progress I'd made was a new plot idea. I'd thought of constructing a tunnel. Tunnels are always good plot stuff because if you get bored with them you can have them cave in and, depending on your degree of boredom, either dig the tunnellers out or leave the buggers in there squashed and move on to something less boring.

I'd transferred the essence of the matter under its Code name to my notebook.

Each evening, Commander Swann dressed in bizarre uniforms of his own design and glittering with Stars, Medals, Orders, and the Sash of King Michael of Bosnia, harangued, with the aid of an interpreter, the twenty captured Portugese illegal immigrants whom he kept under lock and key in Intelligence Canada's interrogation and debriefing chambers in the basement of the National Museum of Man.

Their nightly task was to tunnel from the offices of The Canada Council on Sparks Street towards the United States Embassy a block away to hook into the American power lines. This clandestine activity went under the code name *Operation Sardine*.

Beneath this entry in my notebook was the query:

Opposition tunnel being dug from American Embassy to Canada Council offices by captured Vietnam deserters?

Why?

And beneath that, a note to remind mc that Commander Swann lived mainly on smoked salmon heaped with capers.

But on my own work, my real work, I was solidly blocked. It wasn't the usual kind of block. I could recognize those symptoms easily after so many years — the deepening helpless depressions, the withdrawal from people, the sweating dreams, the growing fears of going outside. I'd had one so bad a couple of years before that I hadn't even been able to leave my room. I'd pissed into beer bottle after beer bottle and crapped in empty Chinese food containers. Unable to wash, shave, dress or undress, I'd lain festering on the bed in the suicidal stench weeping from time to time without effort, watching the progress of the shadows, until one day I noticed the sun was shining, the street glittering with snow, and the images started to fall into place. I fled the noisome room leaving no forwarding address.

This present block was something quite different. I was not depressed. I did not doubt that the book *could* or *would* be done. I only knew it could not be done immediately. I just wasn't particularly interested. I was working on a group of poems which had been sparked by, of all things, the *National Geographic Magazine*. During the summer, an old copy had been lying around the cottage and glancing at it one morning over coffee for want of anything else to read, I'd found myself drawn into a series of photographs.

I remembered the moment vividly. Mike was down on the wooden dock yelling at the kids about life-jackets. Susie was somewhere behind me shaking up a plastic bottle of orange juice. My bare foot had been itchy and I was scratching it over the edge of the wooden bench. And then I stopped scratching it. In the middle of these familiar noises I was suddenly certain that what I was looking at was a new book of poems.

The photographs were of New Guinea and the Cargo Cult. The breezy writing had much the same fatuity as the soundtrack of travelogue shorts produced by the National Film Board but the *images* — the wicker and liane decoy plane, the woman giving suck to a piglet, the wicker tower growing on crazy stilts above the jungle, the plumage of birds of paradise regal above the painted faces. These faces of the Stone Age, ritual in ochre and white bars and dots, these lives accidentally touched by World War II had constructed the incomprehensible and miraculous events into mythology and rite. This impossible juncture of worlds, this attempt by the Stone Age to control the powers had started the movement of words in my mind.

I'd let words and pictures ferment but all I'd produced since coming to Montreal I'd scrapped as sloppy, tired, out of focus.

And the reason was Kathy Neilson.

I have in my time been connected with a wide variety of ladies all of whom have, in a wide variety of ways, made my life more complicated and vexatious. To mention but a few, I have had relations with an excitable girl eager to subsidize the arts who was shortly arrested for having robbed three post offices. With a woman who was being followed. With a woman of unutterable wickedness who set fire to six months of manuscript. Briefly and unconsummatedly with a girl of astounding beauty who, if she were to be believed, suffered from a perpetual menstrual flow. With a woman who attacked me with a pair of scissors claiming to be clairvoyant.

Kathy Neilson was a unique experience, oil on troubled waters, guaranteed balm in Gilead. This unlikely woman was the first woman I'd ever met who made me feel *calm*. An unusual state for me as most of the time I feel like a fragile craft caught in the white water and whirlpools of rage or depression.

It's difficult to convey to someone else why one finds a particular woman more attractive than another, probably impossible to convey exactly why one loves. Kathy was not conventionally beautiful. Had I been trying to describe her appearance to a friend I might have used such words as 'gamin' or 'impish'—but then I would have had to qualify 'impish' and say 'impish in an earnest sort of way' and that wouldn't have made much sense. And 'grave' would perhaps have been better than 'earnest'. And none of this would have captured what I saw. In fact, with her faintly lined face and cropped hair and little sticking-out ears, she even looked at times oddly like a wistful rhesus monkey. But everything about her enchanted me. She seemed to me to have stepped into the real world of my life from the pages of a fairy tale.

Kathy's academic abilities were formidable, her knowledge informed by great love and taste, yet this discipline seemed confined to the neat desk, ranked shelves, and careful files. The rest of her life seemed marked by a quality best described as *scattered*. This quality was expressed by her purse, a nest of a thing crammed with cosmetics, keys, unmailed letters, bills, shopping lists, an aluminum cigar tube containing an emergency tampax, pencils, pens, a Phillips screwdriver, a tin of anchovy fillets. Finding an object in this purse was like a blind groping in a Lucky Dip as she blithely scooped out and dropped bank book, credit card, final notice of this or that, crumpled papers which she paused to read with astonishment.

Her conventionality was but a semblance.

She considered all non-representational art a profitable hoax. She refused to watch foreign movies because they were pretentious. People in foreign movies, she said, were always *looking* at each other. She thought psychology and psychiatry were excuses for behaving badly. She had an almost total ignorance of world politics since the end of the Holy Roman Empire. How could people remember the *names*? She patronized A & P because it wasn't doing as well as Dominion or Steinberg.

She was trying to read a book about Black Holes because they worried her.

She was not interested in the class struggle.

Her favourite books were bloody and atrociously written thrillers. She was working her way through a series called *The Executioner* and had just discovered a new series called *Death Merchant*.

Her favourite food was zabaglione.

I knew with the same kind of certainty that a ball is *caught* while it is still hard in the air, with the same kind of certainty that a shot has dropped a flighting duck before the trigger is squeezed, that Kathy Neilson was the first woman I'd met that I wanted — somehow — to stay with. It was the same kind of knowing that prompts one to start walking round a pool table to position oneself to take the next colour while the cue ball is still rolling down the baize to kiss the first. She fell into place like an inevitable ordering of words, a line's last demanded stress.

What I did *not* know was how *she* felt.

On one of these evenings we'd dined early at a small French restaurant. During dinner Kathy had said that she was sorry but she positively had to work that night. Galley proofs needed correction and she was already days late. I supposed that the proofs must be those I had not looked at that first morning in her apartment. I counted the days and was shocked to realize that the deserts and oases of time added up to just over two weeks. I offered to help, countering her expression of doubt by reminding her that the chore of proof-reading had, from time to time, been my means of livelihood. When I died, I assured her, Hart's *Rules* would be found engraved on mine.

But if she wanted to be alone . . .

No, no, it wasn't that at all . . .

She was sitting at the desk poring over the long sheets, her face side-lit in the pool of light from the Tensor lamp. I'd finished the section of sheets she'd given me and while pretending to re-read I was watching her covertly. There were auburn tints in the black hair. When she frowned, the white scar seemed to deepen. As she moved back down the long pages, her face and shoulders became a dark shape behind the light which was so tilted that its rim dazzled me. And so we sat in silence, she at the far end of the two rooms behind the light, I in the sitting room.

On the coffee table in front of me sat the big lump of quartz glittering here and there with iron pyrites. Some of the flecks of pyrites were flatter than others, dull like dental fillings. I had looked at this rock every time I'd been in Kathy's apartment. I had come to regard it as a hostile presence. Doubtless it had belonged to her dead geologist husband. Or worse, it had been given by him to her dead child.

The crystal sat there, roadblock, monolith, cairn and guardian of *terra incognita*.

Here be dragons.

That Kathy liked me was more than obvious. There were small propriatorial gestures, the intimacy of shared laughter. Her fridge had blossomed with Labatt's Blue Label. But after a beer or two, I would make mention of the hour and leave. She had never mentioned her husband or child. I did not know if Henry Benson had mentioned to her that he'd mentioned them to me. Sometimes she said 'we' but I could not loose the question. Their shades haunted every word we spoke. If she *knew* I knew, what did her not talking of them mean? If she did *not* know I knew, why did she not tell me?

And after leaving because of the lateness of the hour, I would wander the night streets, sit talking with taxi drivers at the all-night café, drink, swap casual lies with other men who did not want to sleep.

Among papers lying on top of the bookcase, I'd noticed some

documents from Foster Parents Plan of Canada. Kathy was helping to support a small boy in Mexico, a waif called Ramon.

Hmmm.

What, I wondered, did one do with a dead child's effects? Last year's coat, the cars and dump-trucks, the hockey cards, the Snoopy pencil-sharpener? How did one dispose of essential treasure — the broken cap-gun, the insides of a watch, foreign coins, dried-up magic markers, special stones accumulated, perhaps, in emulation of Daddy?

No.

Fearful of losing her, I dared not conjure memory of such housekeeping.

And so, not knowing what to do, I'd waited.

And waited.

I heard the heavy slop and slap of sections of the dictionary's pages turning. I reached forward to pick up the lump of quartz weighing it in my hands, turning it to catch the glitter of iron pyrites.

From behind the light, her voice said suddenly:

"Fool's gold."

And in that instant there flashed through my mind her husband, the nameless child, the possible meanings of the remark. It was, of course, possible that the remark was purely denotative. It was possible that the remark was metaphorical, that life itself, men, relationships, children, were 'fool's gold', that only a fool would put trust in them. Fairy gold that turned to withered leaves. That in the assay, even real gold was base metal. Was the remark pointed at me, at us. Fools rush in.

And through this dance, this maze of possible meaning and intent, I replied without a second's hesitation:

"Yes, it's pretty."

And with the words, 'Yes, it's pretty' still sounding in my head, their *silliness* in the strength of what I felt made me break constraint. I was suddenly determined to dance no longer, to end this shadow-boxing with the dead. Emotional minefield or no, I would take my chances to gain the further side.

Still holding the chunk of quartz in my hands, I said,

"Kathy?"

"Ummm?"

"You just said, 'Fool's gold' and I said, 'Yes, it's pretty'."

She looked up.

I set the quartz down. It grated on the glass table top.

"Do you know what was going through my mind?"

I told her.

When I'd finished, she was silent for a second and then she said,

"Oh, *no!*"

"I'm sorry," I said.

"*No!*"

"I'd better go," I said.

She pushed back her chair, proofs sliding onto the floor, and said,

"You'll do no such thing!"

And then in a rush it all came out, the frustrations, the confusions. The same day Henry Benson had told me of the death of her husband and son, he'd told *her* he'd told *me* and she couldn't understand why I'd said nothing. She'd thought at first that it was because she was just another woman I'd taken a fancy to. Well, that *was* the sort of reputation I had. But she felt she knew me better than that. But she couldn't be sure. So she'd held back too. Because if she *was* mistaken about the way I felt, she certainly wasn't going to open wounds for nothing. So she was left not knowing *what* to think. She'd thought she was going crazy. She'd been on the phone nearly every night to her friend in California.

And I'd never made any move to make love to her and she'd been furious because she'd thought it was settled, more or less *obvious* after the reading, at the reception, after the night with the General and Harry and Charmaine and me in her bed. Hadn't I *said* at the reception that I'd been looking for her? *Hadn't* I? And hadn't *she* said she'd been looking for me? And I *had* said in that club, in that Mocambo, that I was falling in love with her. And then — nothing. So she'd thought that maybe I'd just been drunk.

But then I'd been eager to see her all the time afterwards so it didn't make sense *again*.

I was so *obtuse* she could have screamed. Did I remember that evening she'd said she had to wash her hair and she'd been wearing only her bathrobe and she'd bought three bottles of wine and I'd just got drunk and recited Basil Bunting?

And I was the first time she'd felt anything deeply since Steven died. She just wasn't a casual person. And she'd been fairly sure I felt the same way. Things were too *right*. So none of it, nothing, made any sense.

And some nights after I'd said it was late and left, she'd wondered if I didn't want her that way, she was ugly, and she'd just lain there unable to sleep and confused and unhappy and angry and going over and over things in her mind.

She dried her fresh tears with Kleenex.

She calmed down.

She showed me photographs.

We talked for hours until there didn't seem much more, then, to be said.

The ashtray was overflowing.

We fell silent.

"Would you like a mug of cocoa?" she said suddenly.

"Cocoa hadn't entered my mind," I said. "Nor, come to that, had tea or coffee."

I looked at her.

"And, strange as it may seem," I said, "neither had frothy hot chocolate nor creamy Horlicks."

She grinned.

"There's no need to be lewd," she said.

"That's what *you* think!" I said.

"I want to be first to use the bathroom," she said.

Drifting towards sleep, I felt her finger-tips tracing the ridges of the scar that runs from my left shoulder down to the small of my back. Her touch was delicate as if she were reading braille.

"What did this?" she whispered.

"A very bad man with a bottle."

"Tell me about it."

"Shsss."

In the morning, I awoke before her. Her breath was moist against my shoulder. I lay there in the white bedroom looking at the fern in its brass bowl. The candle stick. The misty mountains beyond mountains of the Chinese scroll. On the floor lay the rumpled formality of her white night gown, the neckline pretty with pink and blue ribbons.

Chapter Seven

September had become October. October was drifting by. I was adjusting to the rhythms of the city and of St. Xavier. I had by now a nodding acquaintance with most of the professors in my building and from Kathy most of the essential gossip concerning their activities. It was the custom at St. Xavier to work with one's office door open and a stroll along the corridors was like visiting-day at a private Home.

Some professors left their offices stark and institutional. Some groaned with filing-cabinets and books. Others decorated.

Some had curtains and cactus plants.

Travel posters of olde thatched England.

One had a folding cot.

Office doors were decorated with material that appealed to the inmates — cartoons, slogans, notices cancelling class. Some bore posters advertising such coming attractions as The Renaissance Players in *Gammer Gurton's Needle* and Labia Newman in a series of lectures on Assertiveness Training for Women. Stapled to some doors were folders to receive student essays.

Professor Curll's folders were labelled *Alienation and Madness: Section I* and *Alienation and Madness: Section II*.

Teaching assistants, slave labour in pursuit of the manumission of a doctorate, were crowded four and five to an office which they

97

presumably shared Box and Cox.

Every office supported several tons of free promotional Norton anthologies of absolutely Everything.

Professor Norbert, one of the American specialists in Canadian literature, had an office plastered with reproductions of the work of The Group of Seven—the most constipated retention of artwork outside a Chinese People's Palace of Culture.

Norbert's erudition was enormous. He was exhuming Victorian Canadian verse from yellowed newspapers with the vigour of a grave-digger on piece-work. Two astonishing volumes of this necrolatry had already been published by the University of St. Xavier Press—a tatty off-set operation housed in the basement of the Women's Drop-In Centre. What was even more disturbing, they'd actually sold over two thousand copies. Nothing could impede the invention of a native literary tradition. Intellect hurled itself with glad cries beneath the wheels of the Juggernaut.

The next step would be a Symposium.

Norbert had given me signed copies. I'd accepted them gratefully. They'd go into storage with all the other rubbish in my friend's garage in Edmonton, with all the manuscript, notebooks, dribbles of failed writing, correspondence—everything that I was banking on some university buying to feed the research mills. Bumph for future generations of dung beetles to roll into balls and trundle busily about—balls from which nothing living would emerge.

Balls for ever pupal.

Malcolm's office was tastefully decorated with reproductions of Beardsley drawings of hideous women and dwarves with enormous tools. His desk lamp was a writhing pink-glass art nouveau offense.

The room was usually obscure with a dense fug of hash which he smoked in a soap-stone pipe hand-carved by government-supported Eskimos. This he always proffered whenever I passed by but I never smoke the stuff because it makes me feel more depressed than usual. The block of hash in his filing-cabinet was covered with a thick white skin like Brie—a guarantee Malcolm assured me of its Afghanistan provenance and potency.

Stoned out of his gourd, he claimed to be writing a book which revealed the very secret and very deeply hidden homosexual imagery which riddled the work of H. Melville, W. Whitman, M. Twain, N. Hawthorne, S. Crane, T. Wolfe, and E. A. Poe.

98

His costume was constant — whipcord trousers, leather riding boots, see-through blouses in pink, cerise, lime-green, and virgin white. He looked rather like a naughty Cossack.

Malcolm had no visible arse. Where it should have been was merely flat whipcord. Not a cheek in sight. I've often noticed that about the cruising variety of the other persuasion. This arselessness. Odd.

Dr. Gamahuche's office served as the editorial headquarters of *Lucifer*. He'd shown me some of his duplicate labels. It was all very interesting. Dr. Gamahuche felt very strongly that collecting *bookmatches* was about on the same level as collecting *triangular* stamps.

Fred Lindseer, whom I'd forgiven, was fairly lively in the mornings but by afternoon fell into sodden brooding about Thomas Wolfe and fruit. His office wasn't decorated.

Hetherington was mostly to be seen scurrying about like the White Rabbit with bits of paper. At every encounter, he invariably made strange apologetic noises. On one occasion, he had waved a wad of papers at me and said:

"Pilgrims in this barren land."

Opposite my office, at unnerving intervals, the washroom door did its .303 effect.

The man in the office to my right, Professor Shadwell, took his dentures out when working and placed them on his blotter.

The man in the office to my left, Professor Niddling, was given to long chats with his filing cabinet.

Professor Niddling was friendly in a vague way but obviously didn't know who I was. In the corridor one day he'd thrust upon me an off-print of one of his articles from *Studies in Beaumont and Fletcher* saying:

"You'll enjoy this."

I'd always thought of Beaumont and Fletcher as, at their best, low-grade Elizabethan panto and was mildly surprised that such a dreary pair of crappers could sustain an entire industry but then, to Austin, Texas, all things are possible. After all, they came close to having Evelyn Waugh stuffed.

By and large, St. Xavier was only slightly worse than any other university I'd endured.

My little band of poets was thinning out by the week. Under the demand for work, more than half had already fallen by the wayside as I knew they would. By the third week in October I was left with seven regulars. Mrs. Allaline was in her sixties and had been accepted into Honours English under St. Xavier's Mature Student Program.

The academic qualifications required of a Mature Student were that the student be over nineteen.

Mrs. Allaline wrote poems about cats. She had a voice hoarse from years of cigarettes and whisky and claimed to have graduated in her late teens from a college in San Francisco.

'Graduated in F.U.N., honey,' as she put it later.

By the end of the second session, we'd given up even the pretence of poetry and I supplied the glasses, she the scotch. I scheduled her first to fortify myself for what followed. She'd had more husbands than the Wife of Bath and kept me in tears of laughter. She was as deadpan as Harold Lloyd but switched for the punch lines to a wonderful, leering innocence. She only attended St. Xavier for something to do, to get out of her apartment, to be with people. And she might meet a nice gentleman. She was, as she put it, still good for a buggy ride.

By the end of our third session, she confided that I was the only prof in the whole whodee that didn't give her a pain in the cuz.

Following Mrs. Allaline came a dour young man with an ominous centre-part. He wrote impeccable Shakespearean sonnets weekly about the struggle between flesh and spirit. His given name was Mayo after the Mayo Clinic which had delivered him alive against odds which he described in unnecessary detail. He was obviously destined to become a priest or something Jack the Ripperish but he produced work and produced it on demand and I couldn't think of any way of getting rid of him.

Following him, Angeline, who wore Tuff work-boots and suspenders and was liberated to the point that an offer of a chair was interpreted as a challenge to her endurance to remain standing. She wrote drivel in shortish lengths about being liberated.

She was followed by another Mature Student, a grim woman called Mrs. Strudly who was writing what she described as a 'poem-cycle' about pregnancy and birth and how rotten and unfair it all was. Mr. Strudly had, wisely, deserted her.

Peter Stanley was the only one who showed even a glimmer but the glimmering was fitful. I gave him more time and attention than any of the others but it was a losing battle. I was trying to wean him from the idea of ideas and the strange notion that poetry was somehow connected with sincerity ... He *would* keep on writing

100

about ecology.

> *Now floats the sewage on the tide*
> etc.

I sometimes feel that if I am forced to read one more effusion
on the subject of pollution, ecology, pregnancy, or the fate of the
native peoples, I'll drink lye like Vachel Lindsey who knew when
enough was enough.

After Peter came Frances who was stout. She was of the Plath-
Sexton torrent and wrote formless, rambling, endless, incoherent
verse which was entirely innocent of punctuation. This twaddle
didn't engage even my voyeuristic interests. She took a generally
dim view of life and didn't like her mother or her father or her sister
and was on a diet and had spots and irregular periods and wanted
to go potty and attempt suicide. I found her very trying. What she
really needed was a forceful kick in the arse and a steady job as a
waitress.

None of them read much poetry. None of them read much of
anything except *The Prophet* by Kahlil Gibran. Mrs. Allaline read
absolutely nothing at all except her horoscope.

And then there was Itzik.

Always Itzik.

Itzik inevitably.

Who appeared, against express instructions, on Wednesdays
and Fridays, armed always with absolute sheaves of new inspiration, each batch more awful than the one preceding. On days when I
wasn't there, he pushed poems under my door, crammed rolls of
them into my pigeon-hole in the office, gave wads of them to the
secretary to give to me if I were chance-sighted.

Itzik was everywhere. On the Arts page of the *Xavian*, the one
page not given over to sports results or charges of corruption
against the executive of the Xavier Student Association, there
appeared a weekly Zemermann poem. The Montreal *Herald*
advertised his talks and readings at the Jewish Public Library which
were sponsored by the Pioneer Women, the Workman's Circle, and
the remnants of the Bund. These tiny clippings were pasted onto file
cards and pushed beneath my door.

Itzik haunted me. It had reached the point where on non-office
days when I went into the college to meet Kathy I peered round
corners to see if the corridors were free of his stocky figure with its

buckled briefcase bulging with accusation.

My discussions with Itzik had already hardened into ritual. I laboured to point out to him possible dangers or defects. He sat staring at me like a rumpled and affronted owl. It was obvious he was merely waiting for me to stop. He sat motionless, silent, and impervious. When I finished, he countered.

If I said his diction was slightly archaic, he would say:

'So? Is old bad?'

If I said that rhyme, though it had an honoured place in the tradition of poetry in English, carried certain dangers, he would say:

'So if Shakespeare why not Itzik?'

If I said that dactylic metre was, by its nature, not suited to describe the gravity of a pogrom or a Selection, he would say:

'What is? What metre *could* describe?'

If I suggested that something he'd written didn't make sense, he would say:

'So it's hard to understand. So is life, Mr. Wells, so is life.'

If I were goaded into sharper criticism, he would nod and brood and then relate anecdotes of relatives suspended on piano wire, disemboweled, raped, sterilized, experimented upon, or flayed for use as souvenirs.

Whatever my criticism and however put, he always managed to make me feel like a latter-day member of an *Einsatzgruppe*. He aroused in me exasperation and rampant guilt. Sympathy and shame struggled with anger and reason. I could not *not* care. And after each submission to the horror that had been his life, I felt more and more dishonoured by my weakness.

Itzik was supposed to be confined to Friday afternoons. I'd had a wearing morning full of Mayo, True Confessions, Tuff Boots, and yet more gynecological lament from Mrs. Strudly. This Friday had been the Breaking of the Waters and the thought that *that* was to be followed after lunch by the Parting of the Red Sea sent me hurrying to the bar. Mrs. Strudly had extended her allotted time by twenty minutes of amniotic detail — twenty precious minutes during which strong drink had been available, during which all the submarine sandwiches would have gone from the cafeteria leaving only the bologna with the green relish soaked into the Wonder-bread.

I felt bitter.

I felt like pressuring Hetherington for Compassionate Leave.

102

Kathy had a lunch-time tutorial. She'd offered to make me sandwiches that morning. She was wearing an Irish sweater today that I particularly liked, a kind of pale heather colour. Her nipples were dark brown. She'd bought some Blue Mountain coffee beans. I was feeling agitated and lonely and wanted to see her.

The Faculty Club was nearly empty. Cosimo O'Gorman was in earnest conclave with Professors Grepp and Oldmixon of the Department of Social Realities. Down at the far end of the room, Ms. Mary Merton was shouting at Professor Tibbald, the Dean of Business Administration. The Dean was about five foot three and pinched of feature. He wore a hair-piece whose colour, a light ginger, was so absurdly wrong that it had the reverse effect of a tonsure. Kathy said he was extremely eccentric. No one knew much about his personal life. He lived alone but was reputed once to have requested recognition from the Chair during a meeting of Senate on Finance and risen to say:

"I have known what it is to be married."

Mary Merton must have weighed close to three hundred pounds. The word 'steatopygic' would have been misleading. Were she to undergo an operation it would be less scalpel than flensing. She looked like one of those rudely shaped fertility figures from the end of the last ice age. To be absolutely precise, she was a dead ringer for the Venus of Willendorf.

When I joined them, they were in heated argument about the significance of the fact that men are physically stronger than women. The Dean was convinced that this fact was proof of a natural accompanying mental superiority. Mary Merton could have felled him with a half-hearted blow or crumpled him like aluminum foil. Or sat on him to death. Which would have settled their tedious squabble then and there but she was rabbiting on about anthropological and archeological evidence indicating that the earliest societies were matriarchal and that patriarchal societies were, in the eye of history, a very recent development.

"Progress," said the Dean.

"Rubbish," said Mary Merton.

"What about the Amazons?" I said.

"Myth!" snapped the Dean.

"I meant that they were not only in charge of men but played the male role," I said. "Hunting. Fighting."

"Rubbish," said the Dean.

"And why *not*?" said Mary Merton.

103

"Weren't they supposed to cut their right knockers off so as not to twang themselves with their bow-strings?" I said.

"The word 'knocker' is offensive to me," said Mary Merton.

"I beg your pardon," I said.

"Pure myth!" said Dean Tibbald. "There is *no* historical evidence for the existence of Amazons. No skeletal remains have ever been found."

"Wouldn't prove much anyway," I said, "even if there were."

"And why *wouldn't* it?" said Mary Merton.

"Tits," I said, "don't have bones in them."

"Tits!" said Mary Merton. "Knockers! That's all women mean to you. Just so much flesh!"

"Flesh and blood," I said pleasantly.

"*Blood!*" cried Dean Tibbald, the light of insane logic shining in his eyes. "It's hypothetical, I grant you, but what about this? There are two armies," he said slowly. "Two armies. Two armies composed entirely of women."

"Women," said Mary Merton, "have got better things to do than fight each other."

"Two armies," continued the Dean. "All women. *Now.* What would happen if on the day of battle one army *all had its period at the same time!*"

"You're being absolutely *ridiculous!*" said Mary Merton.

"*But*," said Dean Tibbald gloatingly, "which army would *win?*"

"What," I said, "if *both* armies had their periods at the same time?"

"Exactly!" said the Dean. "Exactly. You grasp the point. The whole thing would be a washout. They'd have to call it off."

He sniffed triumphantly.

"You're both being deliberately stupid and vulgar," said Mary Merton.

"An argument," I said to the Dean, "of extreme trenchancy."

"Rubbish!" said Mary Merton.

"She's sulking," said the Dean, "because she knows her position is untenable."

I nodded agreement.

"She is ungracious," said the Dean, "in defeat."

"There is *nothing* admirable in brute strength," said Mary Merton.

The tiny Dean hammered on the arm of his chair in dwarfish tantrum.

"You're *impenetrable!*" he cried.

And he was probably right.

I went up to the bar for a refill.

Only minutes remained before the bell tolled for the jollities of the afternoon. I'd foregone the bologna and emerald relish and the scotch was filling me with spurious energy which Itzik would doubtless soon sap. I tried to divert myself with obscene imaginings. I tried to picture Dean Tibbald attempting union upon Ms. Merton's unstable mounds. I imagined his death by asphyxiation, his little head, ginger hair-piece askew, trapped between the hot bolsters of her thighs.

But it didn't really cheer me up.

Itzic awaited.

As I started up the stairs, I fell in with Mrs. Herzog, a motherly sort in her sixties who looked like a younger Golda Meir. She ploughed placidly through the Survey course and had been doing so for years. She knitted during her tutorials and munched Oreo cookies. She always carried all her papers and bits and pieces and knitting in shopping bags. I liked her. She spent hours correcting essays and trying to instill the idea of a sentence. A sensibly limited aim.

As we reached the top of the stairs, we saw the dark shape of Itzic sitting patiently in his wheelchair outside my door at the far end of the corridor. I carried her shopping bags into her office.

"You smell of drink," she said.

"Sheila," I said, "I wish I *reeked* of it."

"Friend Zemermann?" she said.

I nodded.

"Have you . . . *read* any of his . . . ?"

"Who hasn't?" she said.

I shook my head.

"*We* get them in Yiddish, too," she said. "In *Der Canader Adler.*"

"What's that?"

"The Yiddish paper. *The Canadian Eagle.*"

"Are they about Treblinka?"

Her features re-arranged themselves into something I couldn't quite read.

"Oh, no," she said. "Nothing like that."

She snorted.

"Nature poems," she said. "Birds. Flowers in the spring."

"What do you mean, Sheila?"

"You've got a lot to learn," she said.

"What? What do you mean?"

She patted my cheek.

"You're a good boy, Jim," she said, "but you drink too much. It's not good for you. It's not healthy."

Itzic was full of a poem he'd just read and on which he'd modelled one of his own during lunch. The poem which had so moved him was "Trees" by Joyce Kilmer. I jumped onto this and started talking non-stop like a salesman latching onto a live one. I explained in minute, painstaking, exhaustive detail the background of Kilmer, that period in American poetry, Kilmer's place in it. Much I invented. In mid-flight, I suddenly realized that I didn't know if Joyce Kilmer was a man or a woman. I was, I realized, quite pissed. I'd had nothing to eat since two pieces of breakfast toast. But the longer I talked the shorter the time left for Itzic's harrowing. I brooked no interruption. I felt invention flowing through me. I was wildly tempted to outline the career and achievements of Kilmer's contemporary, that apostle of the modern in American poetry, that lonely and heroic figure, Shagpoke Whipple. I restrained myself with great effort and concentrated on belabouring Kilmer as the prolonged last gasp of a moribund tradition. I settled for *he*, *him*, *his*. If challenged, I'd claim she was a transvestite. I attacked his flaccid language, ludicrous rhythms, and painful rhymes.

I gave it my all.

Itzic sat waiting.

When I'd finished, he said,

"So 'Trees' is bad by you but it's in *Best-Loved Verses of the American People*."

I fought a rear-guard action against all things 'best-loved', 'the American People' in particular, and 'People' in general.

But then the buckled briefcase was steadied by the withered left arm while the strong right hand undid the straps and clasps.

He handed me the poem.

I put it on the desk in front of me.

The poem was entitled 'Hands'.

I glanced through it. I could see no connection whatever between it and Kilmer. I could see no connection whatever between it and anything. I wanted to hide my head in my arms.

I could feel his steady gaze.

The poem read:

My ghostly family dear and dead
Sit with my father at the head.
My ghostly family sits with Shabbas candles
Drinking wine from cups with lovely handles,
But I alone, with empty cup,
Sit here to call my Song Muse up.
In my canvas chair with rubber tires
I think of Bashele who perished in the fire,
The soap that cleaned those German hands of blister
May well have been my dear loved sister.

Chapter Eight

The Communication Arts Complex stood on the site of what had formerly been a small chapel. In the library I'd seen photographs of the campus taken before its transformation from college to University. The chapel had been an inoffensive little building, Victorian Gothic in style, which had been used by the Fathers of St. Xavier for the daily celebration of Mass.

A few minutes before the time appointed for my tour with Cosimo O'Gorman I wandered across what was left of the playing field towards the front of the Complex. This investigation of the plant had been rather like a scab. I'd been wanting and not wanting to pick at it for weeks.

CAC was a squat, single-storey building with a geodesic excrescence at one end. The dome glittered with tinted glass and panels of coloured funfair plastic while the concrete bulk of the building with its slit windows looked like a mixture of factory and Siegfried Line bunker.

The foyer was hexagonal, mirrored from floor to ceiling, carpeted in purple. To left and right tunnels sloped downwards to some lower depths not apparent from the outside. The tunnel to the left bore a sign saying *CommCepts*, the tunnel to the right a sign saying *CinCepts*. The place was deserted except for my myriad mirror images. I decided on *CommCepts* and followed the easy purple slope until I found myself entering another hexagonal mirrored area. Here, sitting at a desk beneath a small weeping-willow tree, was a lady. I cleared my throat but she did not look up. I retreated up the slope to the foyer and went down the slope that said *CinCepts* and somehow found myself once more in the lower mirrored area again looking at the lady under the tree.

"Hello," I said, "I'm lost."

She was a very superior sort of lady.

"For what," she said, "are you looking?"

"Cosimo O'Gorman."

"Have you an appointment with the Director?"

I assured her that I had.

Her manner was not enchanting.

She chattered buttons on one of those things they have at airports that tell you that your reserved seat unfortunately isn't and green printing began to appear on the screen.

I tried to read what it said but her expression made it clear that I was verging on lèse majesté.

"If you would care to take a seat," she said, "the Director will be free in a few minutes."

"I'd love to have a go on your thing," I said.

I sat on a modern chair near her desk and looked at the rack of reading material.

"Do you mind if I look at your brochures?"

There was no getting away from it. She wasn't a jolly type.

I picked out a large glossy coloured thing that outlined the courses offered by the Complex. It took me a while to work out that this *was* what it was as the cover was a triumph of modern design, the words 'Communication' and 'Arts' being superimposed, fragmented, and repeated like echoes until the effect was something like a rarified colour-blindness test.

I glanced at some of the Course Descriptions.

INTRODUCTORY ANALYSIS OF
COMMUNICATIONAL MEANS (Compulsory)
The course will offer in-depth concentration on various information complexes. Examples of such complexes are theatres, department stores, libraries, the streets of our city, and the highway. The student will be required to select one such complex and perform a written study of the informational aids therein, thereupon, or surrounding which influence perception.

109

(3 credits)

I'd only had two drinks for lunch so it wasn't me.
I read it over again.

THE SOCIETAL USES OF ADVERTISING
This course demands of the student creative criticality. Study will be made of the structural and communicational strategies in campaigns in general terms. Students will experience individual and team creation in an actual campaign and will liaise with professionals in the field from SuperMart Inc. and Miracle Savings City.
(Mode: Self-evaluation. 6 credits.)

I floundered and then sank in the words *focusing on the aesthetic cultural dimensions of the contemporary film and the sensibility of the student within the dynamics of the mass contemporary sensibility.*

This murk put me in mind of Marshall McLuhan. I once tried to read one of his books but after a few pages I could readily understand his interest in non-print modes. His writing was not lucid. It was not, so far as I could see, even marked by lucid intervals.

But then I was absolved from any lingering sense of intellectual guilt as untold thousands of semi-literates like a rush of Gaderene swine embraced the sacred texts and exegesis flourished in the weekend colour supplements of newspapers.

I was tired of the brochure. I was bored by pulling faces at the mirror. The lady at the desk was obviously not programmed for conversation.

I started to hum. I thought briefly of McLuhan, Freud, Marx, Teilhard de Chardin and a host of other boring old farts I'd never been able to read. The hum turned into a boring tune. More of a chant than a tune. It had a dreary, *plonking* rhythm suitable for folk singers. On the principle that stressed syllables are represented by *dum* and unstressed or elided syllables by *di*, the tune went, very roughly,

> Dum di-di dum di dum di dum di
> Dum di-di dum di-di dum di dum
> The first lines came easily:

I've got the hots for Cool McLuhan
Cool McLuhan's got the hots for me.
Don't gimme none of your romantic flannel
I want McLuhan to tune my channel.

I was struggling with a ripish obscenity that involved McLu-han's cool dum-di when there sounded an ethereal ding-dong and the lady under the weeping-willow tree said,

"Would you care to proceed to Hospitality on Level One?"

"Well I'd love to, dear," I said, "if I knew where it was."

She pressed a button and a section of mirror slid open and another lady appeared. She was wearing over-alls.

"Professor Wells to Hospitality," said the tree lady.

I followed this other lady up the purple ramp again. There were no steps, stairs, or visible doors and I was beginning to wonder why the funny men in silver snowmobile suits hadn't appeared with the guns that go *toot-toot-toot*.

"What do you do here?" I said to the lady.

"I work on deconditioned equipment," she said.

"Oh," I said.

In the foyer she pressed a button and a section of mirror slid back revealing a short corridor. She indicated that I should enter. I walked to the facing door and knocked.

"Professor Wells? The Director has been detained unfortun-ately in conference and asked me to entertain you until he arrives. I am Professor Hans Gruber, Head of PAP."

"Hello," I said. "What's PAP?"

The room was white, metal curtains, interlocking cube furniture.

"Publicity, Advertising, and Promotion," he said. "The Direc-tor thought you might wish a drink."

"The Director was right," I said.

Gruber wore gold-rimmed spectacles and was sallow and used hair oil. He looked like a morgue attendant I'd once interviewed in Calgary. He handed me a scotch.

"Do you not . . . ?"

"I permit myself a glass of schnapps only," he said. "At Christmas time."

"Ah, well," I said. "Cheers!"

"I have been out since the early hours with a field-team at Miracle Savings City," he said.

"Oh," I said.

"You are one half way through your day," he stated, "while I am on my way to bed."

There didn't seem much to say in reply to that.

I glanced at the steel engraving in the heavy fumed oak frame which dominated the white room. It was Landseer's *Stag at Bay*.

"The Director," said Gruber, "thought my work might be of interest to you."

"I'm sure it would," I said.

"He suggested that I talk to you," said Gruber.

"I'd be most interested," I said.

He stared at me.

"Watch what I do," he said suddenly.

He tossed a cigarette packet onto a white plastic table.

"*Now*," he said.

He picked the packet up and positioned it with deliberation in the dead centre of the table.

"What is the meaning of this?" he said.

"Give me a clue," I said.

"It is a question of *seeing*," he said.

"Ah!" I said. "If I came in and saw a packet on the table just anywhere I wouldn't pay much attention to it but if I saw it in the exact centre of the table I'd pay more attention to it."

"Good!" he said. "Very good. That is a correct response."

"I *am* glad," I said.

"So!" he said. "Through position I am communicating with you. And if the packet is *so* — erect — then the communication is stronger than if the packet is *so* — supine."

"By Jove!" I said.

"Blue!" he said. "What does blue mean? Blue means nothing. I am right?"

"Right," I said.

"Wrong!" he said.

"Have it your way," I said.

"Listen carefully," he said. "I will now amaze you."

I strongly doubted it. I was getting tired of this *Reader's Digest* condensed wisdom. I was getting tired of humouring this Gruber. It was, I felt, a bit early in the day to be closeted with a buggsy window-dresser.

He was ranting on with Teutonic fervour about blue boxes and 'wolunteers' in some ludicrous test. 73% seemed to figure largely in

112

this harangue. Random sampling. Anecdotal observation. Standard deviations. Suchlike twattery filtered through from time to time.

He seemed quite safe to leave.

I spend a lot of my time living in elaborate stories where *I win*. Influenced in subject matter by the prospect of this visit, I'd started a particularly good one that morning during Mayo's sonnet. I retreated into it leaving Gruber to his fascination with things blue.

I got myself back into the boardroom, back into the titling conference, back with my fellow executives, joggers all, lean, ambitious, ruthless as a pack of whippets harrying a defenceless filet mignon.

Sitting at the head of the table was that living legend of advertising, the man who had saved Consolidated Magma, the man who had put Inter-Foods in the black, the genius behind the rise of Yumnies—Joe Salami.

"I am going to speak," he said, "and when I have finished speaking you are going to speak in the order that I tell you to speak. Is that understood?"

Yes, Mr. Salami.

"We are here to title this book. This book is going to make *Valley of the Dolls* look like it was remaindered. This book is going to sell more copies than the fucking *Bible*. Am I right?"

Yes, Mr. Salami.

"Of course I'm right, I'm always right."

Of course you are, Mr. Salami.

"This book is a Hollywood book. This book is about a man who *fucks* his way to stardom. In the entire history of the printed book there has never been a single volume with so much fucking in it. I have caused to be made a study of this book and there are 817 separate copulatory acts excluding quickies and when he puts it to the same broad 3-9 times on a single occasion which I have counted as one. This guy has a wang on him like a deformed fucking *gorilla*. But this is also a romantic book because it is a love story with a happy ending because this guy is religious and *pure* and is not really *responsible* for putting it to those 817 broads and the dog which I forgot to count. He is not *responsible* because his wang has been *possessed by the Devil*. The end of this book where they tie this guy to his bed and get this creepy old Polack priest to exorcise the guy's dork is horrible like I've never read."

I was staking the whole of my career on a single throw. I had the audacity which the others lacked. But I had something else too. I had *the* title.

I'd seen it staring at me from a packet of my wife's panty-hose. While he was still actually *talking* I stood up and said, "This began to come together for me . . ."

The room froze. Those lesser men thought I'd gone mad.

"Joe Salami is talking," whispered Joe Salami, "Joe Salami does not remember asking persons to interrupt him when he is talking. He feels deeply grieved that this thing has occurred. Joe Salami thinks . ."

"*Be quiet!*"

A pencil snapped.

Salami was staring at me bug-eyed with amazement and outrage.

"The title," I said, "of this book is *this*."

I looked at the faces one by one. I worked my gaze up the table to Joe Salami himself. Into the rigid silence, I said,

"The title of this book *is* . . ."

I waited a few triumphant seconds.

ONE SIZE FITS ALL

With great irritation, I realized that bloody Gruber seemed to be asking a question. He'd spoiled the really good bit where my salary was trebled and I was promoted to being Joe Salami's personal assistant and got to fire all my fellow executives.

"Why should this be so?" repeated Gruber.

I shrugged.

"Always the rectangular is chosen in preference to the oval."

He took his glasses off and rubbed his eyes.

"I would have *thought* the oval *more* sexually attractive," he said.

"I've never tried it," I said.

"What have you not tried?"

"What about sardines?" I said.

He stared at me. He adjusted his spectacles.

"*Sardines?*"

"You know," I said. "Little fishes."

He nodded.

"Well I'd prefer sardines in oval cans rather than rectangular cans."

"That is an interesting statement," he said.

"Because with the rectangular cans you straighten out the little

114

metal tab and get the key twisted on it and then you start turning and you can never get more than three-quarters of the way before you've used up all the key and then you're faced with forking them out in bits or using a can-opener which won't go round the edges properly but if you had oval cans and you'd used the key up the can-opener would go round easier."

"The oval attracts you," he stated.

"I believe it does," I said.

"In this," he said, "you are an aberration."

"Tell me," I said pleasantly, "when did they let you out?"

"I've just got back," he said.

"I thought you might have done."

"How they complained!" he said.

"I'd have thought they'd have been delighted."

"Why are we carrying boxes like labourers they said. We did not pay our fees to labour in stockrooms they said. What are we learning they said. What are you learning I said. I will tell you what you are learning. You are learning *weight*. You are learning *proportion*. You are learning *depth* and *wolume*. You do not *know* you are learning these things *but you are learning them*!"

He was getting Teutonic again so I said,

"It's not unlike the learning theory advanced by Wackford Squeers."

"Squeers? I do not think I know this Squeers."

"Ah!" I said.

"Was he at the University of Southern California?"

"Somewhere in the north of England, I think."

"Squeers," he said again.

"Wackford," I said.

The door burst open and Cosimo O'Gorman burst in.

"Jim! Jim!" he said, all over me, mauling my hand and shaking my elbow too, six foot seven of ill-clad energy.

"What can I say? All Systems Go — and then — Hans! What can I say? My life just isn't my own."

The room was full of him.

"It was a pleasure, Director," said Gruber.

"Indeed it was," I said. "Most instructive."

"Hans," said Cosimo. "We mustn't keep you any longer. You look tired."

He took him by the elbow and escorted him to the door.

Cosimo's suit hung upon him not as awful as the plaid madras

115

jacket but still unfortunate. He was wearing a broad tie hand-painted with a tropical sunrise and palm trees. I had not seen such a tie for more than twenty years. I suddenly wondered, I don't know why, if he wore such clothing as some kind of disguise.

As I wore mine.

As John Caverly had worn his.

Closing the door on Gruber, he turned. His florid, genial face of which there was a lot seemed abruptly less genial. The meeting which had detained him must have gone badly. Behind the flab of his press-the-fleshery and Rotary good-cheer, I glimpsed an O'Gorman less affable.

He pressed the button on the antique domed radio which a depraved taste had converted into a miniature bar and the dome parted again like a missile silo to reveal the necks of bottles.

"Labour under no misapprehension!" he said, exhibiting a bottle of scotch in the manner of a sommelier.

"Fine," I said. "Thank you."

"*Mr.* Robinson," he said.

"Wells," I said.

He seemed not to hear. The conversation was beginning to lose me. He was also beginning to make me feel nervous. His was an undeniable presence.

"A good man on the team, Gruber," he said rattling ice-cubes into the glasses. "There are no doubts about his loyalty."

"Loyalty?"

"You sound surprised."

He stared at me.

"There are minds on this campus," he said, "*medieval* minds."

I nodded slowly under his stare.

"*Hermetic* minds," he added.

He stood soothing the crown of his grey brush-cut with the flat of his hand.

"So, yes," he said. "Loyal."

I watched him carefully.

This was obviously a non-linear mind in action.

There was an uneasy silence.

"A relict," he said holding his glass up to the light.

"Gruber?"

"No, *no*. You have *met* the man? The Librarian? Robinson?"

"No, I ..."

"Horsehair, Horsetail," he said. "That's the name of the stuff, isn't it? The plant that's called 'the living fossil'?"

"You mean you feel . . . ?"

"A hundred pages of a book," said Cosimo, "on a single sheet of indestructible plastic. A library on a silicon chip."

"He doesn't like the idea?"

"Papyrus," said Cosimo. "We are gripped by the dead hand, the *mort main* of papyrus."

Ice-cubes cracked in the glass.

The beginnings of a smile appeared on his face.

"If the man remains impervious to reason," he said, "I shall, of course, strike a committee."

The thought of this committee, its composition and machinations, seemed to recharge his batteries with better humour.

"I've noticed you've been glancing at my *Stag at Bay*."

"Yes," I said. "It's . . ."

"A curve ball," he said. "A little joke I allow myself. You see the point?"

"Well . . ." I said.

"Disorientation," he said. "*That's* the point. You see? A graphic example of what I am informed students call a 'mind-fuck'."

He drained and set down his glass.

He pinged it with his forefinger.

"What," he said, "do we, in essence, *do* here? What is our function?"

I arranged my face into an expectant expression.

"We destroy," he said, "*pre*conceptions. We liberate *percep*tions."

He stood.

He pointed to *The Stag at Bay*.

"The *nineteenth* century," he said.

Dramatically, slowly, he opened his other arm to encompass the room, and, by implication, the Complex itself.

"The *twentieth* century," he said.

He held this crucified position for a moment and then clapped his hands. And then positively rubbed them.

"A world completely dead," he said, looking at the Stag. "But a world in which the *Robinsons* still live."

He shook his head as if wondering at their intransigence or folly.

"Dead, utterly dead. And all the dim centuries preceding

117

washed up on the shore of *that* century. Driftwood."

"I find the Stag rather comforting," I said.

He stared at me.

"In a way," I added quickly.

He chuckled as if to say, *You rogue, you!* and I smiled back at him as though in complicity.

"Washed up," he said, "shattered on the rock of 1839."

"1839?"

"The year of the photograph!"

"Oh!" I said. "Of course. It's so much earlier than one thinks."

He drew up one of the plastic cubes close to mine facing me.

"Shock!" he exclaimed. "That's what we're all about here. A new vision. A new vision for a new age. When my students walk into this building, they're confronted by mirrors. Their static interior images of themselves are fragmented into multiple images. Images in motion. The 'shaving glass' image of self and others, if I can put it that way, is shattered."

I thought suddenly of the boy who'd come to see me about making my poem come alive with snow-related sounds. O'Malley, that was the name. He'd been fragmented all right. The only problem was he hadn't been reconstituted.

"Egypt, umm?" said Cosimo.

I nodded.

He pointed an accusing finger at the engraving.

"The perception of motion," he said, "is the death of the frame."

I nodded once more. It seemed the only safe response.

"Hieratic art," said Cosimo, "in all its guises . . . and hasn't it all been *precisely* that?"

"Well . . ." I said.

"Deployed against us," he said, "are the forces of obscurantism. Outworn pieties bleed us of our possible budget, our necessary expansion, our *needs*."

He was bloody big and very close and all this seemed to call for more than a slow nodding so I said,

"What exactly do you mean by 'out-worn pieties'?"

"Let me offer—what shall we say? An *exemplum*."

He smiled at his choice of word. His tone enclosed it with almost visible quotation marks. I wondered why he found it amusing.

"In September 1939," he said, "General Heinz Guderian in

118

command of the XIX Armoured Corps had sliced through Poland and cut off a large section of the Polish Army. In an attempt to break through Guderian's line and regroup with forces to the south, the Pomorske Cavalry Brigade *rode against Guderian's tanks*."

He paused.

"We can imagine light flashing on sabres, glinting on gold braid, on facings, and froggings. Pennons fluttering in the breeze. The officers in spotless white gloves. Trumpets sounding the advance. Walk. Trot. Canter. The sabre blade sweeping down to signal the charge."

He shook his head.

"An entire Brigade," he said. "Can you *visualize* that?"

I could and thought it magnificent.

"And seconds later," he said, raising a hectoring forefinger, "seconds later the ground erupted. Shell and machine gun fire, men dismembered. Steaming, disemboweled horses. A pageant cut down to a screaming shambles."

I shook *my* head.

"Umm?" he said.

I nodded.

"Umm? Umm?"

This anecdote seemed to have cheered him up no end.

Sir Edwin Landseer, painter of *The Stag at Bay*, was deranged only for the last four years of his life. I suspected that Cosimo had already been ga-ga for much longer.

That or completely criminal.

And in either case needed to be defrocked forthwith.

The tour of CAC was like a royal Progress. Cosimo was everywhere greeted as 'Director' or 'Father' and he, in turn, beamed upon all and addressed them, staff and students, by their first names. In the raw concrete bowels of the building behind the mirrors, the corridors and rooms and rooms off rooms seemed like a maze. I could get no sense of where we were.

I learned that 'educational facility' meant 'classroom', that 'receiver/monitor' meant 'TV set', that 'conceptual resource' meant 'book'. Each educational facility was equipped with sound systems, computer terminals, opaque projection units, projectors for eight, sixteen, and thirty-five mm. film and was wired on a closed-circuit system to the Dome.

The *Conceptual Resource Centre* contained manuals, magazines, and sets of comics — *Superman*, *Batman*, and *Super Friends*.

These were studied by Super-Eight students to learn the rhythms of film-editing, the techniques being nearly identical. I glanced at a magazine which was lying open on the table. The article was entitled:

"Techno Goodies from the Electro Kitchen of the Video Freaks."

Through a mirror, across the purple carpet, through another mirror, and into *Photographics*. The room was windowless and smelled of chemicals. Off this room were small darkrooms. Over a central work table hung a huge developer. Lamps on stands stood about.

"With the advent of lith," said Cosimo, "we have the ability to make comprehensive graphic statements."

I looked about me.

"Lith developer troughs," said Cosimo, gesturing.

"For the . . . ah . . ."

"Lith," said Cosimo. "A complex process but a simple idea. In essence, what it amounts to is taking an ordinary continuous-tone photograph and developing it onto lith to cut out the intermediate grey tones leaving only high contrasts."

"Ah," I said.

"A Line Tone Separation, for example, is made by printing a series of high contrast negatives from an original negative by means of different exposure times. Then a further series of negatives are made on lith by exposing the master positive made from the original negative. Then a series of positives are made by contact-printing the lith negatives onto lith. You follow?"

"Yes," I said firmly.

"And then to produce Line Tone Separation, a lith negative is sandwiched emulsion side out with its corresponding lith positive and light is angled through the sandwich."

"Aha," I said.

He spread out examples of photographics on the table for my inspection.

Line Tone Separation looked exactly like wood-cuts, lino-cuts, and potato-prints. Posterizations turned out to be photographs so buggered about as to look like very bad magic realist paintings.

"The developer," said Cosimo, patting it, "reveals the realities *behind* the reality of the naturalistic record."

"I've never seen such surprising effects," I said.

"And *these*," said Cosimo, "are panchromatic examples of the

Sabatier Phenomenon."

"Good Heavens!"

"They're produced by solarization onto lith and they're characterized, as you see here, by a partially reversed image and the attendant Mackie Line."

"Hmmm," I said.

These horrid things looked like a doodled mixture of Dali, Pollock, and sci-fi illustration.

I stirred them all about politely.

"Creative developing," said Cosimo, "will inevitably supersede the pencil and the brush."

We marched on.

In the *Animation* room, a boy was trying to draw an animal in Confederate uniform. The sheet of paper was grubby with erased pencil lines. The boy said the animal was a chipmunk.

We looked at the animation stand.

As Cosimo closed the door behind us, he said,

"We usually restrict them to cardboard-cutouts or pixilation."

I nodded understandingly.

For some reason, the word 'pixilation' made me think of another word which I couldn't remember which meant 'the removal of unwanted body hair'.

Cosimo gestured at the door of *Audio One* as we walked past.

"Nothing much to interest you, I'm afraid," he said. "Standard studio facilities. We're equipped to record studio-live, off-air, film sync, cassette-to-cassette, cassette-to-reel, reel-to-cassette, reel-to-reel, video-cassette-to-cassette, video-reel-to-video-cassette, video-reel-to-video-reel, reel-to-video-to-video."

This brisk recital brought us to the door of *Screening*.

We stood at the back of the room watching a student's Super-Eight movie of a snow-blower. The snow-blower, the grader, the questing funnel spewing snow into the attendant convoy of dump trucks — all were shot from every conceivable angle. The instructor's voice, like that of a choreographer from a darkened theatre pit, chanted the rhythm of the shots.

"*Long* shot, *Medium* shot. ECU. *Cutaway*. Oh, my God. ECU. *Holy Christ!* LIGHTS! LIGHTS!"

Cosimo took my arm and we went out again into the corridor.

"Do you teach courses on film history?" I said as we walked along.

"There *is* a first year course that's historically oriented," he said, "or was it cancelled this year?"

"And what about individual directors?" I said. "Renoir, say, Bergman, Fellini, Bresson?"

"Well," said Cosimo, "no. They're not really *applicable*."

I glanced at him.

"Oh," I said.

"Let's make our way down here," he said, "to what one might call the nerve centre. To use a biological analogue."

"Nerve centre?"

"The Dome," said Cosimo.

Cosimo unlocked the door to the Studio Control Centre. The Studio was banked with machinery. All the machines were dotted with dials and keys and levers and buttons and tabs and tiny light bulbs and knobs and a variety of holes, cryptically lettered, for wires and jacks to fit into. I was immediately overcome with the glazed boredom with which all machinery affects me. I could remember being taken when a child on educational treats to newspaper offices, steel works, and sewage treatment plants. Of all such trips the only pleasing memory I retain is of having a penny flattened to the size of a quarter under a huge hammer sort of thing. When people *explain* machinery to me, the boredom approaches hysteria and physical pain.

"Ampex VTR," said Cosimo, tapping a thing the size of two large refrigerators, "and up here we have our SEG. As you can see," he said, pointing to all its buttons and knobs, "this gives us fades, dissolves, wipes, mattes, superimpositions, and titling. *This*," he said, "is a CONRAC monitor. Back-up equipment *here* — an Audio Mixer and here we have a Frequency Equalizer. You wouldn't find a more professional studio in the CBC. All our equipment's up to network standards. I'd go so far as to say it's up to the standards of the Big Three."

"It's all very impressive," I said.

The thing called SEG had three little TV screens on it. I studied it with a show of earnestness. Underneath the three screens were twelve knobs. Underneath them were twenty-five buttons, two more knobs and four dials with numbers on and a square meter with a red indicator needle.

"There's more than $350,000 in hardware in Control alone," said Cosimo.

I did an indrawn whistle and shook my head at the same time to indicate awe and admiration.

"Of course," said Cosimo, "with that kind of investment Control Centre's something of a Holy of Holies. It's not until their final year that we allow students to enter into the Studio experience."

I nodded attentively.

"But they become familiar with the video concept during their first three years by using Sony portapaks. We have thirty of them in constant use. Videorover IIs they're called—what you might describe as the Volkswagen of the video world. The portapak VTR uses ½-inch EIAJ helical scan tape and the cameras operate on 2/3 inch separate-mesh vidicon tubes. They do the job and they're a good instructional instrument. But *here*, of course," he said, gesturing out beyond the glass panel into the Dome at the five grey cameras the size and shape of lumpy cannons, "here we use Plumbicon tubes not vidicon and *this* beauty," he said, patting the VTR, "uses 2-inch Quadruplex transverse scan."

"2-inch!" I exclaimed.

It seemed the sort of thing to say.

"Fifteenth generation copies before picture loss becomes apparent," said Cosimo.

He gave the VTR a final pat.

As we went into the Dome proper, Cosimo said,

"Are you familiar with conventional studios?"

"Yes," I said, "I've been in them a few times."

I had nightmare memories of the year I'd won the Governor-General's Award and in a weak moment had allowed my publisher to coerce me into a day of publicity in Toronto. The day had started at 7 a.m. with a radio interview on CBC. It had opened by the interviewer saying,

"The blurb on this book states that you have a 'despairing world vision'. What *right* do you have to such 'despair'? You're presently living on Canada Council money, aren't you?"

Matters quickly degenerated to insult and obscenity and the interview was abandoned. The interviewer then asked me if I'd mind autographing his free promotion copy of my book.

This interview was followed by a TV interview broadcast from the foyer of the Dorchester Motel. The interviewer had not of course read the book and managed four different versions of the title within as many minutes. He then tried to promote an exchange of views between me and a female proponent of vasectomy.

Lunch was spent with a literary critic of the Toronto *Beacon* who described in infinite detail the conversion and remodelling of a slum property he'd bought in Cabbagetown.

Following this, I got drunker with a reporter from *Chatterbox*, had my photograph taken, and then got drunker. My schedule then sent me to a Book Signing at Eaton's where I sat for three hours with one hundred and fifty copies and sold four. Finally, I was escorted at 11 p.m. to a warehouse on the outskirts of Toronto where a Hungarian lady in extreme décolletage and extensive knockers presided over a Cable-TV outfit. She referred to my poems throughout as a novel. My fellow guests were a man who was walking across Canada as a personal Centennial Project and a lady who bred chihuahuas.

I gazed about the Dome while Cosimo stroked his Plumbicons. Thick coaxial cables, microphone extension cables, and other wires more mysterious snaked about the floor. Fill lights and back lights stood about. Key lights were clamped on overhead pipes.

"Colortran quartz-iodine bulbs," called Cosimo.

I stood gazing up. The Dome was criss-crossed about half way up by a maze of girders from which hung thick white rolls like bolts of cloth.

"What are those?"

"You've noticed them!" said Cosimo, beaming and briskly rubbing the grey crown of his brush cut. "Now that's an adaptation of mine—a concept I've pioneered. As a matter of fact, it was written up last year in *Video Universe*. The departure point, of course, was the fly-floor of the traditional theatre but this is computer-controlled. In two minutes I can program this basic dome shape into any variety of spatial environment."

"So you mean they're sort of flies?"

"Any variety of spatial environment," said Cosimo, "vertical *and* horizontal. Flies? Flies, yes, but in no ordinary sense. The cloth is an intense light and audio-reflective synthetic and each environment, as it's formed, feeds the computer its individual light-reading and its impedance on the AGC Circuit of the VTR."

"Incredible!" I said.

"Plumbicons," said Cosimo, "Studio—the whole package cost me close to three quarters of a million."

I stood staring about me.

To my left sat a talk-show set—a couch, an armchair, and a coffee table. Over these hung a boom mike. On the coffee table stood a water carafe and three glasses. I was reminded of something

Gore Vidal had said — that the thought of people sitting at home watching other people talking made him feel very sad.

At the far side of the Dome, a staircase with bannisters rose to end in mid air. A pair of rubber boots stood a few yards from the staircase. Near the glass panel of the Control Centre an ornate throne topped a dais. The three stages of the dais were carpeted in red. The throne, a gothic affair, was painted blue, its scrollwork and finials picked out in gilt.

This obviously random accumulation of props suddenly struck me as purposeful. I don't know why. It seemed like an exercise in the surreal or an exhibition of conceptual art the point of which was eluding me.

I hoped that whatever mummery these props belonged to had been performed with greater expertise than that evidenced by the chipmunk boy in *Animation*.

"What were they for?" I called.

"Oh, some third-year exercise." He gestured dismissingly. "A scene from a play, I believe. Shakespeare or something of the sort. Colour."

I completed a circuit of the Dome. Cosimo seemed abstracted. He mounted the first stage of the dais and stood there with his back to me raising and lowering himself on his toes as if on a springboard over a pool. Slowly, he climbed the next two steps and seated himself on the blue and gilt throne.

I walked over and sat on the lowest step of the dais.

"Is it O.K. if I smoke in here?" I said.

He didn't answer. He seemed not to hear.

I fashioned an ashtray from the packet's silver paper. I took a long and grateful drag. It was my first cigarette since Hospitality on Level One.

"By the blast of God they perish," said Cosimo, "and by the breath of his nostrils are they consumed."

Startled, I glanced up at him.

"I beg your pardon?"

I'd thought for a moment he was making an obscure condemnation of the habit of smoking but he was staring in an unfocused way towards the severed staircase.

The staircase reminded me of the half-demolished building next to my rooming-house, stairs ascending to floorless rooms open to the sky, rooms demarcated by squares of different coloured wallpaper, the last absurdly touching memorials to lives and

125

families.

"Umm?" he said more to the staircase than to me, an interrogative surfacing from some obviously subterranean line of thought.

I cleared my throat to assert my presence.

I ground out the cigarette and lighted another. The match scraped the silence.

"What are the 'high' arts," he said quietly, "what are literature, theatre, opera, painting, orchestras, ballet — what are they but the vestigal traces of another world? Rituals still performed whose significance has been long forgotten. There is a gulf between us and that world, and a gulf between that world and what we *shall* become, a gulf as wide as that which now separates us from pre-historic man."

His arms lay along the arms of the plyboard throne, his thick bony wrists sticking out of the suit. His rumpled black socks revealed white shin. The tropical tie with palm trees lay over one lapel of his jacket. Behind his grey brush-cut were lions rampant.

"Everything in this building, everything you've so far seen," he said, his voice fallen almost to a whisper, "is an irrelevance. A political expedience. Chaff which the wind driveth away. An expedience necessary to attain that vision. Only here. Only here within the Dome..."

His voice trailed away.

He sat in silence for a few moments.

I heard him sigh.

Suddenly he said in a strong voice,

"O sing unto the Lord a new song."

And then, without pause, he said,

"It's become a cliché but unlike most clichés doesn't represent an overwhelming truth. The truth is more complicated."

"Which ... er ... cliché .. ?"

"Film," he said impatiently. "That film marks us off from earlier ages. It contains a grain of truth but not much more. A majority of children now entering elementary school — a majority — have never or but rarely visited a movie theatre. Their visual and social experience of film is entirely confined to TV. Movie 'theatre' and 'palace' — consider such linguistic fossils! We are not of the generation of film. Film has, perhaps unknown to itself, joined earlier cultural expressions as museum pieces. It has become Art with a capital 'A'. Sickly, moribund. No. No, no. The film, all signs to the contrary, is now in its death-throes. Its production costs are too great, its distribution systems archaic, its public attenuated. Economics are against it. The advances of technology have destroyed it. *Which*," he said, "explains the recent rash of high-cost epic spectaculars. Roman circuses. A forceful argument, I think you'll agree."

"Yes," I said, "I hadn't thought of it in that way."

He seemed to be settling into the tone and manner of a lecture.

"Film," he said, "is a *formal* medium, distanced, devised, elaborately artistic. The film concept is in the uninterrupted tradition of the novel—a critical perception, if I may say so, seemingly not available to many. Film is merely a shift in *emphasis*. Ummm?"

"Mmmm," I said.

"TV and video are, of course, the offspring of the film but the parent form has nothing now to teach us. One might, quite properly I think, describe the offspring less as offspring than as *mutants*. The editing techniques of film are not applicable to the video world. We edit in camera. We live in the spontaneous moment. What *is* and our apprehension of it are a single and simultaneous act. The, what I describe as, the *human intrusion* of film editing is greatly reduced. We must, I think, go further even than that. The very *concept* of film with its attendant editing techniques and what they imply about the medium is the *antithesis* of the video function. Film is, in aesthetic terms, though rhythmic, essentially *static*. Video, on the other hand, is of the flow and flux. That quality of distancing, a quality we can reasonably identify as aesthetic, is almost entirely lacking. The over-riding virtue of video is that it has *no aesthetic value whatsoever*."

His voice stopped and the silence extended uncomfortably.

I was reduced to *very* slow nodding.

"Umm? Umm?" he said.

"No aesthetic value whatsoever," I repeated in neutral tone.

"Yes. Yes. The whole *point*, you see."

I could hear the creak of the plyboard throne as he settled back.

I was mildly stunned by the point at which he had arrived, baffled by what seemed to be a logical sleight-of-hand. Had I missed an essential step in his reasoning? He seemed so confident. Point? The whole point of *what*? *Why* was it the whole point? What *was* the point? I felt, I decided, like the bemused loser in a shell

127

game.

"How much," he said suddenly, "do twelve colour snaps cost now? Developed and printed?"

"I'm not really sure," I said. "Six or seven dollars, I suppose."

"And how long," he said, "in the face of Polaroid technology before such film will be regarded as a domestic curiosity like flat-irons or straight razors?"

His tone had required no answer. He grunted. He shook his head. I hadn't the slightest idea what *he* was brooding about but I brooded along with him. I thought of people endlessly clicking and peeling off the paper, the real everywhere reduced to smelly chemical representations, the variegated world raw material for evenings of colour slides.

"Six or seven dollars, you say?" broke in Cosimo. "And an hour, an *hour* of video tape costs us less than eighteen dollars. *And* prices are falling rapidly. Was it ten years ago — eleven — that video became a mass possibility? Has it only been ten? We used iron oxide tape then. At the beginning. But that soon gave way to a revolutionary new tape, a Cobalt doped tape that gave us greater frequency response. All this in ten short years.

But at this very moment, as I sit here talking, magnetic tape of any description is obsolete. Flat-irons. Straight razors. Tape will be superseded, its place taken by solid-state random access memory systems — small chips which will fit into the camera like a cassette. And even now, as I sit here, mass production of true video wall screens is imminent. The monitor will vanish. Holographic 3D video reproduction using the Triniton Tube has passed well beyond the experimental stage. And all this, in turn, means that network TV itself as we know it is now a thing of the past. And this studio, yes, all this — this studio I laboured to build, for which I fought, this too will soon be a museum, its equipment and its possibilities as quaint as a daguerreotype. As quaint as a hand-tinted daguerreotype in a velvet-lined case."

He fell silent.

I shook my head as if in commiseration.

It was the best news I'd heard all day.

But then, sitting upright on the throne, he pointed to the ceiling of the Dome, crying,

"Here am I; for thou callest me."

I watched him carefully. I was beginning to feel much as I imagined members of Idi Amin's cabinet must have felt.

128

He slapped the arm of the throne enthusiastically.

"The progress of the medium is irreversible, unimaginable. We are at a new birth! A cold coming we had of it, umm? umm? Cable!" he half-shouted. "Cable contains our future! Laser! Vistas lie before us unimaginable. The hills must not daunt us — behind them lies a new country. We are but at a stage on the way!"

"The way . . . ?"

"On the way to a total photographic environment!"

He rose to his feet, pushing back the throne. He towered above me. Dusk was gathering and the Dome becoming dim. His features were indistinct, his face a white shape in the gloom. His phosphorescent tie was beginning to glow.

"All the former languages of communication are dead, dead or dying! Let the dead bury their dead! There is but *one* vernacular world-wide, *one* lingua franca, and not to recognize it, to turn from it, to refuse it, dooms us to dead devotions, diseased adorations of the dead forms of the past."

He seemed transported. His voice filled the empty Dome like the diapason of a great organ in a basilica. I felt the plyboard dais shake under his weight as he started down the three steps.

I got up quickly.

He gripped my arm.

"We must *embrace* this birth. We must bend our energies and our being to the confusion of its enemies. In order once again to become whole, in order once again to draw mankind together into a common culture, a common polity, outmoded and irrelevant concepts of art and communication must be eradicated, the delusion of quality discredited utterly."

His grip on my upper arm was shaking the whole of my body with the rhythms of his rhetoric.

"Many of these relics are piously enshrined and the guardians of these pieties mock at us. They mock, they mock and gird. But answer me this. Answer me this. What happened to the stone the builders refused?"

I shook my head.

"What happened to the stone the builders refused?"

"I don't know," I said quietly.

His voice sounded in triumph.

"The stone which the builders refused is become the headstone of the corner!"

He let go of my arm. I did not dare rub it.

129

He was silent for a moment.

"I see a world," he said, his voice touched with tremor, "I see a world in instant communication each part with another, a world of linguistic barriers overturned, a visual world accessible to all men, a world wired to God's Eternal Will."

Silence sifted down.

"A world," he repeated, "wired to God's Eternal Will."

As if tranced, he wandered away from the dais.

The seconds dragged on in their long silence.

He made a slight gesture towards the VTR and SEG.

"'Hear, ye deaf; and look, ye blind, that ye may see'."

He lowered himself to one knee.

He knelt.

Cautiously, the held air aching in my lungs, I made for the door. He remained kneeling, silent, motionless, a dark shape in the gloom of the Dome. When I had gained the door, I turned and looked back.

The paleness of his face was staring up at the blank eye of a Plumbicon. As I broke the seal and eased open the heavy door, I heard his whisper.

"Babel. Babel rebuilt."

Chapter Nine

During the week following my tour of CAC I began to doubt the wisdom of having moved in with Kathy, a move made at her suggestion after she had seen my room and Gagool in the nightdress under the British Army great coat.

CAC had become a focus for my drifting feelings of depression and distress. My brooding exhausted me. I lay in bed. I drank joylessly. I could not summon the energy to shave, shower, or change my clothes. I could feel myself slipping, day by day losing grip. I began to take a gloomy pleasure in my smell.

That Cosimo O'Gorman SJ was starkly mad, I had no doubt. Far more frightening, I had few doubts that he was *right*. Shorn of the trimmings of the New Jerusalem and Babel rebuilt, his vision of a world wired had little in it of delusion. I felt I had more in common with the Stone Age inhabitants of New Guinea than with his new heaven and new earth, more in common with Peking Man than Man Post-Gutenberg. I had long ago been forced to a weary accommodation with the fact that I lived in a country devoid of culture save in the anthropological sense of the word. I was coming more often to doubt if I cared to continue in a world that no longer even understood its lack.

A world enriched by jingles.

Javex Man.

Nihil obstat.

I talked at Kathy obsessedly about television, literacy, the decline of the west, hierarchy broken, the barbarian without the gate. And worse, the multitudinous traitors within the citadel. And Kathy was so reasonable, so *understanding*, without apparently understanding a word. In my sullen rage, she seemed to me like a dotty monk on Iona deaf to the tocsin, earnestly pottering away in the scriptorium with gilt and twiddly bits sweetly unaware of the long ships gathering.

I was irritated by the vacuum-cleaner, the clatter of crockery, *neatness*. I was irritated by her typewriter and bloody George 'Private Ejaculations' Herbert. I was ungrateful for the meals she cooked and which I did not want to eat. I was irritated by her soulful glances at the lowering levels in the bottles of vodka and scotch. I was made furious by the bottle of vitamins she bought me. They were called *Chock Full O' Life.*

Although the dead had been leaving us more and more in peace, she held no sexual attraction for me during that grim week. The past was a receding problem. It was the future that weighed upon me. I felt sick at heart. Our human touching seemed a frail thing, fragile, almost pointless. The darkness was around me, in me, threatening to engulf. At night we both lay tense and wakeful unable to talk or touch. My emotional place, I felt, much as I loved her, was not there. My place was in a room with a sombre wardrobe like a coffin.

I felt her inability or refusal to understand a kind of betrayal. How could she *not* understand?

Vulgar, certainly, tut-tut. Quite deplorable. But people could always turn it off, couldn't they?

It was like bellowing down the ear-trumpet of a Maiden Aunt. She seemed totally unaware the world had shifted in the night, the tectonic plates of the past heaved and buckled, and she looked at the devastated landscape without seeing. How, then, could I make her understand this was but a preliminary tremor? She was so wrapped up in George fucking Herbert that for all she knew the Oxford University Press was already owned by a multinational pet-food company with diversified interests in guano. She'd wake up one morning to find she was editing the *Oxford Book of Bird Shit.*

I punched up the pillows and lay staring at a patch of weak sunlight which was approaching the lower edge of the Chinese scroll. I watched the ascending column of cigarette smoke, its sudden swirls and eddies. I could hear Kathy in the kitchen, the sound of a steel-wire pad on the frying pan. I had pretended to be asleep while she gathered her clothes and made preparations for her day.

I closed my eyes imagining again the bulk of the Complex black against the skeletons of trees on the wintery campus. The dark was stronger, more real than human warmth.

The summons had gone forth. *By General Ludd's Exprefs* Commands . . . Messages whispered. Night knocks on kitchen doors. Clogs on the cobbled streets. The grim men had gathered. Luddite sledgehammers and axes had once smashed the shearing-frames and steam-looms. In parts of Lancashire and Yorkshire the burning mills had lightened the night sky.

A wrecking bar to jemmy the soft Yale lock, down the purple slope, through the mirrored wall into the corridor to the Dome. And then the crowbar to smash the dials, can-open the VTR, disembowel the SEG, rip out the minor wiring and blind the Plumbicons. Then a final game of Russian roulette in the guts of unknown cables until the jarring steel hit the loaded chamber and the voltage illuminated me. Sparks arcing, smoke in wisps, tongues of flame. And in the last milliseconds of life a great light blazing like a thousand key-lights trained on stage and the fading heartbeat of a voice:

TAKE ONE

Take one

Take one

I heard Kathy moving about in the living room and then heard the soft closing of the apartment door. Now that she was out of the way and I wouldn't have to talk to her, I thought of getting up and making coffee but couldn't be bothered with water boiling and filters, cups, and spoons. In the deepening silence after her departure, my thoughts drifted with the wavering cigarette smoke.

Sparks arcing!

Take one.

Posturings, I thought with contempt, bed-time stories for the disappointed middle-aged. As the tap in the kitchen dripped, dripped, I found myself thinking of Marjorie, of the tool box she'd given me as an anniversary gift, found myself thinking, as I so often did of John Caverly, of the Vancouver apartment we had shared, of his firm refusal even in poverty to ride on buses. *He* had never lost courage, never faltered. He held that the only fitting means of

133

transportation for a poet was a taxi-cab with a suitably taciturn driver.

The last few years of his life had been comfortable with grants, awards, and belated honours. He had enjoyed what passes for fame in Canada. His life's work was strangely summarized in a three-quarter page entry in the *Oxford Companion to Canadian History and Literature*, a collocation which gives equal time to every Canadian who has ever set pen to paper or cranked a mimeograph machine. Two slim but laborious works of thematic criticism had appeared which failed to grasp the singing chastity of a single line. His poetry had been widely anthologized so that it could be the more widely misunderstood.

The years of critical neglect were easy to explain. He was guilty of wilful clarity. His work was so lucid, so stark, that there were no thickets of grammatical ineptitude, no coverts of arcane or personal reference, no tangles of ambiguity for the critics to thresh about in and flush meaning out.

Nothing could forgive the grubby shifts to which he'd been driven to keep alive. Nothing could forgive the waste of his best years.

A few days before he killed himself, I received a registered envelope from him. There was no letter. The envelope contained his driver's licence, his social insurance card, a genuine Chargex card, and an unpublished poem typed on thick duplicating paper. I should have realized when I opened the envelope. I probably did. I didn't go to the funeral. I don't like them. I carry the poem with me in my wallet, the paper creased and becoming furry.

On moving to St. Xavier, I had once more changed the licence — this time from Ontario to Quebec. I had visited an office on Cavendish Boulevard with the resounding title *Bureau des véhicules automobiles. Succursales immatriculation et permis de conduire* where the clerk had been blind again to the fact that I'd shrunk a bit. I must have been the youngest looking fifty-year old he'd seen in weeks.

I'd had the licence mailed to the address of a guy I'd met in a bar. I'd spent an evening playing darts, losing twenty bucks to him in preparation. One of my Caverly business cards — *F.D.I. Confidential Investigations* — and some broad innuendo had completed the conquest. His address and telephone number were also stored in the Chargex computer's memory.

The sunlight was just touching the three tiny figures in the misty defile through the Chinese mountains.

Like a dog to its vomit, my thoughts returned to the Complex. I saw again the dark shape in Hospitality of Cosimo's contemptuous *Stag at Bay*. Doomed, yes, but dangerous. Even waddling badgers that feast on the bulbs of bluebells can disembowel the yapping terriers. One day, somewhere, I would face this hall of mirrors head-on, a final stand, the shield-ring shrinking. Futile, romantic nonsense, I knew, but nonsense which to me made sense. A matter of temperament.

Valhalla.

Not Jerusalem.

John Caverly had thought such thoughts as these, perhaps, chosen his ground, died there with some kind of pride.

My stomach growled. It was eating itself. It needed breakfast.

Shield-ring shrinking!

Valhalla!

My final stand was likely to be against Mr. Archambault and his ink-stained cohorts at the Taxation Data Centre.

By registered mail.

I wondered where the tiny figures on the scroll were going. A mandarin, perhaps, on his way to exile in some distant province of the Celestial Kingdom where he would write poems in praise of the succulence of bamboo shoots, of drunkenness, of the ministrations of his concubine. Lacking loyalty, my exile was different. With papers securely forged, I could move through the hostile land, agent, partisan . . . .

Secret agent Wells. Jim the Partisan.

Disgusted, finally, cumulatively, by my self-pity and my endless ability to drift in fantasy, I lay staring at the mandarin, an idea slowly coming into blossom, blooming, ripening towards action. The resolve which was elaborating itself, a token blow against St. Xavier, a sortie, an earnest of what I would wreak upon CAC itself in the fullness of time, would not halt the onslaught of Post-Gutenbergery but might well relieve my constipation. Anything was a gain. I threw back the covers.

"When you get there," I said to the mandarin, "you mind you write good."

Security at St. Xavier was shockingly lax. It is at most vaguely academic institutions. It's because they operate on the horribly mistaken assumption that most people are as much souls of probity as they. The main tactical thrust of Security is usually directed at illicit parking.

The Department of English was an especial disgrace. Within a week of taking up residence, I had had made a copy of the secretary's master-key. The recently arrived IBM Selectric offered itself as a cheering exercise. I would remove it, I decided. I would remove it as a memorial gesture, a John Caverly Fringe Benefit Memorial.

My depression and lassitude seemed to sluice away with the stale sweat under the shower. I used Kathy's pretty pink soap. I sang. With odd stresses, I fitted to an old hymn tune the words:

All our sins are washed away
With fabulous Pink Camay.

I shaved with a new blade — I'd thrown the Philishave away — there were mornings I couldn't stand the noise. I saw things with the clarity that comes after the fever breaks. I took delight in the white purity of the whorl of shaving foam, in the gleam of porcelain, the knurled grip of the razor, all the intricate pleasures to which I'd been blind for a week. I dressed with exaggerated care as if robing for a ceremonial. I positively prinked.

To the bathroom mirror, I declared,

The game's afoot!

In the taxi on the way to St. Xavier I thought about mandarins. How sensible and proper for poets to govern a country! Not your vatic, mimeographed boyos but the winnowed veterans of rigorous examinations in the Four Books, the Five Classics, the poetic forms, and the demands of the eight-legged essay. Thirty-one years of unrelenting study from aspirant to *chin-shih*. Sadly, times change. The exercise of democracy entitles us to choose from men who'd fail a Kuder Preference Test.

I removed the typewriter during the lunch hour while everyone was tucking into the Wonderbread sandwiches. I locked the office door behind me. I encased the machines in a green garbage bag and carried it down to the waiting taxi. By the time I'd dumped it on the back seat, I suspected hernia. By the time I'd humped it up the stairs to Kathy's apartment, I was wondering what, exactly, a *strangulated* hernia was.

"What's that?" said Kathy.

"Typewriter," I panted.

"What for?" she said, closing the door behind me. "We've got two already."

"New one," I said.

136

It bounced on the couch.

I tested my afflicted parts.

"Why do we need a new one?" she said.

"Don't. Pinched it. Sell it. Oh, God!"

I flopped down in the armchair.

"You *stole* it!"

I nodded.

"Xavier. Office."

"*Why*? You can't go round *stealing* things!"

"'Course you can," I said. "That's the easy part. It's selling them afterwards that's difficult."

She stared at me.

"You stole the new typewriter from the office," she said.

I nodded.

"Why did you do that?"

"For a friend," I said.

"And you're going to sell it? Or you're going to give it to this friend?"

"Sell it."

"So you're going to give this friend the money?"

"No," I said. "He's dead."

She sat down on the couch beside the typewriter. The heart attack symptoms in my arm were fading. She was wearing a blue skirt, a white silk blouse, and one of her serious expressions — Botany Mistress at Private School for Girls.

"If you don't mind," she said, "I'd like to go through this again. You have just stolen the new typewriter from the office. You stole it for a friend. But the friend is dead. So you are going to sell it. Have I got that right?"

I nodded.

"Do you need money?"

"No."

"So what you are going to do with the money?"

"Consume it," I said, "conspicuously."

The ensuing silence was meteorological — an unnatural stillness, a cold front, the lull before the storm, etc. etc. I knew that I was behaving badly, knew that Kathy had been hurt and bewildered by my depression and ill-temper, but a quarrel had been looming before this and the typewriter seemed as good a pretext as any for airing the matter that lay between us.

During the past few weeks she had remarked on the hours I

137

kept, my drinking, my drinking to excess, the squandering of my money on long distance phone calls and restaurants, my health in general and my liver in particular. She worried, she said, about what she insisted on calling my 'amnesia' and made frequent mention of cirrhosis. She seemed to equate early rising with health and morality and urged upon me breakfast products which contained bran, roughage, natural fibre, and whole grain.

She did not accept gifts graciously. She harped on my having bought one afternoon when pissed in the company of Fred Lindseer a Victorian *chaise longue*. As I told her repeatedly, she would come to love it when it had been reupholstered. And repaired.

Worst of all, in the manner of a mother pursuing recalcitrant homework, she had on more than one occasion asked me *how much I'd written*.

These irritants, in themselves, were unimportant but they were straws in a stronger wind.

She'd once criticized something I'd done — my requisition of stationery supplies under Hetherington's name I believe it was — as, among other things, 'swashbuckling'. The matter that lay between us was best expressed by the old *mot* that I thought her life could do with a bit more swash and she thought mine could use considerably more buckle.

We sat staring at each other from armchair to couch across the No Man's Land of the carpet. I wondered why her more demure outfits provoked me so lewdly. Which friend? I reminded her of the John Caverly I'd talked about and told her about Fringe Benefits and John in his early days selling cloakroom tickets to people at the tail-end of theatre queues.

"A peaked cap and speed, he always said, were of the essence in that kind of operation."

She was not amused.

"And I suppose," she said, "that you'd also claim that stealing from an institution isn't . ."

"It's not like robbing widows and orphans."

She nodded.

"Your attitudes," she said, "are adolescent. Pathetically so."

I grinned at her.

"A *slum* adolescent."

"I'm begging you, lady, don't turn me in."

"It is not *funny*," she said. "It's public money and I don't approve of *stealing*."

"Nor do I. Most reprehensible. If everyone went around doing it . . ."

She crossed her legs viciously.

"You're damn right it isn't funny," I said. "I'm *agreeing* with you. It's one of the few subjects that still brings me close to apoplexy. *Stealing!* What the hell else do you call deductions at source? *Institutionalized* theft, that's what. And if you contest it, you're in a Kangaroo Court in Ottawa with those paper-shuffling sons of whores as judge *and* jury. *Which*," I said, "is why I withhold all contributions — as a moral gesture. The laws relating to income tax — have you *read* . . ."

"*I have heard*," she said, "I have heard your views on income tax before."

I shrugged.

"Very interesting subject," I said, "income tax."

"And what happens," she said, "if you get caught?"

"I'd hire a good lawyer, I expect, and we'd reach some kind of settlement."

"I am not talking," she said with patient enunciation, "about income tax. I am talking about the typewriter."

"Oh! That."

"Yes, *that*. What happens if you get caught?"

"I won't be."

"But if you are?"

"Nothing. Nothing'll happen."

"Perhaps," she said, "you'd care to explain why?"

I looked at my watch.

"Know what's going on at Xavier now? They've just discovered it's missing. And they can't understand how because the door was locked. So their first thought is that a faculty member borrowed it or Supply's doing something to it. They'll bugger about all afternoon checking that, calling people at home, that sort of thing. They can't believe someone's knocked it off. Probably won't even be reported till tomorrow."

"And what's all that got to do with why nothing'll happen if you do get caught?"

"Did I tell you yet today that I love you?"

A glacial stare.

"You haven't mentioned the subject in a week," she said. "For the last week you've been behaving and ranting like a drunken Solzhenitsyn. A drunken *smelly* Solzhenitsyn. Though I doubt that

139

he would approve of common theft."

"Oh, you old icicle, you!"

"I suppose," she said, "this represents the manic phase of the depressive cycle."

"I wouldn't know, lady. I was never much of a one for book-learning."

"Forgive me for being tedious," she said, smiling a smile of horrible graciousness, "but if you *are* caught?"

"*If* I were," I said, taking theatrical time to light a cigarette, "two wonderful things become operative, as our American cousins say. Silly word. 'Operative', I mean. The first wonderful thing is that they wouldn't prosecute. The second wonderful thing is that they'd be vaguely pleased."

More cold staring. She was doing it very well. I wondered why we both seemed to feel it necessary to *perform* but it was too late to stop.

It was both comic and amazing that a woman with thirty-seven light bulbs made by the handicapped could so affect the manner autocratic. She was always adding to this vast collection of sixty-watt bulbs because she was too embarrassed to say no because she couldn't really understand what the man on the phone said because he had a cleft palate.

I thought how much I loved her and how unpleasant I was going to be.

"Don't you understand?" I said. "To prosecute a member of faculty would be distasteful. Sordid. Why would someone like them *steal* something? *They* wouldn't so if someone they think is somehow like them *does* then there must be an explanation. Extenuating circumstances. Nervous breakdown, perhaps. God *love* the middle class! If a *janitor* stole it, they'd have him in the slammer without a second thought, right? Dishonest janitors *belong* in the drum. But I'm an accredited poet and everyone knows, *them* especially, that poets are *weird*. So that's the explanation, you see. Perfectly understandable. Weird people do weird things."

She leaned back and crossed her arms. Her posture conveyed heroic patience.

"The logic's a bit confused," I said, "but it's their confusion, not mine."

"And what's the second wonderful thing?"

"Ah! The second thing's much more important, Kathy. They'd be *pleased*. They'd be proud that *their* poet, their own accredited funny man, had behaved in exactly the way they suspected he might. They'd love it. Titillating for them, you see. They could gossip about it.

'The guy we had last year stole a typewriter, raped the secretary, buggered the Dean . . .'

Understand, Kathy? They have a basic contempt for poetry and poets. Some of them probably aren't even aware they feel that way. But they do. They do. I'm their Fool. Book of the Month. Fool of the Year. I'm their Court Jester. I can hit the King on the head with a pig's bladder and everyone including the King thinks it's funny. I've got poetic licence, Kathy, the sort of licence you allow pets and toddlers. People like me aren't *responsible*, you see. And that, in turn, makes *them* fair game. Unsporting, really. They're sitting birds."

"You keep on saying 'they' and 'them'. Hasn't it occurred to you that *I'm* . ."

"Of course it's occurred to me. That's what we're arguing about, isn't it? Sides. Taking sides."

"*I* thought we were talking about stealing. All you're doing is knocking down straw men of your own distorted invention."

"Am I?"

"You know very well you are."

"You feel my curve is improbably skewed?"

"I think you're talking offensive rubbish."

"I can't afford your qualified judgements, Kathy. I can't afford nuances and nice distinctions."

There was silence.

Her posture had changed. She was tense and angry.

"Of course," I said casually, "what they'd enjoy even more than on the booze or in the bin is off the bridge. Like poor old Berryman."

She jumped up from the couch, the scar on her forehead almost livid.

"That's a vicious thing to say!"

"Is it?"

I looked up at her from the armchair, meeting her glare as calmly as I could.

"Is it really?"

I let the tense silence extend.

After a few more moments, I said,

"Well, be that as it may, I mustn't dally. I must sally forth to mingle with depraved representatives of the underworld. 'Fencing the swag', we call it. What's the number of White Cross cabs?"

I flipped through the telephone book.

Opening the door and hoisting the huge IBM Selectric, I said, "You know, Kathy, there *is* balm in Gilead."

"What?"

"I love you."

She slammed the door behind me.

The afternoon delighted me. I still felt like a convalescent on the first day out after a long illness. The scene with Kathy was just that — a scene in a complicated play with two more acts to go until its resolution. Futile to try predicting the serpentine plot, the fate of the hero and heroine. The sun was shining. Enough of gloom. Pray for a happy ending.

On the long drive to Craig Street, I pondered strategy. Stealing is unskilled labour. Selling needs the craftsman's touch. The central problem with what sat beside me was that it was, inescapably, an office machine. There were three ways to dispose of it without having to contact a member of the criminal class in some dreary tavern. (Far too risky a procedure anyway as most of the fraternity are well-known to the police and impenetrably stupid.) I could trade it in part-exchange for a new typewriter and then sell that. I could pawn it. Or I could sell it outright to a pawnshop.

The retail price of the damn thing was about $800.00 or so. Its exchange value, then, roughly $400.00. If I tried to work a part-exchange deal, I'd lose heavily *and* I'd have to lay out some of my own money. Not good. The whole thing wildly unlikely. If I pawned it, I'd get less than half its wholesale value. Say $200.00 and that optimistic. My best prospect was to sell it outright to a pawnshop. That would give me $300.00 tops — $275.00 more realistically. They'd resell at about $500.00.

I've had close and meaningful relationships with pawnbrokers in a variety of Canadian cities. I like pawnshops. I like their *flavour* — that faint spicy smell of larceny. Their chief attraction is that all dealings are in cash.

Pawnshops usually conduct their business within the law. They don't have much choice. They're licenced by the police to buy and sell, and too much hanky-panky and pop goes their licence. They're required by law to record in duplicate every purchase, amount paid, date of purchase, description of article, serial number if any, name and address of vendor, and, in addition, they must fill out a printed form describing the vendor's apparel and appearance and estimating age, height, and weight.

A detective sergeant picks up these lists of purchases and description forms twice a week and checks them against the police lists of articles reported stolen.

Contrary to popular imagination, pawnbrokers are extremely leery of buying hot or doubtful items not only for fear of losing their licence but also because if an item they've bought is identified as stolen, they lose both the item and what they paid for it. On the other hand, however, the police usually lean very hard on owners or insurance companies to reimburse the store as the police depend on the co-operation and goodwill of the pawnbrokers.

A pleasing kind of ecology.

But then again, pawnshops don't list *every* purchase. Felonies *are* compounded. Certain dubious acquisitions do tend to get salted away and sold to trusted customers. And baubles, such as gold and diamonds, are temptingly anonymous and protean.

Every pawnbroker I've known has a fund of self-congratulatory stories. They pride themselves on being infallible judges of character. They've got a deadly ear, a honed sixth sense for the story that doesn't sit quite right. And, paradoxically, this ability and their pride in it leaves them wide open for a refined and artistically executed con.

Which was exactly what I had in mind.

As the taxi rolled me along, I considered the garbage bag beside me. Unfortunately, an IBM Selectric is monumentally *unprotean*. Nor would it be quietly sold to a trusted customer. The hulking things need cleaning and repair and the police furnish their officious lists of stolen serial numbers to factories, dealers, and appliance stores. But then, I'd chosen the machine for its difficulty.

Using John Caverly's documentation crudely, the sale would have been mere journeyman work but I intended the transaction as a Memorial. I wanted to perform the near impossible, attempting the pitch without producing any identification at all.

A veritable Everest of cons.

My role, the person I was to be, was beginning to form itself in images much in the way a poem forms. The typewriter so large, so heavy, had broken a table, an occasional table, rosewood, with particularly *gracious* legs. A table that had been my mother's. No. The voice. Get the voice right. A table that had been Mother's. And the machine? He wrote something — poems, why not? — everyone else did — yes, for *children*. And his aunt in Toronto, getting on in years, Mother's elder sister, and somewhat, might one say, *imperious*, had, on the occasion of his recent birthday, ordered a typewriter to be sent.

More about this aunt. Or was it Aunt? Rarely left the house. Ordered her world by phone. Lived with a Companion. And where would he publish his horrible poems? In *Junior Magazine*, organ of the Canadian Red Cross Society, and, inevitably, *The Canadian Author & Bookman*. And in his Parish Magazine of course. Good.

And, diffidently, he was preparing a collection of tales for young readers. Interest had been expressed by Vista Press, the editor there *most* encouraging, determined to submit the book for the Vicky Metcalf Award for writing inspirational to youth.

But where did the bugger *work*? And why was he on the loose on a Thursday afternoon? Social work of some kind. Private institution. Need more on that. Anglican, though.

Yes, he was coming into closer focus now. Well-educated in the social sense, private school, a touch of unconscious or repressed faggery, a background of Family. The carton containing the typewriter had been addressed to *Master* John Caverly. That a rueful admission to illustrate nature of Aunt etc. I began to see the details of his apartment, explored the furnishings. A glass-fronted bookcase, Mazo de la Roche, a childhood copy of *The Wind in the Willows* and all the Swallow and Amazons stories. Arthur Ransome, that was the man.

But these were the quick strokes of a cartoon. I'd have to do better.

Obstinately running beneath all this were the lines by Christopher Smart:
For I will consider my Cat Jeoffrey.
For he is the servant of the Living God, duly and daily serving him.
Obviously important somehow.
Why?

I was deflected into thinking about Christopher Smart incarcerated in the bin for two years and lovely John Clare, compulsory writer-in-residence for twenty-three years at North-hampton General Lunatic Asylum, where, in the unforgettable words of the *Encyclopaedia Britannica* he remained until his death "amusing himself by writing poetry".

Another piece slotted into place. *This* John Caverly wouldn't be seen dead in the street with a garbage bag. For him it would be extremely clumsy brown paper and string. Christ! and my tie! *Wrong.* The suit, very dark blue wool, was perfect. But my tie was a beautiful steel-blue silk. My portrait moved a fraction further into focus.

I leaned forward and said to the driver,

"Can you stop at the first seedy men's clothing store we come to? Something I've got to pick up."

He nodded.

"Sure," he said. "Seedy?"

"Yeah, crummy, you know?"

"Crummy," he repeated. "Sorta rundown?"

"Yes, *yes.*"

I was thinking of John Clare's last letter. I sometimes wish I didn't retain so vividly things read. The letter ran:

Dear Sir, — I am in a Madhouse and quite forget your Name or who you are. You must excuse me for I have nothing to communicate or tell of and why I am shut up I don't know I have nothing to say so I conclude.

Yours respectfully
John Clare

"This the sorta place?" said the driver.

"Yes," I said. "Yes, this might well be it."

The new John Caverly was perfect. The typewriter was positively organic in brown paper. The tie — a stroke of genius even if I say it myself — was *tartan.* A clan with a lot of hideous yellow in it and the knot mean.

The driver put his paperback down on the front seat.

"Y'interested in the supernatural?"

"No," I said.

Cradling the impossible bundle, I stood on the pavement staring into the window of Bernstein's.

For I will consider my Cat Jeoffrey...

What the hell was *that* all about?

I gave a mental shrug and decided to let the adrenalin take over. I pushed open the door and stood there just inside. The emporium was in full swing, shouts, laughter, huddled deals, phones ringing, a drunk trying to sell a chain-saw, assistants replacing trays of watches and rings under the glass counter, producing others, stacks and piles of furniture and oddments antique or merely battered, guitars and musical instruments hanging overhead. I stood looking undecided and rather embar-

145

rassed. I knew that in spite of the apparent chaos I would have been observed. After a few moments, an underling approached.

"Can I help you?"

As to the manner born, I put the typewriter into his surprised arms.

"Well," I said, "I do hope so. I wish to see the proprietor."

Mr. Bernstein, portly in crumpled Shantung, was very pleasant. He received me in his inner office, an untidy cubicle into which were crammed a desk and an immense iron safe. A decrepit bookcase was jammed with tattered reference books on the arts fine and applied. The walls were crowded with thirty or more nearly identical oils of standing horses with stableyard backgrounds. He probably had a horse-man under contract. All the oils had a fine *craquelure* suggestive of a date much earlier than, say, the previous six months. On top of a pile of dusty red ledgers stood a crude polychrome carving of St. Anthony of Padua.

Mr. Bernstein helped me struggle with the layers of brown paper. The machine sat on the desk between us disregarded. He was most understanding about Aunt Dierdre. He seemed quite distressed about the rosewood table and gave me the address of a reliable restorer. We chatted for a while about the identity of the lighter coloured wood of the table's inlay. Mother had always thought it birch. Mr. Bernstein, while no expert, thought birch unlikely. If the table was what he thought it might be, its having been in Mother's family, he thought satinwood likely and sycamore probable.

Mr. Bernstein had certainly heard of *The Canadian Author & Bookman*. He himself, it turned out, had been a close friend of Stephen Leacock. I ventured that plucking up the courage to come to see him after the man in the typewriter shop had been so rude reminded me, well, rather, if he understood what I meant, of the embarrassment of Stephen Leacock in the story "My Financial Career". We agreed the world was a small place. Stephen Leacock and, now, me.

A gift was a gift and Aunt Deirdre *was* Aunt Dierdre. Mr. Bernstein agreed it was an awkward situation. Mr. Bernstein agreed that, given the circumstances, the greater kindness lay in a little white lie.

And quite apart from the fact that I already *had* a perfectly reliable typewriter which had served me faithfully for years and to which I had an almost superstitious attachment — all my poems so far having been composed upon it and *Tales of Canadian Courage* launched, so to speak . . .

Mr. Bernstein could quite understand that. He'd heard of a fellow there who couldn't write unless he had rotten apples in his desk. People were people. In his job that was one of the first things you learned. With some it was typewriters. With others it was rotten apples.

But quite apart from *that*, Jeoffrey had taken most violently against this new machine.

"He's hardly eaten since the thing arrived."

"He hasn't?" said Mr. Bernstein.

"It's the hum, I think. I can't imagine what else it *could* be."

"Some people it might bother," said Mr. Bernstein. "But it's not such a loud hum."

"I tempted him," I said, "in every way."

Mr. Bernstein regarded me over his spectacles across the Selectric.

I shrugged one shoulder.

"He just sulks," I said, "under the sofa."

"Under the *sofa*," repeated Mr. Bernstein, visibly relieved.

Mr. Bernstein, it turned out, had a poodle which was immensely gifted. Such was its understanding of the English language that if Mr. Bernstein wished to talk about the dog to his wife, he was forced to speak in French. Mr. Bernstein did not approve of any variety of canned pet food. One did not know what it contained.

"Now this machine, here . . ."

I listened in goyish wonderment as Mr. Bernstein explained the principles of retail and wholesale pricing, the perilous state of the economy in general, the slump in the typewriter market in particular. He pointed out that, God forbid, such a typewriter could break another person's table. I projected a politely concealed suspicion that I was being cheated and, as actual sums of money were mentioned, exhibited the same sort of embarrassment that a sexual approach would have occasioned.

We settled for $285.00.

Mr. Bernstein told me another anecdote about his poodle.

Mr. Bernstein paid out notes onto the desk at which I did not look. I signed John Caverly on the printed receipt and wrote in the address of the man who didn't play darts as well as he thought he did. I thought I'd done it. There was no doubt I'd been brilliant — that faint suggestion of the feminine in the shrug of only one shoulder. I'd had to fight to hold the other shoulder down. The whole performance was in the Olivier class.

But then, apologetically, explaining that nothing personal was involved, purely a technicality, a police requirement, he asked me if I had any identification.

Slowly, slowly, I took out my wallet. I selected the driver's licence and asked if that was the sort of thing . . . ?

And then, victory snatched from the very jaws, etc. *the old goniff didn't even look at it.* Just smiled, waved it away. He glanced at his watch, scribbled on the form.

Age. Ht. Wgt. Comp. Time.

I stared at the framed Certificate in Gemology behind his head.

It had been done. By Christ, I'd done it!

Hillary and Tensing.

Plant the appropriate bunting.

But I felt too dazed. As he accompanied me out through the store, he asked me to keep him in mind if there were any of Mother's other pieces should I redecorate. He would see what he could do for me.

I found myself out on Craig Street, suddenly exhausted, shivering cold as the sweat began to dry.

From the doorway, he called.

"Canned food, feh! Go where Bernstein goes. Frager's on Fairmount!"

I nodded, smiling.

"Tell him Bernstein sent you!"

I waved.

In an uptown bar, somewhere to sit down, a place called *The Pied Piper*, not the sort of place I usually frequent, I ordered for some odd reason, Kathy's drink, Pernod. The walls were decorated with enlarged reproductions of Daumier's *Humours of Married Life*, the setting reducing their comic savagery to chic. It was the sort of bar that sold pink and green drinks concocted with cream. The girl behind the bar looked as if she'd been expelled from a Swiss finishing school on a morals charge. There was one other customer.

I hadn't the energy to work up more than fleeting irritation about the use of Honoré Daumier. It was the same argument I'd tired of advancing against the culture merchants, the celebrants of the 'culture explosion' allegedly taking place in drug stores and groceries. I held it as obvious that a box of Tampax, *Ulysses*, and a tube of Preparation-H on the same shelf became the same thing. Bach became cough lozenges. Mozart, Listerine. Shakespeare, The Complete Works indistinguishable from the Big Bargain 84-Slice Family Pack of Kraft Slices. The obviousness of it all bored me. Such boosterism was the realm of pop sociologists, Alvin Toffler country — and he was welcome to it.

I didn't want to get pissed, didn't particularly want a drink at all. I should have felt triumphant, exuberant, my cup running over. *Everest*. But I felt nothing of the sort. Nothing but tiredness and an infinite sadness welling up. I sat staring at the colours cast on the grey carpet by the stained glass figure of the Pied Piper in the window. I sipped at the Pernod, my mind drifting with pictures, remembrances. I savoured sadness.

Marjorie: whereabouts unknown. Friendships withered or betrayed. But it was not these. No work of words etc. The lean belly of the year. My New Guinea natives obstinately stuck within the yellow covers of the *National Geographic*. But it was not this.

I played with my swizzle stick.

Arrow or spear?

I'd never been deceived by 'an extraordinary talent in full flower' (*The Canadian Literary Review*) or by 'of major stature' (*Oromocto Times and Recorder*). Rideau Hall with its Governor-General and big bad oil paintings of defunct dignitaries and its military aides like trainee head waiters had not exactly overwhelmed me. I *was* guilty of sometimes basking in the flattery of those who couldn't tell bad from worse but usually when drunk. I could not, in truth, accuse myself of being false to what I knew the best to be.

The essence of the sadness was elusive. Wasted time, work not done, work not done well enough, yes, these I could readily admit. But the feeling was deeper, darker. I felt that my life was somehow changing, was running out of control, that I was edging closer to a dark something that terrified yet attracted me.

Kathy. Kathy was the opposite pole. Kathy was a kind of salvation but there was in me that which prevented my rising, speaking in tongues, stumbling down to the front to sign on with the saved.

In Sunday School the hymn had run:
Stand up, stand up for Jesus
The fight will not be long.
But I and others of the ungodly sang as loudly as we dared:

149

Sit down, sit down, for Christ's sake!
The buggers at the back can't see.
I prodded the ice-cubes about with the plastic arrow.

I remembered signing The Pledge when I was eight or nine. They gave you a badge.

As a dolmen might loom out of a fog sudden and massive confronting the traveller lost on the wild expanses of a moor, the sadness assumed a shape, a shape which expressed itself in the realization: I was getting old.

It no longer lay ahead.

I sat back in the chair staring at the garish figure of the Pied Piper, the magic fluting leading onwards into the fissure in the dark mountain.

Although I knew the poem by heart, I took the creased and furry paper from my wallet and opened it on the table-top. Not his best work. But his last. And mine. One the critics would never mumble with their spaniel gums.

What to Dream About

So many of his poems were entitled, simply, 'Dream'; it was as if they were not separate works but parts of a single narrative, messages sent back to base, recordings in the log of his long journey into the dark.

> *How long does it take you to decide*
> *what to dream about? Do you think*
> *carefully beforehand of women*
> *you never enjoyed and who*
> *would never agree to enjoy you?*
>
> *Do you desire to dream of the deaths*
> *of those you love so your sorrow*
> *will be splendid among your friends?*
>
> *Do you carefully build in your mind*
> *your own car crash the police will announce*
> *in tones that know your loss so well?*
>
> *Do you rehearse your best tragedies,*
> *distilling them into your dreams*
> *night after night before you sleep,*
> *your hair growing grey in your bed*

your pleasant tears huge in your head?

Or do you dream of a real loss,
the bent caverns of the dark sea,
the glass trees rough, shining at night,
no other animal in sight?

Chapter Ten

It was later, much later in the evening. The heat and uproar in the Club Hellenic were building. Only Kathy was cool, her hostility expressing itself in politeness and the consumption of Perrier water. I raised my glass of metaxa to her and inclined my head. After a few glasses, metaxa stops tasting as if it's been manufactured illicitly.

The music was loud, pulsing through my head in remembered patterns, the glittering notes of the bouzouki wrapping me in a shimmer of sound. I imagined the fumes of the metaxa writhing through all the intricate plumbing of my grey matter as through the piping of an elaborate alembic. It was that sort of stuff and I'd had quite a few.

A large, unsteady Greek bumped into our table.

"You are not Greek," he stated.

"No."

"You like Greek?"

I raised my glass.

"*He*," he said, pointing to the bouzouki player, "is Jesus Christ!"

"He's good," I agreed. "Very good."

"Athens. From Athens."

I nodded.

He gestured to encompass the room.

"*All* Greek are Jesus Christ!"

He ploughed off into the throng.

Kathy sipped at her Perrier water. I still felt angry with her and as I looked at her there swam into my mind the word: *cumquat*.

On my return from the Pied Piper and scarcely before I was through the door, there had been another passage of arms, snickersnack, snickersnack. She'd been lucky I felt sad and somewhat contrite. I had waited till she'd wound down and then unwrapped the necklace from its nest of tissue paper. I had bought it on the way home as a peace offering. Mummy-beads with a pendant plaque of Osiris, Lord of the Lower World, delicate faience three thousand years old in greens, turquoise, browns, earth colours.

I had held it out to her on my palms and said,

"Never pass up a chance to spoil the Egyptians."

She made no move to take the package.

"I have no intention," she said, "of accepting stolen property."

She had walked away into the kitchen.

"What do you mean stolen?" I'd called. "I've just bought it."

I had followed her into the kitchen.

"Remember that gag of Dr. Johnson's? The one he yelled at a bargee or a waterman or whatever? 'Your wife, under the pretence of keeping a bawdy-house, is a receiver of stolen goods'?"

"*Leave me alone!*"

We had stared at each other.

The staring had seemed to go on for a long time.

And then I had tossed the beads on the kitchen floor at her feet where the thread snapped and the beads had scattered and smashed, dust and clay.

The silence had been interminable.

Later there had been tears which resolved nothing.

Later still, an edgy cease-fire.

A glittering, mirrored ball revolved above the small dance floor in front of the band. The singer, a dyed blonde clad in a sequinned gown, her face heavy with make-up which did not entirely hide the pock-marks, twitched the lead of the hand-mike in a variety of tired international gestures while the beautiful voice, husky, almost harsh, sang on and on in the sad-sounding cadences of the middle east.

A burst of homicidal yelling sounded from the hatch which opened into the kitchen.

153

I began to drift with the drink and music.

"Was it a vacation?" said Kathy.

"What?"

"When you were there?"

"No, not really. I lived there for a while after university. When I was young."

To a changed rhythm, the singer started a new song singing past the spotlights towards the back of the room ignoring the sloshed couple in front of her who were attempting the *tsifteteli*, a kind of Greek belly dance. A raucous crowd at their table sent a waiter onto the stage with two brandies on his tray. The couple drained them and then smashed the glasses on the dance floor at their feet.

"Why do they do that?" said Kathy.

"Bravura," I said. "Sort of a Greek version of chucking them into the fireplace."

"What," shouted Kathy, as the band started again, "do you think they're singing *about*?"

"All Greek songs," I bellowed back, "are about love or the undesirability of Turks."

I signalled to the waiter and sent drinks to the band. I also procured some beer for myself to wash down the metaxa. Metaxa was thirsty work. The drummer, a middle-aged man in shirt sleeves, produced the usual semi-military rattle with mechanical competence. The bass was a Fender played by a hairy youth who was probably moonlighting from a rock group. The organist was wearing a tartan shirt. Fairly obviously local men, a pick-up group. But the bouzouki player was brilliant, the notes flowing in sheets of sound, rippling from his instrument as he bent poised over it, nodding almost imperceptibly as a signal to the drummer that he was approaching the end of each cycle of improvisation. He was pale and studious-looking, remote. His blue suit and tie gave him the appearance of an accountant in a conservative banking establishment. He did not touch the glass the waiter placed by his chair.

I closed my eyes. The notes he played were the stream of incandescent sparks of arc-welding, the fresh fall of embers, the sudden bloom and slow drift of fireworks down the night sky.

"What?" I said.

Two men were making their way onto the dance floor. One produced a white handkerchief.

154

"It's a dance from Macedonia," I said, "*tsamikos* but they dance it all over Greece. It's one of the classical dances. The kids learn them all in school."

As the music ended and the two men left the floor, a waiter bustled on and started kicking aside the larger pieces of broken glass. Then another waiter stepped up bearing a tray and took from it a handful of dollar bills which he threw up into the air. The bouzouki player looked up. As the bills floated down onto the dance floor, Kathy said,

"What's going on now?"

"Someone's going to dance the *zembekiko*," I said. "It's not one of the classics. Uses some of the steps but it's improvisational, very emotional."

"But why did the waiter throw money in the air?"

"Oh, it's sort of like smashing the glasses. The guy who's going to dance gave it to the waiter to do that. It's money for the band but specially for the bouzouki player because he and the dancer sort of play to each other, you see, urge each other on."

"But don't they pick the money up?"

"No, *no*. Because it's *private*, you see. The man's going to dance because he wants to dance for himself. Because he *feels* that way. It's above money. It's a gesture of—oh, I don't know—*lordliness*, if you like. A waiter'll sweep it up when the club closes. But that's the *point*. They dance *on* the money. Don't you see?"

"It's like Spain," said Kathy. "Like the bull fights."

"Yes," I said. "That's exactly what it is."

"You're getting drunk," she said.

"You might be right."

As the young man danced, the club grew quieter. The bouzouki player dictated his stops, his pauses. The feeling of the dance intensified until it was as if they alone existed, an intricate balance of music and movement, exciting yet grave as if the dancer were somehow aloft on a dangerous highwire which existed only as a bright thread endlessly spun by the glittering notes of the bouzouki. The dance danced on, stately, flowing, sometimes entirely motionless as the young man waited for the very note among many to release movement. And then he swooped into a squat stoop, spun there slowly, then slowly, slowly straightened as if being pulled from the earth by an immense force. He ended motionless, his arms outstretched to the bouzouki which, tempo slowing, rounded to the conclusion of its improvisation.

155

Memories of Greece from twenty years earlier filled my mind. Not the gnarled olive trees of the travel posters, not the presence of the past in the purity of light, not the terrifying roads and brigand bus-drivers of Crete, not the good-natured hilarity as they taught me the steps of the *balos*, the *pentozali*, but that bloody cardboard suitcase bound with hairy rope. For weeks through heat and dust Greece had been for me the burden of that ugly case, Sisyphus suitcase, anchor fore and aft to all I'd sailed from until one glorious morning on an empty beach I'd launched it on the wine dark sea.

The band had stopped playing and were leaving the stand. A most peculiar thing happened. It was as if I were looking at the pattern in a kaleidoscope and the pieces shifted suddenly and then somehow rearranged themselves as they had been before. The bouzouki across the chair, the Fender propped against the bass drum, suddenly struck me as exactly like a cubist still-life and then did not. The bouzouki player carried the glass in his hand. As he edged past our table, he smiled, raising the glass, smiling his thanks.

I stood up and we shook hands. He joined us.

A record was playing and a woman, a glass of beer in one hand, a cigarette in the other, was attempting the *zembekiko* doubtless hoping for the desired insoucience but looking merely tarty.

I looked at the stage again, at the instruments, but they'd stopped being cubist.

"Fifteen year ago," said the bouzouki player, glancing at the dance floor, "no woman would do this thing. Modern. Modern."

"You play beautifully," said Kathy, who'd been obviously moved earlier by the grace of the young man's dancing.

He shrugged.

"I have in Athen book, many book, and study for a thousand year. This is Athen music. Modern. Modern. In *village* is real. Not organ. It must be—" he made the gesture of playing a flute. "Bouzouki have eight string. In village three. In village is more . . ."

"Classical," I said.

"Classical," he said, nodding.

He shrugged again. Sadly, he said,

"All now is amplify . . ."

After he had gone, Kathy and I sat in our separate silences. I wished I could somehow make things right with her but as far as I could see she really wanted me to apologize not for what I'd done but for what I was. We seemed to be on the same side but it was as if she were a general sitting on a hilltop drinking bumpers of champagne while I was in one of the shrinking squares getting the shit shot out of me by the artillery and constantly harassed by the cavalry trotting about looking for a gap. And nothing much ever happened to defeated generals. Did *that* make any sense? Not really. Because if she were a general, she'd presumably have a picture of the battle. And I wondered sometimes if she even knew there was a war going on. That didn't make it much clearer either. I drank metaxa and beer and silently floundered in the mire of military metaphor.

"Heigh-ho for the old global fucking village, eh?"

"What?" she said.

"Poor bastards!" I said.

"Pardon?"

"They don't realize what they've lost. Not yet."

"What are you talking about?"

"They earn more money than they've ever earned before and they have *this* still but gradually it'll all go. And their sons will be ashamed of speaking Greek. And their grandsons won't even know any. Then they'll be *real* Canadians."

"You're just being sentimental, Jim. They were probably living in terrible poverty before they came here."

"Well," I said, "they probably weren't rich and they probably had to work very hard for what they got. But they knew who they were. They lived inside their history. And they ate good food and lived in houses that were lovely even if they didn't realize it. And they turned all that in for a shoddy apartment and a car with chrome bumpers. Fucking sad, isn't it?"

"They don't *seem* particularly unhappy," said Kathy.

"Well, that's even worse, then, isn't it?"

Kathy rolled her eyes.

"Oh, Jim!" she said. "You're being ridiculous."

"How long do you think all this is going to last? This music, say? *Our* indigenous music is a lot of mumbly old French Canadians playing the spoons. That's the *cultural* stuff, of course. Our *preferred* music, the real music of the 'folk' is country and western—every last mindless inhabitant of the true north strong and free yearning to be taken home via country roads to West sodding Virginia."

"Oh, *God!*" said Kathy.

"The whole damn world wandering about stunned with

transistor radios clamped to their nasty heads like growths. And that's nothing compared with joys to come. Just you wait, my old dutch, just wait till Cosimo and his sons of fun slouch to Bethlehem."

"Please Jim, *don't*. Don't take it out on me. I can't stand much more. Don't drink any more. It hurts me to see you like this."

"Pure persiflage, dearheart. Honest. Comedy unalloyed. Cross my heart and hope to die."

"Oh, stop lying, Jim. You're tearing at yourself and you're trying to hurt me too. You're *hating* me."

"I *love* you. I'm just talking about Greeks coming to Canada, that's all. I'll join you in a Perrier water, O.K.?"

I lighted a cigarette. I *was* a little drunk. And I felt rather peculiar, exhilarated but somehow frightened. There was a strange rushing sort of noise in my ears like the surge of surf which seemed to ebb and then rush louder with each heartbeat. And I couldn't stop talking. I could not stop. Faster and faster. Words jumping about in my head like sparks.

"Cosimo and the Vidials. When arrested as a 'found-in', the accused gave his occupation as 'vidialist'. We bring you the mirth and giggles of the Goth Brothers! Alaric the Visigoth and Cosimo the Vidigoth! For their opening number they're going to burn down Rome. One picture's worth a thousand words. True. Profoundly true. But profoundly true only if you can't read. And there's more of them out there, Captain, than there is of us. Which is why, my dear Katherine, we're like dinosaurs standing in a pond having a placid chomp on our nice green weed and wondering dimly why it seems colder. Inaccurate. Way off the mark. Dinosaurs died by Act of God. We're being manipulated to *our* end. For profit.

Literature, sir? Homer, we *don't* carry. There's not the demand. We're a bit low on burning Sappho. But we could offer a discount on *Anne of Green Gables*—a *very* popular line. And there's a special this week on Grey Owl. In the mock-leather, sir? It's whatsit—that tedious bugger who turned out to be a German bigamist. And the Hallmark Cards are at the back."

I sipped the Perrier water.

"And so I welcome this opportunity to welcome *you* to Canada, a country which has been aptly described as a spiritual K-Mart, a description which I can assure you is no mere empty rhetoric. Welcome one and welcome all. My purpose here tonight is to entertain any questions you may have . . ."

"*Sit down!*" said Kathy. "For God's sake, sit down!"

"Do I see a hand at the back? Yes. Food? An interesting topic and one about which I must, perforce, be blunt. The one hope for good food in other than the caloric sense was lost to us by a cruel freak of history. All over France, peasants were dousing things in wine, marinating this and that, cultivating the savoury herb, and generally stuffing truffles up everything that moved. But Quebec— Quebec was unfortunately settled by the one group of peasants in the whole of France whose sole idea of a good nosh was tortière. And the rest of the country was penetrated by people who ate haggis. Our *present* national food? I think that one would have to say that it is a hot chicken sandwich covered with ginger-coloured gravy."

A waiter was pulling my arm.

"My dear sir," I said to him. "Conscription! We are famed, sir, not as militarists but as keepers of the peace. It is a fact, a fact that cannot be disputed, that Canada delayed the unfortunate genocide in Biafra by sending a Hercules aircraft *filled*, completely filled with nutriment."

I took the waiter's hand in both of mine.

"Architecture? In the sense of . . . Yes. I *think* I understand. In *that* sense, Canada doesn't *have* architecture. It has housing-units."

"Please, mister," said the waiter. "Not allowed to drink standing up. Is the law."

"What?"

"You must sit."

"Sure. Sorry."

Remembering Greece, I thought of the beauty of stone. The white buildings shining. One of the islands. Where? Which? I had an intense memory of a taverna, thick stone walls and low ceiling whitewashed, cool, seeming almost dark after the white glare of the street. And I remembered wine in an earthenware pitcher and red mullet fresh from the caiques in the harbour.

"You know, Kathy," I said, "I really don't like the word 'organic'. It's so artsy-fartsy but it really is the only way to describe them."

She was staring at me with a most peculiar expression on her face.

"Are you all right?" she said.

"What do you mean?"

"What are organic?" she said.

159

"What I've just been telling you," I said, "the buildings. The taverna, for example, on that hillside with the fort on top. Layer built on layer. Moorish, Turkish, Venetian, God knows what. All those cultures and all—somehow—*right*, all *one*."

"Oh, yes," she said. "Yes."

I smiled at her.

"All one under the sun."

In the washroom it was much cooler. The urinal was manufactured by T. F. Burton and Sons of Boston. I washed my hands and face. Cooler. Much cooler. The bouzouki player was just going out. I smiled at him. Stavros, I had heard one of the other men call him. It did not seem decorous for me to call him Stavros. I could not say in Greek any of the things I wanted to say to him and he did not understand enough English.

After he went out, I locked myself in the small lavatory cubicle. I stood there resting my head on my arm against the wall. It was cooler there, quiet. After a few minutes, I heard the band playing, the music faint and a woman's voice singing.

My heart was pounding and the rushing noise in my ears and head louder.

I whispered to the wall:

"Stavros, *kali tychi*."

I checked in my wallet. Of the typewriter money, John's money, there was about $175 left after the necklace and drinks and taxis.

I unlocked the cubicle and pushed out through the thick outer door into the heat and noise. There were more and more people. I beckoned to the nearest waiter. I pointed to the band and piled the money on his tray, tens and twenties, all the money I had.

"*Zembekiko*," I said.

"Sir," he said, "this is too much."

"I know," I said. "It's all right. This is a personal thing."

"Five dollars," he said, "ten is much."

"It is for Stavros," I said. "And other things."

"You are drinking?" he said.

"I am not drunk," I said. "Go."

He looked at the money and shook his head.

"Go," I said. "For Christ's sake, we're beginning to sound like Hemingway."

I followed him as he made his way through the crowd. He tossed the bills and they fluttered and drifted. I nodded to Stavros who stared at me.

He started to play. I stood listening, waiting. And then the movement started. I seemed to flow with the main line of the music ignoring the runs of embellishment. At the end of each phase I kept my eyes fixed on the dirty woodblock floor, my mind empty, waiting, not really noticing the shapes of banknotes, the glint of glass. And then after the empty waiting would come again the notes in a bright spray, golden needles of sound.

Poised. Waiting.

A waiter came onto the floor, a tray, a golden glass.

As I drained it I found I was staring straight into the blinding spot.

Glass broke.

Then my left arm and shoulder were moving in a slow curve, my eyes following the path of my hand as I moved again into the embrace of the music. Space roared and fell away. I was lying on the floor.

I heard laughter.

The music stopped.

My hand was near my face and I saw blood pulsing. I watched the blood pump bright under the spotlight and thought: *old.* I felt arms under my chest, felt myself lifted.

And then I was somewhere else and it was cold. I moved my feet and I had no shoes on. There was a sheet. And I moved my feet and my feet rubbed against bars. And then a very bright light shone in one eye and I tried to move away and my head was held down and the bright light shone again.

And later, I heard curtain rings clatter along a metal bar and heard the chink of metal against metal near my head. Liquid stinging. Breath on my face. A voice said:

Hold his head.

And then it hurt like light.

And then shoes came in *squishy—squishy* and a voice, a woman, a West Indian voice said:

This the ECG, Dr. Roberts.

My hand was big and throbbed.

And then Kathy was there. Kathy's voice.

Clinically, said the other voice, *and from what you were saying earlier, I'd say it was delirium tremens. How old did you say he was?*

Forty.

I felt hands digging into my sides.

161

Well, the liver's not enlarged yet.
It was cold. I wanted the sheet.
I formed the words with great care and effort.
"Fucking plumber."
My voice sounded inside my head.
Charming man, your husband. Ever get violent with you? It's a not unusual pattern. And, frankly, Mrs. Neilson, it isn't worth it.
Cold. Very cold. Blanket.
He's not my husband.
Clattery curtain noise again and the doctor's voice calling:
Nurse Braithwaite! Any trouble later with the drunk in here, call an orderly immediately.
The scrape of a chair.
The darkness was rolling back.
The smell of cigarette smoke.

Chapter Eleven

Fun in the Sun! Bermuda! Wonder Vacation for Two! said the
cereal box. There was a strip of blue sea, a strip of yellowish beach,
and a young man and a young woman in bathing suits laughing
their heads off. The colour registration was far from perfect. When
I'd read the English version of the Contest Rules, I read them
through in French.

Kathy continued to say nothing.

Cornflakes crunched.

I felt only mildly Gestapo-ish. My wallet, keys, odds and ends,
and a mess of blood-stained banknotes had been piled on the
bedside table. My hand was bandaged and taped neatly to the size
of a baseball and hurt like hell. The stitches above my left eye were
puffy and black with clotted blood but didn't hurt as much as my
hand. It was, amazingly, only Friday morning, only hours since I
had removed the typewriter, sold it to Mr. Bernstein, and attended
the revels at the Club Hellenic.

I cleared my throat.

"Look, Kathy," I said. "This is silly."

"What is?"

"This silence is."

She widdled her knife around to prevent the honey dripping.

"Can I say I'm sorry?" I said.

"Would it do much good?" she said.

"Well I *am* sorry. I'm sorry I stole the typewriter and I'm sorry I got pissed."

"Well," she said, "I suppose that's *one* way of putting it."

"Putting what?"

"'Getting pissed'," she said.

"What?"

"It was embarrassing," she said, "embarrassing and pathetic to watch you stumbling about on a dance floor and making a fool of yourself and it was embarrassing to have to publically claim your body."

She depressed the lever thing on the toaster.

"It was embarrassing to have to deal with the police when the ambulance came. It was exhausting to sit about in Emergency while you lay snoring and drooling. It was not particularly pleasant to watch them pick pieces of glass out of your hand and face."

I stared at my face distorted in the toaster's chrome side.

The toaster made its preliminary *twinge* noise followed by its *crung* noise.

Kathy plucked out the toast.

"It was humiliating," she said, "to deal with your clothes which were covered with vomit. It was also humiliating to have to beg a taxi driver to drive us here. He didn't much care for the smell either. And nor was it particularly pleasant to be the subject of your aggression."

She widdled more honey on the knife.

"I suppose," she said, "you *could* call that 'getting pissed'."

"Oh, Christ!" I said. "What can I say?"

"Well, that's the point, isn't it? There isn't very much *to* say."

"I *am* trying to apologize," I said.

"Yes."

There was a silence.

"Coffee?"

"Yes, please. Thank you."

"You said," she said slowly, "that when a pawnbroker buys something they have to hold it for thirty days before they can sell it? That that was the law?"

"Yes."

"So St. Xavier will report it and they'll get it back because of the serial number?"

"Yes."

"And the pawnbroker'll be paid what *he* paid by the insurance company?"

"Yes."

"So everything's exactly the same as it was before? The office'll get the typewriter back and the pawnbroker'll get the money back?"

I nodded.

"So it was all entirely pointless, wasn't it?"

I shrugged.

"Except that you, as far as I can gather, consider it some sort of Quixotic gesture."

I stirred sugar into my coffee.

"One windmill down," she said.

She groped about in her purse which was hanging on the back of her chair until she found her nail file.

"Or am I missing something subtle?"

She half turned from the table and started to file away.

"The *Quixote* in Penguin Classics," she said after a while, "is almost unreadable. Flat. No fizz at all. The Shelton translation of 1612 is probably perfection. Like the King James."

"Bugger the Shelton translation," I said. "And bugger King James."

"It's really difficult to understand," she said, "how your poetry can be so sensitive and *you* can be so insensitive."

"What's that mean?"

"You just *don't* understand, do you?"

"Understand *what*?"

"You don't. You really *don't*," she said.

"Look Kathy! I'm feeling a touch fragile this morning. Would you mind not being cryptic?"

She scraped back her chair, stalked out, went into the bathroom slamming the door.

I took several controlling breaths. I was prepared to eat vast wedges of humble pie, whole crow if necessary, but this equation of 'sensitivity' and the ability to communicate telepathically was going a bit far. This mode of communication must be one of the reasons why women seem to get on so well with homosexuals—all their ganglia entwined atwitter.

I glanced at the *Herald* from the day before. The front page photograph was of a female toddler staring at a window. The caption read:

Young Marlene Meets Jack Frost

165

So much for the Fourth Estate.

I went and stood in front of the bathroom door and said, "Kathy?"

"What is it now?"

"I'm very sorry I stole the typewriter and got drunk and hurt your feelings."

"Oh, go away, Jim."

"I still want to apologize."

"*Stupid!*"

"Pardon?"

"I don't care about the damned *typewriter*. I care about what it *means*. If you say you love me, how can you behave in ways that — that put that at risk? If you were in jail? And the doctor said you were drinking yourself to death. Would you do that if you loved me? *Would* you. If there was some kind of future?"

There was a long silence.

I stared at the white paintwork.

The silence quivered.

It was as if a drum were rolling silently, a stylus recording endless fluctuations on a graph. Mortal data. I felt the start of tears. I seemed to have spent too much of my life talking to closed doors. The stitches above my eye hurt as my face crumpled.

"Kathy? Please come out and talk."

"Just leave me alone. *You* go out. Just leave me alone. Leave me in peace."

I stood there a little longer staring at the door.

"I have to go into the university," I said. "Anything you want me to do for you?"

There was no reply.

"I won't be back late."

There was no reply.

My footsteps sounded on the stairs.

The sun was shining but the wind cut at my stiff face. I felt weary and battered in spirit. I would try to talk to Kathy later. Try somehow to make amends. The peaks and troughs scribbled by that recording stylus could not be ignored, erased. Family faces looking up as the surgeon coming through the doors pulls down the mask. Perhaps there'd be no humble pie to eat. *Oh, Christ!* Just cake. I had some memory of a voice saying: *This the ECG.* Another after dinner topic to be approached delicately. Later. And alcohol. In general. That, too, needed its temperature taken. *Oh, Christ!* A melancholy prospect. Brain cells dying never to be replaced. But at the same time, yes, defenceless, all this admitted, whatever I was or wasn't, it wasn't *all* me. Or put it another way, unnegotiably, Don Quixote not only a nobler character than Sancho Panza but, in the ways that matter, *saner.* And then I realized I was mumbling aloud to the bare twigs of a hedge. Very Beckett-like. Well why not? *Oh I know I too shall cease and be as when I was not yet . . .* Who was that? No name. A voice. *Often now my murmur falters and dies and I weep for happiness as I go along and for love of this old earth that has carried me so long and whose uncomplainingness will soon be mine.* A voice from where? *From an Abandoned Work.* Another subject ripe for consideration. *Oh, Jesus Christ!*

But Beckett — boils, piles, and plaints — cheered me up. When I had walked for some ten minutes or so and found that everything seemed to be in working order and that there were no hidden areas of new physical pain liable to strike, I flagged a cab.

The driver was so fat he looked as if he'd been moulded into place behind the wheel. His face and figure suggested a gross Rowlandson cartoon. Honest John Ballocks. Tucked into the neck of his sweater was a bath towel. With one hand he was eating slices of a large, all-dressed pizza from a box on the front seat.

He nodded as I gave him the destination. He worked on what was in his mouth and then wiped his face with a towel.

"Think of a number," he said.

"Pardon?"

"It's my hobby. Any number."

"Yes?"

"No. You've got to tell me."

"Thirty-one."

"Now think of another."

"Eighty-three."

"Two thousand, five hundred and seventy-three," he said. "I do it all the time. Look at the mileage, double it, treble it, anything you like. Street numbers — multiply them by your social insurance number. Anything. I've got a mind like a computer."

"Very interesting," I said.

He adjusted the mirror so that he could watch me.

He engulfed another substantial slab of pizza. Strings of melted cheese connected it from his mouth to the box.

He said indistinctly,

"Give me another. Challenge me! Go on!"

167

"Six thousand, seven hundred and eighty-seven," I said to be polite, "multiplied by five thousand, three hundred and ninety-four."

I looked out of the window and saw yet another sign which said: *Advanced Green When Flashing.* A sign high on my list of irritants. Comparable for incomprehensibility with the language of tax-collectors.

The driver suddenly said,

"36,609,078."

"Correct!" I said. "And now, old cock, if you don't mind, I had a roughish night last night. Got involved in a collision. That apart, when I was at school I was what Educationalists now call 'Math-Avoidant' so I'd be gratified if you'd just stow it, eh?"

I brooded upon the *Advanced Green* sign until we arrived at the Hiscock Building. If he *were* correct, I was probably in the presence of an *idiot savant.* Not a stimulating experience. I paid him with a blood-stained five dollar bill.

"Keep the change," I said, "and multiply it by any large number of your choice."

The campus was pleasantly empty. The Christmas exams were only days away. Courses had faltered to cancellation in the face of mass desertion. The students were burnishing their précis of Cole's Notes and skiing. After Christmas they would return with broken arms and legs and spend the second term collecting ballpoint inscriptions on their casts.

The Office was agog. The disappearance of the typewriter was still exercising the highly trained minds of the English Department. Theories were advanced, actions advocated. Hetherington reluctantly suspected theft and was seriously considering informing the police.

I sat in my office.

I felt, in truth, as unrepentant about the typewriter *qua typewriter* as Mr. Toad about Motor Cars.

In the mail there had arrived from Victoria Press the statements of limitation to be signed for a collector's run of two hundred copies of some of my (relatively) recent poems. In exchange for two hundred signatures I was to receive $800.00. The only surefire way of shifting books in Canada. As investment.

No fountain pen.

I linked twenty-three paper clips.

I inspected my oaken hat-stand.

Across the playing field I could see the edge of CAC and beyond that the Jesuit Residence. Fred Lindseer claimed that the Residence was full of imprisoned priests who were variously loony, senile, steadfast in heresy, or under detention for their flagrant interest in choir boys and youthful sacristans. He claimed as common knowledge that each week the inmates were shown a programme of *Tom and Jerry* cartoons, that each week the Father President heard their confessions in a portable canvas confessional on wheels. It looked, he said, like an Edwardian bathing-machine.

Staring out of the window at the Residence, I drifted into Fred's simpler and more attractive world.

They would, of course, be looked after by a housekeeper. A horrible woman with a religious moustache and burst sneakers. An Irish hag called Bernadette or Bridget who ruled them with sadistic piety. They ate in common in a large, gloomy room decorated with oleographs of faded saints and martyrdoms. Supper was always Irish Stew, a mess kept going from month to month in a blackened cauldron. Discipline was maintained by larger or smaller portions.

Her ladle poised over the pot, Bridget regarded them. Twelve pairs of pastoral eyes gazed at the ladle.

Her catechism commenced with a rhetorical question.

Who emptied the laundry?

Silence.

Who had stiff pyjamas?

Who did diddy-diddy-no-no?

"I didn't. *I didn't.* It wasn't with intent."

You rubbed against the bed.

A small portion, ladled, passed.

One, madder than the rest, said suddenly,

"Her hands are dirty!"

Shut yer gob, yer nasty creature!

The peace-maker spoke.

"Let us think, rather, of some such formulation as 'Hands that are dirty . . ' thus avoiding arguments *ad hominem*, or, as it is in this case, *ad mulieram . . .*"

The ladle banged against the pot.

Latin is it, when you've done what you've done!

A knocking on the door interrupted the development of this promising scene.

"Come in!"

The door opened an inch or so and an invisible voice said,

"Hello?"

"Come in!" I called. "Come in!"

"Is it Mr. Wells?" said the voice.

"Yes it is."

The door opened wider to reveal a small Indian wearing black and white check trousers, white shoes, and a white cable-knit cardigan. He was holding a baggy umbrella.

"Good morning, sir," he said. "I am coming to see you with permission."

"Permission?"

"All is in order. I have a chitty from the Dean."

"Do sit down," I said.

"I am Mr. Bhardwaj," he said. "Would you like a Hall's Eucalyptus Lozenge?"

"No. No, thank you."

He plucked at his plump throat and made loud clearing noises.

"This blithering weather," he said.

Mr. Bhardwaj was somehow succulent, plump as a chicken basted in butter. His black hair gleamed with oil. The handkerchief tucked in the sleeve of his cardigan was strongly scented, a sandalwoody smell. His age was difficult to estimate. Forty. Perhaps a few years more.

"Well, Mr. Bhardwaj," I said. "And how can I help you?"

"I am not a run-of-the-mill student," he said.

"Oh?"

"Indeed no," he said.

We stared at each other.

"I hold my O Levels," he said, "from the University of Cambridge."

I raised my eyebrows, nodding at the same time.

"It is not easy for me," he said, "as during the day I labour for the Federal Government and so am forced to burn the midnight oil."

His expressive face arranged itself to convey gravity.

"I see," I said. "And you're writing poetry? In the evenings?"

His eyes searched my face.

"As a child," he said, "I greatly enjoyed the works of Enid Blyton."

"Ahh," I said.

"Many of my most adventurous hours as a child were spent with Enid Blyton."

170

I nodded.

"Yet," he said, his face and tone suddenly indicating the tragic, "I am now informed she is not a good author."

I shrugged.

"Literary taste," I said, "it's largely a matter of fashion. A whirligig. A lottery."

He planted the ferrule of his umbrella between his white toe caps and began to spin it by the handle. He did this with great concentration.

"Well, Mr. Bhardwaj," I said. "If you could explain exactly what it is . . ."

"In spite of high position," he said, "those blighters forced Daddy to flee."

"Which blighters?"

"Daddy, too," he said mournfully, "was fond of Enid Blyton."

He seemed to be settling into elegiac mood.

Indians, in my experience, are people of strange emotions. During my stint at the University of Western Ontario, one left greaseproof paper packages of curried cauliflower in my mailbox and smiled knowingly whenever we met.

"And so you've brought some poetry to show me?"

"Poetry?"

He sounded bewildered.

"Poems?" I said.

"*My* interest," he said, "is in aeroplanes."

"Aeroplanes?"

"And the frozen North," he added.

"I don't quite . . . ah . . ."

"As in *Desperate Search* 1952," he said. "Directed by Joseph H. Lewis starring Howard Keel, Jane Greer, Paricia Medina, and Keenan Wynn."

"Oh."

"Or *Miraculous Journey* 1948 directed by Peter Stewart starring Rory Calhoun, Audrey Long, Virginia Grey, and George Cleveland."

"You want to make a *movie*," I said.

"Survival against the elements," he said, "as in *The Red Tent* 1971 directed by Mikhail K. Kalatozov starring Sean Connery and the lovely Claudia Cardinale."

"But I know nothing about movies."

"You didn't see *Wings of Chance* 1961 directed by Edward

Dew starring Frances Rafferty, Jim Brown, Rickard Tretter, and Patrick Whyte?"

"No," I said.

"Not *Blaze of Noon* 1947 directed by John Farrow starring William Holden..."

"No."

"...Anne Baxter and William Bendix?"

"No."

"It was very good," he said.

"I'm sure it was but the point is I don't know anything *about* movies. Nothing. Zero. Not a thing."

"Not a sausage?" said Mr. Bhardwaj.

I shook my head.

He sucked the handle of his umbrella for a moment.

"Working as I am working for Transport Canada," he said, "I know so much inside information. It would be invaluable to you."

"To *me*?"

He turned out his palms.

"I am very busy," he said.

I stared at him.

"I am studying and studying for a position in External Affairs — oh!" he said, sweeping out his hand in a dismissive gesture, "—all because they are on their high horse about my qualifications."

"Are you trying to suggest...?"

"*You* are the Writer-in-Residence," he said. "*I* am supplying all the information and *you* are setting it all down on paper."

I shook my head slowly.

Mr. Bhardwaj's expression conveyed immense sadness.

"Not?" he said.

We sat in shared and silent suffering.

"But look!" I said. "How's this for an idea? Why don't you go over to the Communication Arts Complex? *They* make movies. Ask to see Cosimo O'Gorman. In fact, tell him I sent you."

At the door, trying the name over, he said,

"Cosimo-*Oh*-Gorman."

"He's your man."

"Well," said Mr. Bhardwaj, "I wish you a Merry Christmas."

"And to you."

I closed the door behind him.

I sat at my desk.

172

Three-quarters of an hour before the opening of the bar.

Loud in the silence, the urinals opposite flushed themselves.

To the hat-stand I said,

"What the fuck am I *doing* here?"

The most immediate answer to the question was that I'd been bought. Or more unpleasantly put, I'd sold myself. It was difficult to imagine Ezra Pound tolerant on the subject of Enid Blyton, unlikely the sympathetic conjunction of T. S. Eliot and Mrs. Strudly. Would Philip Larkin have sat still for Questions and Answers with the Faculty Wives? Would Samuel Beckett have adjudicated at Fir Tree Elementary School's Public Speaking Contest?

Months now since the yeast and turmoil of words.

To the blotter in its leatherette frame I whispered,

"What have I *done?*"

But I was not granted time to brood further. There was a bump and clatter at the door which swung open to reveal Mr. Zemermann. I had forgotten it was an Itzic day. He crouched over my life like a cat at a mousehole. He propelled himself forward, stopped, reversed into the filing cabinet. Its grey paintwork was already scarred by the handles of his chair.

We exchanged greetings while he performed all the now familiar rituals of settling down for a lengthy chat. He always refused help. He took off endlessly his woollen gloves, overcoat, padded vest, muffler, and woollen hat with ear-flaps. These violent exertions left him red and breathless. He hauled himself higher in the chair. He lifted up his left leg and dumped the foot, then the right. He then pushed both legs slightly to one side so that they lay together.

His calloused palms and fingers were grimy with an ingrained dirt from the rubber wheels. He licked the ball of his thumb and then applied it to the lenses of his spectacles. He gave them a final buff on his lapel and then affixed them.

"So?" he said.

"Umm?"

"A printed picture they sent," he said. "What kind of letter is that?"

"Pardon?"

"With the poems they sent back they sent a man looking through eye-glasses on a stick."

"Who did?"

"The *New Yorker.*"

"Oh, I see."

"It's my name maybe they don't like?"

I stared at him.

There came into my mind the characters the Chinese had used to describe Lord Napier, the foreign devil who would not obey Celestial Edicts and who would not go away. Translated, the characters read, "Laboriously Vile."

Much of Lord Napier's ignorance had been forgiven him in that he came from a dank isle that lacked rhubarb but eventually the Emperor had been driven to write:

Tremble hereat — intensely, intensely tremble!

"The man," I said, "the man in the top hat, the man looking through the eye-glasses on the stick, is what we all get. It's their standard rejection slip."

"For the same price," he said, "they could send a letter."

I thought of cold bread-pudding, a heavy toad, committing suicide by drinking mercury, and how much I liked and admired the Emperor and how much he would have liked and admired me.

"Ah, well," I said.

He produced from the briefcase a manilla folder and from the folder selected a typed sheet. He read it through, nodding, and then passed it to me.

"Something new?"

"Read!" he said. "Read!"

I put the sheet on the leatherette blotter. From the corner of my eye I saw him patting his pockets. I hoped he wasn't going to take snuff again. It was the mottled handkerchief I couldn't stand.

On Winning a Poetry Prize

Unto certain shepherds it is given
The task of making people merry...
For me the blood of many has striven
To make strong my voice, like the cherry
In the cocktail given me by the prize committee
Whose talents are great because they feel pity
For the survivors who still sing
In spite of poverty, heart conditions, and everything
That makes our lives so sad:

174

Because of this I do not feel so bad.
I take this prize today, with speeches sad and funny,
And promise well to use the money.
It will help me publish a new book
At which posterity will look
When I am dead and gone
And have sung my song.

I kept my eyes fixed on the paper.
The morning fell in on itself.
Itzic cleared his throat.
"No!" I said.
"No? No what."
"No, nothing," I said. "Just—in general. *No!*"
"You don't like it?" he said.
The silence extended.
"You read the *Herald* maybe?" he said.
"What? What do you mean *Herald*?"
"Mazel tov your name in the paper."
He passed me a clipping from the manilla folder.

Treblinka Bard Strikes Oil

Middle-aged paraplegic student-poet Isaac Zemermann was awarded first prize ($250.00) in the Poetry Canada Contest sponsored by North-East Oil and Gas. Mr. Zemermann's award-winner 'I do not damn those captors dread and bony' was the unanimous choice of the adjudicating panel of experts in Continuing Education.

'I write as witness for the six million,' said Zemermann. 'My career is being guided by the famous poet and Writer-in-Residence Jane Wells.' The award was presented by Rory McThynne, President North-East Oil and Gas. Mr. Thynne was formerly Vice-President (Sales) of Gas Canada.

"Itzic . . ."
I looked at him.
Light reflected from the gummy lenses of his spectacles.
I felt like an immensely superior boxer being worn down by a heavier, stolid opponent who soaked up all the class and skill and doggedly came on waiting for a chance to smother me in graceless

weight.

"Itzic, have you ever read anything by Joseph Conrad? No? Heard of him? Well, Conrad was an English novelist — probably a great one. But English was not his first language. He was a Pole."

He gave one of his infuriating shrugs.

"Conrad wasn't his real name, of course," I said. "I find I've forgotten what his real name was. But the point, you see, is that very few people, I think, are capable of writing in a foreign language as well as they do in their own. And Conrad, relatively speaking, got quite an early start."

I heard my halting voice. It sounded as if I were expounding a deranged syllogism.

All Conrads are Poles.

All Poles are not Conrads.

What the hell was the punch line?

"It's a question, I think, of *diction*. And of course underlying that . . . What I'm trying to say, I think, is that diction is the tip of the iceberg, if you see what I mean. Diction implies and reflects a culture and a history and . . . and many other things. Do you see what I'm getting at?"

He shook his head.

I touched his poem with my fingertips.

"Well 'shepherds'," I said. "And 'song', for example. The pastoral tradition in English derives from, and I think that's an important word, the *key* in a way to what we're talking about, derives from the Greek and Roman tradition of the pastoral. As, of course, I am sure it does in Polish if in Polish there *is* a tradition of the pastoral as I am sure there is almost bound to be."

I took a deep breath.

"Wouldn't you," I said, "be more *comfortable* in Yiddish?"

He held up his hand as if arresting traffic.

"Polish? Yiddish? What are these? These are dead things, Mr. Wells. They died with Itzic in August of 1942. And with Itzic died three million Polish Jews. Language, studies, literature, everything that was disappeared."

"But Yiddish is still . . ."

"In 1945, Mr. Wells, we began a new life. We feasted on army rations. It was so much, so rich, we threw up. We were given knives and forks for our own. We had blankets, clothes were given us. In our huts that winter there were fires. Coffee some of us were given. *Coffee!*"

I nodded.

"In one of the camps, Mr. Wells, the warehouse where the belongings of the dead were stored, gold and jewels, food, clothes, hair, all their bundles, this warehouse was called by the prisoners 'Kanada'. A place of plenty. There the lucky ones worked. But Itzic was more lucky."

I nodded again.

"And so I say to you, Mr. Wells, Yiddish? What is Yiddish? Polish? So little of history you know Mr. Wells. *Polish?* I *spit* on Poles. English is my language. Canada is my country."

"Yes," I said. "But . . ."

He leaned forward and then squirming, worked his buttocks backwards in the chair and then pushed his torso erect. His face was red and strained. It was as if he were sitting at attention.

He took a noisy breath and began to sing.

O Canada!
Our home and native land!
True patriot love
In all thy sons command.
With glowing hearts
We see thee rise,
The true North, strong and free,
And stand on guard,
O Canada,
We stand on guard for thee.

There was a silence.

He continued staring at me.

"Itzic," I said after a few moments, "I do understand the way you feel. Who wouldn't? And whether you understand it or not, I'm trying to help you. *I* care about what happened too. I care very much. And because I care, I care about the way people write about it."

He shrugged.

"Can't you see," I said, "that these horrors *demand* the best writing possible? Not 'songs'. Not 'shepherds'. Anything less than your best betrays the truth of what happened. You can't approach mass murder carried out by the state with the language of Palgrave's *Golden Treasury*. And that's why I mention Yiddish. Perhaps in Yiddish you could write poems that . . ."

"I write," he said, "in English. My language is English."

"But isn't it true that you *do* still write in Yiddish?"

"I write in English."

"In *Der Canader Adler?*"

"I write in English."

"I'm sure," I said, "that Mrs. Herzog told me that you write in Yiddish in *Der Canader Adler*."

"I write," he said, "in English."

His face was white.

"Now look here, Itzic!" I said. "Let's not play.."

He slapped his hand over his heart.

His teeth were bared as his top lip stretched.

"Itzic! What is it!"

His glasses slipped down to the tip of his nose. His eyes were staring.

I pushed his fumbling hand out of the way and took the small tin box from the inner pocket of his jacket.

"Water?"

A slight shake of his head.

I put one of the small white pills between his lips.

"Shall I phone an ambulance?"

He spread his fingers in a negative.

I stood bent over him. His eyes were closed. The long seconds ticked away.

"Itzic?"

"I . . ."

I bent closer. The word had been more harsh exhalation than speech.

"What? What is it?"

"I write," he forced out, "in English."

"Yes," I said, "yes."

Chapter Twelve

I swung the rented Pinto between the two white-painted wagon wheels which decorated the entrance to Hollis' yard and stopped beside the tilted, rusty mailbox set on a post cemented into an old milk churn. I gave Hollis' collie a gentle boot in the ribs to quiet him down. Kathy and I zipped up our jackets after the warmth of the car. The lights were on down in the barn where Hollis and Eva would be finishing up evening chores.

As we stepped down into the milk house, the warmth and noise enveloped us. The half-wild brindled cats were crouched on the wet floor lapping spilt milk. The motor in the bulk tank was churning. Hollis' portable radio was blaring country and western from his favourite station in Watertown, New York.

We went down the second steps into the barn.

Hollis down at the far end of the first row of bails was stripping a cow by hand and nodded. Eva, beyond him, was holding a plastic pail of milk to two butting bull calves in a small pen.

"Well, Jim?" said Hollis. "How are you weathering it?"

"This is Kathy," I said.

He jerked his head at the cow and said,

"Trod on her tit."

He took off his blue and red cap that said Pride Corn above the peak, wiped his hand on his overalls and shook hands with both of

179

us. Since the summer, he'd become even more bent and shambling with arthritis, his hands red and twisted.

"Get me that penicillin on the ledge there," he said.

He twisted the cow's tail up over her back to immobilize her and stabbed the long needle through the hide of her flank.

Along the limed walls were tacked up a new selection of nudes and calendar-girls. Above the clatter of pails, the bellows and lowings, and the twanging, lachrymose radio, he yelled,

"You'd never think old Eva looked like that with her barn clothes off, now would you!"

Eva had gone up into the loft and was dropping bales of hay down into the two aisles. Hollis cut the twine, stuffed it in the twine sack, and started to spread the hay in front of the bails with a fork.

"Here, let me," I said, taking the last of the churns out for him to the bulk tank. While I was out there, I turned off the radio.

"So you're up to your place?" he said.

"For a few days."

"Cold," he said. "It's drifted in bad up there by the fork."

I nodded.

"I got the sleigh out for you," he said. "Don't get near them heifers, Kathy."

"Is it spreading to the rest?" I said.

"What?" said Kathy.

"Ringworm," said Hollis. "The bugger. Eva's got some coffee on up to the house."

"Hollis? You're sure it's O.K. about Paddy and Prince?"

"Do 'em good," he said. "You're doing me a favour, lad. They're soft yet—haven't had 'em out. I've got to get some wood cut with 'em yet—oh, likely next week when the swamp's froze real hard. Where them dead ellums are?"

I nodded.

"Are you cutting sugar-wood?"

"I'd like to Jim, but doing chores and then the boiling—well, I don't want to get sick like I done last year."

We were standing in front of the pair of black Percherons. Kathy was stroking Paddy's muzzle.

"Aren't they *huge!*" she said.

"The other one's Prince," I said. "And that's Paddy that's slobbering on you."

"Useless buggers!" said Hollis.

He'd raised them from foals and loved them more than

180

anything on the farm, according to Eva more even than her. Their brasses, ribbons, all the many rosettes won at the local fairs decorated the front-room. Their photo in a silver frame stood beside his wedding photo on the china cabinet.

"The Lansdown Draw," he said, "after you'd left. They went like hurley! *Walked* it! Six thousand, three hundred pound in the Light Division."

He went round behind them into the stall and barged them apart.

"Get over, damn you."

In an almost absent-minded way, he opened Paddy's mouth and looked at his teeth. He shook his head.

"There's not many more years in 'em, Jim."

He stroked Prince's muzzle.

"Been thinking any more of a pair of colts?" I said.

He eased his forefinger backwards and forwards under the side strap of Prince's halter. He shook his head.

"I don't know if I've got the heart for it, lad."

Prince leaned his vast bulk against him.

"Get over!" yelled Hollis. "Dog-meat, that's where you're to!"

He evened up the hay in their trough.

We strolled back up towards the house, matching our pace to Hollis' shambling gait. The moon was bright, the stars sharp points of light. The snow crunched crisp.

"Eva's been baking bread and one of your rhubarb pies. Since you phoned, it's been Jim this, Jim that. I've been sick of the sound of you."

The house was warm and cheerful with the fragrance of coffee, woodsmoke, and cooking. Christmas fairy lights were strung about the room, Christmas cards stood on the freezer and were pinned to the curtains. On top of the TV stood a small aluminum Christmas tree. In deference to visitors the sound had been turned to a low murmur but the pictures flickered. Hollis went into the kitchen to change from his barn clothes and wash at the sink. Eva was quickly taking Kathy's measure in conversation about something or other in the Simpsons-Sears Catalogue.

Hollis and I had been friends for years. Five years earlier, I'd bought from him for five thousand dollars six useless acres on which stood an abandoned stone house. I'd been unusually flush that year with a Canada Council grant and windfall money from the sale of some papers to Queen's University. The old house was about four miles from Hollis' farm and about a mile and a half into the woods from Mike and Susie's summer cottage on Stover Lake.

The six acres in which the house stood supported a few large maples, an almost impenetrable forest of spindly saplings which hid a fox's earth, juniper clumps, and prickly ash which grew thicker and more vicious every year.

I spent the summers there, writing, lazing, playing about at the lake with Mike and Susie and the kids, reading. Usually I helped Hollis out with haying and with fencing.

Behind the house was a sway-backed barn in which Hollis stored machinery and straw and all the amazing junk he was always buying when drunk at auctions. He had a sixteen foot high stained glass window propped in there which he'd bid for from a demolished Baptist Church. It was a ghastly depiction of John the Baptist dunking Jesus Christ in very bright blue water while a group of observers who looked exactly like the members of a town council in fancy dress gazed at the spectacle and at some sheep. Hollis always said you never knew when something'd come in handy.

Eva bustled about setting the table.

I watched the near-silent gun battle on TV.

Eva's centre-piece was a white plastic serviette holder whose handle was a garish Christ. On both sides of the holder were the words:

Our Saviour Bless Us Every One.

Eva was a member of a Texas-based church called The Pentecostal and Charismatic Good News Mission.

Hollis was not.

Eva's strange pieties, however, which were little more than a formal expression of her good nature, were oddly mixed with an almost obsessional interest in sexual matters. She knew the sire of every pup for miles around. She always contrived to witness the brief flutterings of the roosters and bantam cocks. Nothing could have kept her from the spectacular matings of horses.

Or funerals.

Her reports on the sex-life of the stock were less comment than pronouncement as the words came out with audible capital letters.

'*Her* tail's not up Just for the Breeze!'

Or of a heifer bred that day:

'There's one felt The Staff of Life!'

Eva bore in the rhubarb pie and we sat and ate hugely.

Hollis overflowed with the local news and gossip. Old Lyman

had lost a finger on his chainsaw. Opening Day, *someone* had sunk the game warden's boat on Stover Lake. Jim Pierce over to Mentzville had caught his wife paying off the grocery bills.

Hollis!

Wayne was having to work out. Up to Smith Falls at the Hershey Factory, couldn't afford to go bulk, poor bugger, the fourth the Milk Board had closed down within two mile. Alton, there, the RCMP arrested him outside the Addington Hotel — drunk in charge of a back-hoe and him being epileptic too with no licence. Gordie Sweet had got another what he called a lodger and one of his girls in pod again and wasn't only fifteen.

Hollis!

"'Course," he said, "who's to tell who? More pricks in her than a porcupine."

"*Hollis!* Whatever will Kathy think!"

"I should think she'd like some more pie."

I left Kathy and Eva listening to one of Hollis' involved epics about a drunken hunt at night which started with the felling of a dead tree thought to harbour coons and the tree flattening Talmudge Orris' snowmobile . . . I walked back down to the barn to harness up Paddy and Prince. The temperature had dropped even lower since we'd arrived. A long way off in the crystal night, dogs were barking.

I backed the pair out and fixed the tongue of the sleigh to the neck-yoke, the whippletrees to the evener. Paddy was restive, stamping his great feet. I loaded the sleigh up with bales of hay and then started them up the hill to the house. I loaded in the groceries and supplies from the trunk of the Pinto and then went to fetch Kathy.

Framed in the fur round the hood of her parka, her face was lovely.

Eva and Hollis stood in the doorway waving, warmth and light spilling out onto the snow as we pulled out between the ornamental wagon-wheels, past the varnished cedar board with their name burned into it in fancy script, out into the deeper snow. My house was some four miles distant through snow too deep for anything but a snowmobile or sleigh. The township plough cleared as far as Hollis' farm but the dirt road petered out then into a wide trail through the bush. We sat on the bales of hay watching the staunch sway of the horses' massive rumps. The only sounds were the runners packing the snow, the creaking of the sleigh's old timbers, the rattle of the rusted bells on the horses' head-stalls.

The pathway narrowed and we had to duck to avoid the lash of branches and twigs. Silence and night closed us in. Intensely black against the whiteness of the snow, here and there, cedars. We were held silent but close in the rhythm of the team's slow plod.

Kathy was the first woman I'd ever taken to the house. The kitchen was the one room I'd made habitable. I'd hammered out the old, rotting plaster and lath to expose the stone. I'd fixed in an old iron stove. I'd repaired the window-frames and replaced two or three sections of rotted floor-boards. In the graciously proportioned living room were stacked four cords of hard maple and some cartons of kindling.

I urged the team up the incline and the path opened out again and then opened further into the clearing and the shape of the house stood before us. The wind had carved the snow into a high curving dune a few feet out from the front door. I guided them round and then pulled them in close. They stood heads hanging. I unbolted the door, lighted the kerosene lamp, unloaded the supplies, and showed Kathy where the wood was.

I left the sleigh outside the barn and led Paddy and Prince inside towards the stalls. I hung the kerosene lamp from a beam. I took off the hames and collars and sweat pads and tucked them between the beam overhead and the boards of the hay loft. I unbuckled the belly-bands and pole straps, and pulled off the backpads and tugs and britchings, hanging all the harness up on nails. I slipped their head-stalls and blinders forwards over their ears and off.

I started to wipe down the lathered sweat with handfuls of straw. Just at the edge of the lamp's circle of light, a cat was watching me. The light glinted on Hollis' discs, beyond them revealed the high red side of his harvester. The barn smelled of musty hay, diesel fuel, the pungency of kerosene. Prince tossed and stamped as I worked his halter on. I covered them both with blankets.

I looked at the neck-yoke and whippletrees before hanging them up. The wood was grey with age and weather, deeply split, the rings rust-eaten. The harness, too, was cracked, the stitching frayed where the tugs joined the split-tug. It had all belonged to Hollis' father. It might see out the lives of Paddy and Prince. But Hollis had no son to care, to mend, to start again.

I carried a couple of bales of straw into the kitchen to use as a mattress. Kathy was crouched in front of the stove. An acrid haze of woodsmoke filled the room. I noticed patches of ice glinting on the stonework round the windows.

I dug out one of the bottles of cognac from the supply box and took two glasses from the battered corner cupboard I'd picked up at a local auction. I blew into them to get the dust out.

"There's something inaesthetic," I said, "about drinking wine or brandy from tumblers or plastic cups. Changes the taste."

"I couldn't care less," she said.

"Don't worry, Kathy. It'll warm up soon."

I spread the straw, covered it with the tarp, and then spread the blankets over that. I put some heavier wood into the stove but it would take time for the stone flue to heat and drive out the damp so that the fire would draw more fiercely. It was still too cold to take off our outdoor clothes.

"Well," I said, clapping my hands, "would you like the grand tour? Including the rarely shown West Wing?"

"No," she said. "Sorry. I didn't mean to sound like that. Tomorrow."

She worked off her boots and got under the blankets fully dressed.

I sat in the rocking chair and downed another large shot of cognac.

"What was that?" she said.

The wind was freshening and tapping the branches of the lilac bushes against the window. The windows and doors were single and unsealed. The bitter draughts were fighting the heat which the stove was beginning to build. I fetched some old burlap sacks from the woodstack in the living room and tamped them along the bottom of the door. Then I loaded the stove with heavy split blocks and closed down the ventilator, doused the kerosene lamp.

I got under the blankets beside Kathy and put my arm around her. We lay listening to the gathering wind, the crackle from the stove's belly and the roar in the flue. The straw beneath the tarp rustled as we moved. There was something about lying with her fully clothed, its strangeness perhaps, perhaps that she was in my house, which was arousing me. I pulled her closer.

"No, Jim, don't. It's too cold. Feel my nose."

And a few minutes later, she said,

"No, Jim. I just feel *numb*."

And so we lay in the darkness, a thin wash of moonlight over

185

the stone of the far wall. Although the cold and handling the team had tired me, desire kept me wakeful. After what seemed a long time, I felt her body slacken and heard the change in her breathing.

Within the thick stone walls and across the floorboards overhead I could hear the sounds of mice gnawing and rolling butternuts about that the squirrels had left. Rats, too, were working away at the plaster and lath.

In the summers, sunlight lying across the boards, the old house was a place of peace. I wrote in this kitchen or in the large living room. I grew a few tomato plants and cucumbers. Sometimes I just sat for hours watching the sunlight on the stone, the colours, the shadows and textures. A mile and a half away at the lake were Mike and Susie if I felt the need of company. And when my body demanded exercise, there were the long fierce hours with Hollis working under the sun until I was too weary to think or feel.

I'd had dreams of windfall riches, the sale of *The Musical Ride* perhaps, bequests from unknown relatives, riches which would enable me to restore the house, insulate, repoint the mortar, concrete the dirt basement, replace some of the rotted cedar beams and in the place of their precarious supports install steel jacks. But the dreams remained dreams and year by year the house grew more dissolute, the domain of vermin and dry rot.

The quarter-section which had originally accompanied the house should never have been farmed. All that remained was two small pockets of land with soil deep enough for corn. Scrub had regained the rest. When the concessions and lots had been surveyed, designated, consigned, they marched across the map ignoring swamp and rock and thin top soil, condemning men to years of fruitless toil, the crops of stone heaved to the surface with each spring breaking their bodies and their hopes.

I'd often wondered about the man who'd built this house, how he'd eked out a living, where he'd raised the money to replace his cabin with so grand a house in stone. I guessed the house had been built in about 1840. Builders worked from Georgian design-books, I'd read, reproducing late into the Victorian years an architecture designed for a more gentle time and place. Some said many of the stone houses in the area were built by masons left unemployed after the completion of the Rideau Canal system.

This house and its neglect — the lack of precise knowledge — these were the essence of our historical poverty. No one really knew. Few cared. Old men said, old men remembered vaguely.

186

Thinking a jumble of such thoughts, drifting towards sleep, aware in the rising warmth of the smell of my sweat and horses, I moved into a vivid memory of an early fall evening with Hollis. We'd gone back into his sugar bush to throw corn into the swamp in the open bay where we'd shoot duck when the season opened. The light was just beginning to go and there was a cathedral gloom under the huge maples. The undergrowth was still rank, rotting branches and ferns. The twilight swamp lay in patches of silver and black. Out in the alders, duck were quacking. Wood-ducks and mallards were flighting in black against the pink sky. We could hear the thrumming of their wings.

And on the way back, deep in the bush, Hollis had shown me a well from which rose pure spring-water. There had never been a farm near, no buildings, no foundations. He did not know who had built it or why. *His* father had shown it to him. It was now masked by brambles. Some of the stonework and the surrounding ground were thick with emerald moss. It was built up three feet high, square, shaped and mortared stones. It was just there, its purpose and maker forgotten.

Tapping at the very edge of sleep, the sounds of the lilac branches in the wind against the window. Old men said that when people built their houses, they always planted lilac bushes by the door. Lilac bushes, they said, were supposed to bring good luck. All over this part of the countryside, clumps of lilacs grew in wild profusion along the lines of a foundation, beside heaps of tumbled masonry.

Lilacs here white and full purple.

So thick in spring almost blocking the kitchen doorway.

The scent so heavy, wasps bumbling against the window panes. Sunlight.

When I awoke, the light in the kitchen was dim. The windows were translucent with ice on the inside. The stove was dead. Kathy lay curled up, the blankets half-covering her face. The stone walls held the cold damp. I eased myself out as quietly as possible and as quietly as possible got the stove going again. I rubbed at the ice on the window with my finger-tip until I'd melted a small peep-hole. In the rising sun, the expanse of snow outside was dazzling as if scattered with brilliants.

I set the coffee pot on top of the stove. My movements awoke her and she looked at me bleary-eyed, her face drawn and pale.

"Sorry," I said. "I had to get the fire going. It's not one of the

Whole Earth Catalogue types, I'm afraid. It goes out."

She gave a kind of groan and pulled the blankets over her head.

The water, as usual, took an age to boil. I poured a mug of coffee for her and knelt beside her.

"Here," I said, "this'll warm you up."

I poured a slug of cognac into mine.

"Are you drinking already?" she said.

"Purely medicinal, my love. Want some?"

While she lay there sipping the coffee, I juggled a hearty breakfast of baked beans and toast, no easy task on that black-bellied little bastard. She sat at the table with a blanket draped around her as she ate. After another mug of coffee, she said,

"Where's the bathroom?"

I cleared my throat.

"There isn't actually a bathroom," I said. "The outhouse is just around the corner on your left."

As she sat down on the blankets to work her boots on, she said, "Where did you get the water, then?"

"Oh, there's a gas-pump in the barn. That well still works but the well outside the house ran dry. Needs a few yards of re-drilling, I expect. I brought a bucket of water in last night. You can't miss it," I said, "it's got a green roof."

She was shivering when she came back in.

"It's not *that* bad," I said. "Eva and Hollis haven't got a bathroom and they've lived here all their lives. Of course," I said, "at night they use what Eva calls a 'vessel'."

She didn't reply, just inspected her face in the mirror from her purse.

"Want to come down to the barn to check on the horses?"

She shrugged.

"What else," she said, "is there to do?"

The snow had been dusted by a powdery fall. I pointed out to her the straight lines of filigree tracks left by deer-mice near the house walls, the splayed confusion of jack-rabbit tracks which crossed and re-crossed the path to the barn. Blue jays were calling, hopping from branch to branch inside the cedar trees in the clearing's edge causing snow to fall in soft dollops.

I checked on Paddy and Prince and spread two bales of hay in their feed-trough.

Stumbling and floundering through the crust, we then tried to

188

make our way between drifts to the swamp's edge.

Sticking up above the snow were the sere stalks of milkweed plants. Each dried pod was split, four gaping sections of husk. The outside of the pods was the rough grey of a pigeon's wing, the inside pale ochre or a delicate satin yellow. They'd always delighted me. Each was like the austere work of a Japanese master.

I pointed out to her in the smaller field the dragging trail of a porcupine, lured out by some earlier, warmer day. We stumbled on. I wanted to show her the nearest of the big beaver lodges.

The stream was still moving, a rivulet of black water which in spring was a torrent twenty-five feet across and where in the summer wild mint grew rooted in rank beds.

I went there often in the summers at dusk to watch the beavers, their heads spreading black and silver arrows through the silver water.

The deep drifts turned us back.

The kitchen was pleasantly warm. I showed Kathy round the house, the large living room with its hewn beams and hand-carved doors, the panelled deep-set windows, the lovely wide staircase curving with the hand-turned bannisters and carved newel posts, the high-ceilinged bedrooms, but all she seemed to be able to see was the neglect and decay, the fallen plaster.

We clattered down the hollow stairs to the kitchen and she pulled one of the chairs as close to the stove as she could and sat huddled with a blanket around her.

I felt even more deeply disappointed than I was prepared to admit. I sat in the rocking chair and poured myself a large brandy. Kathy sat reading one of her thrillers called *The Destructor Hits Detroit*. I wondered if she were so grumpy just because of the cold or because of the outhouse or because of us. Had I done anything *else* recently? The last few days had seemed friendly and happy. Or perhaps it was the onset of her period? *Doleurs menstruels* — an expression I'd read with great pleasure on a box of bilingual pills in her apartment. It had a sound almost liturgical.

I found myself thinking in a confused sort of way about Kathy and the apartment and money and next year. Being in the familiar room brought a picture of myself sitting with the bread board on my knees writing with my ritual Eagle Mirado 174 Servisoft B pencils. By December, I'd usually have received invitations to reside in residence, to give readings, to do the various odds and sods which made up my livelihood. By December, they'd usually set themselves up for the following September. But the mail had delivered up nothing.

A lean year it looked like being. And difficult to understand too. My critical stock was, if anything, healthier than usual. I had been the subject of an extremely long, ponderous, risible article in *Canadian Literature*, replete with swollen footnotes, which had compared my last book with Samuel Beckett's *Whoroscope*.

Fuck it and fuck them. Something would turn up.

But Kathy. What about Kathy? A problem whose logistics I'd often shied from before. How could I fit in what had to be done with staying with her? And would she want me to stay anyway? How deeply rooted was she at St. Xavier? For me, the logical scavenging base was Toronto. And would it be right to try to influence her to move? If she could. I had a considerable respect for her work on George Herbert and had even started reading some of the sermons of his contemporary divines. They wrote pretty well for vicars.

I brought in another armload of wood and jammed three or four heavier logs into the stove.

As Kathy moved aside, across the corner of the cover of *The Destructor Hits Detroit* I saw emblazoned '18 Million in Print!'

"I wouldn't mind," I said, "having *his* royalties!"

She didn't look up.

As I passed behind her I read the sentence at the top of the page she was reading. It said: 'A strong odor was apparent'.

I repeated the sentence aloud.

"Just think," I said, "with so many million copies in print, he'll be cited by future compilers of dictionaries. And then 'apparent' will shift even more preposterously from its root."

I raised an arm, striking an oratorical gesture.

"Thus leading us still further into the linguistic swamp which . . ."

Looking up, Kathy said,

"You know what your trouble is, don't you? You're a puritan. And a conservative. Not a conservative, a *reactionary*."

"Excuse *me*," I said. "I was just attempting a little light conversation."

"What's *wrong* with you!" she said. "What's the matter with the way he writes. It's junk and everyone *knows* it's junk. It's rubbish to pass the time with. And that's all it pretends to be. Why do you have to treat everything like Holy Writ!"

190

The anger in her face surprised me.

"If you really *need* an answer to that question, Kathy, you amaze me."

"You see!" she said.

"No," I said. "See what?"

"You're so goddam earnest and self-righteous all the time. You just *pretend* not to be."

She glared at me.

"What's wrong," she said, "with people reading rubbish for pleasure? Sometimes I think you're *worse* than a puritan. It wouldn't surprise me if you really thought books more important than *people*. It's exactly the same thing with the way you're always going on about that Zemermann creature. What does it *matter*?"

"Wasn't it Faulkner," I said, "who said something about the 'Ode on a Grecian Urn' being worth any number of old ladies?"

"Faulkner," she said, "was a drunk."

"Sometimes," I began, "you . . ."

"Sometimes *what*?"

"I'm sorry if I sound pompous to you, Kathy, but language matters more than most things. And poetry just happens to matter one hell of a lot to me. And yes, I suppose I do go on a lot about Zemermann. And why? Because *Zemermann*, for all that I feel sorry for him, presents himself as a poet and the fucking gibberish gets printed and students — *and* others — *accept* it as poetry. *That's* why it matters, why I'm always 'going on about him' as you put it. Christ! Next thing you know, the bugger'll be getting a Canada Council grant."

"He's already applied," said Kathy.

I stared at her.

"Dr. Gamahuche showed me the form he'd filled in for him. He said the verse shone with a lambent spirit."

She stared back up at me and there was something almost vindictive in her face and manner. When I didn't reply, she picked up her book and started reading again.

I went back and sat in my rocking chair and drank some more cognac. I wondered why she seemed to be aching for a quarrel. I wondered, too, if she'd made up the Zemermann bit to irritate me for her own reasons, but she couldn't have invented 'lambent'. It was too essentially Gamahuchian.

I rocked. I drank. I brooded.

"You know," said Kathy after about half an hour, as though

191

continuing a conversation, "there's something about you. It's as though you're fascinated by self destruction and failure. As though you're drawn to it somehow."

"Failure?"

She gestured impatiently.

"The way you choose to live. This house. You *like* things that.."

"That what?"

"Oh, I don't know!" she said.

I put the glass down beside the chair.

"I never promised you a Hilton," I said. "I'm sorry it's cold. I'm sorry there isn't a bathroom."

"And look at the time!" she said, glancing at her watch. "It's just before ten a.m. and you've already had three big glasses of brandy."

"Cognac, actually," I said. "I only drink brandy when funds are low."

"Joke!" she said.

I smiled at her.

"You *have* got your knickers in a twist, haven't you?"

"You'll never face it, will you!"

"What are we quarrelling about, Kathy? You tell me and then when I know what it *is* I'll face it."

"Sometimes," she said, "I almost hate you."

"Is it the pre-menstruals, dear? Because you're not making much sense and you're not the same jolly companion as of yore."

She slapped *The Destructor* shut and put it in her lap.

"I am talking," she said, "about the way you drink. I had a long conversation about it with the doctor at the hospital when you collapsed. I want to know *why* you drink like that and what you're going to do about it."

"Now, is that the real question," I said, "or is it, as you critics say, the sub-text, the sub-question? Because if all this aggression's about something else, I'd rather get straight on with the else."

"I can do without the attempts at sarcasm, thank you. I'm asking the question I'm asking. Why do you drink so much?"

"I like drinking," I said. "I enjoy it."

"That's not good enough, Jim."

"It is for me."

"You mean that you're saying you refuse to discuss it."

"Not at all. I *do* enjoy it."

192

"But you can't stop, can you?"

"I've never wanted to try."

She sighed. She picked up *The Destructor* and opened it. I heard the glue crack.

"It relaxes me," I said. "I get tense when I'm writing and afterwards I need to relax."

She stared across at me.

"You haven't written a word in weeks," she said. "Months."

There was a long silence. I listened to the crackle in the stove, the shift of logs. The wind outside seemed to be dropping. Each page of *The Destructor* as it turned sounded, sounded like the hollow noise of a spadeful of earth falling onto the boards of a coffin.

"Kathy?"

She looked up.

"Have you heard the expression 'The Floating World'?"

She shook her head.

"It's what the Japanese call a particular kind of print, I think. Ones of the theatre and bath-house and the demi-monde. That sort of thing. But it's not the prints—it's that *name* 'The Floating World'—because that's what it's like for me when I drink. The world floats, becomes unreal. And you meet the strangest people and go to places that don't exist if you're sober. And incredibly funny things happen. You drift. You're part of the floating world and you just sort of float with it. And you can come back with pictures, images. Stuff you can't invent."

"And *that's* why you drink?"

"Don't you understand what I mean? Like the night at the Mocambo with the General. And that guy who collected parrots. Remember that? That's what I mean. There's another world, you see, that's parallel to ours but you have to cross over."

She nodded but didn't say anything.

"Remember that night," I said, "we were in that jazz club and that woman sat at our table and started cutting all her hair off with a pair of pinking shears?"

I shook my head.

"Remember," said Kathy, "all the mornings you couldn't remember where you'd been or what we'd done? Remember the night you collapsed and were taken to the hospital unconscious and covered with blood and vomit?"

"We've been through that. How often has *that* happened? I

was upset, that's all."

"So was I," said Kathy.

"I've apologized," I said. "Often."

She continued staring at me.

"Have you ever thought you were an alcoholic, Jim? That you're killing yourself?"

I shrugged.

"Have you?" she said. "I'm asking you a question."

I looked at her.

"No."

She nodded to herself.

"That," she said, "is exactly what the doctor said you'd say."

I got up, put on my boots, knelt to lace them. I put on my vest and the heavy jacket.

"The doctor," I said, as I kicked the sacks aside and opened the door, "had probably been studying the *Reader's Digest*."

I spent the rest of the morning in the barn looking over the sap-buckets and the cartons of spiles and puttering about among the boxes of odds and ends that Hollis had bought at auctions. His technique was to buy unsorted cartons of oddments at the end of sales when the auctioneer, tired and hurried, was knocking down the remnants at a dollar a box. For something to do, I cleaned and oiled some wrenches I found and brushed a set of files clean with a wire brush.

Lunch was not festive.

Kathy spurned my blandishments so I took out the sleigh myself and drove down towards the lake. There were some rock formations there I'd always liked. Although the wind was cold off the lake, the weather was changing, the temperature rising, the snow losing its crispness. I drove the team down onto what was the dirt access road in the summer and rested them there beside Mike's cottage.

The summer, the shouts of the kids, the *National Geographic Magazine* and that morning of inspiration seemed frozen far, far away.

Dinner was not particularly festive either.

Kathy remained largely silent, polite if spoken to, now reading *The Destructor Penetrates Pittsburgh*.

I loaded the stove and we went to bed early. We lay not touching. I lay awake for what seemed hours. At about eleven, I quietly replenished the stove and then stood by the window looking out over the moonlit snow. Clouds drifted across the moon, then cleared. Then heavier cloud blotting out the light. I could hear the icicles on the eaves beginning to melt, the steady drip on the slabs of stone that had been hauled close to the walls to border a narrow flower-garden perhaps, perhaps a garden for kitchen herbs.

If I wakened in the night, I always stood for a few minutes at the window. I'd seen one of the foxes only once but the sight had given me fierce pleasure.

The memory often occurred in dreams. Not quite the memory. The fox I'd seen had black front feet curiously like a cat's, I'd thought. It had been in summer and the fox had been trotting across the clearing in front of the house. It was one of the most intensely *aware* things I'd ever seen. But in the dream, the fox, the brush a deep black at the tip, was running, no, *loping*, its head turning to look to the sides, and in the dream the fox was loping across a boundless field of snow.

In the morning I awoke before the sun was fully up. Kathy was still asleep, her short hair flattened and getting greasy. The stove had gone out and it was chilly but not as viciously cold as it had been the morning before.

I lay there awhile listening to the sounds of the old house in the wind, the creaks, the irregular, inexplicable sounds.

I extricated myself from the blankets taking care not to waken her and went into the living room to fetch kindling and wood. I stood in the empty room in the grey light for a long time thinking how much I would like to strip the green paint from the panelled, recessed windows. How I would like to sand the brown paint from the eight-inch floorboards until they were bright again, then stain them very lightly to bring up the grain, then wax them by hand so that I could see the room, the sunlight filling it, see it beautiful again for one last time before the roof finally went and weather finished off the old place. A fine, meaningless task for the summer perhaps?

The smell of the coffee awoke Kathy.

Breakfast was mainly the munch of toast, the tinkling of the teaspoon stirring sugar against the ironware pottery mugs.

Politely, apologetically, Kathy asked if I'd mind very much if we went back to Montreal. She hadn't been sleeping well. It was so cold. There was so little to do because of the depth of the snow. She hated sleeping in her clothes. She was beginning to actually smell and she wanted to be warm and to lie in a long, hot bath . . . She *did* like the house, and the countryside was beautiful but really, even I would have to admit that the house wasn't exactly *practical*—not, at least, in the winter months.

I burned what garbage I could, and carried out the rest to the pit in the scrub behind the house. While Kathy packed up, I went down to the barn and harnessed up Paddy and Prince. Where it had been trodden, the snow had turned to watery ice. The temperature had risen so dramatically from the day before that there was a faint fog.

I took the team up to the house, picked up Kathy and the supplies, and then guided them slowly down the incline onto the trail where they settled into a seemingly effortless plod.

After a few minutes, Kathy said in a bright voice,

"It's just like a Christmas card, isn't it? One of those Dickensian ones with stage coaches and ostlers."

"Mmmm," I said.

I urged them up over the hump in the snow where a culvert ran under the trail and a brace of partridge exploded from the etched brown grasses and stiff sedge in the ditch. Prince shied, barging Paddy, and I had to stand and shout to straighten them, hauling back on the rein.

The familiar landmarks, the cedar stand, the special place where I took Mike's kids to gather puff-ball fungus, the rotted manure pile where you could catch milk snakes, the wrecked car where wild bees had nested two years before, the familiar landmarks passed one after the other until we swung into Hollis' yard.

Eva stood in the doorway smiling.

"Too cold for us, Eva!" I called.

"I'll put some coffee on!" she called back.

Down at the barn, Hollis joked about the cold weather shrinking things so you could hardly find them, and pencils that didn't have no lead, but I noticed his eyes were going over his precious Paddy and Prince. I showed him where the tugs were fraying at the split-tug.

The area in front of the barn was a sheet of ice, covered with thin water. The day before he must have slaughtered a cow and cut it in half with his chainsaw. The four hoofs fringed with hair lay on the ice. Kathy was staring at them. The great white sack of the stomach, what Hollis always called the 'inwards', lay on the manure pile.

196

Water was seeping in fissures under the ice, a network of meandering veins of movement. Blood, red and pink, moved with it down the slope towards the corn crib.

After the usual banter, after coffee, after Eva had overborn our denials of hunger and we'd eaten rich wedges of chocolate cake, we loaded the Pinto, said our goodbyes and headed back along the country roads towards the 401 and Montreal.

I settled into a steady speed. Neither of us seemed to have much to say. After half an hour or so, Kathy switched on the radio and found a strong FM station in Ottawa which alternated Bach with a friendly dimwit who in reverent tone, mile after mile, interviewed a woman who handwove and hand-dyed wall-hangings which she referred to throughout as 'fibrous constructs' and then after a dose of Pete Seeger the same man interviewed a terribly enthusiastic man who'd written a book about cat astrology from which one could discover whether you and your prospective pet would be compatible.

Kathy asked if I'd mind stopping for coffee and I pulled into the next of those barn-like gas stations, one of the Canada's Heritage chain, where Canada's heritage, a few old flat-irons, tobacco-cutters, jack-planes, and butter molds are displayed next to the White Owl cigars and Spearmint gum.

We sat in a booth with the coffee and watched the cars and trucks stream by.

I lighted a cigarette.

"I'm sorry, Jim," said Kathy.

"Oh, don't be silly!" I said.

"I want to be warm, Jim. Can you understand that. I *need* to be."

"We can stay," I said. "Sure. Have another coffee."

She put her hand on mine.

"I don't mean it that way," she said.

She looked out of the window at the traffic.

I suddenly understood her to be referring to her dead husband and child.

I nodded.

I stared at the sugar container.

She squeezed my hand tight.

"I *need* to be warm."

I nodded again without looking at her.

I pushed my empty cup and saucer aside and eased out of the

booth.

     I stretched mightily.
     I tried to smile.
     "Well," I said. "Wagons roll!"

Chapter Thirteen

I rang Hetherington's front door bell at the appointed time and stood on the ice-covered step holding a bottle of wine. Large plastic toys stuck out of the snow of the front yard. A light came on and then the door opened and a piggy, teen-ish boy stood staring at me.

"Hello," I said.

He regarded me without curiosity.

The paunch of his T-shirt said:

Had any lately?

"Aren't you going to ask me in?"

"Why should I?" said this fat boy.

"Because your father invited me to dinner."

He seemed to be considering this.

He retreated as I pushed my way into the little hall and heaved my coat on top of those mounded on the pegs.

"What's your name?" I said.

"What's yours?" he said.

I wondered if he were defective or drugged but decided he was simply unpleasant, surly with avoirdupois and adolescence. I followed his expanse of back down the short passageway. This opened into a larger hall with doors leading off it.

"They're in there," he said.

"Thank you."

He started up the stairs and then turned.

"That's mistletoe," he said, pointing to the chandelier. His face was lit with something close to animation. "You can kiss women under that," he said, "and get hold of them."

I stood on the threshold of the large living room looking over the dramatis personae. The room crawled with children. Julia was draped in dun-coloured cloth, possibly hessian, and looked even more than usual like an extra from the opening scene of *The Mayor of Casterbridge*. The cloth was gathered at her waist by what might have been a tie. On her feet were gold, high-heeled evening shoes. She was sitting in a wickerwork throne of Asian manufacture.

Hetherington himself was kneeling on the floor at the far end of the long room dabbing at an infant's bum. He waved a wad of brown Kleenex in greeting.

"Do," cried Julia, indicating the couch, "shovel away some debris." And taking the proffered wine, said, "Wine! How scrumptious!"

I sat.

"Somebody get the poor man a drink!" said Julia.

"What's black and red," said a studious-looking child with a big head, insinuating himself, "and goes 'Urrghh!'?"

I smiled and shrugged.

"A nun," he said, "with a knife in her back."

"Lemon or olive?" said a girl in a maroon school tunic and knee socks. She had the same accent as her mother. She was probably about eleven but looked a corrupt fifteen dressed in the clothing of a younger child for the entertainment of business men.

"That's in a martini?" I said.

"One would hardly put lemon or olive in scotch," said this child. "Would one?"

"Urrghh!" said the small boy and deliberately fell off the couch. He lay on the floor and said, "Urrghh!"

"Oh, *God*!" said Julia. "He's started!"

"Daddy!" shouted another child. "Rab's started."

"Rabindranath!" called Hetherington.

I stared.

Julia caught my expression.

"Dick used to *adore* Tagore," she said.

"Urrghh!" said Rabindranath.

It was odd to hear Hetherington called anything but Hetherington but of all names 'Dick' seemed somehow inevitable.

The corrupt child reappeared with my drink.

"Oh, *God*, Cecilia!" said Julia, pointing to Rabindranath. "Can't you *do* something?"

She did.

She kicked him in the back.

He crawled off.

"With you in a jiffy!" called Hetherington.

Julia raised both feet and indicated the gold shoes.

"Thirty cents," she said. "At the Salvation Army. Aren't they absolutely 1930?"

Hetherington reappeared with a drink and sat beside me on the couch.

"Well," he said. "Cheers! And all the . . . ah . . . belated best for the New Year! I really do feel most apologetic, should have done this ages ago, of course, but Julia has been . . . *is* . . . ah . . ."

"*Wonderfully* and restfully enceinte," she said. She patted the middle of the dun-coloured cloth.

"Congratulations!" I said.

"I do find I feel most acutely alive," she said, "when the oven is with bun."

With outstretched leg she warded off the staggering advance of the cleaned infant. What could be seen of the leg was hairy.

"Not," she said, "that I *like* them but I *do* enjoy the being pregnant and the *having* of them. It gives one an interest."

Hetherington smiled in his hunted sort of way.

The infant advanced again. It was naked except for the diaper.

"Peeny boo!" it cried.

It pointed to the ceiling.

"Peeny boo!" it said piteously. "Peeny *boo*!"

"What's that mean?" I said.

"Peanut butter," said Julia. "Aurelia! be a dear child and fill your sister."

From an ancient reticule she produced an amber cigarette holder and a tin of cheroots.

"*Do* replenish this, Cecilia!" she said, extending her glass. "And attend to your father and Mr. Thing."

I stared beyond Cecilia. The smell of vinegar had invaded the room. A small female child was spooning white powder into a beaker. With each spoonful, a dirty tan foam rose up the glass and surged onto the carpet.

"That's Lavinia's chemistry set," said Hetherington.

201

I nodded.

"Dinner," said Julia, sipping her replenished drink, "will be unaccountably delayed."

"I know this is a frightful bore," said Hetherington, "but I wonder if we might talk shop for just a moment?"

"Certainly," I said.

"Kill...ah...two birds," said Hetherington.

"Of course," I said.

"Well," said Hetherington. "It's this Zemermann business."

"Oh, you heard about that?"

"Mr. Pringle called, you see. Fortunately."

"Who's he?" I asked.

"From the Print Shop," said Hetherington.

"About his heart attack?" I said.

"Pringle?" said Hetherington.

"No, Zemermann," I said.

There was a pause.

"I have it!" said Hetherington. "Could we possibly be talking about different things?"

"Well," I said, *"I'm* talking about Zemermann having a heart attack in my office. Did you hear about that?"

"No, actually."

"He had some kind of attack," I said. "His heart. He had tablets. I was being critical of something he'd written—in the kindest way, you understand—and suddenly.."

"Quite," said Hetherington. "Quite. It's happened more than once, actually, in just those sort of circumstances."

I looked at him.

"What are you getting at?"

"Well, not sitting examinations, for instance," said Hetherington. "Work not done. Failing-grades. Those sort of circumstances."

"I'd like to be certain," I said, "that I'm understanding you."

"Did his wife phone you?" said Hetherington. "Subsequently?"

I shook my head.

Hetherington nodded.

"She phoned me you know, on a similar occasion. Jolly distressing. Called me a murderer. Among other things. Of course, the poor woman was somewhat distraught and many of her what I took to be imprecations were not actually in *English* but ..."

It was both rude and difficult to force Hetherington into a direct fully-formed and definitive statement but it suddenly seemed important to try.

"Dick!" I said. "You seem to be implying something. What are you implying?"

He gazed at the ceiling.

"What *do* I mean?" he said.

He opened then closed his mouth.

"I'm not really sure. But it *does* seem that these . . . ah . . . attacks . . ."

"You're not saying he . . ."

"I'm not saying he's a slippery customer," said Hetherington. "I'm not saying that at all."

"Why bring it up, then?" said Julia. "I would have understood you to be saying *precisely* that, Richard. It really makes me quite cross when people don't just say exactly what they mean. *I* always do."

She tapped ash from the cheroot onto the carpet.

"You mean," I said to Hetherington, "that these attacks might well be too convenient to be . ."

"Not," said Hetherington, "that I'd wish to be quoted on the . . . ah . . ."

"Good God!" I said.

We sat silent for a few moments.

Cecilia brought more martinis. My heart was warming to this child. First she's sunk her sturdy brown Oxford into Rabindranath and subsequentlty provided a steady flow of drink. As kids go, not a totally bad kid.

I brooded about Itzic.

"You know," I said, "I just can't figure the guy out. I don't know what he wants. He doesn't want to *learn* anything. He just sits there. He's — well, implacable. What *does* he want?"

"It's quite obvious what he wants," said Julia. "He wants everybody to feel sorry for him and he wants to be famous."

"Famous?"

"One can tell that he's utterly ruthless," said Julia, "by the way he propels his wheelchair."

"Now, *really*, Julia!" said Hetherington.

"Don't 'really' *me*!" she said. "*I* have not forgotten that unutterable 'Meet the Students' evening. Not that any sane person would wish to. Meet them, that is."

"Oh, Julia!" said Hetherington.

"He described my sausage-rolls," she said, turning to me, "as

203

unclean."

"All he *said*," said Hetherington, "was.."

"It is beyond me," said Julia, "quite, quite beyond me why everyone *bothers* with the man when he's so obviously beyond any possible pale."

"The whole situation," said Hetherington, making tentative movements with his hands, "is endlessly *delicate*."

"*One* of them," said Julia, "vomited in Lavinia's toy chest. Why?"

"Pardon?"

"As is," said Hetherington, "this episode with Pringle."

"What *is* this about Pringle?"

"There is nothing delicate about it at all," said Julia. "You're merely indulging in preposterous special pleading. *Were* he not a Jew, *were* he not a cripple, *were* he not allegedly subject to heart attacks, and *were* he not a survivor of concentration camps, one would tell him to piss off."

"Really, Julia!" said Hetherington.

"*I*," she said, "would tell him to piss off anyway."

She drained her martini and rang the glass down on the table.

"But then," she said, "*I'm* not academically gifted."

Hetherington crouched nibbling at his lower lip.

Julia sucked an olive.

"You see," said Hetherington suddenly, "the sum involved was in excess of $1,500 and these monies are linked directly with the Department's budget which really, however distasteful the task, one must watch like the proverbial hawk, rob Peter and one must pay Paul, which is not to say, of course, that one suspects any members of the Department of dishonesty but rather that *thoughtless*, or should we say, *unthinking* use of the... ah..."

"What...?"

"...ah...reproductional facilities," concluded Hetherington.

I took a large mouthful of martini. This was the longest single speech I had heard him utter. It made me wonder, fleetingly, how he could perform so consistently such a straightforward activity as sexual intercourse.

"Nor," he added, "do I for one moment doubt the warmth of your intentions."

For a lunatic second, I thought he'd somehow discovered that I'd knocked off the office typewriter.

"Dick," I said, lighting a cigarette, "I don't quite follow..."

"But I thought we really ought to get to the bottom of it."

"Yes," I said.

"So quite apart from any question of financial feasibility, I think the primary question must be—did you?"

"Did I what?"

"Select them."

"Them?"

"Mr. Zemermann's poems."

Conversation with Hetherington was rather like the apparently aimless snippings of a pair of scissors through sheets of folded newspaper which, unfolded, revealed snowflakes, dinosaurs.

I nodded.

"He did bring me a great wad of poems," I said. "Weeks ago. Horrible. And he asked me to choose the best thirty. Yes."

"And did he say why he wished you to do this?"

"He said something about getting a book printed."

"Ah!" said Hetherington. "Aha!"

"Aha, what?"

"And did he say *where* the book was to be printed?"

"No. He didn't say anything about that. The last one was done by a vanity press in New York. Who'd publish the stuff if they weren't paid to?"

"So you made no promises? Just picked out the better . . . ah . . . ?"

"What do you *mean* 'promises'?"

"Oh, dear!" said Hetherington. "It's *so* awkward. Because Pringle himself, you see, was not actually present when—it was that young man with an earring."

I wanted to haul Hetherington up and slap him repeatedly.

He sighed.

"*Somehow*," he said, "the impression was given—I think that's probably the best way to put it—that the Department was paying for an edition of one thousand copies of a booklet of Mr. Zemermann's poems."

"You mean, he *said* that the Department . ."

"No, no, you see, *that's* the crux. The young man with the earring—it's all really a matter of assumption. And the . . . ah . . . title page *did* say 'Selected by James Wells'."

I stared at him.

"*Singing Bones*," he said. "Selected by James Wells."

"Well, Jesus Christ!" I said. "But you've put a stop to it,

haven't you?"

"Actually," said Hetherington, "more of a *hold*, really. You see, *had* you authorized the . . . ah . . . we might have been, *legally* speaking . . ."

He made one of his spastic manual gestures. And then started to pluck the elasticized top of his sock.

"Well now you know I *didn't* authorize anything," I said, "what are you going to do to him?"

"Do?"

I nodded and stared at him.

"Stall," he said. "I shall have to stall until we've taken legal counsel. Until we see if your act of selecting does in itself constitute some sort of . . . ah . . . The problem really is that nothing is quite clear-cut, as it were. You see, the young man with the earring claims to have no memory of the . . . ah . . . and neither was a work-order completed so we're really all in rather a fog of — a fog of *intention* rather than of . . ."

"I can't believe this," I said.

"But it does rather *seem*," said Hetherington, "that Mr. Zemermann is in some way culpable yet . . ."

"Culpable!" I said. "He's bloody criminal!"

"Just what *I* was saying," said Julia. "Utterly ruthless."

"Oh, Julia," said Hetherington.

"*And*," she said, "he has hair, actual *tendrils* growing out of his nose."

"Yet the law," said Hetherington, "is infinitely . . ."

"He doubtless lurked in his wheelchair," said Julia, "until only a menial was in charge and then simply said, 'These were selected by a member of the English Department'. Something along those lines. Hoping for a *fait accompli*. Always plump for the butler."

"I just can't believe," I said, "that anything even vaguely legal is in question."

Hetherington shook his head.

"There was a Portuguese janitor," he said, "who drank from a five-gallon drum of commercial cleaning fluid."

"What's that got to do with it?"

"I mention him as an example," said Hetherington. "The sort of thing that can happen."

I drained the martini.

Julia held out my glass and hers. Her fingernails were painted dark green.

"Do!" she said to Cecilia.

Hetherington sighed.

"Far, far from simple," he said. "Quite apart from any legal questions, if legal question there be, the man *is* Jewish and he *was* imprisoned in wherever it was that he *was*."

"One wearies," said Julia, "of listening to such tiresome *balls*. Why should one not be entertained?"

She leaned forward from her throne and placed her hand upon my knee.

"Recite," she said, "a poem."

"A poem?"

"One of your own."

"Most of my poems aren't particularly entertaining."

"How drab of you," she said.

"But I still don't see," I said to Hetherington, "why you can't make him pay for it."

"No work-order exists, you see," he said. "Washee, as it were, but no tickee. So he could just deny the whole thing. Claim he asked for something entirely other — a Xerox copy, say, and there he is — home and dry. *Or* . . ."

"There are limits," said Julia, "to the tedium I can endure. For lack of anything more amusing, I shall prepare dinner."

She bore her drink before her. She was unsteady in the golden shoes. The hessian dress was in the basic shape of a medieval sack. Except for the trailing pieces. I was suddenly reminded of a photograph of Dame Edith Sitwell.

"*Or*," said Hetherington, "he could claim to have understood you to have authorized . . . I'm afraid it's all jolly far from simple."

We sat in silence.

Trying to get a grip on the direction and meaning of the conversation had left me feeling vaguely concussed but one thing seemed relatively clear — Itzic was not what he claimed to be. I had to hang onto that. Itzic was not what he seemed to be. And that knowledge absolved me from further complicity and humiliation, from the dead weight of his awful importunity.

The whole matter sat like a rich, unopened present. Later, I promised myself, in suitable quiet and seclusion, I would gloat.

Rabindranath reappeared, now dressed as a wolf cub. He sat on the floor and pushed a car about making *brmmm-brmmm* noises.

The other children were upstairs and threatening to come

207

through the ceiling.

Cecilia was lying on the floor with a big book.

In a jolly, visitor's voice, I said, "And what are you reading about, Cecilia?"

"Ritual prostitution," she said.

Julia reappeared with a bowl of peanuts.

"I had purchased a vast fish," she said, "but I find I lack the necessary fortitude."

"Can I . . . ah . . ?" said Hetherington.

"That's very dear of you, Richard, but it has *looked* at one."

She waved a dismissing hand.

To me, she said,

"The coloured pictures in cookery books are so enticing, don't you find? Yet one's results so always disappointing? Actually, I enjoy a jolly good cheese sandwich eaten *whilst looking at* coloured photographs in cookery books — pardon, Richard? Of course I have no intention of serving cheese sandwiches. We have no cheese. We shall order Chinese food. They bring it in a motor car. But of course you're *used* to that. It never ceases to amaze me."

She made an unsteady exit.

"Do hope you don't mind," said Hetherington. "She's been feeling a little under the weather with her . . ."

He patted his stomach.

That, I thought, and the effects of the best part of a large bottle of dry gin.

Her end of the telephone conversation sounded in the hall.

Hetherington leaned back and placed his hand over his eyes as if in pantomime of deep thought or pain.

I looked at Rabindranath who looked odd. He was sitting with his back against the wall. Both hands were gripping the edge of the carpet. His eyes were closed. He was making a steady humming noise.

I quite understand. Do stop saying 'No substitutions'!

Rabindranath started rocking backwards and forwards.

I do feel you're becoming rather obsessional about Complete Dinners A and B. Quite. And a Complete Dinner is not at all what I require.

With each backward movement, Rabindranath was banging his head against the wall.

Do let us eschew Complete Dinners. Yes. I'm sure you're the dearest of men . . .

The contact between Rabindranath's head and the wall was now audible. He was settling into a steady rhythm. He was quietly chanting his name: Ra*bin*dranath! Ra*bin*dranath! Ra*bin*dranath! And with each stressed *bin*, he was banging his head, hard.

"Dick?"

"Ah?"

I pointed.

He grabbed a cushion and, hurrying over, crouched interposing the cushion between Rabindranath's head and the wall. A reaction, I thought, somehow quintessentially Hetherington. He started talking to the child, a low murmur, words inaudible.

"Don't be alarmed," said Cecilia. "It's rather a *thing* of his."

Aurelia did not even look up from her magic painting book but continued eyeing it and sipping from the jam-jar of painty water.

Julia entered and headed for her glass. She sank into the wicker throne, rearranged vagrant lengths of hessian, and said,

"I do find conversations with Chinese *debilitating*."

She glanced at Rabindranath.

"I suppose," she said, "one ought to get him looked at."

The phone rang.

Hetherington looked up but continued cradling Rabindranath. He said "Ah . . ."

Julia creaked in the throne but flopped back.

"Could you be so kind?" she said.

I went into the hall and picking up the phone said, "Hello?"

"No, it isn't. Dick's in the middle of a slight crisis. Can I give him a message?"

"Oh, is it? Well, look, you could tell me what to say and I could stick my head round the door and call to him. O.K.?"

It's Irving. It's a matter of life and death.

"Irving who?" said Hetherington.

I consulted the phone.

Irving Misky. It's about SOB.

"What's SOB?" I said to Hetherington.

"Save Our Buildings," said Hetherington. "I'm vice-president."

They're knocking down the Carroway House on Sherbrooke. The same company as last time. Irving thinks they haven't a permit and he thinks they'll just pay the fine like they did last time.

"Has he informed the police?" said Hetherington.

I popped back round the door frame to the phone. I was

209

beginning to feel like something from a Punch and Judy show.

Irving says the police are there but they won't do anything. He says he thinks they've been paid off.

"What?" I said to the phone.

Irving says that when the conservatory shattered, something in his heart broke too.

"Yes?" I said to the phone. "Yes. Hold on."

Irving's mobilized the members—"wait a minute"—*and there's a reporter from the Herald*—"yes?"—*and every single body is needed to*—"could you repeat that?"—*to form a living wall.*

"To what?" said Hetherington.

To form a living wall.

To oppose the wrecker's ball.

I was feeling pleasantly drunk and was pleased with the serendipitous rhyme of the last couplet. Irving quacked away at the other end and every now and then I conveyed the gist of the matter to Hetherington who was still cradling Rabindranath.

Irving is very upset.

Should Irving phone CBC-TV?

Should Irving alert the Pollution people?

Hetherington was visibly torn.

"Tell him . . ." he said.

Dick says—

"Ah . . . Oh, God! . . . ah . . . You'll think me frightfully rude . . ."

You'll think me frightfully rude.

"No, no," cried Hetherington. "I was saying that to you. Look! Tell him . . . ah . . ."

He propped Rabindranath against the wall, pointed to him, gestured helplessly, and scurried out past me. There were noises in the small entrance hall and then the front door slammed.

"Hello, Irving? Yes. I think he's on his way to join you. Yes. Yes. Nice talking to you, too, Irving."

Rabindranath started to bang his head against the wall again. Aurelia wandered across and poured some of her paint-water on him. He stopped. I sat on the couch. Julia looked glazed.

There was silence.

After a couple of minutes, the fat boy who had let me in came into the room and said,

"Where's Dad gone?"

Julia turned her torso and focused on him.

210

"Your father," she said, with a limp hand, "is building a living wall."

He didn't say anything — just stared a bit — then went out. He could be heard going up the stairs.

Cecilia turned a page.

Julia began to snore.

Cecilia's long, honey-coloured hair hung about her face. She had eased off the ugly brown shoes. As she read, she was working the woollen knee-socks down until they hung off her feet like nightcaps, like deflated balloons. And then her bare feet, long toes. I watched her. My glass was empty. I took Julia's. Her mouth was open. The snores were moderating into an indrawn burble.

Cecilia's toe nails were rimmed black with dirt. A large part of the attraction of nymphets, I realized, was their *grubbiness*. I wondered why. Grubby women were not attractive at all but the tide-line round a nymphet's neck seemed oddly aphrodisiac. Was muck somehow innocent? Was innocence an aphrodisiac? Was I depraved?

It was quiet in the large room. Rabindranath, Aurelia, and Lavinia had disappeared. The infant had disappeared. The fat boy had disappeared. The noise from upstairs had stopped. I sat awaiting the arrival of a Chinese dinner for eight.

I cleared my throat.

"Is that something you're reading for school?"

"*The Golden Bough*?" she said.

"Not approved stuff, eh?"

"Miss Minge," said Cecilia, "favours Gerald Durrell."

"Do you all go to the same school?"

"I go to The Grove because of Mother and the others go to The Free School because of Father."

"And what's that like? The Free School?"

She pushed the sweep of hair back from her face.

"It's the sort of school," she said, "that only uses exercise books made from recycled paper."

I nodded.

"And what about The Grove?"

"Latin," she said. "And navy blue knickers. But actually I quite like it."

I grinned at her.

"And what do you plan to do when they let you out?"

"Do you think I'm attractive?" she said.

211

"Yes," I said. "Very. Why?"

She shrugged.

"I wish I were more *nubile*," she said. "You ought to see my friend Tania."

I oughtn't, I thought.

She sighed.

"Anyway," she said. "I don't expect to live much past my majority."

"Really?"

She polished her fingernails on her tunic and then inspected them.

"Last week," she said, "an acquaintance of father's was here sitting where you are. And I was lying here reading. He's excessively *ordinary* — what mother calls 'a person'. Rather plebian, actually, but I kept glancing up at him like this — it's what Tania calls 'licking an ice-cream'. Actually, Tania's irredeemably vulgar and a bit of a cow. But anyway, I could *feel* his eyes on me. So I turned on my side like this, and then I kept this leg straight and drew this leg up like this and I vamped him unmercifully and do you know what?"

"No?"

"I saw his roger stir."

"Cecilia!"

"Well I *think* I did."

I cleared my throat.

"Put your leg down," I said, "and behave yourself."

She giggled.

The plastered Julia groaned.

"You live with Kathy Neilson, don't you?"

"How do you know that?"

"Father was talking about inviting her here with you but he thought you didn't know he knew and that mentioning it might not be quite the thing. Poor old daddy!"

"Hmmm," I said.

"She's quite nice, isn't she?"

"Well," I said, "yes."

"Do you love her? And does she love you?"

I looked at the table top, at the smeared empty glasses, the ashtray full of cigarette ends and the brown stumps of cheroots. At the pile of olive pits furred with cigarette ash.

"Yes and yes," I said. "I suppose."

She rolled over onto her elbow and said,

212

"What does 'suppose' mean? Do tell me. I'm genuinely interested in things sexual."

"Well," I said, "I love her and I think she loves me but I'm not at all sure that she *likes* me."

"I don't quite *see* that."

"Well, we seem to annoy each other, you see."

"But can't two people magnificently *hate* each other and still be in love?"

"I don't know," I said.

"Mother and father," she said, "don't think the same way about anything at all. In fact, they seem quite separate except for *breeding*. But I do think they love each other."

She frowned.

"Still in a way, they don't really *count*, do they?"

"Hmmm," I said.

"I read a novel about the Civil War in America," she said, "about a man and a woman who hated each other extravagantly because they were both so proud they tried other people, lots of people, for years, but in the end they came back together again because everyone else was unsatisfactory. Because they had this all-consuming *thing* for each other."

"Well . . ." I said.

"I do think it's terribly important to live passionately, don't you? I mean, given that one is going to die."

"I suppose so," I said.

A profusion of lilacs, masonry tumbled.

"That's what I'm going to do," she said.

"What?"

"Live terribly passionately."

Chapter Fourteen

I was greeted on the first day of the second term by the secretary, lank hair, blemishes, and officiousness. She habitually spoke of things 'going through the paper channels'. This hair was secured by a leather thing with a wooden skewer through it. She reminded me that my marks for the first term had been due on the final day of the first term, that all marks were to be submitted to the Dean of Arts, were to be countersigned before submission by the Department Head, were to be entered in triplicate on carbon-backed forms for a total of nine, were to be expressed as percentages, were to be transferred after approval to a computerized master-list *using the special pencil*, that the final mark was arrived at by the addition of the first term's mark and the second term's mark, that this mark was then subject to division by two *etc. etc.*

And much more.

Rather than that, I made the rounds.

Malcolm offered me a glass of grapefruit juice and a B12 vitamin pill. He was wearing a necklace of sharks' teeth he'd been given for Christmas by a seventeen-year-old boy from Texas whom he'd met in the lavatory of the Voyageur Bus Terminus. He and this Texan catamite had spent the vacation ingesting an hallucinatory drug called PVC or somesuch, but the boy had turned out to be a runaway wanted for auto theft and armed robbery and had become what Malcolm called physical and had caused Malcolm pain and now Malcolm was in positive fear for his very life and obviously hadn't had such a good time for ages.

Ms. Merton and two maenads from the Women's Drop-In Centre were stapling up posters round the corridors. At each encounter, the helpers stared at me in silent loathing. With their unwashed hair, unwashed ponchos, and wall-eye, they reminded me of two half-breed gunmen in a Marlon Brando western. The posters advertised a journal for women by women called *Women Speak!* to be produced by the women of St. Xavier. In the centre of the poster, in extreme close-up, were a pair of lips and some teeth. Which prompted the fancy that if you were mounting a search for the sasquatch or the *vagina dentata*, a reasonable starting point would be deep in the underwear of Ms. Merton's henchpersons.

Lindseer's room was sadly empty. Fred had secured a temporary post at the University of Maine at Orono to teach Thomas Wolfe and Service English to jerk-offs.

Dr. Gamahuche expressed the hope that the vacation had replenished the wellsprings of creativity and showed me two rare empty matchboxes manufactured in Germany during the Weimar Republic.

Professor Norbert had unearthed a lot of poems written by an early Canadian lady with three names the middle one of which was Primrose. He was very excited.

The folders stapled to Professor Curll's door now read: *Alienation and Madness: Section I (Term II)* and *Alienation and Madness: Section II (Term II)*.

I sat in my room with the carbon-backed forms and looked over the names of my poetasters and felt glum. Next door, Professor Niddling was in spirited colloquy with his filing cabinet.

This business of allotting marks expressed as a percentage made me feel resentment and a reluctance which bordered on principle. It was not that I was opposed to making judgements and nor was I opposed to expressing those judgements in numerical terms. It was not really a question of defending the innocence of the Muse against the advances of the dirty old Academy. After all, my charges were not poets. They were semi-literates with delusions of grandeur. Who, in his right mind, would claim a toe-hold on Parnassus for Mrs. Strudly?

No, it wasn't what now appeared to be called *000234 Creative Writing* — it was *me*. I objected to confirming in the three-piece administrative minds of St. Xavier the notion that poetry was, after all, much like anything else, that poets, just like anyone else, could be bought. I regarded this mark business as a demand for a formal, public act of self-abasement.

I had rehearsed my distaste with Kathy but she had been short, unsympathetic, claimed I was behaving like a professional virgin.

How stings the truth! as Poet No. 4, Peter Stanley, would undoubtedly have written.

I thought of the Director of Continuing Education plump in his bonhomie and natty gent's suiting with his gold-plated pen and pencil set by Cross who as the barman in the faculty club poured from the bottle always urged: *Con brio! Con brio!* How deeply satisfying it would be, I thought, to maim him.

I sighed and prepared to add my half-credit to the farce. On a scrap of waste paper I noted my highest and lowest marks between whose bounds the rest could be bunged in. The obvious choice for the highest mark was Mrs. Allaline because she didn't write anything at all. Equally obvious, the lowest mark was Itzic. I plonked them in at 98 and 51 and then slumped back trying to decide whether Tuff Boots got up my nose more than Mrs. Strudly.

The phone rang.

It was someone called Corey. Edward Corey. He was with External.

"What do you mean, 'External'?"

"Affairs."

He apologized for the lack of advance warning but he had two writers under his wing. Russians. Touring the country. A visit sponsored by the Secretary of State. Professor Hetherington was laying on an audience. Would I, as Writer-in-Residence, as a matter of courtesy, be agreeable to dining with the writers beforehand and generally . . .

"Well, who *are* they?" I said. "And why does the Secretary of State want them here?"

The Secretary of State wanted them here, apparently, as part of a continuing gesture of international good will. Cultural reciprocity. And so forth. The two celebrated writers were Kutuzov and Borkh. I said their names didn't ring a bell. Borkh wrote poems and Kutuzov wrote —

"*What!*"

"Fairy tales," repeated Corey.

"Well . . ." I said.

I felt dubious. They were obviously members of the Writers' Union or Literary Guild or whatever it's called and thus extensions of the State. Was it being implied that I somehow represented the Canadian State? Could my conscience allow me to give aid and comfort to these hack emissaries of the USSR?

The Soviets stood high in my world heirarchy of scumbags. But then, so did many other countries. But then again, most of the other scumbag countries contented themselves with torturing a few hundred here and there. A few thousand. Russia since 1917 had wacked off more than forty million for the greater good, a figure which made Hitler seem a model of restraint.

I thought of the long list of writers and intellectuals the Soviet Union had killed, imprisoned, or treated for mental instability. But then again, honesty compelled me to remember the sheet awfulness of much of their writing, the ineffably boring short stories which used to appear month after month in *Encounter*, a bad investment for the CIA as it had been difficult to sustain indignation at fever pitch when actually confronted with yet another story by Abram Tertz.

"You mean *tonight?*" I said.

"Six o'clock," he said. "Chez Son Père."

According to *Where to Eat in Canada*, some of the best grub in town.

"Ask for me by name," he said.

"Right," I said. "Six o'clock."

And hung up.

Hmmm.

What did he *mean* 'Ask for me by name'?

It occurred to me that I'd never met a man from External before, nor, come to that, an actual, living Soviet Russian. I considered *The Man from External* as a thriller title. Ottawa again. Which was their building? I thought it was the one where you got passports, the Lester B. Layered-Fudge-Cake-Building on — was it Sussex Drive? The fact that I didn't know was indicative of something or other. I certainly knew what went on in Moscow's Dzerzhinsky Street. And who the hell *was* the present Secretary of State? I decided that the most comfortable way to think of the evening ahead was as research, as raw material for *The Musical Ride*.

Upon which I had got no further.

The problem was only partly sloth. After much mental

struggle, I'd been forced to admit that writing a thriller set in Canada verged on the impossible. Impossible because nobody knows what a Canadian *is*. We're invisible to ourselves and to the larger world because we have no stereotypes.

Even Australians have the distinction of being universally deplored.

The whole world knows what happens when a beautiful woman is shipwrecked on a desert island with an Englishman, a Frenchman, and an American. The only activity credible for a Canadian in their company would be standing on guard as a one-man peace-keeping force.

The problem had become unpleasantly clear to me when I was casting the movie version of *The Musical Ride*. A character actor like, say, Peter Sellers, can produce from his hat Englishmen, Americans, Indians, Frenchmen, Arabs, Mexicans *etc. etc.* But what would he do if asked to sketch in a Canadian? What would he wear? What mannerisms might he assume? How would he speak? How would he suggest to an international audience *Canadian-ness*?

I had, of course, postponed my grapple with the problem by making Commander Swann British. And weird. My American secret agents were a piece of cake. American agents actually looked American and actually did talk of terminating people with extreme prejudice, caricatures before I'd even started. Russian heavies, too, were pretty standard stuff. But that still left the major problem of the minor characters. Canadians they had to be. And it still left the problem of setting which had to be Ottawa, a place which even to Canadians has the reality of an ill-made stage set.

Hmmm.

Seventeen minutes until the opening of the bar.

Tuff Boots: 61

Mrs. Strudly: 59

Edward Corey as Commander Swann's aide?

Fat Frances: 52

There you are! said Professor Niddling's voice from next door. *You little file!*

To an outside observer, the scene at the table in the alcove in Chez Son Père would have suggested six people gripped in some intricate, fascinating task such as defusing an ultra-sensitive trembler bomb or cutting perilously into the living tissue of a human brain. All eyes were fixed on the woman's face, and her eyes and lips, as she rumbled away in Russian. Then, all eyes switched to Kutuzov as *he* rumbled away in Russian. Then, all eyes switched back to the woman whose face was always impassive, her voice a monotone. She said:

"Viktor Alexeivich says that in Moscow there are also large quantities of snow but that Montreal has a more sophisticated system of snow-removal than has Moscow."

The relaxation after each of these ghastly exchanges was visible.

The meal seemed to have been going on for hours.

When I had arrived, it had not previously struck me that the buggers *wouldn't speak English.* This was bad. The implications of it all had unfolded slowly. There was to be a whole evening of this bomb-defusing stuff. It wasn't going to stop. It was going to go on. And on. There was to be a bomb-defusing reception. But prior to that the buggers were going to chunter away telling us fairy tales and sodding poems for fucking hours *in fucking Russian.*

The mental strain of it all was too awful to contemplate and as it was all paid for by the Department of External Affairs anyway I was applying myself to lowering as much drink as humanly possible without vomiting so that during the actual fairy tales and poems I would be in a state as near comatose as the occasion would allow.

Edward Corey was a small greyish man in a grey suit and had neither said nor done anything spyish or diplomatic. Hetherington was being Hetherington but worse than usual. The occasion was exaggerating his compulsion to be polite and it was he who had initiated most of the exchanges. He had introduced as rollicking conversational topics: the weather, travel in aeroplanes, Montreal's subway system, the weather in the different seasons of the year, the weather in the different seasons of the year in different parts of the country, the problems involved in laundering clothes whilst travelling, food.

Of which Viktor Alexeivich and Pyotr Gregorevich had put away large amounts. But not as much as Madame Irena, the official interpreter, who was pointing now to that, that, that, and *that* on the proffered tray of *pâtisseries.* She was the size of a Sumo wrestler and looked like an incompetent female impersonator. Her hair was a nondescript brown and built up on her head in diminishing mounds like a large but disciplined horse turd.

Kutuzov and Borkh were an extreme disappointment. Their suits were not ill-made, neither was endowed with epicanthic eye folds, nor did they have stainless steel teeth. They were just ordinary. Except that they spoke bloody Russian.

They, too, had been going pretty heavily at the wine. Doubtless better stuff than the people's vintages to which they were accustomed, the old Côtes de Vladivostock and the Château Praesidium.

I felt Hetherington under the table take hold of my hand.

Oh, no!

But he was pressing something into it. It was a twenty-dollar bill.

"What?" I whispered.

"Jolly good of you to rally round!" he whispered.

"Round what?"

"Dinner. The meal. Paying the delivery man. Slipped my mind before. Frightfully sorry."

I made a think-nothing-of-it face and took up my wine glass.

Hetherington nudged me and whispered,

"Had it for breakfast."

Pyotr Gregorevich had finished his coffee and had taken out of his pocket and was pushing about on the tablecloth a souvenir of Canada, one of those bristly toy seals made of real seal skin. As he steered it about, he kept making a loud noise best rendered as *hrank! hrank!* He then beat the toy seal repeatedly over the head with his pâtisserie fork and said:

"New! *Fond!* Land!"

He beamed.

"Ha! Ha!" said Hetherington. "Quite. Newfoundland."

Pyotr Gregorevich hit the seal on the head again.

"Seal!" cried Hetherington. "Wallop! Wallop!"

"New! *Fond!* Land!" said Pyotr Gregorevich again.

"*New*foundland," said Corey.

"Newfound*land*," said Madame Irena.

Oh fuck me! I thought.

Viktor Alexeivich started to rumble.

All eyes fixed on him.

Madame Irena cleared her maw of an apricot tartlet.

All eyes turned to her. She said:

"Viktor Alexeivich says that in Russia fur-bearing animals are also hunted and form a valuable part of the country's economy."

She got stuck into an éclair.

Corey consulted his diplomatic watch, summoned the waiter, settled the bill, and arranged two taxis.

The cityscape rolled by as I sat jammed between Corey and Kutuzov. Kutuzov, the writer of fairy tales, should have been the little one but was large. Borkh, the writer of poems should have been large. Nothing is ever the way it should be. I, personally, I thought, would rather admit to being in the tertiary stage of syphilis than publically admit to the perpetration of fairy tales. But then, on the other hand, perhaps his tales were socially conscious. About the tractor fairy or something.

Corey even managed to sit somehow neatly, on his knees his neat, square briefcase on the side of which stamped in miniscule gold letters were the intials E. C. Initials which might just as well have stood for Efficiency and Correctness.

He'd said on the phone — what was it? Something I'd been thinking about, needed for *The Musical Ride.*

Yes, there it was.

"What you said," I said to him, "about cultural whatname — reciprocity — what are *they* getting for *these?*"

"Oscar Peterson," he said.

I nodded to myself bitterly as we passed a huge, neon pestle and mortar flashing on and off above a pharmacy. The message accompanying the pestle and mortar was in Greek. I nodded again. There you are! Bloody impossible. Try to think of something culturally Canadian and you come up with a brilliant Negro who makes his living mainly in the USA and learned his craft from Art Tatum, an even more brilliant Negro American.

The audience was vast. External must have cracked the whip. The auditorium seethed with students of engineering, business administration, dentistry, sociology, social realities, CACS, and herds of bewildered older people who must have been Continuing Ed. For which they'd get their money's worth tonight, poor buggers, and no mistake.

As we tried to make our way through the crush with Hetherington making . . . *ah* . . . noises, I heard Ms. Merton who was jammed in front of us saying to one of her sidekicks how interesting it was going to be to hear the *rhythms* of poetry in another language . . .

If a stop was not put to this sort of thing, they'd be importing

221

Bantu speakers, Mongols, Masai bards to recite the eight hundred heroic epithets traditionally recited of their sacred cows.

I saw Kathy who beckoned and jabbed at a seat she'd saved a few rows back. I returned the wave and then pointed at Madame Irena and Corey and shrugged and made a garrotted face.

Corey sat neatly, hitched up the crease in his trousers, placed the neat briefcase on his grey knees, extracted a thin white wire from it and a tiny ear-plug and sat staring at the stage. Deaf! And the poor little fucker was too conscientious to accept this God-given gift!

Madame Irena heaved her bulk up the three steps at the side of the stage like a seal. I encouraged the waves of xenophobia to flow over me. I wondered if under the bell-tent-like evening dress her Russian armpits sprouted goat beards. The thought of her naked made the thought of Ms. Merton naked positively attractive.

Madame Irena's introductory monotone droned on telling us how famous in the USSR were Kutuzov and Borkh, what endless numbers of books flowed from the fertile brains of Kutuzov and Borkh, how beloved in the USSR were Kutuzov and Borkh.

She could have made a fat living as a stage hypnotist.

Kutuzov kicked off.

I kept looking at my watch in wonder and disbelief. It went on. And on. It was like listening to the soundtrack of an Ingmar Bergman film. But worse. Compared with this, a Noh play was funnier than Charlie Chaplin. The KGB probably used Kutuzov to read fairy tales to captured Americans until they *begged* to confess.

Their *style* wasn't uninteresting, though, for the first minute or so. They gestured and whispered and bellowed and made exaggerated faces like the actors in melodrama. Especially Borkh.

Even more amazing, though, was the play of expression on Corey's face. Tension. Fear. Delight. His eyes never left the stage. His hands were clenching and unclenching. Why, then, hadn't he spoken Russian in the restaurant, in the cab? Perhaps these poems and fairy tales really *were* meaty stuff.

He grinned and, as if in applause, mimed a pounding on the lid of his briefcase.

Doubtless some Ural witticism.

He leaned over, grinning, and whispered,

"Cournoyer scores *again*! Assist by Lemaire."

The wretched show eventually ended with some interminable dolorous-sounding I suppose poem by bloody Borkh whose voice

222

trailed away into a sort of I suppose groan. Difficult to tell with Russian. Then he just stood there. When it didn't all start up again, the audience expressed its relief, its sense of release, in frenzied, hysterical applause. Kutuzov and Borkh bowed and bowed. Students whistled and stomped and made ape noises. Massive laughter swept the crowd as some wit shouted *Encore!*

The grateful mob fought for the exits.

But there was no escape for me.

I had been designated pig-in-the-middle.

Official Charlie.

The reception in the Faculty Club was a select and sedate affair. Miniscule open sandwiches, unwilted and unsoggy, were on offer by a waiter in a clean, white jacket. And the stuff on the sandwiches wasn't Xavian either. The Department of External Affairs must be, I decided, a power in the land. The Reverend rubicund Father President was gracing us with his presence, guarded loosely by Cosimo O'Gorman in a plaid vaudeville suit. There were some Deans. There was a Director or two. And a scattering of professors to give the affair some body. Another waiter with professional aplomb was circulating trays of *champagne*. I tasted a glass cautiously. It actually *was* champagne.

It wasn't of Canadian origin.

And all *I'd* got was Duck.

I glared at The Reverend Rubicund's pectoral cross and thought darkly of prophets not being without honour.

I was so intent on reaching Kathy that I bumped into tiny Dean Tibbald in his ginger wig. I hadn't noticed him. Knowing his dislike of the feminine, I said, bending and indicating Madame Irena,

"How about *that* as an example of Soviet womanhood!"

He whispered,

"They use steroids, you know."

I was in the middle of trying to convey to Kathy and Henry Benson the tense horror that had been dinner when my elbow was firmly taken. Collared by Corey, I was led to an arrangement of chairs around a low table where Madame Irena, Viktor Alexeivich Kutuzov, and Pyotr Gregorevich Borkh awaited.

As the champagne man passed, I whipped another glass off his tray and said,

"A triple cognac on your way back, there's a good fellow."

He inclined his head.

Suave stuff, this.

It was like a movie.

I had consumed a great deal of alcohol in Chez Son Père but not enough to have dulled the pain of the reading. I felt, justifiably enough, truculent.

The Russian rumbling began.

"Pyotr Gregorevich wishes to know if there are in Canada many magazines which publish the works of literary writers."

"Yes," I said. "Many."

More rumbling.

"Pyotr Gregorevich wishes to know the name of the magazine which has the largest circulation."

I stared at the obsidian eyes of Madame Irena.

"The *TV Guide*."

I still hadn't got over my disappointment with Kutuzov and Borkh. They had none of the hallmarks of Soviet beastliness. For years I'd glanced through fiction full of OGPU men, NKVD men, Beria boys, KGB nasties, and here I was stuck with a big twerp who wrote fairy tales and a little twerp who wrote poems of inordinate length.

Where, I wanted to cry, *are your shoddy suits? Your metal teeth?*

I felt distinctly disgruntled.

Of Corey I hadn't really expected much but even he hadn't referred to the buggers as 'Ivans' which is only standard practice.

A vast balloon of cognac and a section of arm clad in white samite materialized.

"Viktor Alexeivich wishes to know if there are many Canadian fairy tales."

"They are confined," I said, "largely to the native peoples. To the Eskimos and Indians. They are not actually fairy tales as such but legends and myths. Mainly myths which deal at great length with all the usual mythical matter. They have been recorded exhaustively and it seems that scarcely a week goes by without some new tome appearing bulging with yet more myth. But still the most famous myth of them all is called 'Eskimo Nell'."

Corey frowned at me.

I warmed the huge snifter in both hands and raised an eyebrow at him.

I was beginning to feel like a plastic duck in a shooting gallery and decided, along with Clausewitz, that the best method of defense was attack. I asked Madame Irena if Borkh and Kutuzov would like me to explain to them the nature and workings of literary life in Canada.

Rumbling.

Yes. They would like that very much.

"Well," I said, "it's really very much like literary life in the USSR. But then again, in certain ways it isn't. Both systems, for example, are State-supported. There is, in Canada, you see, an institution called The Canada Council. This Council or Praesidium is given money by the State to support the arts."

I could feel the cognac warming me as I warmed to my theme.

"Let us," I said, "follow the career of an imaginary young writer. He or she wishes to be a writer and so writes. Writes let us say poems or stories. He then sends them to one of the literary magazines. These literary magazines are supported by The Canada Council because few people will pay actual money to buy them."

I lighted a cigarette.

"We now come to the second stage. When our young writer has written and published in these magazines let us say a dozen stories, or say thirty poems, he applies to the Council for a grant. If the Council decides he ought to have one, money is sent to him to live on while he writes *more* poems or stories."

The rumble of Madame Irena's translation was becoming a background noise, ignorable.

"Now," I said. "When he has written enough stories or poems to make a book, he sends the manuscript to any one of the publishers he chooses."

Kutuzov was nodding away.

"Again," I said, "our systems are similar for these publishing companies are not actually capitalist enterprises. They, too, get grants from The Canada Council to enable them to publish the manuscripts."

There were loud interruptive rumblings from Borkh.

"Pyotr Gregorevich wishes to know why, then, there is not just one publishing company."

"Tell him," I said, "that it is a complex question but that I hope all will soon become clear."

I took another swig of cognac.

I leaned forward.

"We now come," I said, "to the big difference in the two systems."

Corey sat impassively with folded arms.

"I have heard that in Russia," I said, "books are very popular. Huge editions are printed. Hundreds of thousands of copies. Excited queues miles long form before dawn to lay hands on the stuff hot off the press."

"*Da*," said Kutuzov.

Borkh nodded.

"This," I said, "does not happen in Canada. In Canada, people do not read books. They do not like books."

Surprise, disbelief, consternation played over the faces of Borkh and Kutuzov.

It was like telling a story to small children.

I was beginning to enjoy myself.

"What then *does* happen?" I said. "What happens is this. The publishers of the books send them to book shops where people can buy them. But the people do not buy them. They will not. So the sellers of books wait in despair and then they send the books back to the publisher."

I raised a lecturing finger.

"And so," I said, "a year later there is a curious kind of Canadian festival called Remaindering when the publisher sells the books for much less than it cost to make them. And then, as a result, The Canada Council has to give the publisher even more money."

rumble-rumble-rumble

"No, Pyotr Gregorevich, it does *not* make sense. And so The Canada Council formed a Committee to solve the problem."

I left them in suspense for a few seconds.

"And this is how the Committee of the Council saw the logic of the problem. If the Council paid the writer to write, if it paid the magazine to print, if it paid the publisher to publish, *it must pay the reader to read*."

Kutuzov's eyes were as big as the eyes of the dog with eyes like saucers.

"But how was the Council to do this? The Committee of the Council knew that people would cheat and just *pretend* to have read the books. So the Council invented two ways. First, just as an experiment, they said that if any Canadian or landed immigrant bought a State lottery ticket and failed to win the money then, instead of just throwing away the useless ticket, he could take it to a bookstore and the bookstore would sell him any Canadian book for half-price."

I took another swig of cognac.

"But *still*," I cried, "the people would not buy the books."

Borkh shook his head.

"Can either of you guess why? You can't?"

They stared at me.

"Because," I said, "the people are sly and cunning and knew that if they waited for a year they could get the book not for half price but for five cents at the Remaindering Festival."

Kutuzov was about to say something but I held up my hand to stop him. My exposition of the subject, I felt, was gathering the pleasing repetition of poems for children. This is the house that Jack Built sort of thing.

"So," I said, "what happened in the end was that the Council took up the *other* suggestion of its Committee. If the Council paid the writer to write, the magazine to print, the publisher to publish, and *still* the people would not buy the books—the only thing left for the Council to do *was to buy the books itself*!"

"And so," I said, "every year all the books printed are gathered together into huge crates called Book Kits Canada and are sent as compulsory gifts to underdeveloped countries, hospitals, institutions for the blind, prisons, and lunatic asylums."

Corey leaned forward.

"Professor Wells," he said, "is making a joke."

rumble-rumble

"Da?" said Kutuzov.

"Not da at all. He *has* to say that because he is an Official of the State."

"Take it easy," said Corey.

"Denouce me," I said, "to the Council! You know I speak the truth."

All four of them were silently staring.

"In Canada," I said quietly, "all literature is, in effect, *samizdat*."

I sat back well pleased with both the form and accuracy of this exposition. With an airy wave of my balloon, I summoned the waiter in wondrous white and instructed him to refill it. There was much inter-Russian rumbling going on.

Stick that, I thought, up your samovar.

If any of them were KGB, my money was on Madame Irena as full colonel. It's always the chauffeur or bootboy who rules in the embassies. Kutuzov and Borkh were obviously star trusties but Russian trusties didn't seem to be trusted too far. Though it beat me why they'd want to flee from the oppression of sales of 100,000 copies to the freedom of the lottery of Canada Council grant application forms.

It was more likely they were on a mission to assess the intellectual strength of the West and weaken it by reading to it in Russian.

I wondered if Madame Irena could possibly be a man. When viewed from certain angles...

My little passage of arms with Corey seemed to have put a damper on the conversation which was a merciful release but then Kutuzov looking very mournful started to rumble.

"Viktor Alexeivich wishes to know if there are then no writers at all who are beloved."

"There are two," I said, "who are somewhat beloved. There is a very large one who writes about railways and a small one who writes about whales."

Pyotr Gregorevich looked worried too.

He wanted to know if then there were no *poets* in Canada who were beloved.

I thought for a second of John Caverly with brains and blood spattered and sliding on the white tiles of the bathroom of a cheap Vancouver hotel.

"Poets," I said, "are *especially* unbeloved."

He looked very sad.

"Once," I said, "there used to be poetry popular among the masses but now, under the baneful influence of television, such folk poetry is dying out."

"Pyotr Gregorevich wishes to know if you could quote a short example of such folk poetry."

I frowned.

I assumed a solemn voice, a *declaiming* voice, and said:

> *There was a young Fellow of King's*
> *Who cared not for whores and such things:*
> *His height of desire*
> *Was a boy in the choir*
> *With a bum like a jelly on springs.*

Madame Irena rumbled for a very long time and when she'd

228

finished Pyotr Gregorevich looked slightly bewildered.

I shrugged.

"Much," I said, "is lost in translation."

He nodded.

"I could," I said, "give you another example."

"I think you've gone far enough," said Corey.

Looking at Pyotr Gregorevich, I said:

> *An Argentine gaucho named Bruno*
> *Declared, 'There is one thing I do know:*
> *A woman is fine*
> *And a boy is divine*
> *But a llama is numero uno'.*

While the rumble of translation proceeded I smiled at Corey.

"I've always thought," I said, "that the *enjambement* there was a matter of considerable *finesse*."

"You are letting down your country!" he whispered.

This promising exchange was interrupted.

"Pyotr Gregorevich wishes to know at what age writers receive their pensions."

"Writers do not receive pensions," I said. "But when they are old and worn out those who have won the Governor-General's Award during their careers are given sinecures by The Canada Council. They are set to work in one of the publishing houses writing captions under the hockey photos."

Corey said,

"That is flatly untrue! Professor Wells is drunk!"

"Your denials," I said, "ring hollow!"

I stood up with my empty glass.

Corey stood up too and put his hand on my arm. I felt a sudden lurch, a slide towards the attraction of the dark.

"I think you've had *more* than enough to drink, Professor Wells."

With a kind of joy, I knocked his arm aside and said intensely and loudly enough to be heard by Madame Irena,

"I do not fear you, Corey! You can abuse my body but you will never kill my spirit!"

"For Christ's sake!" said Corey.

"Do not trifle with me, Corey! If you will, stifle, but do not trifle!"

"Jesus!" said Corey. "You're—"

I turned my back on him.

To Madame Irena, I said,

"I must visit the bathroom. If either of these gentlemen would care to be shown . . . ?"

Borkh rose eagerly.

As we walked away, there was a lot of excited Russian rumbling going on and Corey's voice plaintive. The bathroom was not in the Faculty Club but outside and at the end of a short corridor. As soon as we were inside, I put my finger to my lips. Then I cupped a hand to my ear and pointed to the corners of the room.

Borkh stared.

I scribbled on a sheet of paper from my notebook:

Corey is agent of Swann. Canadian counter-intelligence NOT Section B of RCMP. Repeat NOT. CANADA COUNCIL IS. Headed by Commander Swann. With CIA Swann now tunnelling to Soviet Embassy Ottawa. Power lines goal. New technology. Codename: Operation Sardine. Further details soonest mail. Coded on The Vertical Mosaic *by John Porter. Available bookstores.*

The bathroom was tiled white, lit by insane fluorescent lights. Borkh had not moved. I made a quick pantomime of looking in all the cubicles. Then I rushed from basin to basin turning on all the taps at full blast. I flushed three toilets.

I beckoned to Borkh.

He looked terrified.

I folded the note.

"Give this to Madame Irena," I said.

The rushing water sounded like the rushing in my head.

Borkh gawked.

"This," I said, tapping the paper. I mimed furtive giving.

"Madame Irena," I said.

Borkh frowned.

"If you do not," I said, "the KGB will get you. Dzerzhinsky Street."

I pointed at his chest.

"You in Lubianka Prison. *Lubianka.*"

He stared at me as if waiting for me to do a card-trick.

Trapped in a lav with a gormless Slav.

KGB? KGB?

It was on the tip of my tongue.

230

"Komit Gosudarstvennoi Bezopastnosti!"

His eyes widened.

He took the paper and started to say something in Russian, from its intonation a question.

I put my finger to my lips.

He seemed to be under some strain. He bolted himself into a cubicle.

I leaned my hands on the sides of the washbasin and stared into the mirror. I felt that I could weep. Kathy said my greying hair was attractive. Kathy was going to be angry again. It wasn't that kind of old I cared about. It was being tired. Used up. Too old and tired for the words to move again. I felt frightened. I stood in the roaring white-tiled washroom waiting for Borkh to emerge.

Chapter Fifteen

"... so I thought that a *cycle* is really a circle and a circle stops where it starts — you know what I mean — so as I'd started with conception which is the interruption of menses, then, to be *really* cyclic, I'd have to return to the re-establishment of regular menstruality. The flaw in my thinking, you see, Mr. Wells, was that I hadn't written about the afterbirth and post-partum hormonal imbalance and depression."

I let my head nod as if considering these technical problems of composition. She was wearing the pink crimplene pant-suit again. Under which lurked the possibility of pink, crimplene skin. Or *grey* crimplene skin. What engendering juices could have flowed in this arid woman to have provoked Mr. Strudly to the folly of paternity? To the folly even of penetration?

I was awaiting the arrival of Itzic Zemermann.

This, the first Friday of the second term, was to be our first encounter since my non-dinner at Hetherington's. Wednesday, my other contractual day, had been cancelled by Kathy by phone as I had not been feeling quite myself following Tuesday's Soviet festivities.

"Mmmm," I said. "Yes. So it's the *birth*..."

I felt extremely tense.

"... severing of the umbilical cord but *now*..."

I nodded again.

Although I had thought and brooded and agonized over what I was going to say to Itzic, *how* I was going to say it, although I had rehearsed the scene in every possible variety of way, I still had no clear idea of anything except that the matter was somehow of vital importance and that there was in me a core of extreme anger. I was no longer even sure if it was anger directed completely against Itzic or whether Itzic had become in some way some form of catalyst. For something. Whenever I tried to reason the why, the wherefore, the how, my thoughts flowed as into sand becoming nothing more than a dark stain.

I stared at the green blotter which I had been decorating with ballpoint stick-figures in a frieze of sword-play.

On Tuesday night the Director of Continuing Education had driven his car into one of the few elm trees on the campus not suffering from blight. There was a measure of satisfaction in that.

I saw that my pen had listed on the side of the blotter:

mossy dell
mons veneris
pubic mound
pubes
Brillo pad

"I beg your pardon, Mrs. Strudly?"

Her nasty nasal voice repeated the question. It was like a bass mosquito stuck in your ear.

"Well, I'm not Dear Abby," I said, "but you might try to stop thinking of conception as the interruption of menses."

She clutched her thin black binder and stared at me.

"What do you mean?"

"*Or*," I said, "and you see, I really don't *see* this as a technical problem, you could just *add on* the afterbirth and the . . . er . ."

"Well that's what I thought, really," she said.

"Good!" I said, standing up. "You have a go at the afterbirth, then, and then next week we'll . . . er . . . go into it."

I sat in my room and waited, my room with its bare walls, grey filing cabinet, oaken hat-stand. I looked at my watch again. The room was almost exactly the same size as a prison cell. It did not allow for pacing.

Opposite, the urinal stalls flushed themselves and then the cisterns refilled themselves, groaning, knocking, whining slowly into silence.

And then it came. The bang of the edge of the footplate against the door, the fumble with the handle, the door slamming back against the wall to reveal Itzic bent to propel himself through the gap.

He wheeled himself forward, stopped, hurled his torso to the side to slam shut the door, forward, stop, reversed with a clang into the filing cabinet.

I stood up, and nodded.

"Good morning, Mr. Zemermann," I said.

"*Mr.* Zemermann. *Mr.* Zemermann!" he panted. "Over the vacation we've become strangers?"

He began the long struggle with his muffler and woollen helmet, the contortions with his overcoat, the scarlet, panting struggle with his padded vest, the disposition of his lifeless legs.

He took off his spectacles, licked the ball of his thumb, applied it to the lenses. He huffed on them, buffed them on the slack trouser material of his thigh, affixed them.

I might just as well not have been there. For all my hours of resolution, my scenarios, I felt helpless.

He hauled up the bulging briefcase and with his good hand attacked the straps and buckles.

The withered hand lay on the manilla folder holding it in place while the good hand was turning papers.

He grunted.

He leaned forward from the chair with the sheet of paper.

I took it.

It read:

My Lute

In life there is much good
And so I say to my lute
"Sing, lute, you must tell
How my songs come from your deep well.
Sing my song of dreadful cheer
And cause people's hearts to be less drear."
I almost perished one awful night
But I am here to bring them light.

I read this slowly.

It was innocuous enough compared with the dactylic doings of the Gestapo and similar doggerel I'd previously endured but it was enough. It was what I had needed. I read it again.

It acted as a detonator.

"You 'say to your lute', do you, Mr. Zemermann? Do you possess a lute? What *is* a lute? Have you more than the vaguest idea? Have you ever handled a lute? *Seen* a lute? Because I'm fucked if I have!"

I slapped the sheet of paper.

"Where in God's name," I said, "do you *find* language like this!"

I stared at him.

He stared back.

"Lutes!" I said. "I may well be mistaken, and correct me if I'm wrong, but I think they were last used some three hundred years ago to accompany the jolly chaunting of all that jug-jug, twit-twittery. They were strummed upon, Mr. Zemermann, by lovelorn swains. They were listened to, Mr. Zemermann, by languishing bits of crumpet with tits like dumplings, during evenings given over to apple-bobbing and swilling from the wassail bowl."

I glared at him.

"Lutes," I said, "my *arse!*"

He shrugged.

His affronted owl shrug settling its plumage.

"One likes the rabbi," he said, "the other likes the rabbi's wife."

"*Pardon?*"

"I should please everyone?" he said. "So lutes you don't like."

"I don't like lutes, Mr. Zemermann. I don't like songs. I don't like singing. I don't like shepherds *and I don't like sheep!*"

"If you're feeling maybe a little off colour," he said, "I could come back on Wednesday?"

I ripped the sheet of paper in half, in quarters, into tiny scraps. I hurled them at the wall.

"Dr. Gamahuche said such verse he'd . . ."

"Dr. Gamahuche," I said, "is a buffoon."

He stared at me through his smeared lenses, doubtless secure in his knowledge of the lambency of Dr. Gamahuche's opinion.

"There are matters between you and me, Mr. Zemermann. The first of them is the matter of your selected *Singing Bones*. I don't like being *used*, Mr. Zemermann. I am not saying anything, at the moment, about the circumstances of the printing of this material. That is a matter for Professor Hetherington to pursue. But you do *not*, Mr. Zemermann, lend *my* name to your dubious enterprises without *my* permission."

I sat down in the swivel chair.

"But that is not the chief way in which you have used me. You have done worse."

He said nothing.

He just sat.

"I find all this," I said, "and what I am *going* to say extremely painful and embarrassing."

I opened the screeching file-drawer in the desk and took out a bottle of scotch and two of the glasses I kept there. I poured two stiff drinks.

As I stood up, I handed him a glass and said,

"I am going to talk to you about poetry, Mr. Zemermann. I want no comments from you, no interruptions of any kind. Is that understood?"

He did not reply.

"Is that understood?"

He shrugged assent.

I took a sip of scotch and went over to the window and stood with my back to him. I looked out over the playing field. It would be easier to say what I wanted to say if I didn't have to look at him.

I stared towards the concrete edge of CAC.

"There's a line of verse, Mr. Zemermann, from a not very good poem by a very minor poet that's somehow lodged itself in my mind."

I think continually of those who were truly great.

"It's from a poem which isn't even about poets or poetry but all poets, all *real poets do* think continually about those who were truly great. Not with envy. Not with a selfish ambition. But with humility. They walk with them."

I rolled another sip of scotch around my mouth.

"Old Wordsworth," I said, "decribed poetry as 'the breath and finer spirit of all knowledge'. Yeats spoke of it as 'the chief voice of the conscience' and for all his fairies at the bottom of the garden and Spirit Guides, he was probably right."

Below me a file of jogging professors slogged round the field in the slush and mud.

"When Yeats died, Auden wrote an intensely moving poem in his memory and I'd like to quote to you, Mr. Zemermann, a couple of verses of that poem."

236

Time that is intolerant
Of the brave and innocent
And indifferent in a week
To a beautiful physique

Worships language and forgives
Everyone by whom it lives;
Pardons cowardice, conceit,
Lays its honours at their feet.

"I believe that, Mr. Zemermann."

My breath fogged the glass.

"I know it's unfashionable to be earnest about anything, but I believe that."

Track suits, red, blue, green, there a yellow one. Toiling past.

"And I'd like to quote you something else of Auden's. It's the last line of a sonnet in tribute to Edward Lear."

And children swarmed to him like settlers. He became a land.

Tears started in my eyes.

He became a land.

I rested my forehead against the cold windowpane.

That was what Caverly had become.

John.

I watched the coloured track suits.

As Auden had himself.

The urinals flushed, groaned, knocking in the pipes, the cisterns filling whining slowly into silence.

"I couldn't feel more continually concerned, more outraged than I do, Mr. Zemermann, about the Nazi extermination of the Jews. I can only hope that you will believe me when I say that. I have said the same thing to you before. It was, you may recall, a conversation last term during which you lied to me about writing in Yiddish and at the end of which you suffered, or claimed to suffer, an attack of angina."

I opened the window's cold brass catch and then forced it home again.

"What you suffered, Mr. Zemermann, what you saw, what you felt, I don't think I can understand. I have read, seen photographs, seen documentary films of those camps, Mr. Zemermann, and I must confess to you that my emotions could not grasp what they were seeing."

237

I paused.

"And then, those horrors past, a senseless fate struck again and left you crippled."

I kept on staring towards the edge of CAC and concentrated on making what I was looking at an exercise in perspective. I took a breath and plunged on.

"Yet, Mr. Zemermann, there is a sense in which you're a fraud. At about the time they were strumming on their bloody lutes in England, and I suppose it's lutes that put me in mind of this, there were rogues wandering about called Abram-men, thieves and beggars who pretended madness to receive charity. Elizabethan con men, I suppose you'd call them. There was a cant expression 'to sham Abraham' which meant to pretend distress or illness to get off work. It's a harsh accusation to make, Mr. Zemermann, but I think *you* 'sham Abraham'. Such as our conversation about your use of Yiddish. You trade on your afflictions. And worse, you use poetry as a vehicle of that trade.

I wouldn't be saying these things to you if you were like the rest. But you aren't. You publish. And you profess poetry. And you profess it to a public too ignorant to know the difference.

Your subject matter is events from which no decent person is free. And there are many people, particularly in places like this, Gamahuches, who are all too willing to take upon themselves the sufferings of the world instead of getting on with their jobs. It's these people, kind, properly liberal, suffused with guilt for every damn thing in the world, guilty that they're even half-alive, these are the ones who've encouraged you, tolerated you, allowed you to use them."

I rubbed the windowpane clear with the sleeve of my jacket.

"Well, Mr. Zemermann, you can count me out. Poetry isn't self-aggrandizement. If anything, it's the opposite. So I'm not going to be used by you any more in *that* way. And I'm not going to be *drained* by you, drained of emotion and strength to feed whatever the hell it is that you're feeding. Find someone else to batten on."

He gave a loud gasp and started to say something.

"*No!*" I said. "I told you not to interrupt. And I'm not finished."

I could hear him moving.

"Poetry, Mr. Zemermann? You've never written a line in your life that wasn't drivel!"

He dropped his glass.

"Leave it!" I said sharply. "Leave it alone. This is unpleasant for both of us. Let's not prolong it."

The puffing professors in their coloured suits were performing clumsy exercises, a gross chorus-line.

"I can't prevent you from betraying language," I said. "I can't prevent you from publishing your gibberish. I wish I could. And there's nothing I can teach you. I've tried but you've exhausted me. So what I want to do is this. I want to come to an agreement. Strike a bargain with you. And the deal is this.

I don't want to read any more of your fucking songs. Not a single lugubrious word of it. And I don't want you to set foot in this office again. Come to see me, I mean. In return for which, I'll gladly give you a credit for this farcical non-course I'm supposed to be running."

I groped in my jacket pocket for cigarettes and matches.

"Well?"

He didn't say anything.

"Is it a bargain?"

I turned from the window.

He was slumped over the left side of his wheelchair.

His head was hanging. His spectacles lay across his wasted thighs, the side pieces sticking up.

"Mr. Zemermann?"

I bent over him.

"Itzic?"

I touched him.

He was unarguably dead.

Chapter Sixteen

On the evening of the day of Itzic's death I arrived home very late with a Family Bucket of Kentucky Fried Chicken and a man called Owen who had been forsaken by his wife and who worked in a factory that made armatures. There had been a juke-box in the tavern and Owen had played Tammy Wynette singing "Stand By Your Man" until the owner of the tavern had refused to change any more bills into quarters and had unplugged the juke-box because of complaints.

Owen had suggested a game of blackjack but Kathy couldn't find the cards.

The hours after that were confusion, the divisions of the day, the times of waking and sleeping blurred. I was drinking. I remember only fragments. I remember Kathy insisting that I eat a bowl of cornflakes in the middle of the night. I remember waking to darkness and to daylight. White tiles and yellowed grout in the glaring bathroom, the stumbling floor. Kathy in a nightgown, her feet bare, frying eggs and bacon. And talking. Every meal seemed to be breakfast.

Whenever I started from sleep, my neck and hair damp with sweat, the images of my sleep lingered, a vast pair of spectacles such as those which advertise an optician's store but smeared and behind the smeared lenses eyes which regarded me with hurt. An endless institutional corridor and at a distance, tiny, but advancing with the jerky movements of a mechanical toy, a wheelchair. In a courtroom I stood in a glass cage. There were microphones, wires, and speakers which amplified proceedings at unbearable volume. Complex recording machines, red needles quivering, spun slow reels. My poems were being read aloud to me in an unknown foreign language which I somehow understood.

Waking, I went over and over every scene with Itzic straining to fix everything that had been said, trying to capture every nuance, striving to establish an accurate transcript so that motivations could be evaluated, actions judged.

But the closer I tried to grapple with words the more slippery they became. Words led to other words, words far from my intentions. Some by repetition became meaningless sound. Others, accusatory, turned to patterns, pleasing rhetoric.

His death lies at your door.

Said my head.

Slain not by bloodstained hands but by hubris, by a heart hardened . . .

I could not still the mad babble.

The contemptuous glance of counsel:

Not, members of the jury, with a knife but just as surely with sharp words . . .

On and on, this incessant verbiage betraying the reality of his death. Betraying: the slack mouth, the enlarged pores in his nose, the disposition of limbs under the red blanket, the way one of the blue-uniformed men had worked and tugged the balaclava helmet onto the lolling head, the rubber wheels along the corridor whispering.

I remember the whiteness of Kathy's blouse turned grey in patches with the dampness of my tears.

I sat in the bathtub cold with the water run out and dismissed Kathy's palliatives. Had not Faulkner said that the writer's only

241

responsibility was to his art? Had not Faulkner said that if a writer had to rob his mother he should not hesitate for the "Ode on a Grecian Urn" was worth any number of old ladies? *And had I not agreed with him?* Could she deny that? At Christmas? In my house? That she had provoked me was irrelevant. And why would she have said what she said were it not true? The hair on my legs and arms was dark and flat as if combed, stiff, simian. And why would she have said what she said if she had not *felt* it to be true?

There my case rested.

Kathy undid the string and brown paper and inside was a pair of pyjamas in a plastic bag. She said they would help me to sleep better. I did not see why. Feeling clean and new, she said, was always relaxing. I remember putting on the pyjamas and looking down at myself. And then I ripped them off. Buttons, the jacket tore. And I remember her face and shouting at her:

They're striped!
Striped!

I ripped open a new carton of beer and restocked the fridge. The level in the bottle of scotch was dangerously low. After endless hours of talk and argument and after hours of solitary consideration, I had come to see that I was not solely responsible for Itzic's death. As Kathy had said, he could have died at any time. And the fact that his heart *had* been weak did not necessarily invalidate Hetherington's suspicion, Hetherington's *certainty*, that previous 'attacks' had not been genuine. But these points and others like them now filled me with impatience. They were like managing to join together two small bits of blue perhaps sky or perhaps sea in a thousand-piece jigsaw puzzle of a naval engagement.

Had the university not embraced the fallacy that a university ought to be a democratic institution, Itzic and I would never have met in the first place. His death in my office, even my *being* in an office in a university, was part of a complex fabric. Examining a thread here, a thread there, would not yield up the secret of the pattern. It was not even altogether fanciful, I thought, as I shifted a bottle of purple horseradish to make room for another can of beer, not fanciful at all to think of Itzic's death as having been foretold in de Tocqueville.

It was a complicated matter and though I had been, in a sense, instrumental, there were endless ramifications and it was to these ramifications that I was giving myself up.

"You may think," I called to Kathy from the kitchen, chocking one ice cube on top of another and crackling more scotch over them, "you may think I'm merely in my cups but mine is not a lone voice."

She was lying on the couch.

I sat in the armchair again.

"Hello?" I said.

"What?"

"Not a lone voice at all," I said. "Research is on-going. Scientists put TV sets in playpens. Kids thought it was their mother. They developed towards it what is known as an affective relationship. When the sets were withdrawn and the mothers put in the playpens 13% more children exhibited symptoms of marked regression as measured on the open-ended Neilson scale."

"I'm *trying* to read," said Kathy.

"Plus or minus, of course," I said, "one standard deviation."

She did not look up.

"Ever heard of 'Television Knee'?" I said.

"Why don't you try lying down again?" she said.

"The American Medical Association reports a significant increase in damage to the patella and lower lumber regions in men and women between the ages of 18 and 40. People get it by engaging doggy-fashion so as not to miss their favourite programmes."

I lighted another cigarette.

"Talking of which," I said, "I had a doggy when I was a kid. And my father gave me this booklet called *The Care of Your Dog.* Some such title. But there was a sentence in it I've always remembered. Do you know what it said?"

"What?"

"Well, *I* thought it was interesting and there's no need to be snappish. Knowledge is power. This sentence said: *A dog's sense of smell is so acute it can detect one drop of urine in a million drops of water."*

"Amazing," said Kathy.

"Well, it *is*," I said. "Mine was defective though. It couldn't detect its food bowl. And it died by not being able to detect a railway train. It is from that period of grief that I date the decline of my interest in science. But it certainly makes you think."

"Mmm," said Kathy.

"Guys that work down in the sewers in New York, they're issued with the exact timing of all the commercial breaks during peak viewing hours. Did you know that? Before that, before they'd figured out what was going on, they'd lost men swept out to sea, every 8¾ minutes on tidal waves of excrement."

I wandered over to the window.

"'Viewing,'" I said. "Isn't that a foul word? Like 'authoring'. Though 'viewing' does somehow suggest that *lobotomized* quality, I suppose. Could you *say* it? Could you say, 'Last night I viewed the CBC news'?"

"*Please*, Jim. Just try to be quiet for a bit."

"I used to be embarrassed," I said. "In restaurants. But now I read it all out *in a loud voice*: I would like two farm-fresh free-range golden eggs with extra-lean back bacon from your farm in Windsor, preceded by the sun-loved orange juice. Not that it makes any difference. They have no sense of shame. I once got punched in the eye in an Italian restaurant for trying to explain to the proprietor the conventional use of inverted commas. Know what I read the other day? The word 'fanzine'."

"What?" said Kathy.

"Fanzine. It means 'fan magazine'."

I stared out into the night.

"There's a whole world of it out there," I said.

"Won't you eat *something*?" said Kathy. "A sandwich?"

"I'm not hungry."

It was snowing again.

"I was on a bus once," I said, "sitting next to this fat woman. Very jolly sort. And she'd just been to collect her husband's ashes. She had them in a Loblaws shopping bag with some tangerines. Not *loose*. In a sort of pot. And she said they weren't at all like fire ashes. Not powder at all. Do you know what she said they were like?"

"What?" said Kathy.

"*Fish scales.*"

"Hmm!" said Kathy.

I turned from the window and wandered across to the table. I

picked up the chunk of quartz. I considered it and said,
'I knew him well. A fellow of infinite jest.'

"Don't drop that!" said Kathy. "You'll break the table."

"Did you read that book about Nixon's presidential campaign?" I said. "Know the book I mean? The first campaign in history that was waged purely on TV. An ad agency sold him like — well, soap or like a vaginal deodorant where you're not allowed to mention vaginas or what, exactly, the product does or why. Which is a fitting comparison when you think about it. But you know the name of the guy that directed it, made all the commercials? Shakespeare. Honest. Frank Shakespeare."

I put down the quartz.

"Kathy? let's say that the statistically average viewer . . ."

The doorbell rang.

Kathy jumped up.

"That'll be Betty," she said going out.

There was conversation in the hall.

She came back in with a Bayer aspirin bottle, the large size, full of pink liquid.

"What's that?"

"It's some of Betty's stuff to help you sleep. You haven't slept for more than two or three hours at a stretch for three days and you must, Jim. You need to. You're going to get really sick."

"Yes, but listen, I've been thinking about this . . ."

"I'll listen if you'll eat a couple of sandwiches."

I followed her into the kitchen and poured the last of the scotch.

"It doesn't matter what the *actual* figure's supposed to be, alleged to be," I said, "but let's say that people watch television for 35 hours a week."

"Cheese or pâté?"

"Now even the smallest kid knows that redskins *don't* bite the dust, right. They know it's all actors, it's all pretend."

"Um-hm."

"Everybody knows it's a convention, understands it as a convention, right?"

"I suppose so," she said. "Before you eat those, you've got to drink this."

She poured the pink stuff into a glass. The taste of raspberries masked a taste harshly chemical. I shuddered and chased it down with scotch.

"Where was I? *Convention*. Right. Black and white — blah — blah."

I waved a hand to dismiss the obviousness of these lines of argument.

"So the central point is that it's all understood as *unreal*."

"Oh, God!" said Kathy. "What if it's synergistic!"

"*What!*"

"Alcohol and the whatsit. The pink stuff."

"Listen! Pay attention. Like a steel trap the mind is closing on the problem."

"Do you think I ought to phone the hospital? To enquire? What did Betty say it *was*?"

"*When I've finished*," I said, "when I've finished, you can phone Dial-a-Prayer if it's any comfort."

"*Seconal!*" said Kathy. "That's it!"

"That Arbus woman," I said, "is clever but nasty. Exploitive. But all those arty photographers plagiarize painters anyway so we're not concerned with them. They're not the point. Where were we? *Unreal*."

"Doesn't it happen with cheese and something?" said Kathy. "There was a murder case in France."

"So following on from *that*, it means that the photographing of something that *is* real instantly makes it *unreal*."

She stared at me with a worried expression.

"So much," I said, "for *cinéma verité* and other such Gallic *merde*."

"Or was it insulin?" she said.

"*Kathy!*"

"Photographing real things makes them unreal," she said. "Yes. That's a bit of a jump, isn't it?"

"No," I said. "It precisely is not. How else could people eat their dinners while watching genocide or the Viet Nam pleasantries?"

"Mmmm."

"*Because*," I said, "they know it's John Wayne. *Or* they don't even see it at all. A snippet of war, a homerun, floorwax, a touch of starvation in the sub-Sahara — it's all the same thing."

She nodded.

"Miracle Whip," I said.

"Mmm."

"Remember Biafra?" I said ripping off the tab from a can of

beer. "Brought to you by Inter-Foods? Makers of Yummies? For Which Your Dog Begs?"

I bumped the door of the fridge shut.

"*Please* don't have another drink," she said.

"Remember those horror movies where the only ones unaffected by It or Them were the young reporter and his girlfriend? They gaze out over the stricken city. He says, 'Terrifying things have happened to people's brains'. Well he was fucking well right."

I drank from the can.

Kathy's eyes followed.

"Look!" I said. "If I'm going to be synergized it's already got half a bottle of scotch to work on anyway. I love you very much and absolve you from all responsibility. I shall cease upon the midnight with no pain. O.K.?"

I set the can down on the table.

"*Now*," I said, "all the foregoing is not at all original. *But* — and this is where it gets more complicated — although it's true that movies and TV and photography render the real unreal, it's equally true that a growing number of people no longer really believe that things *are* real *unless* they see them on TV. Or, with a slightly different emphasis, the things they see on TV are more real than the things they see for themselves."

"Careful!" said Kathy, moving away the empty scotch glass.

"*Well?*"

"But you just said," she said, "that they don't see things on TV."

"What I *meant*," I said, "was that they don't see *real* things. Or perceive the real as real. They see fiction as real, or the real as fiction, or both. Or possibly neither. I haven't got that bit worked out yet."

"Are you feeling drowsy?" said Kathy.

"It gets confusing, you see, because it seems that the only things that are really believed to be true, *felt* to be true, are the things that are known to be untrue. Which is confusing. Unless we're talking about art which we aren't."

"How do you feel?" said Kathy.

"Fine," I said.

But I wasn't. I was feeling weird.

"But," I said, "if the real becomes unreal then it ought to be believed but it isn't."

I stared at the colours and writing on the beer can. Somewhere,

247

it seemed, there was something wrong with the argument. I felt secure enough about its general sweep and conclusion . . .

"Jim?"

"Umm?"

"What's making you think about all this so much?" said Kathy. "All this stuff about photographs and TV?"

I stared at her in amazement.

Her inability to grasp arguments, to see the point of things, sometimes astonished me. Her incomprehension seemed genuine.

"What I've been talking about all night," I said.

"What?" she said.

"Concentration camps!"

She regarded me.

"What I said to Itzic!"

"What?"

"What I *told* you. That I'd said I'd seen photographs and film of concentration camps but I couldn't grasp — emotionally — what I was seeing."

"Oh, Jim!" she said. *"Please.* You must stop this — this blaming yourself. It wasn't your fault."

"No, no," I said. "It's not that. I'm just trying to work out what's going on. There's a *reason* for all this, you see."

She looked at me and nodded.

"How do you feel now?" she said. "Sleepy?"

"Fine," I said.

"I think we'd better go to bed," she said.

"Perhaps it *is* like a horror film," I said, fumbling with my shirt buttons. "Perhaps there's a sort of photo world. Like living in a negative. Perhaps there's a paraworld. Understand what I mean?"

I had trouble with my trousers.

"They're all schizophrenics, you see, and they move between the world and the paraworld until they live in the paraworld all the time. And then they can't come out any more."

I lay in bed and Kathy sat on the edge and held my hand.

It was worse lying down. Horizons receding.

Waves.

I made a last effort to make it all very clear.

"It's central to the whole thing — what I'm working on — that American evangelist. Do you know who I mean? With a name like a dentist?"

"Yes," she said. "Mmm."

"He tells sick people to put their hands on the screen to be healed. Can you imagine that? How sad?"

Her hand was stroking my hair.

"People alone in rooms pressing television sets."

"Go to sleep now," she said. "Go to sleep."

"So sad."

"Yes."

Waves.

The light switched off.

Sad.

I felt her lips on my forehead.

I awoke in the mid-morning. I lay for a few minutes half-held in a dream of driving through a hopeless maze of lanes in Mount Royal Cemetery looking for Itzic's grave and always arriving back at the place I'd started from and the taxi driver repeating:

If only we knew the exact location of the bereaved.

I opened my eyes and stared at the grain and texture of the white wall.

I felt weak and filleted.

I closed my eyes again.

One summer at the house, it was a memory that often intruded, the sort of memory that nudged at me as the germs of poems did but a memory too singular and odd to lend itself to anything but recall, one summer I had borrowed Hollis' truck to take a growing collection of rubbish I couldn't burn down to the municipal dump.

The dump was deserted. Even the pressed-board shack like a sentry box with the word 'Office' daubed on it where Floyd sat over his kingdom in bifocals was empty. The day was hot and still. The open trench was burning. Dense clouds of white, acrid smoke and the stench of rotting garbage hung over the site. Somewhere further down the trench, tires were burning. I backed the truck to the edge of the trench and started to chuck the plastic fertilizer bags of garbage down onto the cardboard boxes, the split green sacks of liquifying waste, the tins, cloth that had once been clothes, rusted machine parts, bicycle frames, the wreckage of an old incubator.

Resting for a moment, I looked across at the holes in the strata of the grey clay's opposite wall and remembered old Floyd's telling me that the fires didn't worry the rats none, burrowed deeper and waited the bastards, come out again when it was cooked.

As I stood there at the edge of the trench, I heard music from somewhere in the pall of smoke. I walked along and peered down onto a heap of green garbage bags and old paint-cans. A grapefruit rind. The fire was burning fiercely there, feeding and climbing on oil and paint, crackling up through the dry twigs of a dead bush, and the music faded and a gabbling voice said:

And now here's a timely message for all you sweltering folk out there in Summer Land. Hurry . . .

And then a sudden breeze rushed the flame fiercely and there was silence.

I rolled over and stared at the hanging fern.

Kathy said the fern was called *Nephrolepsis* which I wished she hadn't told me because it sounded like a disease connected with synapses which if it existed I felt it likely I had.

While she was making coffee and toast, I went into the bathroom. I studied myself in the mirror. I didn't feel too bad, considering. Nothing a few aspirins wouldn't cure. The stubble on my face was thick and itchy. The bristles were beginning to grow grey. I dislike being unshaven. I'd reached the Yasser Arafat stage. Whose hairiness is one of the central mysteries of contemporary politics. He is either unshaven or incapable of growing a beard. And presumably he isn't incapable of growing a beard because if he can grow *some* it seems likely he can grow more. But if he's unshaven, how is it that every photograph shows him *at the same stage of unshavenness?* Does he go into seclusion for four or five days after each shave? And if so, why? Something to do, possibly, with the Koran?

I looked at the hair on my chest.

Sad and stealing messengers of grey.

Kathy called me.

I went into the kitchen and sat at the table. I sipped the coffee.

"Feeling better?" she said. "Less upset?"

"Terrific," I said. "I feel fine, love."

"I thought for a while you'd died," she said, "until the snoring started. I had to sleep on the couch."

"I'm sorry, Kathy."

"Well it was my fault. I phoned Betty and she said the bottle was supposed to be for two nights."

I took some aspirins and buttered the toast.

"What are you frowning about?" she said.

"Nothing. I was just thinking about Yasser Arafat."

I rubbed my bristles.

"You'd look horrible with a beard," she said.

"Well, more about *photographs* of Yasser Arafat."

"Oh," said Kathy.

She put her toast down and looked at me, that grave, considering look.

"And you know something else that's significant?"

"What's that, Jim?"

"Well, family gatherings and suchlike where everybody takes Polaroid snaps of everybody and then everybody passes them round looking at them to see what everybody looks like. There's something very peculiar about that. Isn't there? Don't you think so? The picture more real than the person? You know, they're taken with flash bulbs and Aunt Emily stops being Aunt Emily and becomes this rabid creature with bright red eyes and everyone says how much weight she's put on. While she's actually *there* and they wouldn't dream of saying such a thing to *her*."

"I suppose it *is* a bit peculiar," said Kathy. "There's apricot jam if you . . ."

"A lot of implications there, you see."

She looked at me and put her hand over mine.

"It wasn't you," she said. "It wasn't your fault."

"I love you very much," I said.

"Yes," she said. "I know."

We were silent for a moment.

"Coffee?" she said.

"But you see where I'm going, don't you? It's Aunt Emily, you see. Or the *reverse* of Aunt Emily. *That's* the point. It isn't the enormity of it you can't grasp or the horror — which is what everyone says. It's that you know it isn't real."

"Mmmm," said Kathy. "That *is* interesting."

She nodded.

I put the top on the jar of jam. She put the butter in the fridge.

Clatter of plates and knives in the sink.

"You know, Jim," she said, "you haven't been out in days. Why don't we? Go out for lunch?"

"Sure," I said.

"I can do some shopping and then we'll find somewhere . . ."

"Fine," I said. "Good idea."

251

As I was standing under the shower, I realized that I was far less anxious than I'd been feeling. Everything necessary was *there*, just beyond reach, and would resolve itself in its own good time. A magician's impossibly knotted rope a simple pull would untangle.

Kathy had phoned for a taxi. We stood waiting in the entrance hall by the mailboxes. Hot air from the register blew on us. A woman passed by outside bundled up to her nose against the cold.

As the cab carried us along residential streets, I watched mailmen, dogs on their busy errands, toddlers in bright snowsuits being hauled over snow banks. A woman on a porch between cedars sprinkling salt from a yellow paper sack. As we approached the downtown area, traffic began to clot, the cab sitting, the meter ticking.

"What you see through a window," I said, "isn't at all what's there."

"What?"

"Ever thought how much *glass* there is?"

"Glass? What do you mean?"

"Well," I said, "being in a car's rather like watching a movie, isn't it?"

She didn't reply.

"Oh, look!" she said. "That's the place Malcolm was talking about—where they sell buffalo steaks."

"Did he tell you about his latest?" I said. "The one from the sauna in Central Station? They lie in bed and Malcolm licks the tattoo on the guy's bicep."

"He's a very good cook," she said.

"But what I mean is," I said, "well—take the track between Hollis' place and mine. If you walk it, you know how far it is. Your muscles map it. But if you drive you don't know. You see things through glass like a movie. You see but in another way you don't see anything at all."

She turned towards me and said,

"Jim, I *do* understand and I understand how you feel. But it's in the past. You have to try to forget about it. Other people have lived through worse."

"If you're walking," I said, "you see individual plants and you can see *why* they're there. Why this grows here but not there, the depths of the rock, where the water runs."

"I'm hungry already," she said. "Are you?"

"But from a car," I said, "through glass, you just see 'a field'."

"I suppose you're right," she said. "Still, we can't go back to that, can we?"

I shrugged.

The cab drew up at one of the entrances to Place Duplessis and I paid the driver. Place Duplessis was one of the newer constructions, four massive octagonal towers which contained stores, banks, offices, and apartments. The towers were interconnected by a maze of shopping galleries. Every few yards there were coloured maps to tell you where you were. On the maps the towers were called 'Nodes'. Uniformed ladies at Information Centres directed the hopelessly trapped. Wherever the eye looked there were angles, vistas, slopes, overhead walkways, diagonal gantries, all of raw concrete, the whole doubtless expressive of some new human vision which I didn't want to know about.

Attempts had been made to soften the concrete with green architectural shrubs in tubs. Soft music played. Escalators conveyed torsos and legs up and down. Moving walkways trundled people into the horrible boutiques. Electric waterfalls ribbled over abstract plexiglass. People threw pennies into pools.

A woman wearing a clown costume was giving helium-filled balloons to children. The balloons sat in the middle of the air. They said: Place Duplessis. They had ears.

On Concourse Three south of Node One, Kathy stood at the mouth of a boutique flipping blouses on a clattering, circular stand.

"Is that the size or the price?"

"It's awful, isn't it?" she said. "And you just can't *buy* cotton. I think it's disappeared."

"Like blotting paper," I said. "I don't like it here. It's like a sort of secular hospital."

Concourse Three opened into a concrete clover-leaf. A diagonal row of moving heads was visible on Concourse Four. I extended my arms into a rifle position and made *bang* noises.

"Hit three," I said, "and you get a balloon."

"Stop being silly," she said. "People are staring at you."

She wandered towards the escalator. I trailed after her.

"Have you ever read Frank Lloyd Wright?" I said as we were carried upward. *"The Natural House?* Interesting book. It makes *Mein Kampf* look like an exercise in self-effacement. Mad as a hatter. Hello? Katherine? I'm *talking* to you."

"Just keep your voice down!" said Kathy, turning round. "Just stop it."

"He was quite wrong about glass, of course," I said, "but he talks of scaling buildings down to fit the normal human height. And then — get this — he says *'ergo 5' 8½"* tall. This is my own height'. I enjoyed that. Good God!" I said, pointing, as we were deposited on Concourse Four. "Look at *her!*"

Competing perfumes wafted from a strange sort of hut thing thatched with palm fronds where a gaunt creature sat under a sign that said: *If he Asks... It's Terracotta.* Her cheek bones were covered with round patches of pale brown make-up. Her hair was short and drastically thinned and plastered on her head as if with Brylcreem. Her lips were brown too.

"Just *look!*" I said.

"Shss!" said Kathy. "She's a model."

"I didn't think she was Pocahontas."

I stared as we passed.

"*If* he asks!" I said. "He'd be fucking well *bound* to say *something*, wouldn't he? You ought to buy her a sandwich. Her clavicles stick out further than her tits. I hate it here. I'm warning you. I'm beginning to feel not well."

"Just look at these," said Kathy and disappeared into a boutique whose window was full of deformed boots and orthpaedic clogs hung on barn boards and wooden wagon wheels. A window-dresser in paper slippers was in an agony of creative indecision about what to do with a rusted scythe.

In the window opposite stood dummies draped with furs, wigless, and wearing sun-glasses. The baldness made them look peculiarly obscene and degenerate. Made them look like unrepentant collaborators.

Eaton's depressed me. Alexis Nihon Plaza made me feel hysterical. This was like being in a concrete realization of one of Piranesi's *Carceri d'Invenzione.*

How joyous it would have been to see grim men in fatigues advancing down the walks smashing in the glass, herding out the dazed consumers, tossing grenades into the boutiques of embroidered jeans, into the Krazy Kitchen Korner with its electric knives, gas-powered-wine-cork-removers, microwave hot-dog-warmers, and digital-egg-timers, how joyous the raging of molotov cocktails amongst the Gucci and Pucci.

"Oh, there you are!" said Kathy. "I thought you'd got lost."

"Get me out of here. Where's the way out?"

The escalator carried us downwards. Suspended *Nephrolepsis* appeared and disappeared.

"Oh!" said Kathy. "I *must* get some Liquid Paper stuff and thinner. They'll have it in here."

It was a chain bookstore.

"Oh, Christ, *no!*"

"I know," she said, "but it *is* convenient. And then we'll go for lunch. Promise."

While she wandered off towards the back, I stared numbly at the hundreds of inconceivable book bargains. Everything was sealed in plastic so that it couldn't be read. I drifted past the sections: Organic, Diet, Woodstoves, Classics, Sexual Inadequacy, Parenting, How To.

Stopped.

How to: *Become a Person*
           Overcome Depression
           Survive on Roots and Herbs.

Drifted on.

Posters. Posters of rock groups. Of androgynous teen entertainers.

Pictorial History of—stared—*Trotsky.*

Joy in Sex.

'Strength Through Joy'

Under a large maple leaf, Canadiana. Pioneer stuff. Railway stuff by the large man. Native Peoples stuff. The Great Spirit sealed in plastic and selling like hot cakes. *The Book of Canadian Weeds.* Piles of that perennial favourite *Great Canadian Disasters.*

I came to rest in front of a table heaped with remainders. A dangling card said: *99 cents.* I stared without really seeing at spines and coloured covers. Some were paper, some cloth. *Now a Major Motion...* I read. *Based on the TV Series...* read another. I picked up a book with a picture on the dust-jacket of a girl in a white dress under trees draped with Spanish moss, in the background the portico of a white house, let the pages flip, antebellum heiress stuff. Then stood staring shocked at what had been beneath. Everything sharpened. The slight flutter of the fluorescence. The orchestral arrangement piped by the muzak of a Beatles tune. I stared at the book. Staring at me from the book's back cover was John Caverly.

It was his *Collected Poems.* There was a pile. There were nineteen copies. The book had been published three years before. Or was it four now? I picked up the top copy and stood there holding it against my chest and gazing towards the front of the shop. Across the gap of the entrance passed a balloon with ears.

Memories locked my throat in pain.

At the end of the launching party for the book I clutched, after the last smile, the last flash bulb, the last courteous answer to the last tedious question, I'd helped John back to the Royal York hotel. I'd been shocked at how tired he was. In the elevator he had stood with feet planted, head hanging.

Kathy was beside me nudging me saying something.

I turned and looked at her.

I pointed.

I gathered up the nineteen books and carried them to the cash register in the front. The girl knew nothing. The manager was a polite young man. I asked him whether the books had come directly from the publisher or through a jobber, whether there were more. He said that, regrettably, company policy did not permit him to divulge information of that nature. There were, he said, no regional variables. All the stores were serviced, he informed me, by Central Ordering at Head Office in Toronto to which all such queries should be communicated.

I thanked him for his help. I paid for the books with a Chargex card. The Caverly one. It put the card out of play but the sacrifice seemed appropriate.

I raised my wine glass in salutation to the five copies of the *Collected Poems* on the mantelpiece and sipped. Other copies stood on the glass table, the desk, the bureau, and the window sill.

On the way home from Place Duplessis, I'd stopped off at the Maison des Vins and bought a bottle of Château Lafite-Rothschild (1961) and a bottle of Château Margaux (1966).

The price had made me blench but the occasion demanded.

I looked up at the books over the rim of the glass.

"He was dead wrong, you know."

"Who was?" said Kathy.

"Shakespeare. All that posterity stuff. Such as,

Not marble, nor the gilded monuments
Of princes, shall outlive this powerful rhyme.

256

Ha!"

I set the glass on the arm of the chair.

"Silly William!" I said. "Posterity? We're talking about *shelf-life*, William. Can't you get that through your wig? If the groundlings in the grocery haven't gobbled it up in three weeks, off come the covers. Here's a scene for you. This is the Bard authoring in Toronto. One of the trade editors takes him out for lunch at The Three Small Rooms and after they've had a snootful, the editor — who's an ex-teacher or ex-salesman — the editor says:

'Well, we've been going through the financials, Bill, and I guess it's no secret we took a bath on *Macbeth*. And now you've come up with this — right, *Hamlet*. Now *you* know it's good, Bill, and *I* know it's good but what we're looking at here is the bottom line.' Exit pursued by Bear.

"Ah, Katherine! My lovely Katherine! What a falling off there's been! When Byron published *Childe Harold*, Lady Caroline Lamb sent him a letter with clippings of her pubic hair. What do *I* get? Letters from Mr. Archambault of the Taxation Data Centre. That's what I get. And threats from his bully-boy — a Ms. Thing of the Civil Litigation Section of the Department of Justice."

I got up and stood in front of the mantelpiece. One of the dust-jackets had ridden up. I tapped it down with my forefinger. I moved one of the books back so that the five were in line.

"It's as well he's dead," I said. "I'm glad."

Kathy sighed.

"Jim?"

"Umm?"

"No," she said. "I don't know. I'm sorry. I don't know what to say."

"Your life's work," I said, "remaindered in a cook book and tit poster emporium."

There was silence.

"But what can you *do* about it?" said Kathy. "What can anybody do?"

"Well, yes, that's the rub," I said. "But we can start with our publisher. A little inter-personal communication seems needful. They give courses in it at community colleges."

I found the number in my notebook.

As I started to dial, Kathy said,

"But what *good* will it do?"

"*Good*," I said, "is precisely the point. Shining in a naughty world. Being a sunbeam for Him. You in your small corner and I in mine. Didn't you go to Sunday School?"

I listened to the mysterious clickings on the line and then to more clickings as the call was redirected from the switchboard of Avery and McLeod to McLeod's office. Avery was defunct.

"Don't talk nonsense, Maria," I said. "'In conference' indeed! It'd strain his intellect to confer with a myna bird. Yes, of *course* it's me. Wake him up for me, will you? Yes. I need to have most urgent words with him. Certainly I'll hold. Thank you, Maria."

I nodded to Kathy.

"Charles! What a pleasure to hear your voice. Yes, it *has* been a long time. You're well, I trust? And your wife and little ones? Good. Good. Ah! Yes. There is indeed a particular reason for my call. I found myself today in a sort of bookstore, Charles, and in this store I happened upon a quantity of Caverly's *Collected Poems* for 99 cents each. I presumed that you had remaindered them because you're bringing out a much larger edition in paper but..."

"*Not*? Really. Um-hmm..."

I listened to his practiced flatulence for a couple of minutes throwing in an occasional 'umm' and 'ah' here and there and then said,

"I'd say it was about two or three years ago that your language began to deteriorate, Charles. You started to talk funny. You started to talk about 'product' and 'units' and markets being 'soft'. And when you begin to talk funny, Charlie, it's a sure sign that you're *thinking* funny. No. You listen to me.

Your problem, Charlie, is that you've stopped trying to be a serious man. No, I don't want to hear about reality, Charlie. I don't want to hear about saturated markets and cash-flow. That's the adult equivalent of swapping bubble-gum cards. Let's talk like *real* grown-ups. The reality, Charlie, is that you've dishonoured John Caverly and you've betrayed his work and you've..."

I listened to his furious quacking.

When he paused for breath, I said,

"In the middle Victorian years, Charlie, so I've read, it was widely believed that intercourse with a virgin was a cure for clap. And as a result, there was a roaring trade in virgins. And some unscrupulous whores, Charlie, if you'll believe this, used to insert lumps of alum in their doodahs which had the effect of puckering them up like startled clams. Now what you need, old Charlie, in the state you're in, is to find some sort of equivalent of a lump of . . . *hello?*"

I looked at the receiver and then replaced it.

"And I hadn't finished," I said. "In fact, I'd hardly got started."

Kathy did not look up and said nothing.

"Another windmill down, eh, Katherine?"

She shrugged.

"Do I detect disapproval?" I said.

"Disapproval?" she said.

"What do you *want?*" I demanded. "What *should* I do? Nothing? Roll over, paws in the air? You want me sober, sombre, prudent, cautious, neither a borrower nor a lender be? Jesus Christ! What the fuck do you *want!*"

"What about your next book?" she said. "Is he likely to want to publish it after you've . . ."

"You have that the wrong way round," I said. "The question *is* — would *I* wish to associate with a corrupt man?"

"And you can find another publisher just like that?"

"Sure. I expect so. Possibly. *I* know what'd stir McLeod about. A bomb threat! A communiqué from . . . *Parents Against Pornography* . . . or from *Action for Canadian Righteousness*. Len Peters could phone it in tomorrow from a call-box in Toronto. He'd like that. It's too late today. Where's your concordance? Ah! Here we go. Look up 'wrath' and 'abomination'. There's bound to be lengthy entries there. Try 'woe' as well. Nothing like a fundamentalist bomb threat right after your porridge."

"You don't *really* intend doing that!" said Kathy.

"Certainly."

"You're not serious?"

"The wrath of God is revealed from heaven against all ungodliness."

"Jim!"

"Romans I:18."

"Well," she said, "it isn't going to be revealed from *my* phone."

"Where's the corkscrew?"

"This wine's far too special just to *swill*," she said. "I'll get dinner and we can have it with that. Cheese and bits, O.K.?"

"Just as a point of information, I'm *not* swilling it. I'm drinking it in memory of and in communion with one of the best poets this country's ever seen. And which it doesn't deserve. And, of course, which it doesn't *want*. Know what I read in the *Herald* the other day? Here's a piece of Canadiana for you, the authentic expression of the true North strong and free. Protestant churches in Ontario are opposing the sale of wine in food stores on the grounds that they don't want people to assume that wine's a natural accompaniment to food. Marvellous, eh? Porridge for ever!"

"Porridge?"

"Calvin. Knox. Every glutinous gobful reinforces the idea of a better world and the undesirability of this. Why do you think they're called *Quaker* oats? And they all came *here*. The porridge people. To make everyone else eat porridge and to stop them from drinking wine."

"Which we are going to have with dinner," said Kathy, getting up and taking the bottle from the glass table.

While she was in the kitchen, I scribbled down in my notebook the outline of a communiqué—the satanic cancers spawned by Avery and McLeod and subsidized by the hellish Canada Council: pornography, profanity, impurity, godlessness, lewdness, evolution, viciousness, vandalism, and pig-pen morality.

I crossed out the word 'bomb' and substituted 'explosive device'.

I picked up a copy of the *Collected Poems* and sat holding it. The cover was purely typographical, dark brown print on a light ochre, warm and pleasing. I turned the book over and looked at the photograph again. On the wall behind his head the David Milne watercolour—a frenzy of seagulls and wings in a strange perspective. A couple of years before he'd died, John had been trying to persuade McLeod to publish Milne's journals and correspondence but presumably the market had been soft.

And not shown in the photograph there would have been on the tabletop a silver-plated ashtray he'd removed from Rideau Hall, a mushroom-shaped piece of coral, and a child's wooden pencil case.

I took the book into the kitchen with me and put it on the table beside my plate. Kathy had furnished her favourite meal—what she always called 'bits'—cheeses, olives, bread, celery, herring, salami, and salad. She filled the glasses with Château Margaux.

"You know," I said, "this book represents twenty-five years' work. A life-time of talent worked down to a fine edge. And do you know what the print-run would have been? This is a guess—but it's an informed guess—two thousand copies. And subtract from that the number given away for promotion and the number sold to libraries and the number purchased by the Canada Council for

Book Kits Canada and the number remaindered and what you're left with is one thousand copies — one thousand copies bought by people who actually wanted to read it. And *that* works out to one copy for every 23,000 Canadians. Cheers!"

I speared a chunk of herring and chewed.

"And 23,000 people," I said, "is a good-sized Canadian town. With one owner in it of this book. Ever allowed yourself to think of a town like that? There's the cinema showing American movies, the six Chinese restaurants specializing in Canadian-Chinese-Italian food, a lot of banks, real-estate agents, and insurance companies and a shop that sells birthday and get-well-soon cards. That's the main street and it's dying.

In the streets behind the main street there are the churches of thirteen different denominations.

Then on the fringes of the town there are two shopping centres — Woolco, Canadian Tire, Consumers Distributing, and McDonald's Golden Arches. And then the road peters out into service stations and agricultural equipment dealers and widely spaced houses with big lawns and on the lawns there are plastic swans and painted concrete nigger-boys holding fishing poles or lanterns. And beyond that, there might be a drive-in that shows adult movies, a motel with a gracious dining room featuring Surf N' Turf and Wayne Ogsby at the Organ and beyond that fields with Holsteins and then the bush starts."

I poured another glass of wine.

Sediment stirred and clouded.

"And the only social cement," I said, "the only social bond, is buying and selling. Big Bucks. Top Dollar. In the towns, it's merchandise. In the country they sell each other parcels of bush."

Kathy said nothing and seemed to be staring over my shoulder. It was as if I wasn't there.

And then she said.

"Mmmm! I think this is quite the best wine I've ever had."

I stared at her.

The moment extended.

And then I said,

"Yes. It's — did I ever tell you that story about . ."

"Bismarck?" she said.

"No. About two noblemen who were tasting a vintage wine? And offered a glass to a passing peasant to see what he'd say? Well, he stood there for a while rolling it around and then he said, 'Ah, dear Sirs, it seems to me that God is descending . . . in velvet trousers'."

She smiled and nodded.

"True story," I said. "Or genuinely apocryphal. What's the difference?"

"It's a nice story," she said.

"Why can't I make you happy?" I said.

She looked down at her plate.

With the tines of her fork, she arranged the pits from the olives in a row.

Silence extended again.

"Umm?" I said. "Kathy?"

She sighed.

"Where's all this sort of thing going to end?" she said.

"All what sort of thing?"

She shrugged.

"I don't *know* exactly what I mean," she said. "Anger, I suppose . . . violence . . . You, yourself. *You* don't seem able to be happy and if *you* can't . . ."

I nodded slowly.

I picked up the book.

I nodded again.

"I loved *him*, too," I said.

I got up and looked in the cupboard above the sink for the cognac.

"For you?"

She shook her head.

"What's happening, Kathy? What's happening to me? Happy? Happy! In a few short months I've turned into a guy who harangues fucking *corpses*. I can't stop thinking about what I said to him. To Itzic. Foolish of me, priggish perhaps. Oh, I was so confident! Standing there reciting Auden like a credo."

"Auden?" she said.

"I didn't tell you? Those stanzas from the Yeats poem? Oh, God! Oh, yes, just picture *this*."

> *Time that is intolerant*
> *Of the brave and innocent*
> *And indifferent in a week*
> *To a beautiful physique*

Worships language and forgives
Everyone by whom it lives;
Pardons cowardice, conceit,
Lays its honours at their feet.

"Yes," I said, "a charming scene and one that has tended to linger, as they say, in memory."

Kathy got up from the table.

"... *beautiful physique*," I said. "Christ, how *could* I!"

I watched her wrap the pieces of cheese in Saran Wrap and tumble the rest of the olives back into the container that had a band aid stuck on it that said 'Olives' in magic marker. The letters had spread and become fuzzy on the band-aid's nubbly surface.

Anyone else would have had a label or nothing at all. I felt a rush of affection.

"But there was something else about that poem, Kathy. Something I *didn't* tell Itzic. And I've been thinking about it. I've been thinking about it a lot. What I so proudly spouted were the verses as Auden first published them but when he brought out his *Collected Shorter Poems* — 1965, I think it was — he'd revised a lot of his earlier work. And he cut those verses out. *And* the one that followed them. The one about Kipling and Claudel? And in the last few days I've been wondering *why*. Because they were a bit doggerel, do you think? Or because the syntax is a bit scrambled? Or because of the awkwardness of that near-rhyme in the third stanza? *Or*," I said, following her into the living room, "or do you think it was that by 1965 he no longer believed in what he'd written?"

I sat the squat cognac bottle and my snifter on the glass table.

"Where are we if they're *not* true?"

I watched the flare of the match.

"If we're *not* pardoned?"

Kathy settled herself on the couch. With her feet, she eased off her shoes and let them fall on the floor. I was reminded, suddenly, of Hetherington's daughter. What was her name? Cecilia. Kathy pulled the cushion down under her head.

"I don't know, Jim," she said. "I don't know what to say to you. But it's obvious that you can't go on like this."

I nodded.

"No," I said. "You're right. I can't."

I dropped the spent matchstick into the ashtray.

"'A dazzling display of concinnity and elegance'—that's what Auden urged upon poets in his last book before he died. But who was he figuring on dazzling?"

I spread my fingers round the bowl of the snifter.

I sat for some time in brooding silence.

"Remember," I said, "the first time I met Henry Benson? After that reading last term? I've been thinking about something *he* said, too. We were talking about culture and change—some such thing—and Henry said, 'Perhaps we've been at the end of something for longer than we'd care to admit'. Remember that? Well, we're not merely at the end of something, Kathy. Worse. Far worse than that, we're at the beginning of something else."

I sipped the cognac and glanced across at her.

Then looked.

She was asleep.

It seemed I was doomed to impart gems of wisdom to the sleeping or the dead.

I slumped back in the armchair sipping the cognac, watching cigarette smoke spiral, my thoughts drifting. I found myself thinking of the two chill days that Kathy and I had spent at my house at Christmas. And from there I drifted, as I so often did, to thinking of all the restorations I'd like to make until the house was once again alive. The stone re-mortared. The chimney pargeted. The floorboards sanded. Rotted fascia boards replaced. And the crumbling ceilings rebuilt—not strapping and sheets of gyp-rock nailed home with crude local hammers but plastered, medallions and cornices, a trade now as exotic as thatching, the only practitioners of the craft Italian immigrants.

I had a vision of it all in the late spring, the land unlocked, the house alive, the dance of young-leaf shadows on the polished boards, lilacs murmurous at the kitchen door.

Kathy stirred and hunched her shoulder, pushing deeper into the cushions of the couch.

I stuck my nose into the brandy snifter and breathed deeply.

It struck me as amazing that the French could produce *this* and at one and the same time the unspeakable Sartre and Gauloises. I thought of one of Johnson's *dicta*, '. . . he who aspires to be a hero must drink brandy'. I held the dark bottle up to the light. I could see that soon I'd be half-heroic.

I thought again with affection of Henry Benson, stooped, bemused, his hearing-aid switched off, looking rather like the eleventh earl reduced by penurious circumstances to opening his house to paying mobs disgorged from charabancs.

I thought of Henry's 'end of something' and then of that beginning of something new. Of that something already begun. 'The ringing grooves of change' — endearing of Tennyson to have got it wrong. The old order changeth and all that and doubtless old farts had always bemoaned what it made way *for* — but *this*!

Nobody, despite the capsuled in-depth prognostications of *Time Magazine*, nobody could yet see the emerging shape but it wasn't too difficult to guess at the nature of the beast.

Expressions of the beast were, I thought, at random: supermarkets, glass, androgyny, fast food outlets, TV, youth, ball-point pens, clothes made from man-made fibres, the USA, travel, instant coffee, packaged holidays, pocket calculators, welcome wagons, shopping malls, therapy, gas-ripened tomatoes from Florida and California, Florida and California, candles, the occult, anchor-men, psychology, flowered bathroom tissue, pundits, egalitarianism, personality, functional illiteracy, communication, fun, powdered potatoes, leisure, love, relating . . .

Fill in the blanks.

Using the special pencil.

What really fascinated me about the whole vision, I decided, was that none of it came from those who consumed it. None of it was an expression of human need and aspiration. It was a world steered by hucksters and foundering under its freight of sleaze. It was all, all of it, the creation and manipulation of merchants and ad-men and the psychologists in their pay who nurtured in the great and stunned unwashed the desire for vaginal deodorants in five flavours, microwave mousetraps, and CB radio sets to fill with adolescent and constructed slang the appalling prospect of silence.

Disney World.

I stared into the amber depths of my cognac.

But the one manifestation which seemed to embody all the rest, the weather-vane, the indicator of true North, was television. Not entertainment but anesthesia, a life-long twilight sleep. Lulled from the crib by Mr. Dressup and stared at in passive and geriatric wonder right up to the day before Mr. Joyboy screwed down the casket's lid.

Each evening a blue, flickering twilight settling over the land as Canadian morons watched American morons winning bedroom sets.

I sloshed more cognac into the glass.

Half-heroic.

The Twilight of the Gods.

No, there'd be no götterdämmerung, no bards to sing the exploits of the dead.

Shelf-life. Half-life.

That was me and the people like me. The half-life of a dying culture, our faint emanations recorded on the peaks and dots blooming on the monitor's screen, dated, ancient timbers, fabrics, shards.

The glass arrested at my lip, I stared at the glints of fool's gold in the chunk of quartz as if at a crystal ball. What had been but vaguely apprehended for days, unclear, unformed, was suddenly obvious, the impossible knots in the magician's rope unravelled.

Of course.

A world wired.

This was my inexorable discontent. *This* was what had remaindered John Caverly. *This* was the cause of Itzic's death.

A feeling of great mental easement filled me.

I looked across at Kathy. At her black hair against the floral cushion.

This, then, was the power that thwarted what I so much wanted with her, *this* was the power that refused me the warmth she needed, that imprisoned her behind the magic wall of briars, that turned my heart to iron and ice.

I studied my smeared glass.

What was it she'd said? Something about my not being able to go on like this? I nodded to myself. Quixotic, too, she'd called me. But he at least had saddled up and sallied forth.

I looked at myself with distaste.

An aging dreamer.

Drunk.

My last heroic act, the theft of a typewriter.

I sat in the armchair staring at nothing.

At nothing.

Kathy's stirring on the couch brought me back.

I took John's last poem from my wallet, unfolded once again the worn creases, sat holding it, remembering his always quizzical smile.

Do you rehearse your best tragedies,

distilling them into your dreams
night after night before you sleep,
your hair growing grey in your bed
your pleasant tears huge in your head?

I nodded to myself.

"You horrible old bastard, John," I said aloud. "You horrible old man."

I smiled.

I got up and knelt in front of the fireplace. I placed the poem on top of the ornamental pyre of white birch logs and set fire to it. I watched the paper bloom, curl, blacken.

At the door, I turned to look back at Kathy, blue veins at the back of her knees like the crayon rivers I once drew. Then quietly I let myself out of the apartment.

Mike, the janitor, lived in two dingy rooms in the basement beside the furnace and the two washing machines. He was an affable guy with unusual tattoes who was working at three different jobs to save money for his return to Nova Scotia. He told me nearly every time we met how it would be. It was a story that sustained him.

He would send word ahead of his arrival. His beloved younger brother whom he had not seen in four years would be there to meet him. He would step down from that train. He would drop his bags. They would shake hands. And then right there on the platform, boy, they'd square off and fight by Jesus till one of them dropped.

While Mike rootled through the big trunk in which he kept his tools and supplies, I swigged from the bottle of Molson's Canadian he'd given me and stared at the television set. On the wall above it was affixed a huge red lobster. On the screen, people were shooting at each other from behind chimney stacks and a policeman with a loudhailer was loudhailing and then cars were screaming down a race track to a chequered flag and a presumably famous person held up a can of motor oil and said he always used it.

I stumbled up the dim basement stairs, odours of washing machines and roach spray, to the glass doors of the entrance hall, looked out at the driving snow. I pushed against one of the heavy doors and felt the cut of the wind. I would need coat and boots.

I went back up to the apartment and got the key in the lock. As I entered, Kathy was sitting up. Her face was soft from sleep like a child's and reddened on one side with the impress of the cushion's fabric.

"What's that?" she said. "And where have you been?"

"I didn't mean to wake you," I said.

"What *is* that thing?"

I took my overcoat from the closet.

"What are you doing?" she said. "Where are you going?"

I turned and looked at her. I still wanted to make her understand.

"You know how I feel? I'll tell you how I feel. I feel bewildered. *That's* how I feel."

I dropped the overcoat.

"Look," I said, "the sort of thing I mean, this chair. It's supposed to be whizzing about all over the place but anyone can see it isn't. Do *you* understand that? *I* don't understand that. And Black Holes which we're supposed to know are there precisely because they aren't or something and because they're made of nothing which is the opposite of something and they suck things into themselves like celestial vacuum cleaners. Do *you* understand that? *I* don't understand that. Einstein — who in hell knows he wasn't selling us the Brooklyn Bridge?

There's cables and lasers and fucking things that see round corners. There's brains in bottles. Armed social workers. There's a new master-race.

Of arseholes. Cloned from rectal polyps. Oh, yes, I can see from your face. You think it's just horror stuff from a triple-feature drive-in. Of course you do. But it isn't. They're in the kitchen, in the closet. Watch it next time you take out the ironing board.

I mean, what the fuck's going *on*?

As far as I can see, ours is the only recorded century where there's a premium on ignorance. If you're fucking stupid or disadvantaged or whatever they call it, you've got it made. We're fucking drowning in sentimental sludge. That's what killed Itzic, too. In part. Know what an 'individual learning station' is? It's a desk. I found that out. All those poor black bastards who can't speak English patronized at institutions of higher learning with credits in Street Smarts, Intermediate Motherfucking, Advanced Jive. We've got Black Studies, Women's Studies, Gay Studies, Golden Age Studies, Geriatric Studies, community courses in how to fuck, buy, and die.

And over here, ladies and gentlemen, *hurry along, please*, here in the Cecil B. De Mille Gallery, artifacts of the Language People who were finally destroyed *circa* 1950 by the ruthless invasions from the north of the hairy Picture People.

Know what they wrote as the cause on Dylan's death certificate in New York?

'Insult to the brain'.

I think it's catching."

I shook my head.

"There's nothing left for me, Kathy. Nothing except a few individuals. And trying to love them. And I've not proved much good at that, have I? An ex-wife I don't even know where she is. Bars and taverns in a few cities where my friends are drinking-friends. And John. Oh, I *knew*! I knew when I got that letter. I might have found him. I might have got to him in time. What is it they use nowadays for the messy ones? Used to be blankets. Plastic bags? Heavy-duty Glad bags?

And you. And then there's you. You told me you needed to be warm and I understand that. I do. You've got more sense than me. But I can't help it, Kathy. I can't help it. It's darker where I am."

"You're very drunk, Jim," she said. "And feeling sorry for yourself isn't going to make things better, is it?"

She plumped up the cushion and replaced it.

"Once," she said, "I had a husband and a child."

I nodded.

There was silence.

And then I said,

"I *am* sad and I *am* sorry, Kathy, but I'm far from maudlin."

"Well, whatever you are," she said, "I wish you'd stop brandishing that thing about. You're going to break something."

I looked almost with surprise, at the blued octagonal steel with its curved claw end.

"How right you are!" I said.

What she had said struck me as vastly comic. I felt a grin growing, a grin that turned into a laugh, into laughter until my eyes were wet.

"How very right you are!"

"What's the joke?" she said. "And what *is* that?"

I weighed it in my hands.

"It's called a wrecking-bar," I said.

"What do you want it for?"

"To wreck something."

"*Now* what are you talking about?"

269

With a military turn of my wrist, I consulted my watch.

"At 22.30 hours," I said, "General Ludd will launch Operation Plumbicon. The Communication Arts Centre, code-name CAC, will be infiltrated. At 22.35 hours penetration of the Dome will be effected. And then I'm going to smash the buggery out of all of Cosimo's little toys."

"You're drunk and not very funny," said Kathy.

"True," I said.

"And what's given you *this* brilliant idea?" she said.

"It'd take too long to explain."

"Because of all that stuff about TV and photography and . . .?"

"*And* Itzic. *And* John. *And* on. *And* on."

I zipped up the side of my boot.

"Oh, don't be *ridiculous*, Jim! You'd be arrested immediately."

I nodded and zipped up the other boot.

"And if you did something like this," she said, "you'd go to prison."

"Or the bin," I said.

"And that doesn't bother you, of course."

I looked up at her.

"I don't really think it does," I said.

The realization surprised even me.

The words lay flat on the air.

I seemed to hear them echoing in my head.

Kathy stood staring down at me. I could read in her eyes the consequences to which I'd given no thought.

The tense silence extended.

Then she said,

"Look, Jim! I don't understand all this. I just do *not* understand this. *Really* understand, I mean. Why don't we have another drink while you tell me about it?"

"Kathy!" I said chidingly. "I may be pissed, my love, but you'd never make it on the stage."

I shrugged into my overcoat.

"Well I'm coming with you, then."

"Not inside, you're not."

"Shall I phone a cab?"

"*No!* Dispatchers keep records. Keep yourself out of this."

She got her coat and boots from the closet.

We started down the stairs.

Half-way down, she said,

270

"Wait! I forgot my purse!"

I stood there on the stairs listening to the clatter of her boots, the key, the door. It occurred to me how indecorously the mundane penetrated even the most solemn of events. Like the Queen's horse staling at the Trooping of the Colour. It occurred to me that the same thought had occurred to Auden. And it then occurred to me that it occurred to me because it had occurred to *him*.

Which was doubtless where the idea of *horses* had come from.

How undignified, how inappropriate to the pitch and moment of my enterprise it was to delay what I hoped would be a junior Armageddon while a woman collected comb and cosmetics.

I stood under the dim lightbulb smiling.

Outside, the wind was driving thin snow in stinging gusts. Away in the dark above the necklace of headlights, the warm beacon of a cab. Chains on the tires clinked and thumped.

Kathy sat at the far side of the cab hugging a great leather purse big enough to hold a week's laundry. We did not speak. There seemed nothing to say. Now-familiar street names, neon lights performing, 24 hour SERVICE, *Advanced Green When Flashing*, sidewalks largely deserted save for a few muffled Moscow figures bent into the wind.

The windows of the cab were crusted with snow. The light inside the cab was odd, shadowy, as though rising towards some surface as the chained tires trundled us under the spaced sodium lights. We were, I thought, three mysterious figures cast in plaster by George Segal.

I stared into the arc of the windscreen-wipers. The radio played music. Crackle and static from the dispatcher's voice, answers to unheard questions from other vehicles somewhere else. My eyes followed the backward, forward, backward, forward of the wipers.

The driver clicked his microphone and said urgently,

"31. 31."

The radio, the other radio, made the noise it always made when it was time for news.

"31. 31."

The man who read the news said 'as of this hour'.

A woman in Outremont had murdered her husband.

"31. 31."

The murder weapon was a barbeque appliance.

"Anything for 31?"

A barbeque *appliance*?

Fork?

Pair of tongs?

What did it *mean*?

The radio made the noise it always made when the news was over.

The campus was deserted. It was quickly cold outside the cab. I decided to go through the tunnel underneath the Hiscock Building which would bring me out at the Engineering Building not many yards from CAC.

I unlocked the door with the Hiscock master-key. As the door opened, the draught fluttered the papers tacked on the corridor's notice boards. Reminded me of something. Keats. The lovers after their fruity midnight feast fleeing into the stormy night. What was it — 'the long carpets rose along the gusty floor'. Must have been thin carpets. Something unethereal about the name Fanny Brawne.

Like the Blue Plate Special.

Our footsteps echoed.

Spray-painted student wit soaked into the raw concrete.

A notice on an office door said:

Contemporary Theology Cancelled Today.

Past the rows of green lockers like upended mortuary trays.

Our footsteps echoed.

The door at the far end.

Unlocked.

Relocked.

Cold again.

Light spilling down the steps of the front entrance of CAC.

Coir matting fixed up the steps in a central strip.

I took the claw of the wrecking-bar and worked it into the division between the two glass doors just below the lock. The doors moved making a grinding noise.

Inside, mirrors.

Many me.

The perception of motion is the death of the frame.

I banged the claw further home with the heel of my palm. I tested the depth I'd got with a slight pressure. The claw slipped and then bit. The metal of the door frame shone where it had been skinned.

sparks arcing
take one
take one

272

As I changed grip and prepared to lever outwards, I said, "Kathy..."

From the corner of my eye I saw all the mirrors fill with movement.

The pain was a black explosion in my head.

Somewhere far off, far, far away, I heard the fading clang of fallen metal.

Chapter Seventeen

The first thing I saw seemed to be a pineapple. Or two pineapples. Or more like a pineapple overlapped by half of another *wavering* pineapple. Then I vomited.

This seemed to happen often. Pineapples. Or in the middle of the air an upside-down glass bottle.

Followed by vomiting.

Often the voice came.

Sometimes there were lights and noises and other voices. They all hurt my head. They made me very angry. Most of the time these noises and lights were like a distant naval battle below the horizon, lights flaring in a dark sky, swollen noises rumbling. But at other times the noises and lights screamed and seared.

When the pains were naval battle pains, I made the noise in my throat. When they were the others, I made the noise in my cheek bones and nose.

And then I saw what seemed to be a nurse.

"Hi," she said.

She didn't overlap as much as the pineapple but she still overlapped.

Her white clothes made a loud noise.

She pulled something out of my nose.

At another time, in the dark, I heard myself groaning. The

groans were inside my head and outside. Lights blazed. She gave me a clear red capsule. It was like a plastic ruby. It shone.

At a different time, perhaps another day, a doctor said,

"Can you tell me your name?"

"Jim Wells."

Talking hurt my head.

"What's your mother's name?"

"Elizabeth."

"Where do you work, Jim?"

"No."

"Very good," he said. "Just relax. Don't worry about it."

"About," I said, "what?"

And then I vomited. Clear yellow liquid beside my face. The voice came. The voice was the nurse. She seemed to be Chinese.

Perhaps it was the next day. There was a dazzle place on the ceiling where the sun glanced off the upside-down bottle. The dazzle hurt my head. The doctor said to the nurse,

"Vomiting?"

I looked at their faces.

"I can't move," I said. "Why am I tied up?"

They didn't reply.

I wondered if they could hear me.

He released the blood pressure thing. As he had pumped it, my head had inflated and thundered. He peered into my eyes with a light and breathed on me. His tie smelled of cigarettes.

He said my pupils were equal. He tapped my knees. My legs jerked. He scratched the soles of my feet with his car-keys.

"Good!" he said.

"Good?"

"You've got a negative Babinski," he said.

"Your tie smells," I said.

"Good!" he said.

Time began to resolve itself more clearly into day and night. I stopped vomiting. I made discoveries. I discovered that I was tied to the bed in a sort of canvas strait-jacket; that one arm was free but that the other was strapped down and attached to the i.v. bottle; that the hair on the back of my head was shaved off and there was a puffy pad taped there; that a catheter joined me to the drainage bag that was strapped to the bed-frame.

Four times a day I had valium and aspirin and if she said I was shouting I had a red capsule which was chloral hydrate.

275

I had heard one of the doctors say to the nurse 'something, something, *Lactated Ringers*'. I had thought that this was the name of the disease I had but was relieved to discover that it was the name of what was in the i.v. bottle. I was relieved because 'Lactated Ringers' sounded like a disease which afflicted cattle. Bot, bloat, scours. But what I had, I discovered, was cerebral contusion. That seemed to mean concussion. But worse.

But how?

'You hit on head', the Chinese nurse had said, giggling.

At every visit, she said,

'What *your* story, morning glory?'

If I tried to reason with her, she gave me valium; if I demanded a pillow or a cigarette, she said:

'You shouting you *weally* sick'.

The pineapple was one pineapple and it was definitely a pineapple. I spent a lot of time staring at it. It crowned a wicker basket of apples, pears, oranges, and grapes. The corners of the basket were filled with crumpled silver foil on which rested almonds and brazils in their shells.

The car-keys doctor came again and said he was going to tell me two magic words. They were 'inchworm' and 'fish'. He was then going to look in later on and see if I'd remembered them. He did. I had. I lay in bed and listened to passing feet and the elevator button dinging. Braced up on the wall and tilted downwards towards the bed was the grey dead eye of the TV set.

The day after the magic words, the other nurse released me from the strait-jacket. The Chinese nurse removed the i.v. apparatus.

'You much better,' she said. 'Tomollow eat *dericious* food.'

I asked her if it would hurt when she removed the catheter. The last word I heard before I fainted was 'lubbish'.

Time passed, drowsy, easeful.

Breakfast was jello.

I noticed for the first time that tucked into the far side of the wicker basket of fruit was a white envelope. I stretched out and got it. Inside was a card with a picture on it in blue of a bluebird. From its beak the bluebird trailed a banner on which were the words: *Get Well Soon!* Handwritten under that were the words: 'On behalf of all the members of the English Department — Dick'.

I started to laugh — only Hetherington would send a pineapple to a man in a coma — but abruptly stopped as pain began to uncoil.

When I next awoke, Kathy was sitting near the bed. She was reading a magazine. She was wearing the heather-coloured sweater I particularly liked. I looked at her carefully. She did not overlap at all.

"Oh, Jim!" she said.

I thought for a second or two and then said,

"I'm sorry."

She stared at me.

"Whatever it was," I said. "I'm sorry. I must have done something."

"You don't remember anything?"

Her eyes searched my face.

"I have this feeling," I said. "I suppose I might have done something, gone too far. Or something."

Fat tears started to roll down her cheeks.

"You were unconscious for *four days!*"

"I like that sweater," I said. "You look lovely in it."

She started to sob.

"But you *do*," I said.

The weeping continued.

"What's the matter?" I said.

I stared at her.

"I'm sorry," I said. "Really."

She seemed a bit potty.

The thin nurse, not the Chinese one, came in and said,

"I'm sorry, Mrs. Neilson. I'm afraid you'll have to leave now."

"Yes," said Kathy. "I'm sorry. It's just..."

"Tomorrow, perhaps," said the thin nurse.

Kathy nodded.

"It's just that he seems so..."

"Dr. Chawn," said the nurse, "would like to have another word with you before you go..."

At the door, Kathy turned and seemed about to speak then disappeared.

The pain in my head had declined from forked lightning in an exhibition sky to a sullen groundswell, a momentous heave and slosh.

Events all seemed like a chaotic play in a church basement. Entrances. Exits. Incomprehensible speeches. At any moment the vicar would pop up and explain that owing to circumstances beyond control...

I really couldn't be bothered.

I lay in the bed and felt myself drifting again towards sleep. Thoughts, slow and laborious, tried to form themselves. It was like wading through mire, floundering through snow. Kathy was unhappy, upset about something. But I didn't know what the something was. There were things that I didn't know. That I *didn't* know didn't really worry me, but what did worry me was that I wasn't worried because I felt that I probably *ought* to be worried about whatever it was because... because Kathy was crying.

Tears.

The moist eyes above the slipped spectacles were reproachful, hurt. And then the lumpish figure of Itzic seemed to merge with that of my mother, the wheelchair turning into the familiar armchair, the fabric worn and shabby. The wool looping and looping from the paper bag at her side, needles clicking, eyes moist above the slipped spectacles, reproachful, hurt.

The noise awoke me. The lights were on and I found myself staring at a nurse's rump. She was pulling back the sheets and blankets on the other bed. There was a clattering of metal in the corridor outside, a kind of ratchet noise, and I turned to see an orderly backing into the room guiding a bed on wheels. The Chinese nurse followed.

On the cot lay the body of a man. I sat up and stared. He looked like a corpse. His face was grey. His breathing was loud. Both his eyes were blackened and the whole of his upper lip was so badly bruised it looked as if he had a moustache. The orderly and the nurse heaved the body onto the bed and then straightened him out.

"You got company for you," said the Chinese nurse.

"What happened to him?"

"He had surgery," said the Chinese nurse.

"Why is he all bruised like that?"

She pointed at her forehead.

"Tumour on brain."

I stared at him, at his head. There were no bandages, no shaving.

The orderly drank my orange juice and wiped his mouth on his sleeve.

"How?" I said. "How did he have an operation?"

"Up his nose," she said.

She giggled and covered her mouth with her hand.

The man started groaning. Each exhalation was a groan.

"Why is he all bruised like that?"

I stared at the grey sweaty face.

The nurses started talking about someone called Norma. Norma had had her hair dyed. Norma had quarrelled with Betty because Betty had refused to swap shifts even though she knew Geoffrey was coming in from Toronto.

The groaning seemed to be getting louder.

I watched their faces.

"Look!" I said. "I don't know what happened to me. You said I was hit on the head. What do you mean 'hit on the head'? Did something fall on me or did someone hit me? Or what? What happened to me?"

"It O.K. not to remember," said the Chinese nurse.

The orderly, a swarthy man, stuck his wrist between the two women and pointed at his watch.

"Digital," he said.

"What a nice watch!" said the other nurse.

He looked at her, frowning.

"The watch," she said, pointing. She beamed and nodded extravagantly. "*Very* nice."

He smiled and shrugged.

"Digital," he said.

"You have no right," I said, "not to tell me what happened to me. This is ridiculous! I refuse to be treated like a child!"

"We're not deaf, eh?" said the other nurse.

She took the clipboard from the end of the bed and then said to the Chinese nurse, "Oh! One of Dr. Chawn's."

"Well?"

"Mustn't get excited," said the Chinese nurse.

"For Christ's sake! I'm *not* excited. I'm asking you a civil question to which I have every right to an answer."

"Shouting hurt your head," she said as she followed the orderly out.

"Dr. Chawn," said the other one, "wants you to be calm. If you're not calm, we can't make you better, can we?"

"Who's Dr. Chawn?"

"Dr. Chawn's going to help you get better."

The Chinese nurse came back in with a glass of orange juice. She gave me a red capsule.

"Tomollow," she said, "much better."

I lay back feeling anxious and obscurely disquieted. I closed my eyes. I listened to their shoes — *squishy-squishy* — and to what they were saying. They were talking about Norma again. The grey man was groaning. The rattle of the curtain being drawn between the beds. And then their shoes went away. I wondered what the word 'oedema' meant. The tingling started and my body became more liquid and began to lose shape and as the gloomy red waves rolled in, I started to feel afraid. I struggled against the red weakness. The voice was there. I could hear groans and cries.

The next morning, after the fog of chloral hydrate had cleared, I *did* feel much better. I felt physically stronger and much more alert. And bored. I was awake before the nurses came. I listened to the bruised man behind the curtain for a while and said, "Hello?" but there was no answer. I listened to the corridor noises, voices. I stared at the pineapple and the oranges and the apples and the pears and the grapes and the nuts — a mound of *nature mort*. The jello woman arrived with her trolly. She gave me a bowl of what she said was cream of wheat. After her, the lopsided girl with the moustache stomped in and clattered empty dishes. She didn't speak English or French. Then a new nurse bustled in ahead of a doctor, swished back the curtain, revealed the bruised man. The doctor held the man's wrist for a few languid moments while chatting to the nurse about cross-country skiing.

After they'd gone, I recited as much as I could recall of Book One of *Paradise Lost*. I stared out of the sky part of the window to see if a bird would fly past.

One didn't.

And then Kathy peered round the door.

Coming into the room, she said, "How do you feel, Jim? They tell me you're going onto the Soft Diet today."

"I've already been," I said. "It's cream of wheat. Kosher cream of wheat."

She pulled up the chair.

"This hospital," I said, "is Jewish."

She nodded.

"It's for everyone," she said. "It was nearest."

"The jello was kosher too."

"Jello?" she said.

"Something to do with shins," I said.

"*Shins?*"

"Shins," I repeated. "Why, I don't know. But what I *do* want to

280

know is what I'm *doing* here. How did I get here? What happened? What's the big secret?"

She started at the sepulchral groan and stared at the dividing curtain.

"It's all right," I said. "He's unconscious."

"Well," she said. "It's difficult to know exactly where to start . . ."

She began to explain events, my guilt over Itzic's death, my drinking, the remaindering of John's book, my theories about television and my conviction that CAC had been, in some way she hadn't quite followed, responsible for killing Itzic, and as she talked shapes of that evening began to stir and shift.

"Hold it!" I said. "Just hold on a minute. I was waiting for you in the hall. On the stairs. In your building. *Yes.* I *do* remember that. You went to get your purse. We were going somewhere. *Yes!* That big leather thing from Morocco. I was thinking about Ronald Firbank."

I felt excited.

I noticed her changing expression.

"No, it's all right," I said. "I *was*. I can remember that. It was about you too, somehow. About the Queen's horse staling during the Trooping of the Colour and I remember thinking that Firbank said that 'staling' was his *most* favourite word in the English language. Who was it," I said, "someone, he said to somebody, 'I adore italics, don't you?'"

She was staring at me.

That Katherine look.

"No! I'm not nutty. I'm remembering. I *am*. Go on! Go on! We were in a cab, weren't we? Why?"

I watched her face as she talked.

She seemed hesitant, ill at ease.

"A wrecking bar?"

I stared.

"CAC? Did I really? With the bar?"

She stopped.

I had a sudden glimpse of the foyer of CAC filling with mirrored movement.

"You!" I said. "*You* hit me on the head."

Her eyes moistened.

"The purse," I said. "It must have been in the purse."

I lay back for a few moments in silence.

She blew her nose.

"I didn't know how hard to do it," she said.

I stared at the ceiling, the discoloured bit that resembled the eastern coast of India and Burma.

"It made this *noise*," she said.

The bulge of Burma was actually flaking.

"Tell me," I said, "purely as a matter of curiosity, what exactly did you hit me *with*?"

"The quartz," she said.

The orange juice trolley rattled past in the corridor.

"The quartz," I repeated. Then I said, "Well, what the hell! Here I was beginning to think I might have done something awful. Caused an affray or incited to riot or something."

I smiled up at her. She was wearing gold studs in her ears. Blue eyeshadow and mascara. Her perfume was faint but luxurious, exciting.

She opened her purse and started to rummage.

I chuckled but then winced.

"So," I said, "all I'm suffering from is a head full of fool's gold. Talking of which, are those earring things new? *Most* becoming!"

"Jim . . . ?"

"Hey!" I said. "Listen!" I sat up again. "The campus is private property, isn't it? And we were on it legally, right? Members of faculty. Do you know," I said slowly, "I'd be surprised if they couldn't be held responsible. You know — for *insurance*!"

"Jim!"

My mind was full of Hetherington's Portuguese janitor.

"Jim," she said. "*Please!*"

She produced a disintegrating Kleenex.

"What?" I said.

She closed the purse. The clasp clicked.

I listened, watching her face.

As she was speaking, her fingers were twisting the Kleenex until it was furry.

"The *police!*" I said.

"I thought you were dying," she said.

The scar on her forehead was standing out, a white ridge.

I shook my head slowly.

"And St. Xavier?" I said.

There was a long silence.

"Do you realize what you've *done*?" I said.

"Do *you?*" she said.

I stared at her.

"Whose side are you *on*, for Christ's sake!"

Tears started to roll down her cheeks. She wiped a gathering tear drop from the corner of her mouth. Tears glistened in the mascara.

"I'm . . ." she started. She looked away. The corners of her mouth were quivering as she struggled to control her voice. She said,

"I'm not on anybody's side."

Silence extended.

I lay back on the pillow.

She looked at the tiny gold wristwatch she ritually wore when she was going to go anywhere. The link bracelet, too, was gold and heavy.

"Look at the time!" she said. "I'm late. I really have to go."

The watch was broken. The hands always stood at eleven-thirty.

"Yes," I said. "Yes, of course."

She stood up and made as if to put the chair back against the wall and then didn't and walked towards the door. She hesitated in the doorway for a second but then looked down and went out. I strained for the sound of her footsteps in the corridor.

The long hospital day dragged on. It was punctuated by lunch and then, later, by the orange juice woman again. Lunch was sort of fish blanketed in white, viscous sauce. The potatoes were reconstituted. The bruised man didn't eat his chicken soup. I spoke to him but he didn't answer. I took his soda crackers. Establishing the flaking patch on the ceiling as being the western coast of Burma, I managed, after great concentration, to locate Singapore just beside the second ceiling globe.

A tubby nurse with a clipboard came in and looked at us.

"And which one of you is Mr. Wells?"

"That's me."

"These are for you," she said, giving me a writing pad and two brand new pencils.

She made a tick on her clipboard.

"Why?"

"To write on," she said. "That'll be nice, won't it?"

She popped out.

The pad was white, the pencils Eagle 224 HB. I doodled for a while and then did some stick-figures. Then to introduce drama, I started stick-figures sword-fighting. This turned into a full-scale battle covering the whole page, a mêlée involving a welter of clubs, swords, pikes, maces, crossbows, arquebuses, and corpses.

I wrote *Kathy: Katherine: Kathy Neilson: Katherine Neilson: Kathy.* Then I wrote Kathy in capital letters with shading and serif embellishments.

Did more stick-figures, doodled the afternoon away, watched through the window the decline of the light.

The tubby nurse came back and took the pad and pencils away.

"Why?" I said.

"You can have nice fresh ones tomorrow," she said.

"Can you get me a phone?"

"This isn't my ward," she said.

Dinner was unspeakable. Pasta of a sort.

I asked the thin nurse for a phone. Phones, she said, were only put in rooms in mornings. In the morning I could have a phone.

I cajoled.

I begged.

Love, happiness, life itself depended, I told her.

Rules, she informed me, were rules.

Nasty language, she said, was the one thing she didn't have to tolerate.

When the Chinese nurse started her shift the hospital noises were muting into night. I asked her for a phone. I begged. I promised not to make a noise. When she plugged in the jack, I dialled Kathy's apartment. The phone rang and rang. I tried Betty's apartment but there was no answer. I tried Kathy's number again but somehow got connected to the X-Ray Department. The receiver was wet with sweat. My heart was hammering. I tried the Faculty Club, her office, the apartment again.

"Hello?"

"Kathy?" I said. "It's Jim."

She made a slight sound — exclamation, indrawn breath perhaps.

"Kathy?"

The line was live but silent.

"Hello?"

Then the receiver was replaced.

The burr persisted.

I switched off the lamp. My eyes soon adjusted to the dark. I lay listening to the bruised man's breathing. Later, the smell of coffee percolating at the nurses' station quickened the room. The door was ajar and I lay staring at the path of light from the corridor lying across the floor. I found that I was thinking about a book with blue covers I'd had when I was a child, a book about a bear cub called Mary Plain who lived with a man she called The Owl Man because he wore spectacles. The line of light on the floor reminded me of something to do with the part in his hair, the white stripe Mary had called it, which had reminded her of — was it badgers?

Much later, I heard the approach of footsteps, the light widening, the dark shape of her standing in the doorway.

"Mr. Wells?"

I pressed my face into the pillow.

"Why you clying?"

I imagined the capsule's melting in the heat of my body, the red tinge drifting through me like dye, like the uncertain smoke of leaves, like paint from a brush uncurling and misting down through a jam-jar of fresh water. The shapes and sounds of the room slowly faded. Time seemed suspended. The air was still, humid, heavy with the scent of bruised wild mint. We were at the stream below the old barn where the water ran in rills and trickles over the rock ledges into the widening pool. In our concentration, we were breathing through our mouths. Kathy's skirt was tucked up into her white cotton knickers. We were children. Further downstream in the marsh where the cattle had churned the mud, a bullfrog was booming. Tapping and knocking, a woodpecker was working a dead elm tree at the pool's edge. We could hear the slither and scratch of its claws. She was watching me with solemn eyes under the fringe of black hair. I was pointing and pointing down along the white string with its bacon bait trying to get her to see the crayfish pincers under the wavering ledge.

The morning was soggy and bleary. I wanted to go back to sleep but was pestered with shaving and orange juice and cold toast until I was alive with irritation. I lay staring at the shape of the TV trying to organize my thoughts, trying to assess my situation.

I felt bleak.

I recalled the conversation I'd had with Kathy after I'd stolen the typewriter. I couldn't see any holes in the argument I'd advanced. Though I wondered again exactly what she'd said. And to whom. Merely that I'd been drunk? Or had she gone further? Given chapter and verse? But whatever. The university, I felt sure, would not press charges. Hetherington *had* sent me a pineapple. On behalf of the Department. And if the university didn't press charges, presumably the police themselves couldn't.

Though the involvement of the police might complicate the question.

But beyond *that*, there were endless irritating ramifications.

My employment would presumably be terminated. I would plead nervous strain, total collapse brought on by Itzic's death. *Future* employment — there was *another* complication. These kinds of things got about. Sexual pecadilloes, minor peculation, gross aberrations — all were acceptable, welcome even, but the line would be drawn at an attempt to destroy the very plant. Invitations to write in residence would tend to dry up when at learned symposia Dean spoke to Dean.

Wells? Our experience of him, frankly, was non-viable.

And then there was The Canada Council — they'd have to be placated, a letter which would strain creativity to the limits.

"Dear Dick," I said aloud.

It sounded silly.

"Dear Richard," I said.

From behind the curtain sounded a groan.

"Yes," I said, "you're right. Given the situation, I'll make it perfectly formal. 'Dear Professor Hetherington . . .' How about that? Do you like that better?"

"Here we are," said the tubby nurse coming through the doorway pushing a wheelchair. "Just sit on the edge of the bed and put this robe on."

"Now what?"

"You're coming to stay on my ward," she said.

"Why?"

"Because now your head's getting better, Dr. Chawn's going to be looking after you until you're ready to go home."

As she wheeled me along, I kept my eyes down. I felt ridiculous with bare ankles, the hospital gown like a shift, the bathrobe too small. I didn't want to meet the glances of the legs and boots sitting on benches outside offices and chattering along the corridors. We went down in an elevator. Along. Up in an elevator.

We were disgorged in front of a nurses' station. The nurse parked me beside the counter behind which stood a plump middle-aged woman in a white knit jump-suit. She had elaborate hair and a Florida tan. From her rhinestone glasses depended loops of chain.

"This is Mrs. Udashkin," said the nurse, "our volunteer."

I smiled and nodded.

"He's for a profile?"

She started assembling cards and papers and examination-booklet-looking things from the bank of filing cabinets.

"And that's your hematology," she said, putting down two labels, "and your urine."

I tilted my head and managed to read the titles of a couple of the booklet-things:

The Godfrey-Weber Manifest Anxiety Scale.

Rev. Series 3: Braat-Mordant Attitudes and Feelings.

Pieces snapped into place.

The bruised man's nurse saying: 'Oh! One of Dr. Chawn's'. Whom Kathy had seen. More than once — the thin nurse saying to her something about 'another word with Dr. Chawn'. The general evasiveness. The appearance and confiscation of the pad and pencils.

This was, I realized, looney toons.

I glanced at Mrs. Udashkin's red talons.

Twenty Questions.

With the Ha-Ha men.

The tubby nurse trundled me along to a room where the door stood open. There were two beds. Beside one sat a man dressed in ordinary clothes. The television was quite loud, a choir, surplices, organ pipes.

Sunday.

"Here's a companion for you, Mr. Curtis. That's it. Just sit on the edge of the bed, Mr. Wells. And we'll hang up the . . . there we are."

Mr. Curtis looked thirty-five or so. He had thinning, ginger hair. His spectacles were rimless. He was wearing a tartan shirt, grey flannel trousers, a brown cardigan, and furry slippers.

The room didn't look like a hospital room. There were magazines on an occasional table. Two small orange plastic armchairs. Pictures on the walls.

Mr. Curtis, after a brief stare and a nod, had returned to gazing at the TV.

He sat neatly.

While the massed choirs hummed, a man was playing 'Amazing Grace' on a trombone.

"Mr. Curtis?" I said. "Do you mind turning it down a bit?"

"Ernie," he said.

"Jim," I said.

He stood up and took off his spectacles. He put them on again. He walked over to the TV, brushed the top of the cabinet with his fingertips, examined his fingertips as if for dust, then walked back again.

"It isn't loud," he said. "I always have it on like that."

"It *is* loud," I said.

"No it isn't. Excuse me, but that definitely isn't loud."

I'd noticed that his grey flannels were hitched too high exposing sock. I was reminded again of Fiona, a young actress I'd been friendly with in Vancouver. Whenever we were out together, she'd given me pointers about her craft—movement, posture, clothing. Pants at half-mast, she'd claimed, was the most obvious mark of crazies. And ever afterwards on the streets, in stores, I'd obsessively noticed trousers.

I thought about my situation for a few moments.

"I'm sorry, Ernie," I said. "It's not that I want to quarrel. I suffer from pain in my head. I hurt myself, you see."

"I'm sorry then, too," he said. "But that definitely isn't loud."

"I fell," I said.

I smiled at him.

Wasted effort because he was turning away to watch footage of the Holy Land, a shepherd wandering along followed by a straggle of sheep.

"And how long have you been here, Ernie? That is, of course, if you don't mind . . ."

"Three months," he said.

"And how long do people usually stay?"

"Until they're not troubled anymore," he said.

I nodded.

"Three months seems a long time," I said.

"I haven't been able to cope," he said.

I nodded again.

"It was, well it involves, involved my wife."

"Ah," I said.

There was silence for a moment.

"Cope?"

"Well," he said, "it all started when I came home from work one day—or rather," he said, "I should say that's *my* perception of when it started. The concensus in Group is that that is not the case.

288

And I'm not trying to say that Group's wrong but for the purpose of trying to . ."

"For just *talking* about it," I said.

"That's what I mean," he said. "Exactly."

I nodded.

"Anyway," he said, "when I got off at my stop there's a florist right there and there was a sign on the sidewalk. A sandwich-board sign? 'Cash and Carry. Roses. $3.25'. So I thought I'd purchase some for Mary. They were thornless. I hadn't known about that. That there *were* thornless roses."

He paused.

"I prefer the bus for work," he said.

I nodded.

"Just as convenient," he said.

"Sure," I said.

"It was just like any other evening," he said. "I picked up the *Herald* at the United Cigar Store as I always do — a creature of habit, that's what they say in Group. But when I got home with the roses she wasn't there. And that wasn't usual. Nor was there a note on the fridge. She always used the children's magnetic letters. To leave notes."

The tale unfolded.

He became more animated.

He recounted events with a strange and growing enthusiasm and in a sequence which suggested frequent rehearsal.

He'd called from work at varying times of day and there'd been no answer and he'd caught her out in subsequent lies. Book matches in her purse from restaurants, phone calls that when he answered were wrong numbers, hidden under her silk scarves and squares a tiny bottle of new perfume she'd claimed she'd bought out of the housekeeping money.

She'd started shopping on Thursday and Friday evenings whereas before she'd gone on Saturdays. On occasion, she'd returned from Steinberg's flushed with alcohol and smelling of peppermint.

His suspicion and jealousy grew apace.

"I grew so sick that I used to get her soiled underthings — it's pathetic, isn't it? — her soiled things out of the laundry and sniff them to see if I could smell, well, traces of men."

Nodding, feeling a horrible embarrassment for him, I looked at a point just beyond his face.

"You see," he said, "I was denying her the opportunity to grow, to become a person in her own right."

I stared right at him.

"And then," he said, "I was so weak, you see, that I tried to punish her in the most terrible and inhuman way possible."

He had my sympathy.

He held my eyes with his.

"I attempted," he said, "to take my own life."

I shook my head very slowly.

"In the garage."

This recital over, he turned back to the TV where a woman was spraying some stuff on a shining table top and then cuddling the can against her cheek.

I lay back on the bed.

The wheelchair sat beside it.

I stared at the wheelchair for a while.

On one wall was an El Al poster combining an airplane and an aerial view of Jerusalem. On another a reproduction of a Chagall, a bowler-hatted lover in mid-air offering a girl a posy. To the right of the TV, which was crowded with foul crunching children munching, was a poster of big teeth and gums illustrating the correct employment of dental floss.

My only course of action was a mouth resolutely shut. Any loose chat about CAC, any exposition of the relationship of frozen french fries to the decline of the West and they'd plug me into Hydro Quebec.

Christ!

What had Kathy *said*?

I had a sudden memory of Fiona in Vancouver naked except for a necklace of red coral, inverted nipples like kittens' noses.

I stared at Jerusalem.

At the teeth and gums.

Gradually, I became aware of faint, irregular sounds beneath the babble and laughter from the TV and turning over on the bed saw Ernie sitting in his orange plastic chair staring at the screen tears running down his cheeks.

"It's O.K.," I said. "Ernie? Don't cry. Things'll work out."

I sat up.

"Ernie?"

A moan sounded from him, quavering, almost falsetto.

"Ernie! Come on!"

"What," he said through his tears, "what do *you* know? You know nothing."

"Look at me, Ernie," I said. "How can I talk to you if you're staring at that fucking thing!"

He looked down at his knees.

A tear-drop hung from the edge of his nose.

After a moment, he said.

"I suppose you think it's unmanly to cry."

"No," I said. "I don't think that, Ernie."

He blotted his eyes with a Kleenex.

"I don't think that at all," I said.

His lower lip was tremulous.

"*That's* better," I said. "It'll be all right. There's no need to cry."

"That," he said, "there's what I mean."

"What?"

"That you don't know anything. Coming in here!" he said indignantly. "Of *course* there's a need to cry."

"Well, sure," I said, "we all . ."

"*No!*" he said. "That's *why* you're here."

He seemed almost scornful.

"You won't be leaving here," he said, "until you've *learned* to cry."

I stared at him.

"What do you mean, 'learned'?"

His face was blotchy red and white.

"Until you've learned to cry," he said, "and then learned not to cry."

"I'm not sure I'm understanding you," I said.

He was polishing his glasses with a Kleenex.

He sighed.

"Of course you don't understand," he said with offensive patience. "That's what you're here to learn. How can you understand what you don't know?"

"Mmmm," I said.

Seemingly quite composed, he turned back to the TV.

A handsome housewife beamed as her winsome Labrador pup bolted down a bowlful of Yumnies. A vet in a white lab coat who happened to be in her kitchen said that Yumnies contained, in addition to immediately available protein, calcium, iron oxide, iodized salt, and assorted vitamins. The puppy tried to climb into the empty bowl. The vet smiled at the lady. The lady smiled at the vet. The vet and the lady smiled at the dog.

"I'd prefer," said Ernie, without turning his head, "that you didn't smoke."

I blew smoke towards the ceiling.

"No kidding?" I said.

The afternoon was packed with incident.

The tubby nurse took blood samples, urine specimens, and a saliva sample. She weighed me and measured my height. Then she wheeled me along to a bright room with yellow curtains and a carpet where she handed me over to a Dr. Nimitz who was tall and long-faced and had buck teeth.

Stuffed toys sat on a bench.

Dr. Nimitz asked if I felt well, if I felt relaxed. I told him I did. He asked me if I were agreeable to writing some diagnostic tests. I told him I was. He gave me a new pencil and I completed:

The Godfrey-Weber Manifest Anxiety Scale.

Rev. Series 3: Braat-Mordant Attitudes and Feelings.

The Stanford-Binet Vocabulary Test.

The Tumm Pictorial Absurdity Test.

He then asked me if I felt tired and I assured him I didn't. Whereupon he timed my performance on a test starkly entitled *Nufferno* and enquired if I felt up to a *Porteus Maze.*

I was then returned to the room where Ernie was watching TV. Ernie was still being haughty. He said that of *course* Dr. Nimitz wasn't the leader of Group. That it wasn't *accurate* to speak of *a* leader. Or even of a *leader*. That Dr. Mendelson, *Mendelson*, moderated.

I looked through the copies of *Maclean's, Family Circle,* and *Reader's Digest* on the occasional table. I read all the usual hints on how to cut fuel bills and add zest to marriage and concoct appetizing meals from hamburger. In one of the copies of *Reader's Digest* a previous loony had drawn arrows pointing to the genital areas of all illustrated women. The arrows were drawn in blue ballpoint and carefully fletched. Beside the feathering, neatly printed, were the words 'Castro's Cuba'.

I lapsed into staring at the television. I watched it for the remainder of the afternoon and all evening. After two or three hours I'd stopped wondering about mass society, etc. consumerism etc. the global village etc. After two or three hours, I'd stopped wondering about anything at all. I just lay there feeling dull, exhausted, sodden.

The next morning bright and early Tubby was bustling in and out, words of good cheer, varied medication for Ernie who had real pyjamas, pale blue with white piping on the jacket. Scrambled eggs, the dirty dishes woman, local news blaring on the TV, traffic reports, the possibility of freezing rain, a smiling woman performing yoga exercises.

The local news and traffic reports were from Burlington, Vermont. I pointed out to Ernie that we were in Montreal, Quebec. He denied that the TV was loud.

Then there were puppets.

After what seemed hours of the *Reader's Digest*, Tubby brought me a pair of paper slippers and conveyed me in the wheelchair to Dr. Chawn. She left me in the ante-room facing Dr. Chawn's secretary who was wearing headphones and transcribing a cassette. She did no more than glance. In a beribboned pot on her desk a chrysanthemum flowered. Bronze. I thought of the bronze chrysanthemums I'd seen in Kathy's apartment that first morning I'd awoken there. It seemed a long time ago. Dr. Chawn's door was sound-proofed with black quilted leather. I sat in the wheelchair breathing deeply attempting to get a grip on my early morning ill-temper and abraded nerves. On my left was an occasional table piled with copies of *Reader's Digest* and *Maclean's*. On my right was a dwarf tree with podgy leaves like swollen ears.

I looked up as the door opened.

Dr. Chawn was a small man, only three or four inches above five feet, dark, Indian, perhaps West Indian. His eyes were large and intense in the thin, austere face.

He beckoned.

"Please."

I extricated myself from the wheelchair, stumbling over the footplate, and followed him into the office. The floor was carpeted. One of my paper slippers came off and I had to poke about with my bare foot to get it on again.

"Awkward," I said, "these things."

I smiled.

He stood watching me in silence.

"Please sit here."

He went round the desk.

The desk-top was a dark matte brown and bare except for a cassette recorder, an intercom, an ivory coloured phone. From the centre drawer he took a block of graph paper and a folder. On the graph paper he placed a fountain pen. His black leather chair creaked back.

His eyes were fixed on me. He regarded me in silence. He gave the impression of being coiled, compressed. I felt so uncomfortable I had to fight the urge to babble. From beyond the door, faintly, almost inaudible, the sound of his secretary typing. Then he opened the folder and started to read.

I glanced round the office. It was lined with bookshelves, journals, abstracts, ranks of books in uniform bindings, red and gilt, doubtless the Proceedings of some dreadful Society or Association.

Looking up, he said,

"A B.A. degree from the University of British Columbia. That is the extent of your formal education?"

"Yes," I said. "Yes, that's right."

He turned back a sheet in the folder and frowned.

"And your weight? There's no entry here."

"Yes," I said. "Yesterday. One hundred and sixty-three pounds."

"Which would be . . ."

Beyond a suggestion of something British in the cadence of his speech, he had no accent that I could hear.

". . . in kilograms . . . seventy-four, seventy-four point one."

When he spoke, gold glinted.

He made a note on the graph paper, the handwriting miniscule.

He took out a bulging file of printed forms and cards.

"And if you would complete this."

It was a list of childhood diseases.

As I ticked off the common items, I said,

"My childhood seems absolutely uneventful."

I looked up and smiled.

"Nothing dramatic at all, I'm afraid."

His face remained impassive.

"My interest in your childhood," he said, "simply concerns the ability of your heart to withstand unaccustomed physical stress."

I nodded.

And waited.

From the folder had fallen a yellow card. Printed on it were the outlines of two hands, the thumbs and fingers numbered. It looked like something from a fortune-teller's tent.

"This interests you?" he said.

"I was just — ah — just wondering . ."

"They are used," he said, "in clinical hypnosis. The subject designates one finger as a 'yes finger' and another as a 'no finger'. This is the record of that designation."

"I see," I said. "And are you going to hypnotize me?"

"I?" he said.

I looked at the dark eyes.

"Dr. Nimitz," he said, "sometimes employs hypnotism."

"But you don't?"

"Dr. Nimitz," he said, "is interested in the underlying causes of behaviour. My interest is simply in the amelioration of symptoms."

He made a steeple of his fingers. The fingernails were milky, tinged with blue.

"I am concerned, in your case, with increasing cortical inhibition and decreasing cortical excitation."

"What does that mean," I said, "exactly?"

"The production of extroverted behaviour patterns," he said.

"I'm afraid you've lost me," I said. And as he did not reply, added, "With your explanation. I wonder if you could . ."

"This afternoon," he said, "I wish to start preliminary measurements. You're familiar with the EEG?"

"Yes," I said, "but . ."

"To determine your sedation threshold," he said, " we will take a continuous frontal EEG record while you receive intravenous amytal at forty second intervals."

"Amytal?"

"Sodium amytal."

"But what does it do?"

"It's a barbituate."

"I don't mean that," I said. "I don't understand . ."

"Ah! Threshold!"

"Well, no . . ." I said. "The whole . ."

"A purely routine diagnostic procedure," he said. "The Shagass threshold establishes the position of the patient on the obsessional-hysteric continuum. It's a measure of tension and manifest anxiety and from . ."

"But . ."

"And from these data we determine the necessary dosage of successive depressant drugs."

"But what do you mean by *patient*?"

He stared at me.

He sat back and gripped the bridge of his nose between thumb and forefinger.

"I don't think I understand your question," he said.

My armpits were wet.

I smiled.

"Well," I said, "I'm not particularly tense and, manifestly, I'm not particularly anxious so I don't really understand how or why you're thinking of me as a patient."

"I see," he said. "I think you're simply misunderstanding the clinical use of the words 'tension' and 'anxiety'. It's more than likely," he said, "that Dr. Nimitz and Dr. Mendelson will wish to repeat the series combining an amphetamine with the amytal. This is, of course, their particular interest."

"What is?"

"Such a combination," he said, "inclines the patient towards elation and according to the literature the attendant loquaciousness has sometimes resulted in an abreaction."

"Pardon? In a what?"

"Amphetamine," he said, "*as a depressant* is still something of an uncharted area. Certain studies have suggested that the depressive psychopath responds favourably—particularly those with a persistent theta rhythm in the EEG. I am not entirely persuaded but . . ."

He shrugged.

I stared at him.

"Are you suggesting," I said, "that you consider me a psychopath?"

He looked at his fingernails and then looked up.

"The term in clinical usage is merely denotative, Mr. Wells."

I could feel the sweat through the thin gown sticking to the chair.

"Dr. Chawn!" I said. "I have been polite and cooperative and I have not complained about the way you have evaded answering questions."

"Evaded?"

His eyebrows rose.

"Put crudely," I said, "you seem to consider me in some way crazed and you wish to wire me up and inject truth drugs into me. Is that right?"

He stared at me and everted his lips.

"Because, you see," I said, "I don't want you to do that."

296

I met his eyes and stared back.

My heart was hammering.

The silence extended.

"I see," he said.

"Look," I said. "Other than having been hit on the head, there's very little wrong with me. I grant you that I might not be statistically normal or average or whatever but what does that amount to? Nor are you. Right? By virtue of your education, I mean, income, that sort of thing. And as for tests—well on a battery of tests anybody would show characteristics of *something*."

He stared over the steeple of his fingers.

"And even if I *were* a little peculiar, that wouldn't prevent my earning a living and so forth. Would it? 'Functioning', that's the word."

He nodded.

"It is, of course," he said, "your legal right to refuse treatment."

I sat back in the chair.

I crossed my legs, tugged at the bathrobe.

"Take Marshall Blücher, for example," I said. "A bit late for the Battle of Waterloo but a respected and competent commander. Of that there's no question. Yet apparently he lived his whole life in fear of giving birth to an elephant."

I smiled and shrugged.

"On the other hand," said Dr. Chawn, "providing that you can be shown to be dangerous, it is *my* legal right, and reponsibility, to detain you."

"*Dangerous?*"

"You will then be taken before a board of review which is empowered to order compulsory treatment."

"*Me? Dangerous?*"

From the desk drawer he took a wallet-folder. He opened it and spread papers on the desk top.

"You seem to forget, Mr. Wells, the circumstances under which you were brought to this hospital."

"I admit," I said, "that I was drunk and behaving foolishly but.."

"We are not talking of a childish prank, Mr. Wells. How would you explain your desire to break into the Communication Arts Complex and destroy university property?"

A good question.

'Complex' seemed to sum it up.

To enter into any explanation about Itzic and CAC, the demented O'Gorman, the paralysis moral and emotional caused by television, seemed unwise. Any thread of explanation led inevitably to the subject of frozen french fries.

I shrugged.

"I was drunk," I said.

"And were you drunk when you stole the university's typewriter?"

What, I wondered, had possessed Kathy, with her general scorn for psychiatry and all its works, to spill so many beans. Had she been gulled by his alchemical patter, seduced by his vision of vagrant enzymes and wayward secretions? I thought of Kathy in the heather-coloured sweater, crying.

I'm not on anybody's side.

Naïve to the end.

"An instructive statement," said Dr. Chawn. "What do you mean, 'needed the experience'?"

I was beginning to feel like a novice chess-player seeking a way out of check on a ravaged board. Every possible move seemed threatened by knight or bishop, pawn or rook.

"I'm writing a novel," I said, "and I needed a scene involving a pawnshop."

He raised his eyebrows.

"And this gives you licence to steal?" he said. "To behave as you will? To disregard others? You feel yourself above normal social constraints?"

"This board," I said. "Who's on it?"

"It would be made up of psychiatrists and laymen."

"Would you be on it?"

"No."

"But you'd present your . . . your findings?"

He inclined his head.

"Hmmm," I said.

"*These*," he said, "are the records from the Royal Victoria Hospital."

"I was *dancing*," I said.

"With corroboratory notes from Dr. Roberts concerning your violent attitude."

"I was dancing," I said, "and I fell down."

"Police report," he said, pushing the paper aside. "And *here*," picking up another xeroxed sheet, "from your notebook, a bomb threat against your publishers. A bomb threat purporting to come from an organization called *Parents for Canadian Righteousness*."

"A joke!" I said. "For heaven's sake, man, a joke!"

He regarded me.

"A joke," he repeated flatly.

"*Yes!*" I said. "Yes!"

"I see."

He spread some xeroxed sheets with his fingertips.

"Your poems . ."

"Don't tell me," I said. "I've got a 'despairing world vision'. It's on the dust jacket."

"I do not pretend to expertise in literary matters," he said, glancing at one of the sheets, "but these tend to complement in every way the profile which . ."

"Did *you* make these copies?"

He looked up.

"They were furnished by Concordia University."

"In violation of copyright," I said. "An act of theft, you see, Dr. Chawn. Theft just as much as if they'd crept into my bedroom at night and stolen the money out of my pants pocket. Have *they* a licence to steal?"

He looked at his watch.

"Am I boring you?" I said.

He creaked back in the black leather chair.

"And then," he said, "there are the tests you wrote yesterday."

"What's wrong with them?"

"Dr. Nimitz and I are in agreement that your performance was an act of deliberate non-cooperation."

I nodded slowly.

"And not cooperating," I said, "or doing whatever you want equals aggression or hostility, doesn't it? Yet more incontrovertible evidence of a violent and dangerous disposition."

I stared at his impassive face.

"It's a case of Heads-I-Win-Tails-You-Lose, isn't it?"

He did not reply.

I tied a couple of knots in the cord of the bathrobe.

"What did you say that man's name was?" I said. "The threshold man?"

"Shagass?"

"Perhaps he pronounces it differently."

Dr. Chawn steepled his fingers on his chest again.

The silence extended.

I looked at the squiggly black writing on the graph paper.

"These paper slippers," I said, standing up and shedding them, "are sweaty and unsanitary."

He leaned forward, and pressing a key on the intercom, said, *Nurse Teitelbaum, please.*

"There's no need to be nervous," I said.

I walked over to the window and stood looking down into a parking lot, rows and rows of cars in the snow.

Soft smoke was piling out of a tall brick chimney.

Where the base of the chimney joined a long low building, pigeons huddled.

I undid the bathrobe feeling the sun's warmth through the thin hospital gown.

The sunshine was crisp on the churned snow, the ruts and ridges all defined by shadows blue and mauve. Steam was rising from the wet roof of the chimney building, wreathing, hugging the shingles, shifting in sheets, eddying as though it were smoke from a fierce fire within. A pigeon sailed out against the sky, banked, swept from view.

The voice behind me spoke again.

"Pardon?"

Nurse Teitelbaum was a man.

A large man.

Dr. Chawn looked up from the notes he was writing on the graph paper and said,

"Interesting."

"What is?"

"Marshall Blücher."

"What are you talking about?"

"He's one of your central fears, isn't he?"

"He is?"

"You fear that had he been cured of his delusions, he wouldn't have been a successful soldier."

I stared down at him.

Then smiled.

And smiled.

He looked beyond me and nodded.

Behind me, Nurse Teitelbaum said,

"Mr. Wells?"

As he held the door for me, I said,

"The sun's getting stronger every day."

"Yes," he said, closing the door behind us, "we're through the worst of it."

The secretary was pounding at the keys.

As I got myself into the wheelchair, I said,

"And if we get any more, it won't last long."

"Yes," he said, "there's only — what is it now? Twenty-eight, twenty-nine days to the official beginning of spring."

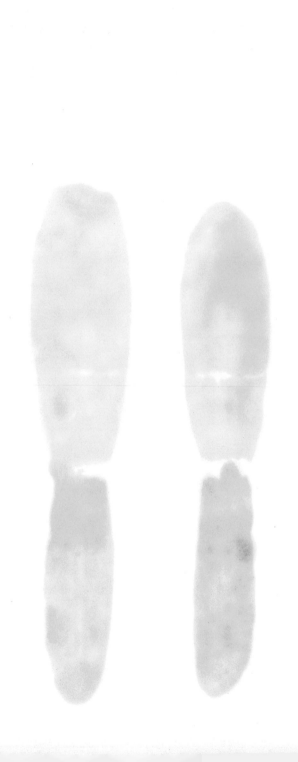

DATE DUE

GAYLORD   PRINTED IN U.S.A.